Barbican Press

1 Ashenden Road

London E5 0DP

website: www.barbicanpress.com
email: info@barbicanpress.com
Tel: 0207 6841790 m: 07507 554731

16th December 2014

SUBMISSION FOR THE JOHN W. CAMPBELL MEMORIAL AWARD

We are proud to submit James Thornton's SPHINX: THE SECOND COMING for this year's award.

Manda Scott wrote of SPHINX: '"Sphinx is Intelligent, inspiring and innovative. The combination of past, present and future is genuinely original and the ideas are fantastic.'

We hope you enjoy your own journey into the book.

Happy Judging!

Martin

Martin Goodman: Director

BIOGRAPHY

James Thornton is one of the world's leading environmental lawyers and a Zen Buddhist priest. He founded and runs ClientEarth, the leading environmental NGO, working throughout Europe and in Africa. The *New Statesman* called him 'one of ten people who could change the world' while the *Big Issue* termed ClientEarth a 'fleet of armour plated tanks in the battle to secure our future on planet Earth.' This is his second novel.

ALSO BY JAMES THORNTON

Immediate Harm

A Field Guide to the Soul (non-fiction)

SPHINX:

THE SECOND COMING

JAMES THORNTON

Published by Barbican Press in 2014

First published in Great Britain as a paperback original by:
Barbican Press, 1 Ashenden Road, London E5 0DP
www.barbicanpress.com

A CIP catalogue for this book is available from the British Library

ISBN: 978-0-9563364-4-6

Typeset in Garamond by Mike Gower

Cover Design by Jason Anscomb: www.rawshock.co.uk

Printed by Lightning Source, Milton Keynes

FOR MARTIN

A shape with lion body and head of a man
A gaze bland and pitiless as the sun,
Is moving its slow thighs, while all about it
Wind shadows of the indignant desert birds.

--from '*The Second Coming*', William Butler Yeats, 1919

Prologue

I was on my way by train to the mountains of Switzerland, to visit the psychiatric hospital where Carl Jung was trained. There I would meet with a brain scientist, a colleague working on the physical substrate for human consciousness. I had decided to take the overland route from our house in the wild French Pyrenees. It would give me a chance to visit a friend at the 13th century chateau of his aunt, a countess. The chateau was one of her many estates, and I was told that it was charmingly situated near the Abbey of the Grand Chartreuse.

From the station I hired a car for the excursion along French country lanes. Losing my way, I stopped in a village bar. It was 10 a.m. on a Sunday morning and the habitués were already knocking back the local white wine. They argued among themselves about how to describe where the countess and her chateau could be found. I picked out the thread running through their haze, and arrived at the chateau just in time for a pre-lunch pastis.

The visit went well. Spry for ninety-two years old, the old countess produced a fine salmon from her own river as the main course. An onion tart to start, and raspberries from her garden for dessert rounded out the meal, washed down with a pleasant local red, and followed by her own liqueur. We spent hours chatting dozily under an arbor of white roses.

I declined to spend the night in the countess's chateau, preferring such old piles by daylight. In the late afternoon I returned the car to Grenoble. A sophisticated provincial town that incubated the French Revolution, Grenoble is where Stendhal was born and where Champollion decoded Egyptian hieroglyphs. The town was nearly full and I began to regret turning down the offer of a bed in the chateau as I was turned away from one hotel reception desk after another. I worked my way down from the five star hotels through the four and three stars before walking at last, with a little trepidation, into a two star. Little did I know I was about to receive what Henry James called a donée, the germ of the tale that became this book.

The man behind the distinctly two star counter was Arab-French. He was reading what appeared to be an esoteric tome. He looked up, fixed me with a stare, and said, "What is your work?"

I explained I was a lawyer who runs an international brain science institute. This pleased but did not placate him.

"And you studied philosophy?"

I admitted that I'd taken my degree in philosophy from Yale.

"You are also a writer?"

I admitted I was, uncertain what was coming next. His accuracy was better than your average palm reader.

"And you like science fiction?"

Admitting I did precipitated his explosive leap over the counter.

"You are the one!" he yelled, grasping the lapels of my khaki traveling suit, but leaving the tattersal shirt unwrinkled. "You must write his story!" He spoke as if his life depended on it. His eyes were wild and I thought him slightly mad. "The story of the Sphinx! You must bring him alive in all his power and glory. You must write how he is the bridge between the gods and humans—you know he is a chimera, with an animal body and a human head—this symbolizes his divinity and humanity. He is made of different stuff. He will transform our genes and bring about the next stage in the evolution of the human race! But for this to happen, you must bring him to life. I have been waiting for years to find you. I tell you this: you think me crazy, you will ignore me and try to forget what I tell you. Yet I am no fool. I am a member of a learned society at the University. And I will also tell you this: it does not matter that you try to forget me, for you can never forget your duty to the Sphinx. Now that I, his messenger, have discovered you, now that you have walked into his web, you cannot escape. When you try to forget, the Sphinx himself will come to you in dreams. He is famous for it. You will see. It all depends on you now. You must make it real! You *will* bring him alive! The next stage of human evolution will begin. It must happen!"

I told him as politely as I could that I'd think about it, in order to dislodge from him the key to my room. Once out of his company I didn't give another thought to his ravings. I ate dinner with my traveling companion in a restaurant with too many dried flowers under glass bells, a view of the Alps and a three-course *prix fixe.*

The next morning I awoke covered in boils. It didn't take long to recall that this was one of the plagues of Egypt. I lay listing them in my mind, staring in the half-light at the dingy ceiling: the plague of frogs, the plague of locusts, the death of the first-born sons, the plague of boils. There were others. I couldn't remember all the plagues inflicted on Egypt, but boils were surely on the list. My traveling companion in a separate bed was untouched by them. The plague had covered my chest, back, and legs. The boils took four months to heal. I say that the boils healed, but while the blemishes vanished from my skin, something festered still.

For two years I ignored the prompting of the boils and fought against writing the Sphinx's story. I turned my mind to professional tasks. But the memory of the boils kept returning. At a certain point the dreams came, dreams of the Sphinx, just as the mad hotelier had predicted. Perhaps he had been afflicted with them too. Perhaps that is how he came to think of himself as the messenger of the Sphinx, and gained the power to afflict me.

The Sphinx told me to work on his behalf. Such a command had also been given to a pharaoh of the New Kingdom. By that time the Sphinx's statue was already old. It was buried in desert sands up to the chin. Thutmose IV was then a teenager, one of several princes who might succeed to the throne of Egypt. He went out hunting for the day. After lunch, he decided to take a nap. He sheltered on a comfortable sand dune right under the Sphinx's chin, to take advantage of its shadow in the hot desert sun.

The living Sphinx came to Thutmose in a dream. The Sphinx told the prince to dig his statue out of the desert sands. Thutmose was told he would succeed to the throne and become a great pharaoh if he did this. His dream of the Sphinx changed the pharaoh's life 3,500 years ago. He dug it out of the sands. He erected his Dream Stela, a high flat panel of rock between the Sphinx's paws, where the story of his dream is detailed in hieroglyphs. The dream served both the Sphinx and Thutmose well. The Sphinx was worshiped as a god, and Thutmose did indeed become a great pharaoh.

The Sphinx changed my life in dreams too.

When the Sphinx first came I was unprepared. One night I found myself standing by the Nile. Though my body was in my bed at home, this was no dream.

I felt the sand between my toes. I heard the palm fronds snap and sway in the breeze. It was dark. There were no lights only stars. Then out of nowhere the Sphinx stood before me.

He bowed his head low to honor me. The Earth shook.

He spoke and the sound resounded in my skull.

"Welcome, Way Opener. I am The Bridge Between Gods and Men. It is time for my return. You are my Way Opener. I need your help to enter into your time. I need it now. Make my Way ready. Tell my story. Tell my story and I will become real in your time. Tell my story and I will save your species."

Then the Sphinx went silent and vanished into light.

Back in my bed I was wet with sweat.

More than anything else, I was eager to forget the burden the Sphinx had given me. What was his story? Where was I to discover it? What made me the Way Opener for the Great Sphinx? Did my species need saving?

But the Sphinx was not interested in my qualms.

The Sphinx left my dreams and entered my ordinary reality. When I sat down to write legal or scientific documents, an alternative stream of logic kept flowing from my pen. I had begun against my will to channel the true story of the Sphinx.

I can normally focus my mind as I choose, but in this instance I finally had to give in, and devote myself to the task of letting this incredible story come through me. While I must make the ludicrous confession that I channel material from some unknown sphere, like spiritualists and mediums I once scorned, I have nevertheless maintained some aspects of my professional training. While I channel, I also edit. I have confirmed this story by traveling to Egypt and by months of research in the recesses of the British Library at St. Pancras.

Unwilling as I have been to bring this story to the light of day, I had to tell it. The plague of boils was warning enough. The Sphinx commanded me to exhume him from the past. I do so in this book. He told me to tell his story. It is recorded here. Just as the mad hotelier foretold on that fateful day in Grenoble, this story changes everything.

Part I
Grave Games

When I entered the room of Shoju, the rhinoceros of my previous doubt suddenly fell down dead.

—Hakuin Zenji, *The Five Ranks*

1

Four lights appeared, changing shape and brightness, as if each light were a window into higher dimensions. The colors spilled off into fractal shadings, each light centered on a color: red, yellow, blue, and green.

The lights morphed. They became a baboon, a falcon, a crocodile, and a lion. These four gathered companionably on a bedrock outcrop.

The Wild Nile raged as they watched. The river would not tame itself for another three thousand years. Then it would accrete the Black Land grain by grain. Only then would people enter, tentatively at first. They would set up villages and gorge on fish that the river, now relaxed, would offer them.

While they gorged, people in the west would go hungry. Sophisticated astronomers and farmers, the western people's land would turn against them. It would get steadily drier until green savannah became sand punctuated by oases. When the oases dried, the people would leave what was now the Red Land and move east. They would meet the simpler river people in combat and camaraderie until they fused into the world's first nation state: a ribbon of life a thousand kilometers long ruled by King Scorpion, the first pharaoh.

The four companions had watched the Nile Valley for a very long while. The time was ripe for the next move. They chose the Giza Plateau, whose bedrock stood above the floods, as their point of purchase on human destiny.

Their visit would usher in the Zep Tepi or First Time.

"We have work to do," said falcon.

"We must enjoy bodily recreation inside these gorgeous creatures, after business," crocodile said, enjoying the snap of her jaws.

Baboon scratched and nodded, while eyeing a stand of date palms that flanked the Nile.

"To work, then," said falcon, stretching her wings, then refolding them and preening.

They all turned to lion. The game was his to call. He had taken the lead from the beginning.

"The local people are emerging from their childhood. I will stay," continued lion. "I will indwell here, and participate lightly."

"I've been watching the lord of this galaxy," said crocodile. "He's not entirely stable."

"It's because of his origins," said baboon. "It's hard for a black hole to achieve a clear sense of identity when it's a composite."

"I've never understood why," said falcon irritably. "There's no inherent problem. Small galaxies cannibalize each other all the time. Their central black holes merge. Sometimes the merger is friendly, often not. But there's no reason they can't work out a joint point of view."

"Most of them stabilize, of course," said baboon. "They work things out, move into a corporate personhood, and concentrate on gobbling stars and burping new universes."

"That's what worries me here," said crocodile. "The lord of this galaxy starves himself. Occasionally he'll eat stars, but his habits aren't steady. He'll sometimes go without eating for a long time, as if he's trying to kill off part of himself. I worry that he'll be tempted by the mindstuff of these humans."

"Eating mind," said falcon thoughtfully.

"We've seen it happen," said crocodile. "I doubt these humans are strong enough to resist if he starts sucking their souls."

"Stop him right now," said falcon, strident. "Why wait? I see no profit in going easy on unstables. A galaxy lord has responsibilities. If he won't honor them, intervene."

Lion had been listening. He was not yet sure of his feelings. He addressed falcon. "What would you do?"

"Restructure him. Strip out the personae that are causing the instability."

"Restructuring a black hole doesn't always work," said lion. "It can destroy the galaxy. It's unpredictable."

"I don't have any trouble wrapping up a galaxy that's not functional at its core," said falcon.

"This is the most promising planet in this universe, and this universe has been evolving such a long time."

"You're always so hasty!" said baboon. "Why worry about this universe? We can always make another."

"It's not the time so much as the conditions. We may never recreate such optimal conditions in any reasonable number of universes."

"It's your call, old friend," said crocodile, and snapped her jaws. "We don't mean to be unhelpful. We just know that the closer you come to success, the more painful failure would be."

"We'll leave the lord of the galaxy alone for now," said lion. "I've kept this a free universe from the start. If he eats mind, it may be just the challenge the humans need to accelerate their growth."

Baboon, falcon, and crocodile nodded at lion.

"How will you use the edge of your awareness?" said baboon.

"I'll let it interact with the people who come here," said lion. "I'll let my awareness bring forth gods for them. Whatever gods suit their needs."

"Perhaps they'll resemble us!" said crocodile, with a delighted snap of her jaws.

"What can we do to help, before we go?" said falcon. She was the closest to him, and she felt his imminent loss.

"There is something," said lion. "I'd enjoy it if we did it together. I want to make something here that will captivate their imagination, and last as long as their species."

"What do you have in mind?" said crocodile.

He showed their minds mountains. Mountains along the Nile and in the western lands. Mountains sharp and pointed. Mountains falling into perfect geometries, helped by wind and rain.

"I want to raise mountains to grip the autochthonous spirit," he said. "This land has four elements: the river, the sun, the land, and the people. It has four protectors: the four of us. We will raise four-sided mountains for them to wonder at. We will raise three of them—one for each of you, my companions."

"And what of you?" said falcon.

"I have learned something from this creature's shape," lion said, pushing his paws forward, stretching his spine and yawning. "You will see."

They joined their minds and saw the Giza Plateau. They visualized the three pyramidal mountains they would raise. They would fashion something beyond the capacities of the people who would wander onto the scene.

Baboon wondered into their joined minds whether they should make the pyramids in a material beyond the people, making each a single crystal of diamond or transhuman metal.

Lion thought not. Better if the pyramids were not too remote from anything humans could do. He wanted to encourage them, not crush their spirit.

Crocodile wondered if the pyramids shouldn't contain puzzles to trip the edge of lion's awareness should humans find and solve them. All agreed quickly. They played with images of what the first puzzle should look like, until they reached the same geometric solid, an ikosikaitrigon.

They arrived at the twenty-three sided figure because of a mental shorthand they used. When thinking of a species that interested them, they used as its signifier a certain kind of image that came easily to them: a three-dimensional solid with as many sides as the species' number of chromosomes, each side of the polygon bearing in simplified signs the key elements of the species' genetic signature. Such mental images served as a universal code. Since each signifier so designed was different throughout the Multiverse, there could be no ambiguity as to what the signifier pointed to.

The most natural thing was to leave humans' own name as their puzzle. When they achieved the sophistication to read it, lion would leave his meditations to engage more actively. The solution pleased them. They would conceal it in the most interesting of the three pyramids.

2

They decided to take their time building the pyramids. They would do it stone by stone.

Their animal bodies had been sedentary. They got up and moved, enjoying the experience of living in these creatures. There was always something to learn by being embodied. The restrictions it imposed brought a corresponding vividness in point of view. They decided to inspect the stone on the plateau for its building qualities, and quarry the best that was there. Lion and baboon were delighted to be on the move, and falcon's wings bit into the sky.

Crocodile, though, soon reached the limits of her new body. She lumbered slowly on short legs to keep up with the others. Walking across the plateau, try as she might to enjoy it, was distinctly unpleasant. Her body was not built for long walks, and so she decided to listen to its wisdom. She found a comfortable spot to bask in the sunshine. With her eyes closed, crocodile saw through the eyes of the others.

When the other three found the stone to work, lion and baboon held up their paws.

The stone shuddered like a live thing and cleaved itself away from the lower bedrock. It shivered into blocks that raised themselves into the air. The four left marks on the blocks to suggest humans might have done the work, to make the pyramids appear friendly to the people who would live here. Baboon took the lead in visualizing these details. Her presence in an ape body gave her an intuitive feel for how human apes might work such material.

They began with the Great Pyramid. They visualized its base courses, and the stone blocks flew to do their bidding, fitting seamlessly. They flashed ideas to each other for the pyramid's internal structures. Lion saw three chambers. One deep in the bedrock, two high in the pyramid. He shared his sense that humans like trinities, and would be moved by finding three chambers disposed from the depths to the heights.

They had agreed on their ikosikaitrigon, and lion led in fashioning it. They conceived star shafts and built them true as they raised the great blocks and set them soaring to join their kind in the mountain rising on the plateau.

In the highest of the three chambers they made an open granite box. It would serve as a trigger for those who came, opening the speculative mind. It would also serve as a capacitor, a place where humans could tap directly into some of the awareness lion would leave active. "Let their kings awaken while lying here," he thought to the others. "I will guide those who are receptive."

He decided to seal the entrance, and open it in invitation later, when the time was right. He would also implant in the mind of mankind the idea that men had built the pyramids. Arguments down through the ages would focus on *how* they were built, but few would doubt the pyramids were the work of human hands.

The four companions finished the pyramid's body and bent their minds to finding a source of pure white limestone. When they did, they called it to them, and clad the pyramid in a blazing white sheath.

They saw what they had done and they were pleased. To conceive and execute such work with local materials remained of keen interest long after they were able to manipulate galaxies and birth universes. There was nothing as satisfying as a good creation, at any scale.

"Except," thought baboon while stretching, "some relaxation after." She reminded them that they should take time to experience these bodies. The others agreed, crocodile the most readily, as torpor called out to her now.

They dropped their mind link and focused on the sensoria of the species they inhabited. Lion moved off into the green savannah that would become the Western Desert. He hunted gazelle in rapid bursts of speed. He felt the fragile necks break in his bite, the hearts pumping fountains of hot arterial blood down his throat.

As night fell, crocodile slithered into a lagoon where an old bull hippo lay dying in the shallows. Joining in a frenzy with a dozen other crocodiles, she locked her jaws on the hippo's flank to tear the flesh from his body. She flipped herself over in a corkscrew motion: onto her back, belly, and back again, and was rewarded with hunks of hippo flesh quickly gulped down.

Falcon spent the afternoon hunting larks, ripping the warm entrails out with razor beak to hawk them down. The night saw her watching the stars from a high cliff on the western shore.

Baboon got her dates fresh from the tree. She then ambled into the local baboon troupe in a way calculated to make sure her baboon body carried the seed of the local alpha male. She was not disappointed.

3

They met the next morning to continue their work. Lion teased them with their enjoyment of bodily form and its hot quick life. "Are you tempted to stay behind in these forms when I go indwelling?"

They heard behind his question an anticipation of loss. He would be giving up the exercise of much of his power and the experience of their rapport.

Falcon answered lion's question. "No, but depending on what form your gods take, maybe I'll visit from time to time as one of them."

"I have a thought," said crocodile, replete from her night of feasting. "But let's finish our other pyramids first."

They completed them in the way they had done the first, settling on simpler internal arrangements, letting them speak through their crystalline presence.

"Will you build temples to spur them on?" said baboon.

"One in front of the token of my indwelling. I'll leave it half built, concealing more puzzles. Perhaps a few others."

"What will be the token of your indwelling?" said falcon.

"It's time, so let me show you." Lion got up and stretched. He walked some distance from the central pyramid toward the Nile. Here he sat down facing east. He increased his size until his bulk was proportional to a pyramid. Then his lion mane shifted into a headdress, and his lion features into those of a man.

The others were taken with the transformation. Moved by the thought of their impending separation, they joined for the cycle of a day and a night in the most intimate openness of shared mind. As they began to differentiate, crocodile offered her thought.

Each of the three would leave a live atom of awareness to indwell with lion. In this way they would stay in subliminal contact with his meditations and know when he returned. They saw his indwelling as a retreat. He would explore aspects of the self he was ordinarily too engaged to be aware of. They would resonate with him and he could know through their presence of their abiding union.

"And when you emerge?" said falcon.

"It depends on who the people have become. I may simply enjoy them. Enjoying them is the goal for which we set this universe in motion. Or I may intervene to help, though reluctantly. Or I may destroy them."

"That would be painful," said crocodile.

"I don't see it as likely."

"That's why I mentioned the lord of this galaxy. I agree it's not likely if he does his duty. Then circumstances should favor them. But if he strays..."

"I'll study things minutely and render judgment. You will know when I come back."

As the others prepared to go, they released their animal bodies. An alligator waddled toward the Nile; a baboon skittered to a grove; a falcon was away in an eyeblink.

Three lights appeared before the great lion. Then each of them spilled out a rainbow to arc over him and furl itself within a pyramid.

The huge man-lion smiled and turned to stone.

The three lights passed into the sky in the direction the Egyptians would later call Rostau.

4

The two men went by donkey, humbly. They bore none of their insignia of office. They wore no cosmetics, not even kohl eyeliner fresh-ground on a slate palette. The younger man, somewhat vain of his appearance, had not been in public without his eye shadow since the day he first got access to it. Nor was he wearing any of his customary jewelry. He had no rings or amulets, not even a simple gold and enamel eye-of-Horus on his smooth bare chest. No man or woman at his level would ordinarily go out naked of makeup and jewelry, dressed only in a linen kilt and skullcap.

The older man did not feel the lack. The simplicity of pilgrimage suited him. He was becoming more and more focused on what lay beyond the horizon of time. As he got older, he valued the rituals and ceremonies more. He saw deeper into the way they calmed the troubled mind. He had come to begrudge his morning toilet, and this was strange to the point of uniqueness for a man at his rank. A bevy of servants bathed, shaved, perfumed him and did his makeup every morning. It simply ate too much of his day. What had been once so enjoyable had become a distraction. He consoled himself that it was a kind of ritual too, so he let the servants chatter while they preened him and he watched the shadow move across his sundial, the first in Upper Egypt.

They had come from Upper to Lower Egypt, taking a boat north along the Nile from Karnak to Memphis. They were welcomed into the hostelry of the temple of Ptah, helper of mankind.

Ptah's temple complex was a separate city within Memphis; he had emerged as the chief god of the pharaoh's capital city. Resplendent white walls and its vast size made Memphis justly admired as the greatest of all cities.

Unas, the older man, was High Priest of Amun-Ra, in the god's modest home in the provincial town of Karnak. Unas had decided that it was time to take Qaa, the younger man, on a pilgrimage.

Qaa was to succeed Unas when the time came. Unas had made his choice because of the young man's exceptional qualities. He was gifted at writing and maths, and his personal beauty and charm allowed him to hold the attention of anyone he chose. He was from a family noble enough to feel comfortable in Egypt's Great House, and he was ambitious.

The god needed Qaa's ambition. The only hesitation Unas had was that Qaa took seriously the famous admonition to priests:

Do not be ascetic. Eat and drink and make love. How can the gods be happy if you are glum?

In any case, it was time to go on a pilgrimage. He would show Qaa something of the nature of both gods and men.

They stayed only overnight in Memphis, since Unas was eager to get to Saqqara. Shortly after dawn they were already on the edge of the capital, well outside its great white walls. Dust was in the air, stirred by the feet of men going to work the fields and fish the Nile. Children played and dogs barked. The smell of the day's bread rose from smoke holes in the adobe houses.

Unas and Qaa rode on their donkeys. All the other donkeys bore burdens other than men. In the absence of jewelry and makeup, their mounts and the fine quality of their linen kilts were what set them apart from the laborers, who stared at them with open curiosity.

Giza and the pyramids lay to the northwest. Before visiting the pyramids, Unas would take Qaa to Saqqara. He wanted the young man to see the smaller stepped pyramid first. Unas had a strategic reason to show Qaa the structures in this sequence.

The Saqqara road took them through what had been savannah. When Memphis was young and the people were working to domesticate wild animals, it was always green here. By the time they succeeded in domesticating the pig and goose, dog and cat, the land was noticeably drier. By the time they abandoned the attempt to domesticate the hyena, ibex and giraffe, and the city's great white walls had been built, the land had dried to its present state. Tired and thirsty, it could flush with green blades and wildflowers after a rare shower. Butterflies and bees would appear along with bee-eaters to hunt them down while life's brief bloom lasted.

The blessing of a recent shower meant the men rode through a living land. Qaa appreciated the desert wildflowers. His donkey trod herbs whose rising scent inspired deeper breaths. It felt strange that he had come here with an old man to study death.

"There it is," said Unas, as Djoser's Step Pyramid came into view. A stone ziggurat inside an expansive corbelled curtain wall, it was a most impressive sight.

"It's wonderful!" said Qaa. He had seen nothing to equal it. "Can we go in?"

"If you can find the way in," said Unas. "There are many doors. Choose."

The Step Pyramid was faced in polished limestone and surrounded by an enclosure the size of a city. At regular intervals in the walls, which stretched to six times Qaa's height, were doorways. If this had been a city of the living, Qaa could see why there should be so many passages through the walls. But why in a city of the dead?

Then he recalled that it was not properly a city of the dead, more a Great House for one dead man, the now deified pharaoh Djoser. Many priests were in attendance, living within the sacred precinct carved from the world by the walls. Still, so many doors made little sense.

"I don't see why there should be so many, sir, but any of them should do. I'm keen to see what's inside. It seems like a much more impressive temple than our own."

"You choose the door you think best and approach it. I will wait here till you have been invited in, and then join you."

Qaa rode up, somewhat at random, to a nearby door. It appeared as good as any other. He climbed off the donkey and walked up to it.

Sand, still cool, crunched under Qaa's bare feet. Qaa knocked hard to show his decisiveness, only to pull back his knuckles in pain. The cedar door was stone. It was no door at all.

Flashing anger at being made a fool, Qaa went to the next door. It looked right. He knocked much more tentatively this time, only to find the same thing. A stone false door cunningly contrived.

Qaa denied the impulse to look back at Unas, who would be, he was sure, laughing at him. At this second false door, Qaa's anger changed to admiration. He tried one after the other, nine in all, along a thousand meters of wall. The sand was now hot under his feet as he returned to Unas.

"Perhaps your experience bestows greater wisdom than my persistence."

Unas laughed lightly. He had been right to choose Qaa. "Follow me. In this as in all ways, I will give you the key."

Unas spurred his donkey forward. Qaa fell in behind him. They rode over sand, since there was nothing as clear as a path leading to any door. Unas seemed to choose casually, selecting a door that Qaa had not tried. It looked like all the others.

While they approached the door, unseen eyes watched them. Without a knock or even a word from Unas, the door swung open before them. Two young priests bowed to them from inside its threshold. Unas spurred his donkey forward and Qaa followed. Qaa found himself in a corridor leading through the walls into the pyramid enclosure. The corridor was so dark compared to the open sky he had left behind that Qaa was momentarily blinded.

Just as his eyes adjusted to the dark, he was blinded again.

They rode into the great South Court. It was open to the burning turquoise vault of heaven. Across its broad paved yard, Djoser's Step Pyramid, all fifty meters of it, rose before them.

The pyramid was covered in highly polished white limestone that focused the light of the Sun god Ra into an overpowering dazzle.

Qaa felt an unaccustomed awe. There was a power here he had not felt before. While his eyes struggled to take in the pyramid's shining form, his lungs relaxed in the precious incense wafting from altars throughout the pyramid compound. Expressions of power and refinement at this level were entirely new to him. As Qaa let himself float in the splendor, his awareness of the people around him dimmed. Priest attendants had to ask him twice to dismount from his donkey before he understood what they were talking about. The attendants took the donkeys, and offered Unas and Qaa refreshment. Qaa simply drifted along with Unas, until the high priest came to meet them.

By now they were in a luxurious apartment. Their feet had been bathed and they had drunk a light fruit-flavored beer.

The High Priest of Djoser's Funerary Temple looked the part. He was tall and severe and regally dressed. Qaa came to full attention when the gold and lapis lazuli of his collars and cuffs caught the light. Qaa had entered a world that combined luxury and holiness. It was the world he had always hoped to find.

For the rest of the day, Unas and Qaa accompanied the high priest on his rounds. They went from altar to altar around the vast complex. At each, they made offerings of food, drink, flowers, and incense. A hundred altars bore the pharaoh's image. At each the offerings were piled high. Djoser's *ba*, the celestial soul that only gods and pharaohs possess, had gone to join the imperishable stars. But the pharaoh's *ka* was still present, still alive within the sacred precincts. It would live for as long as it was remembered with offerings. Because Egypt was eternal, Djoser's *ka* was sure to live forever.

The chants, prayers, and offerings were not unfamiliar to Qaa. They were close to those he had been trained in, if different in detail. What was unfamiliar was the luxury of the offerings.

Everything that was placed on an altar in Djoser's memory was of exceptional quality. The flowers were the largest, most perfect, and most numerous blooms Qaa had ever seen. Among bundles of narcotic blue lotus were exotics new to his eyes.

The beer and wine were so choice that their smell alone was intoxicating. The meats and cheeses, bread and fruit piled up high on the altars were of the quality only pharaohs could afford.

That night they ate with the high priest, who was an old friend of Unas. The high priest's paunch suggested the attention he gave his table. Qaa was not disappointed. The food was of the same quality offered on the altars.

Qaa and Unas sat together at a pedestal table of alabaster. The high priest had his own table nearby. The room was large enough for a banquet, but just the three of them dined, served by twice as many. Qaa had never before tasted wine, and would never forget the red and white he drank that night. Nor the choice cuts of beef, gazelle, and giraffe they feasted on. He tasted honey for the first time and vowed to have a life that afforded him the chance for more.

The high priest was proud of his table and delighted by Qaa's unfeigned enthusiasm. His severity put aside, he explained that the temples for the dead pharaohs had farms and suppliers just like pharaohs had while alive. Djoser's temple owned cattle farms in the Delta, vineyards in Faiyum, wheat fields and farms spread throughout central Egypt. The offerings to the *ka* must be the equal of what Djoser enjoyed while reigning. After their use in ceremony, the offerings fed Djoser's priests, ensuring an enthusiastic cadre of servitors.

"Next time you come through, we'll have a banquet. We honor the memory of Pharaoh by serving his *ka* the banquets he enjoyed. Courtiers come from Memphis. We feast on sumptuous dishes and choice wine. Young girls dance for our entertainment. Young men oil themselves and wrestle. And music, wonderful music, flows like the River!"

Qaa was a willing captive of the picture the high priest conjured. Unas smiled indulgently and sipped his wine. He had enjoyed such banquets and the access they offered. The high priest continued.

"It has been six generations now since the blessed Imhotep, architect of genius, built this memorial to Pharaoh. For all these generations, my family has served here. When I was your age Qaa, I wanted to be a priest at the temple for Khufu at the Great Pyramid. But the pyramid temples at Giza have always gone to priests in the royal family, and I have become content here. Sometimes even the demands of this life become oppressive, and I long for a small temple to a provincial god in a backwater town like yours. How fortunate for you to be far from the demands we have to put up with, with the Great House so close, and all its courtiers and pests."

Qaa was feeling the wine. He watched the oil lamps flicker over the blue enamel walls as the priest spoke. Table servants refreshed their drinks and brought more choice plates. What was building in Qaa was outrage on behalf of Amun-Ra, his god.

"How can you call the great Amun-Ra a provincial god?"

The high priest laughed and addressed Unas. "You have found a sincere one. That would not be easy to do in the capital." Then he spoke to Qaa. "It is good to be jealous on your god's behalf. But if you wish to advance his interests at court one day, you have much to learn about the ways of the capital."

"How can I advance the god's interest? Surely he does that."

"Who will help your god if you do not? Who will get him farms and fields to ensure his offerings? Who will earn the income to keep him in precious incense? Unas, does your temple have endowments of farms and cattle?"

"We must rely on donations from a few of our local nobles. I am working on some of them, cultivating them. A few, I hope, will make an endowment."

"You see, Qaa," said the high priest. "You have much to do for your god, and the court is the place to do it. Who better than Pharaoh Menkaure to provide for your god's legitimate needs? Menkaure can be generous when a case is clearly made."

They fell silent for a moment and listened to the reed flutes and evening devotions chanted in a nearby shrine within the compound.

"But I shouldn't fill your head with politics, Qaa. Unas has brought you north to experience the Opening of the Heart. It is a rare privilege, very rare. Only the high priests of Ptah, chief god of the royal court, have this experience. There is a single exception—the high priests of your god. Unas, you must explain to me some time how you wangled this. Qaa, be sure to learn what you can from Unas while you have him!"

He paused for a comment from Unas, but none came, so he continued, "And it is about to become the rarest of all privileges. I hear that Pharaoh Menkaure will have the Great Pyramid sealed up again. So you may be the last man to have this initiation."

"I knew it was a great privilege, but not a unique one," said Qaa.

"Time to retire, gentleman," said the high priest. "I trust you will sleep well, and I will wish you safe passage in the morning."

Qaa and Unas slept in an apartment modeled on a guest suite in Djoser's palace. They were the departed pharaoh's guests and were treated as such.

5

They set out early, after a light breakfast of dark beer and bread. Their donkeys would bring them to Giza by midday. Saqqara had filled Qaa's mind with questions. He would brood before broaching them with Unas.

Unas was enjoying the absence of conversation. It was said that if a master found one true student, he was favored by the gods, and his life a success. Unas was a master, and equally deft at ceremony, magic, and priestly politics. Grateful to have found Qaa, he believed him the one true student on whom he could build his hopes.

The pyramids rose from the desert as if to greet their approach. Their enormity excited Qaa; their high polish dazzled him. It was all so much more powerful than Djoser's Step Pyramid, which had so recently seemed the pinnacle of the world.

Unas hurried them to the temple of Khufu at the foot of the Great Pyramid. The high priest, who expected them, welcomed them himself. Because preparations were already underway for Qaa's Opening of the Heart ceremony, luxuries were dispensed with. They were received simply. They sat on the floor cross-legged on rush mats in the old style, and lunched on beer, bread, and raw onions.

Only two pharaohs separated Khufu from the reigning Menkaure. The high priest was an old man and a cousin of Khufu. His parents had known Khufu before he went to join the imperishable stars.

The elderly courtier-priest entertained them with courtesy and stories. After lunch they rested in the courtyard of the high priest's house. They dozed on couches placed under the sycamores for respite from the midday heat. Their lunch and rest would help them through the night. During the ceremony, both would fast and neither would sleep.

Toward dusk, Unas prepared Qaa. "The Opening of the Heart is a powerful initiation. If successful, it ushers you into the ranks of the mages who can call upon the gods. We will see if the gods favor you. If you are granted a vision I'll help you understand it and integrate it into your life. The ceremony itself is simple: we enter the Great Pyramid and climb to the King's Chamber. An open sarcophagus is there.

"You should know that these three pyramids were already here when our people were first called by the mildness of the river. The pyramids sat here majestic, perfect, and inscrutable. For several thousand years our ancestors lived near them, feeling their power, called to worship. When the man appeared who would become King Scorpion, something happened. The Great Pyramid opened. Some god-made magic opened the passage in its mirror side. Scorpion entered and found the sarcophagus. He lay in it and had a vision that has bound the Two Lands together ever since. Tonight you will lie where he lay. Are you ready for this?"

"I am."

"Are you really ready?"

"I am!"

"Then let us purify ourselves. Let us wash and remove our body hair. Let us honor the gods."

They washed themselves. Then they removed all body hair save eyebrows and eyelashes. They worked on each other in turn, shaving the hair with a flaked flint blade for razor. Then they were taken to a sanctuary that gave access to the pyramid. Because the entrance was well up the polished side, a kind of ladder led through the temple roof and scaled up to the entrance.

Unas and Qaa climbed.

It was dark now and two attendants carried lamps. Entering the stone passage, Qaa felt fear and elation. He followed Unas. They emerged from the narrow entrance passage into the Grand Gallery and climbed into the King's Chamber.

Unas settled Qaa into the stone sarcophagus. "You will become cold as the stone robs your body's warmth. But you will survive."

Unas made silent prayers over Qaa and then sat down by the head of the sarcophagus.

"He too will get cold," thought Qaa, "and all for my sake." Love for Unas, his teacher and friend, entered his heart. Then Qaa prayed. "My heart is the seat of my mind and soul. I dedicate my heart for all eternity to you, Amun-Ra, great god. If I can be of service, grant me a vision tonight."

Unas told the attendants to withdraw with their lamps and return for them at dawn. The chamber became dark with a perfect darkness. It was silent as the inside of a stone.

They waited and prayed. Qaa became uncomfortably cold, and shifted to lie on his left side. He continued to pray, and perhaps fell asleep.

He fed burning coals to the fire to make it as hot as he could. He wanted to purify the gold thoroughly, and so the fire must be as hot as possible. The heat grew. He went around to the side, from where he could see the gold. It had melted like luminous butter, molten and pure. While he watched, it became like the face of the Sun. Then he realized something was wrong. The gold was moving, flowing. It would overflow. Without thinking, he went up and touched it, trying to take care of it. The molten gold did not burn. Instead it flowed into him and filled him.

Qaa awoke with a start and found he was shivering. The contrast with his vision was so extreme that he laughed explosively into the darkness.

Unas asked him what had happened and Qaa told him the story.

"You have been given a gift more precious than gold."

"Was this a vision?"

"Of a very high order. You must tell no one else, to keep its power in your heart. Gold is called 'the flesh of the gods'. It has filled you with Amun-Ra's light. You are his true servant now. Stay quiet and keep your heart open, while we wait for Amun-Ra to fill the sky with morning." Unas was moved. Qaa could hear it in his voice.

When the attendants returned, Qaa and Unas left the pyramid, climbing down. The elderly courtier-priest spoke briefly with Unas and was pleased to hear that Qaa had received a vision. Unas then asked that he and Qaa be left alone. They talked over a breakfast of brown beer and bread spread with fava bean paste.

"I will open my heart to you now that yours has opened," said Unas. "I told you these three pyramids were here before our ancestors arrived. The gods made them, I am convinced of it, though I don't know which gods. But men are not content to revere the gods. Here in the fabric of this temple you see impiety. Khufu built his temple here to claim this pyramid as his own. Khafra did the same at the next pyramid. Our Pharaoh Menkaure is doing the same again, at the smallest of the three. Humans delude themselves into believing they built these great works, and claim them as their own. Other pharaohs imitate the gods' work. You saw Djoser's tomb. On the way south I'll show you Sneferu's two pyramids at Dashur. One is bent and the other incomplete. They are failures."

"This upsets you?"

"It is important we know our place. We are not the gods. A pharaoh's *ba* may join the gods, but the great gods are still the great gods."

"Where do I fit in?"

"You have been chosen by Amun-Ra. Here is how we will serve him. As you heard, our god lacks endowments. We must change this."

"By going to court?"

"In time. But you have much to understand first. You and I will lay our plans for future dynasties of pharaohs. We will help them give up the arrogance of trying to build pyramids. We will teach them to cut tombs in rock in the valleys west of Karnak. We will make it into a valley of royal tombs, a Valley of the Kings. Imagine whole dynasties buried there."

"What does that mean for Amun-Ra?"

"Let me make it clear to you. Tombs need nearby temples to make offerings for the pharaoh's *ka*, temples that must be maintained forever. Amun-Ra is the local deity. He will be the god that protects the pharaohs for millions of years. Imagine the vast endowments that will flow to him. Karnak and Luxor will become the greatest and richest temples in the world. When a god's endowments are great he is recognized as great. We will see that Amun-Ra is recognized as the greatest of gods. When the other gods are forgotten, he will still be served."

"Will you teach me how to work at the court on the god's behalf?"

"Not only that, I will teach you all I know of magic. If you keep yourself pure of heart, you will be able to compel the gods themselves into action."

"Even Amun-Ra?"

"Yes."

"When do we start?"

"We started long ago, and we will continue until I leave this body and you carry on the great work. Perhaps our work will continue in other lifetimes, too."

6

The Sphinx enjoyed his indwelling, from its first moment down to this time, when Unas and Qaa lived in mortal bodies. With limitless time and no hindrances to action, both enjoyment and suffering were choices. His indwelling opened the possibility of suffering. He was becoming attached to people. If they failed and he chose to destroy them, his suffering would be extreme. Sometimes he was grateful that the future was irreducible.

The Sphinx touched these people as gently as soft rain, promoting the growth of the planet's first great civilization. Later he would wean them. Eventually he would leave them to grow on their own. He would return to render judgment.

The Sphinx let his mind go to the river. He felt its great body, its power and intelligence. He felt the life teeming within it from bacteria to hippos, from perch the size of a man to tiny bilharzia that parasitize fishermen and blind them.

He felt the savannahs on the west bank drying out like sponges left in sunlight. He saw the towns, now in the sand, where he had taught the people how to set up stone circles and track the stars. He had guided the same people towards the river when the oases dried. He enjoyed their amazement at the pyramids and Sphinx.

The monuments had worked their purpose, triggering awe. Because the river provided abundant food and its floods made farming easy, awe could mature into inquiry.

It was the people from the Red Lands, the ones who had invented astronomy, who pushed the questions. The pyramids were so much greater than their circles. How could they be built? They were made of stone, like nothing else. How could one build in stone? They were precise in their alignments. What did this mean?

Out of their questions the first great god was born: Ptah, god of the inquiring mind.

The Sphinx dedicated the edges of his awareness to the Egyptians. Whenever a person made a sincere request to higher powers, or pursued an idea with a clear heart, the Sphinx let them encounter the penumbra of himself.

The god Ptah was born when the astronomers wanted to know more. They wanted a working calendar. They wanted to know how to use star alignments for buildings. They wanted to know how to measure the Nile's floods, and how to build in stone.

Ptah answered their needs. The Sphinx let the intentions of the postulants call forth an image, a story, and a personality. The god became real and temples were built to him. A priesthood grew who studied mathematics, the stars and engineering. Ptah inspired the priesthood and they changed Egypt.

They invented the nilometer to predict the height of the annual flood. They became good chronologists and master builders. Ptah became their creator god since he helped create so much. He became the main god at Memphis, the pharaohs' capitol on the Nile in Lower Egypt, near Djoser's Step Pyramid.

The Sphinx projected Ptah in human form, as a man holding a measuring staff and dressed in a simple close-fitting gown. The Sphinx made Ptah in the image of mankind, so they should know that all his power and potential lay coiled within themselves.

The Egyptians became infatuated with the presence of gods, and he never rejected a sincere request for communion.

He loved these people. They were open and joyful. The half-human, half-animal nature of most of the gods expressed the way the people enjoyed their own animal natures. They liked to sleep late, make love, dress up, drink, and have parties. Life was not long, but one could make it pleasurable.

He also loved his gods. They were parts of himself he had never expressed before, born of his relationship with the people. Crocodile had been right: gods took the forms of baboon, falcon, and crocodile, and they were great and powerful. The gods were as multifarious and overlapping as life in a jungle, or the conversations at a banquet. His lion guise became an aspect of many gods, from the sun god to the mother goddess' angry moods. Thousands of gods dwelt in the land of Egypt, from those who resided in a single hamlet to the chief gods of the nation. No one would ever systematize them, for the Egyptians understood that the gods were as variable as the shape of hope.

While all of this happened in the edges of his awareness, the Sphinx focused inward. He moved beyond human concerns. He touched the living Earth, which he loved like all his kind. He felt the luxuriance of the Earth superorganism. He felt its confidence, bold and unquestioning. Life on the planet was nearly four billion years old, its teeming udders of being a constantly evolving miracle.

At first he wanted to merge with the superorganism. He wanted to know every detail of all that is born, evolves, and dies on the planet from inside. What bliss this participation would bring. Then he stopped himself. It would be too great a risk. He would intervene. It would be almost impossible not to. He would know when the least sparrow fell from the sky. How could he not help?

He must leave Earth independent. Otherwise it would become no more than the theme park of his imagination.

So he went into the core of his awareness, into that poise from which he experienced existence directly and he no longer acted.

He watched the Multiverse being born out of emptiness again, and again, and again. Its continual rebirth defined the smallest meaningful unit of time. He appreciated the passage of time and the rebirth of the Multiverse as identical. Reality's re-creation of itself became his recreation.

He touched the child he had once been, sitting by a waterfall. That child's wonder lived within him now as he sat by the waterfall of existence flooding into time over the cliff of Nothing. He would stay here during his indwelling, letting his appreciation ripple out to all beings.

Meantime, the penumbra of his awareness engaged the Egyptians. He would let their gods evolve. As the people mastered the skills Ptah offered, other gods would dominate.

He liked the feeling of the small provincial solar deity Amun-Ra. He was becoming fond of Unas and Qaa. Unas had the aggression of a strong life force, and the will to channel it towards the god. Qaa had enough love of luxury to compel him into the pharaonic court. There he could elaborate the long-term trap for the dynasties that Unas was designing. Qaa had merited his vision. He would know the flesh of the gods.

Amun-Ra would prosper. He would make him a great god, in time perhaps the greatest. Then Amun-Ra and all the other gods would fall silent. The Sphinx would withdraw his awareness, letting people find their own way.

Until one day someone found and solved the puzzles that he and his three companions had set. Then his gods would reawaken and call him from stillness. He would return and render judgment. Whether he offered the people a festival or the sword would depend on them.

7

Six people watched the sunset from the veranda of the Al Minah Hotel. They sat in a semi-circle facing west. Five of them had just arrived in Cairo; one was a permanent resident.

The Sun melted like a globe of molten glass into the desert west of the Nile, as it has every day since the First Time. It melted into the Valley of the Kings west of Karnak, where pharaohs carved their names in stone and set their souls to join the gods beyond the stars. It melted into the Red Land west of the pyramids, sending their triangular shadows into the land of the living.

The adults were mesmerized. Maria noticed them glancingly. Her attention went to her son Cliff, who was fidgeting.

Cliff had come with her from Berkeley, where she was a professor of ethnobotany and he was a senior at Berkeley High. He was in love with computer science, and his skills were already beyond his teachers'. Maria saw a problem waiting to happen. She got the University to accept Cliff for one programming course. After that life made sense. Cliff sat through the rest of his boring high school classes, while pattern recognition algorithms danced in his head.

Cliff had an elusive beauty. His skin tones were as rich as the Egyptians who moved among them with drinks. Their skins ran to coffee with milk. His was honey with almonds, thanks to his Japanese father and Latina mother. Cliff was graceful even when fidgeting.

The fingers of Cliff's right hand tapped on his thigh. Maria waited to see which way he would break.

"Mustapha, when can we dig?"

Maria turned toward Mustapha at the abrupt question. The elegantly dressed Cairene was more amused than shocked. Mustapha was the Director of the Supreme Council of Antiquities. He had the discretion to make or break the research plans of anyone who wanted access to the ancient monuments of Egypt.

Mustapha had a high forehead, black hair combed straight back, and a thick mustache. His brown eyes were almost black. He was by turns implacable as an Old Kingdom statue then intimate and funny. Unpredictable as rain in the desert, he was playful but like a lion is playful.

"Cliff my boy, why are you interested in digs? That's Jack's business. I thought you were here to help your mother."

"I'm helping Jack too. Mom doesn't need much number crunching."

"Jack?" Mustapha turned to him with a smile. "Your permit request doesn't mention this member of your team."

"The boy is good and I can use him," said Jack.

Maria watched the last light of day gild Jack's face. He was blond-gold and handsome in an old-fashioned way. Professor of Egyptology at Chicago's Oriental Institute, Jack had fallen in love with Egypt as a boy. Now in his late forties, he was the world's leading expert on the Sphinx. His inherited fortune was large enough for him to supplement the university's stingy research budgets for Egyptology. Jack wore perfectly laundered khakis, a white cotton shirt and handmade shoes.

"Come on, Mustapha." Jack lacked the patience to play bureaucratic games. "Don't joke with me about my permit requests. Wolfgang's a puppy from Heidelberg. You let him sail through, while you keep me waiting. You've been drinking with me on this veranda for twenty years during every digging season, and this is how you treat me?"

Mustapha represented the race that invented bureaucratic games more than 5,000 years ago. He looked over at the puppy from Heidelberg. Wolfgang at 31 was a double Ph.D., in physics and engineering. Slight, with cropped black hair and ice blue eyes, he had the bad boy look of a German rock star. He slouched, sneered easily, and looked like he would be happier on stage, where he could drink in the adulation of thousands.

Petra, his younger girlfriend, sat next to him drinking shots of arak. She was blonde as he was dark, with equal eyes of ice that looked like they should melt in this climate. Petra was a painter who had started her own women's art collective. An elaborate tattoo snaked across her shoulders. Her pierced ears and eyebrows carried enough studs to have caused hell at any metal detectors she passed through on her way here.

Mustapha studied Jack before replying. "Jack, I value Wolfgang's research. He's going to run a mini-robot up the mysterious shaft in the Great Pyramid, the curious one leading from the Queen's Chamber. I want to have a look through the second door we found at the head of the shaft when we cut through the first one. The mystery of what is behind this second door needs looking into. I regard it as the most pressing matter in Egyptology. I endorse Wolfgang's methods because they will cause no harm. You on the other hand Jack my old friend, are becoming impatient. I worry about what you propose. As you know, the time when we could damage the monuments to satisfy our curiosity is over. We must proceed cautiously and make sure we conserve them."

"Look, Mustapha, give me a break. I've devoted my life to studying the Sphinx. The last thing I want to do is hurt her."

"Her, Jack? I've never heard you call the Sphinx 'her,' old friend."

"Well. Anyhow, you know I'm studying anomalies about the Sphinx. My gut tells me it conceals chambers and passageways. You won't let me dig, so I have to use seismology. Last year we laid down passive microphones. They're sensitive enough to pick up earthquakes in Peru and family fights in Cairo. We compiled the data. It looks like the way sound is transmitted under the Sphinx, there has to be open space there. But the shapes just don't make sense."

"So now you need an active matrix of sound," put in Wolfgang, animated for the first time. "What is your plan, explosions?" Tight wrinkles of delight fanned out from the corners of his eyes.

"That's my problem—and Jack's," said Mustapha gazing west.

"The charges are the size of kids' firecrackers. There's no scenario under which they can cause harm."

"I am the guardian of the monuments. If we begin to allow blasting, where can we safely draw the line? When does legitimate inquiry lead to irresponsible damage? Can't you look into something else Jack? So many unanswered questions remain."

"But this is where my work has to go," said Jack, tenacious in the twilight.

"Look guys, I see a possibility here," Wolfgang offered. "Maybe we can do it with music. Maybe we can put music through the sand and watch the waveforms. The physics is a little weird, but maybe. Jack, let me think about it and let's meet tomorrow night."

"Until I get my permit, I'll be here every night," said Jack.

"And I hope after that too," said Mustapha. "I am on this veranda every night as a witness to the sunset. The research season is so much more charming than the rest of the year because of your lively minds. I hope to hear of your new discoveries every evening."

He stood, picked up his walking stick and the white panama hat that complemented his linen suit, tipped the hat to the ladies and said, "Until tomorrow my friends."

They watched him walk off into the night and the mysteries of Cairo.

8

Wanre was a lightly boned biped with golden skin. His people were graced with flowing manes of hair across a rainbow of colors. Wanre's head displayed none of this luxuriance. His head was shaved to show he was adept in a form of inner technology as old as his people.

Wanre had agreed to become Speaker of the Consilium for a cycle. He had long served the Consilium. On its behalf, Wanre had become an expert on Earth. He sat on a committee that monitored Earth's progress. The Consilium tracked civilizations at the end of Level 2, when a civilization going global can awaken or self-destruct.

Wanre's tastes were simple: sparsely furnished rooms around a courtyard. These were in keeping with the style of his home world Leucandra. Beyond his window was a lake. Long-tailed airdragons, the largest of their kind on the planet, flew the stately quadrilles of their courtship. He watched as they twisted their tails into complex knots and drew the results across the sky.

Wanre looked beyond the airdragons to the nearby mountaintop. Dense bloom washed the mountain's flanks like distilled summer sunshine. The eyrie of Toran, the Second Speaker, was at the mountain's top. Toran had left her home planet on a spiral arm of the galaxy to build her eyrie near Wanre while they held office together. He welcomed her proximity. She enjoyed flying in the soft warm air of his planet, now that she and the airdragons understood each other.

Thinking of Earth, Wanre's mind turned to a newly agreed system for classifying civilizations. It would be easy to take this system for granted. Future generations wouldn't understand the time and energy it had cost them.

He ran through the taxonomy in his mind. *Level One*: the species is intelligent, self-aware and has built a civilization, but lacks advanced information systems. *Level 2*: They have advanced information systems and nuclear and biotechnology but no global civilization. *Level 3*: They have experienced a global awakening beyond the disparities in wealth and power that make the use of nuclear and bio-weapons attractive. *Level 4:* They have fashioned a global society assonant with nature. *Level 5:* They have evolved galactic travel and demonstrated a capacity for peaceful co-existence. They are ready for recruitment into the Consilium.

"Obvious once stated," thought Wanre. "But that is the hallmark of all great ideas."

Wanre had grown fond of Earth as he studied it. He was concerned for its future. He knew that most cultures do not make it into the Consilium any more than most salmon from a clutch of eggs survive to spawn, or most spiders ballooning into the world on parachutes of silk live to reproduce.

The airdragons over the lake comforted Wanre. Large predators in view evened the psychological balance of his next meeting. This morning Wanre must meet with two other Earth experts, the co-chairs of the Committee on Earth Assessment. Benben and Bulbul were the two halves of a symbiont from a galaxy within his home universe.

He did not like them. In their presence he had to control his prejudice against parasites. Their race had evolved into symbionts or it would never have made it into the Consilium. His intuition sensed a lot of the parasite left in them.

The male Bulbul was much smaller than the female Benben. While she was large and stood erect, he looked like a worm. His body was draped around her neck like a scarf, his hind section attached by suction and teeth to a hole in the top of her head. His face appeared at the level of her chest.

Political correctness, of which Wanre was no fan, said that he should venerate the harmony such symbionts had achieved. But Benben and Bulbul seemed designed to blunt his attempts at open-mindedness. To him they always looked faintly ridiculous and smelled mildly evil. Despite the vaunted mutuality of symbionts, he found that this pair cast the shadow of the parasite.

It also irked him that while the two always agreed with each other, they disagreed with him on everything from Consilium policy to the best place for lunch.

"Enough," thought Wanre. "Let me still my mind before they appear."

Benben's green skin set off her topaz eyes. Bulbul, wrapped around her neck, gave a rakish smile. Of the two, it was the wormlike Bulbul that Wanre preferred. He admired the ability to be rakish in someone who was an off-white grub, wrapped around his partner's neck, his hind end implanted in her head. Wanre knew that Bulbul could survive two days, Benben a little longer, if they were decoupled. He imagined taking Bulbul out for a drink unplugged.

"Nice digs you got yourself here, old boy," said Bulbul with a wink.

"Welcome," said Wanre, rising to greet them. "Please have a seat."

"No thanks," said Benben. "This is urgent." Wanre had heard that earlier in her life she was an artist, and charming. One could sit with them for hours drinking tea, talking of art, consciousness and politics. While he believed the reports he had never experienced the charm.

"You've been avoiding me," said Benben. "Our committee hasn't met in months, but we have business that is vital."

"Calm down," said Wanre. "What is so vital?"

"The Earth. We must intervene."

"There's nothing particularly interesting about the Earth. It's nearing the end of Level 2, but so are over a thousand others that we're watching."

"I've followed it closely for over thirty years, and I'm convinced that the Earth is different, that it represents a danger to the Consilium of a kind we've never seen."

"What evidence do you have?"

"I am completely convinced. You block the gathering of any evidence. You've delayed the committee from meeting and you don't take the threat seriously."

"I've made the best data collection methods available to you, techniques that none of the other world assessment committees have access to. We've followed all the standard protocols and seen nothing on Earth particularly out of the ordinary."

"These methods are of no use to me whatever. You ignore what I have known for three decades: Earth is a danger and we must intervene."

"You know the Consilium doesn't intervene in a Level 2 culture, except in the rare case where it's threatened by a higher level rogue. Even that's happened only a few times since the Beginning."

"Don't give me that. We credential solo ops to mess around down there whenever we feel like it."

"Solo ops can be credentialed, yes, but on Earth there haven't been any for a long time. Interventions just don't work very well. You know there's an informal convention against them. So unless you have a more coherent argument to make, I'll simply have to move on to other business."

"Don't you get so goddamned officious with me. If you continue to ignore what I know is true, I will work with others. I will take it over your head to the Council."

"Go right ahead," said Wanre wearily.

Bulbul felt the flush of Benben's brain chemicals suffusing up through his hind segment, and made a moue.

9

"Come on Petra, it's time to get up," said Wolfgang. The day's first sunlight came through the shutters, fingers of fire reaching into their room on a day already gone hot. He was eager to get to the pyramids.

"Oh, it's so early! I don't want to do anything today, Wolfie. Remind me not to drink so much arak tonight, or else to drink it all night through. I don't want to feel like this again tomorrow morning!" She stretched her arms over her head, spreading her blond hair over the pillow into the sunlight streaming in.

"Look, we have to get an early start. We have to drive the equipment over to the pyramids in the Mercedes, and I have to get into the Queen's Chamber."

"I know, I know. Give me a minute to shower, and why not order some hot coffee so I can wake up."

Wolfgang moved to the phone to order their continental breakfast. As he picked up the receiver, he watched Petra. She was out of the bed and on her way to the bathroom in a single languid movement. He ordered the breakfast, put the phone down and followed her. His gaze was detached yet transfixed, like a cat watching a goldfish in its bowl.

Wolfgang had spent months building a small robotic device. His minibot was designed to climb up a slender shaft from the Queen's Chamber of the Great Pyramid. Wolfgang's was the third robot to climb this shaft.

The first robot found a polished limestone slab at the head of the shaft. Was it a magical door into the afterlife for the pharaoh's soul to pass through? It could hardly be for the living: the shaft runs over sixty meters from the chamber; it is only twenty centimeters high and as many wide. No human could ever access this polished limestone door until the invention of a robot small and powerful enough to crawl all the way up to the end bearing a light and camera.

The next robot was a National Geographic effort. A team of some seventy people were involved. There was worldwide coverage, with the robot's efforts livecast on the Net. The robot was equipped with a cutting tool. It drilled through the polished limestone door to find yet another door.

What lay behind this second door? Blank solid rock, or treasures of knowledge purposely sealed away for millennia until anthropoid apes crossed an invisible line in the evolution of intelligence and created the technology to open it? Wolfgang intended to find out.

10

Wanre was troubled. He felt sure his meeting with Benben and Bulbul was the start of a long struggle. So he took his normal medicine for a troubled mind.

He went out from his courtyard, latching the gate behind him. A visitor from Earth would judge Wanre's world primitive. Seeing villas in the lush landscape, the visitor might take them for holiday homes. When he found no cities but only what looked like jungle villages, the visitor might conclude the locals were no more advanced than an indigenous tribe.

Yet Wanre ran the Consilium from here. All the instrumentalities he needed were folded into the living tissues of the planet. Wanre walked near the lake and watched the airdragons, half a dozen adult dapples, do barrel rolls. He walked on and came to a fork in the road. Left lay the woods. Right led around the lake to Saiki's villa then climbed the mountain to Toran's eyrie.

He turned and entered the woods. Morning light slanted through the trees and awakened their blossoms. He felt relieved and happy. His irritation at Benben and Bulbul receded to the edges of his mind.

Wanre sat down in the scented shade. He put his left hand on a tree trunk and his right on the ground. He closed his eyes, emptied his mind and relaxed.

A sweet memory of childhood came. He recalled the story of the green magi who appeared near the end of Leucandra's Level 2. The green magi cultivated the talent to see into the life of all the planet's organisms. They could understand in an intuitive flash what it was like to be any animal or plant. They knew from inside the hunger and the feeding, the rutting and the mating.

The green magi felt the flower seduce the bee and knew the bee's suck and swoon. They understood the subtle moods and cues that bound things together. They knew the needs of each species and all their interactions. They saw the flows of energy and poison, understood the interior of altruism and aggression. They saw webs of light dance down through the wealth of creatures. They tasted the teeming udders of being.

Seeing into the intimate lives of the species, the green magi began to take teachings from them. They learned how to penetrate the wisdom of the living world and extract its solutions. The book of life on Leucandra, billions of years old, became their grimoire, their book of spells.

The green magi became so adept that they could *see* the patterns that evolution makes in time like wind in tall grass. They decided to share the results. This sharing brought Leucandran culture into assonance, the moment when a species leaps beyond its own mind and learns to read and follow the book of nature. Their species rebuilt its infrastructure to mimic natural systems at the level of fine structure and comport with them overall. Assonance represented the maturation of their species, the *volte face* in which it stopped trying to force nature to fit its notions and began to harmonize its every move with nature's great pattern. Those activities that did not harmonize dropped off the screen.

Scientists learned to ask the genomes of species and suites of species where they were pregnant for change. Along which vectors could the genomes readily move? They developed the soft science of combinatorial biologics, to speed up the genomes' natural dispositions for change. Their culture reaped vast rewards with little risk.

Wanre's left hand felt the rough damp skin of the tree. His right worked its way through grassy plants to the soft ground. When his mind went quiet, he felt the energies flowing all around him and fell into appreciation. He knew himself part of the One Thing, the web of life on his planet. He felt microorganisms around him decompose what had died in the woods. He felt trees draw in the nutrients thus released. He felt the trees make pollen to feed creatures of the air and fruit for those who walk and climb and spread seeds far and wide. He felt all their separate energies fuse into a whole and he *saw*.

When he had seen the physical exchanges of energy through the living tissues, he began to see things more refined. With open eyes he watched large flakes of light rain down on the forest. The light came down like immaterial snow. Invisible to most, he knew it as the stuff that made life flourish.

Wanre resided in the rapture of the real for as long as time allowed.

Then he felt something soft hit his head and fall into the grass. He opened his eyes and looked down to see a bunch of purple flowers before him. A scream from above drew his eyes to two airdragons, common blues small as his hand, chasing each other through the treetops. Wanre laughed lightly at their play.

He became aware of his duties. He thanked all the living things, stood up, and walked home to his office.

11

"Hello Wolfie," said Petra. "Where have you gone, lost inside some pyramid?" She smiled. She had gotten used to him disappearing in mid-sentence when a solution to a problem he was working on entered his mind.

"Just in love with my chocolate brioche," he said. "Where were we? Yeah, the plan for the day."

He laid it out quickly. She would drive one Mercedes and he the other. They were in the hotel garage parked and ready. He'd done that yesterday. There were six boxes. Each had three. He had the minibot, computers, and recording equipment. She had the cables, high rez monitors, and box of spares. Mustapha had agreed to close the chamber while they worked in it and post guards to protect the equipment.

"Anyhow, I've got tracers in the equipment that no thief could notice but I can see from a hundred kilometers. And the Egyptian Secret Service would help me to track it down. "

She looked at him as if for the first time, wondered how much she didn't know about him, and where what she didn't know was going to take her.

"We'll assemble the hardware in the Queen's Chamber. We start there. Today I'll just run diagnostics. I've built the whole system to military specs, but it's traveled a long way and I want to know of any problems with the minibot before she crawls up the shaft."

"How come the Queen's Chamber?"

"Because that's where the treasure is buried: behind the little door at the top of the secret shaft. What a trip, huh? I need to get to that door, that cute little door, that sweet little polished white limestone door that lies all the way at the end of the shaft, and put my probe through the hole in it. Then I need to cut through the second door and see what hides behind that."

"How can you cut through the solid rock?"

Wolfgang had designed a laser that cuts through stone like a surgical laser cuts through human tissue: carefully and persistently until the job was done. It would work on granite and other stone matrices. Wolfgang knew that Egyptians worked in hard stones. They made statues and vessels of diorite, an impossibly hard stone, bending it to their purpose as if it were soft wood. Some say we could not work diorite so well today without diamond cutting tools.

Fascinated by such technical mysteries left by the ancient Egyptians, Wolfgang was prepared for diorite and other super hard stones. His laser was tunable so it could be reprogrammed for whatever he ran into. The laser was carefully packed away in a titanium box that Wolfgang had loaded into the trunk of one of the cars.

He wanted cars as reliable as his own designs for this expedition, and so had decided on the pair of diesel Mercedes. He bought them in Israel, through security service connections. The Mossad had used these Mercedes, old and battered, since purchase, so he was sure they were well maintained: two white 350SDL Turbodiesels, tank-like things and tough as trucks. He assumed they were well bugged too. He was happy to have his whereabouts tracked by old friends who may just come in handy if things ever got really hot in the desert.

Wolfgang thought of himself as a consultant, never a spy. At the University of Heidelberg, his expertise in physics and engineering focused like crosshairs on quantum cryptography. He used the randomness of the subatomic world to produce unbreakable codes. As was natural for a professor with such interests, Wolfgang worked with the German intelligence service, the Bundesnachrichtendienst or BND. When the BND started a project with the Americans on secure communications, Wolfgang began to consult with both the CIA and NSA. He got on well with the Americans. When the Americans set up a joint working group on quantum codes with the Israelis, Wolfgang was sent to the Middle East and made Mossad friends.

He helped Mossad with a series of decryptions. The work involved breaking novel codes that were giving Mossad trouble. To Wolfgang the codes were soon transparent. The result was a series of raids on the Palestinians in which dozens died. Wolfgang learned to distance himself from the results of his work.

Over time, the Americans funded more of Wolfgang's research and demanded more of his time. They also wanted his loyalty. The CIA asked for regular reports. This did not seem problematic to Wolfgang. He would report on internal politics in his university department. As his funding became ever more American, Wolfgang filed more extensive reports. Now that he was in Egypt, he was expected to report on what he was doing and what he observed. Wolfgang was a consultant, he reminded himself, not a spy. Some electronic postcards to his friends seemed only reasonable for all the support they gave him for his research.

They descended to the hotel's garage and the valets brought the cars.

"OK, this one is yours," said Wolfgang. He handed her the keys. "We went over the route. Keep the Citadel to your left, turn right onto the Sixth of October Bridge. It will take us over the Nile. From there it's easy, you basically turn left, follow the road and you'll get to the pyramids. You want to follow me?"

"Maybe you should be the one to follow me instead."

He liked her pluck. "There will be parking reserved for us when we get to the pyramids. Here," he said, taking something from his pocket with a flourish. "My new trick. This fits over your ear like so." He placed a soft-covered wire loop over her left ear, and arranged the microphone bar across to her cheekbone. "It's a communicator that will let us talk to each other while we drive. Voice-activated," he said with a quick smile, putting on his own unit.

They got into their cars, which started up with a diesel clatter. Edging away from the hotel, they plowed into the early morning congestion, noise, and funk of Cairo. Off to the left was the medieval Arab quarter. Above it all loomed Saladin's Citadel and the Muhammad Ali Mosque, its minarets pencils against the sky.

As Petra drove over the Sixth of October Bridge, she saw feluccas plying the Nile below. The boats seemed incongruous in modern Cairo, and sent her thoughts to ancient days, a time when no high-rise buildings flanked the Nile, and no highway bridge spanned it. She felt herself wanting again to be a tourist. She would love to go by boat all the way up the Nile to Luxor and Karnak, the great temples near the Valley of the Kings. She had to see the paintings and frescoes in the tombs. After Wolfie uncovered his secrets in the pyramids, she would get him to take some vacation.

Wolfgang and Petra pulled the cars into their reserved spaces in the visitor parking at Giza. It was 7:45 a.m. The Great Pyramid would be opening an hour later than usual, at 9 a.m., to let Wolfgang run his equipment into the Queen's Chamber without tourists in the way. The Queen's Chamber itself would remain off limits until Wolfgang had finished with his project.

Nearby in the parking lot was a tour bus full of Americans on holiday, here to see the sights. Their tour company was surprised by the late opening time, and so they had an hour to kill. Instead of walking around to see how the temples, causeways, pyramids, and Sphinx all fit together, they huddled in their bus, engine running to keep the air-conditioning going. As Wolfgang and Petra opened the trunks of their cars they drew the tourists' attention. Padded faces turned towards them, the eyes within restless and bored, caught in the quandary of wanting entertainment but unwilling to step into the heat to find it.

Wolfgang took out two lightweight dollies and assembled them. He piled three titanium equipment boxes on each one and strapped them down. He slung on a small backpack. Then offering one of the dollies to Petra, he said, "Let our adventure begin."

The tourists watched Wolfgang and Petra stroll with their equipment toward the entrance denied to them until 9 a.m. Their looks turned hostile over the Coke and jelly doughnuts they were using to fortify themselves for the rigors ahead.

At the entrance, Wolfgang turned and gave the tourists a jaunty wave. He showed the guard a permission letter from Mustapha. The letter bore all the flourishes of Egyptian bureaucracy. The guard bestowed such a careful examination on it that Wolfgang wondered if he was waiting for baksheesh. Then following his own logic the guard became satisfied and waved them through.

They stopped for a moment just inside the Great Pyramid. It was Petra's first time and she did not want to rush the experience. The relative cool surprised her. The temperature outside had soared already. Here by contrast it felt like entering a cave cut into a mountain, a cave that had been inhabited forever.

"You know," said Wolfgang playing tour guide, "this wasn't the original entrance. That's higher up. A big Mameluke blasted this opening. His descendants are probably terrorist mullahs."

"Or worse: tour guides for busloads of large people."

"Come on, I'll show you how they sealed this place from the inside with thirty ton granite blocks."

12

When Maria arrived at the Egyptian Museum she always thought of the Louvre. This building too bore a French imperial imprint. Before finding the desk she was assigned, she dropped by to see Mustapha. The nameplate on his office door gave his title: Director of the Supreme Counsel of Antiquities.

"Good to see you in your lair again," she said.

He rose politely, using his knuckles against the surface of the desk to raise himself. His red silk tie arced forward to touch the desk's edge and brush against it as he stood.

"Ah, Maria you come like spring to our hot desert." Maria was wearing a yellow silk blouse with a pale blue cotton skirt. "You have come back to sit with us in what remains of our patrimony. What was not stolen by Egyptian grave robbers before the Christian era, or by the British, French, and Germans during it. Please sit down" He was smiling beneath his mustache. "We have little left but you are welcome to enjoy it. Coffee?"

"No thanks."

Mustapha took a moment to appreciate Maria. Her dark hair came below the ears. Her high cheekbones were Castilian. Her nose and shoulders were broad enough to remind him of women in Aztec carvings. He mused that her features traced the relationships her forebears had entered into from Spain to California. He knew she was the first in her family to go to university, finishing her doctorate at Berkeley with scholarships based on merit. He liked the way she moved through the world. "What brings you here this year?"

"Last year, you remember, I was researching the theory that Egypt became great by discovering beer—that the cultivation of the whole Nile Valley came about to produce the grain for its fermentation."

"Yes. The theory is charming, though I'm not convinced until the cocktail hour approaches."

"You won't believe what I'm up to this year." Sparring with Mustapha was to her mind Cairo's most refined pleasure. Continuing, she said, "Psychedelics."

"Your parents—or maybe your grandparents—must have used them in the '60s. Are you continuing their rebellion in your academic sphere? Is that the best way to advance your career?"

Unwilling to be drawn, she said, "Ethnobotany is a fertile field where divergent points of view can blossom."

Mustapha smiled. He liked a woman who could turn his thrust with metaphor.

Maria continued, "I was studying grain in the ancient world. My beer theory was part of that. The work with grain led me, through one of life's little surprises, into studying the Greek Eleusinian Mysteries from the Golden Age of Athens and before. In the Eleusinian Mysteries, the initiates drank a psychedelic brew as their annual communal sacred rite."

"Hmm," said Mustapha, neither encouraging nor interrupting.

"It looks like the Eleusinian Mystery brew was based on ergot fungus growing on grain, like LSD. So Euripides, Aristotle, Alexander the Great and every other Greek you've heard of took acid. As a scientist I have to wonder if the cult of Eleusis, with its sacred psychedelic communion, wasn't important to the flowering of Greek civilization. Now I wonder if the Greeks learned their psychedelic botany from the Egyptians, just as they learned most other things of interest from them."

"You are gaining in wisdom, Maria, and becoming a woman after my own heart," said Mustapha lightly.

"So I did what research I could at the Smithsonian and other American collections. I have a hunch that priests were using psychedelics in ancient Egypt by the 18th dynasty."

"Akhenaten?"

"Certainly."

"And from what sources—grain again?"

"The sacred acacia tree is everywhere in Egyptian art and was worshiped throughout the country. Other than papyrus it's always struck me as the most emblematic plant of ancient Egypt. It's a member of the pea family and its seeds are loaded with DMT, a natural psychedelic. All you need to make it effective is a leaf with the complementary chemistry. There's a very good one endemic to Egypt and known to the ancients: Syrian rue. If you mix the two together..."

"You go to wonderland." Mustapha was becoming interested. "Do you think it was used here? By the priests?"

"Probably. I'm here to find evidence. The priests of ancient Egypt were expert botanists and chemists. I doubt very much that such an important plant medicine would have escaped them."

Mustapha rested his palms on his desk. "What they achieved in those early years of the Old Kingdom was never surpassed in all the subsequent 3,000 years of Egyptian culture. Or to my eye in the 2,000 years since pharaonic Egypt became a memory. How did such a supremely sophisticated culture emerge out of nowhere? I wonder if this intuition of yours has anything to do with it."

"Either that or their culture was a gift of their gods," Maria said. She was thoughtful. "Or perhaps both: maybe the priests spoke to their gods with the help of the sacred acacia?"

"I know less than I'd like to about the mysteries those ancient priests practiced," said Mustapha. His gaze fell on the glass paperweight on his desk. It contained a small figure of Amun-Ra, the ancient Sun god, sitting still and quiet inside like the germ in a crystal seed waiting to grow into life. Mustapha was pondering Maria's ideas when his phone rang and called him back into the present. "Excuse me, I'm not expecting a call, but I must take it."

He answered, frowned, and turned to Maria. "I must take this call in private. Forgive my rudeness."

"Time for me to get to work," said Maria.

"Until we meet again," said Mustapha, "Perhaps tonight on the veranda of the Al Minah." She smiled and left, closing the door behind her.

He said into the phone, "You know not to call me here."

"Forgive me but it is unprecedented. You must come at once."

"Then I will come," said Mustapha. He put down the phone, rose to find his linen coat, panama hat and walking stick, and soon was on his way.

13

Cliff rode in Jack's white Range Rover. This would be Cliff's first view of the pyramids and the Sphinx. Jack wanted to give the boy that experience. In Jack's view, every person's life divided into before Giza and after Giza. Meeting these ancient monuments was the ultimate coming of age experience. As to those who never made it, well the world is full of people you just cannot talk to.

They parked and got out. Cliff wore black jeans with a black tee shirt. He complemented these with black sandals and a black baseball cap. He believed in themes and completed it by donning his black sunspecs. Cliff closed his door with a solid thunk, but no other sound came from him. He stood and stared.

Jack let a little time pass. He took Cliff's silence as awe.

"So what do you think?" Jack felt as proud as if he had built the pyramids and Sphinx himself.

"So radical. I had no idea."

Pointing to the pyramids, Jack said, "Imagine these babies as they were originally. They were clad in white limestone top to bottom and polished like a mirror. The Great Pyramid was the tallest building in the world until the 19th century."

"What beat it?"

Jack laughed. "Damned if I know. I guess the Eiffel Tower."

"Sort of a cheat. Doesn't amount to much. It's skinny, mostly open-air, made of factory metal and certainly won't last as long."

"You're becoming a historical reactionary in your first ten minutes here. Good sign in a budding Egyptologist."

Cliff was still staring at the pyramids and not quite listening. "Can we climb them?"

"I'm afraid not anymore. I did when I was your age. It was easy then. You could come here, slip some baksheesh to a guide, and he'd take you up by a safe route. There have been a lot of deaths by falling since then—at an angle of fifty-one degrees you tend to keep falling once you start—and so the local authorities have really cracked down."

"Even at night?"

"I'm afraid so."

"What about Mustapha, can't we wangle a permission?"

"We're already pushing his envelope. But look, we'll have some pretty special time inside when Wolfgang gets his equipment running. Right now I want to show you something about the Sphinx."

They walked around the recumbent Sphinx, taking it in slowly. The great statue was timeworn yet still immensely powerful. It may have lost its nose in a fit of human intolerance, but the Sphinx still smiled its Mona Lisa smile long after Ozymandias and the ancient empires had turned to dust.

"We don't really know who built the Sphinx or why," said Jack. "A stela bearing the name of Pharaoh Thutmose IV was set up between the paws. But that no more proves he built it than some kid's tag, spray painted on a New York City subway car, proves the kid built the car or owns the subway."

"What about the pyramids?"

"No more evidence there. Standard Egyptology says they were built in the Fourth Dynasty of the Old Kingdom, around 4,500 years ago. I'm not convinced. To me the 'standard view' has become a dirty word for when bright people put their heads into ancient manuscripts and tombs like an ostrich puts its head in the sand."

"What are they hiding from?"

"What I call the Holy Anomalies. A series of them that the standard view just doesn't want to know about. One: no name of any pharaoh figures in those three pyramids there, other than a single bit of graffiti. Two: the pyramids are without decorations or funeral texts painted on their walls—there are no 'pyramids texts' in these pyramids. In all the lesser pyramids we see the walls proclaiming the name of the person buried there, and the walls swarm with prayers to help the deceased get across to the other side. Not our three Giza pyramids. So I'm pretty sure they were never tombs. Three: the star shafts of the Great Pyramid look like they are aligned for a time 10,000 years ago. But remember, the standard theory says these pyramids were built just 4,500 years ago."

"Is there any science to support the standard view?"

"That's the problem. Egyptology is not a science. Physics was already a science with Aristotle. Egyptology started a couple of hundred years ago with Napoleon's expedition to Egypt. Most of what it's done until about 10 minutes ago has been grave robbery."

"You're pretty radical!"

"Not hard to be radical among a bunch of Egyptologists. If they were really scientists they'd head straight for the anomalies and burrow in until they had teased out answers. But the field mostly draws people who like the fact that nothing in Egypt changed for thousands of years. They have their story of who built the pyramids and they don't want that to change either. You can also see why I wind up funding a lot of my own research."

"So the standard story doesn't make sense, and most of the players don't want to know why. Room for a major breakthrough?"

"Hope so amigo, it's what keeps me coming here. That and the wonder—who *did* build the pyramids and *why*. Look, I want to show you another Holy Anomaly."

They walked over to the northern flank of the Sphinx. Cliff was surprised to find a high sandstone wall. He had always imagined that the Sphinx sat on the sand in the open desert, with sand dunes stretching around it from the Nile to the horizon. Instead the Sphinx sat on a stone platform that was open only to the front. Behind its back and around the flanks were walls.

"This thing wasn't built but cut out of the living rock. Like Mount Rushmore. There was a small mountain here that was probably somewhat Sphinx-shaped to begin with. They cut away just enough stone to reveal the figure, leaving the statue in an enclosure open at the front with walls on three sides. What interests me are the defects in the surrounding walls. Take a look." Jack pointed at a series of ripples in the sandstone wall. Smooth, rounded, and irregular, they did not look like they were designed by the ancient builders. "What do these ripples in the stone look like to you?"

"Closest thing is some eroded hills we were hiking through in Colorado last summer."

"Exactly, erosion. I thought so too. So I had a geologist friend who consults for NASA on erosion on Mars come here to look. I flew him in. He gets right here where we are standing. 'Yep, ' he says, ' erosion by rainwater, no doubt about it.' Now here's the killer. You remember when it last rained here?"

"I don't know, five or ten years?"

"Now it's your turn to get radical, Cliff."

"OK, 500 years."

"Right direction only more so. Turns out it is 7000 years since it rained here, give or take a sprinkle. Let that sink in: 7000 years. It wasn't always desert in Egypt, with only a narrow ribbon of green flanking the Nile. On the contrary, it was Eden. It was lush green all the way from here to Morocco. Then the climate crossed a cusp. You know Mandelbrot math?"

Cliff nodded, delighted Jack knew about this stuff.

"Well," Jack said, "the climate system found a new homeostasis. It did it virtually overnight. It took only 10 years or so for this place to go from Eden to Sahara."

"And so," Cliff said, excited, "the erosion of the walls had to have happened while it still rained regularly."

"Remember, these walls are here because they cut the Sphinx out of the living rock. So tell me, how old is the Sphinx?"

"More than 7000 years old!"

"That, my boy," said Jack, "is a pretty piece of reasoning." He pointed to the Sphinx. "It puts this unsigned masterpiece lying here in front of us in the same age range," he pointed to the pyramids, "as those other three unsigned masterpieces over there."

"I'm signing up for your team. How do we find evidence to blow the standard view apart?"

"Under the Sphinx. That's my hunch. Other NASA friends have leaked me some Geomonitor Satellite images based on a sensitive kind of mapping sonar. Nothing clear, but it looks like some caverns under the Sphinx."

"That's what Edgar Cayce said."

"I think he said in front, but that's all new age hogwash to me. Far as I'm concerned, 'new age' rhymes with 'sewage'. I don't believe in aliens and I'm not interested in psychics. I want the goods."

"Grave robbing?"

"Well maybe, but for science," said Jack with a smile that would blind a camel.

14

Mustapha strolled down the corridor from his office towards the lobby of the Egyptian Museum. He was perhaps the last man in Cairo to carry a walking stick for effect. When colleagues twitted him about looking like an Egyptian official from a Humphrey Bogart movie because of his signature white linen suit, panama hat, and walking stick, he suavely pointed out that Egyptians had made linen since pre-dynastic times. His walking stick he fondly called his magic wand. As to the panama, well, what defense does style really need?

He told his secretary he was going out for lunch on foot, to explain why she did not need to call the car and driver he had at his disposal as Director of the Supreme Council of Antiquities. He was going to investigate the unexpected phone call he had received while Maria, with unhappy timing, was sitting in his office.

He had in fact no intention of walking, and was headed for the garage where he kept an inconspicuous Fiat Cinquecento for unofficial expeditions. When he reached the Fiat he opened the driver's door and folded the seat forward. He laid his walking stick down across the back seat, took off and carefully folded his linen jacket. He amused himself with the line 'If you take care of your costume, it will take care of you,' as he laid his jacket on the rear seat. It was too hot to wear it, given that the Fiat's air-conditioning consisted of its folding roof flap. Finally he placed his panama on the folded jacket.

He drove through the mad press of Cairo with the serenity of a mother cat whose kittens jump all over her in an aimless haze of busy motion. His destination was only a kilometer from the Museum. He passed the site of the old Opera House, which had burned down when he was a young man. He mused that there had been a pharaonic splendor in building it for the visit of the Empress

Eugenie on the occasion of the opening of the Suez Canal. In its place stood a parking lot, and he judged this a fit monument to the present era.

He drove into the Midan Ataba, and turned onto the Sharia Muski, heading toward the Tomb of the Khalifs. He entered the Fatamid enclosure and Cairo's medieval Arab Quarter. Parking off the Sharia Muski, he got out and reassembled his costume. He walked at a magisterial pace for two blocks and turned into a narrow alley. For another ten minutes he drifted, apparently at random, through the warren of alleys that make up the quarter. He stopped before a nondescript building of stone turned blackish brown by time and the patina of pollution. The numberplate was broken, and the building looked like it might have been a warehouse built by a rich merchant when the quarter was new. It was now in desuetude, the small windows shuttered.

Mustapha took out his key ring and inserted a high-tech security key into the apparently old lock. The heavy wooden door swung open easily on silent hinges. He flicked a switch that lit a single bulb and stood in a stone vestibule.

He descended by a spiral staircase, until the light from the bulb above was gray mist. At a landing he switched on another single bulb. The landing became a circular room. Before him was another door, this one of steel. Mustapha opened the lock with a second high-tech key. He threw a switch and descended another storey. Here the building entered the water table of the Nile. Beads of condensation clung to the walls, as if the stones were sweating from the effort to hold the building together.

Mustapha came to a landing made of high carbon steel. In front of him was a bank vault door. He reflectively ran the thumb of his right hand over the tips of his right fingers, touched the lock and flicked it left, right, left, right, left. It clicked, and the vault door swung open onto a stone chamber beautifully made, the style ancient Egyptian. The walls bore hieroglyphs in gold, red, and lapis lazuli, all as fresh as when they were carved and painted. He admired them for a moment and then closed the vault door behind him with the quiet tact of a good husband closing the bedroom door in a hotel.

In front of him stood massive doors of cedar worked in hieroglyphs depicting the afterlife. He ignored them for now. He had preparations to make. He stood his walking stick in a granite jar, hung his hat and coat on their respective hooks, and undressed until he was naked. He knelt at a small altar and offered a silent prayer. Then he rose and opened a wooden chest covered in more carved and painted hieroglyphs. It held the accoutrements he would need. He put on a white linen loincloth, and over this a starched white linen kilt. He lifted a gold pectoral collar over his head and lowered it to his shoulders. From the heavy collar hung an image of the Sun disk in beaten gold, and a breastplate composed of divine images. The collar, Sun disk, and breastplate covered his chest down to his navel. He put on linen sandals. He placed a gold and lapis lazuli cuff on his left arm. It covered his forearm from elbow to wrist. On his right arm he placed a cuff fashioned of gold and jasper. On his head he set a gold diadem of the Sun disk supported by scarabs. He took his staff from its alabaster jar. The staff was two meters high and made of cedar covered in electrum. At its tip was an ankh, the symbol of light and truth.

Mustapha stood before the doors and struck the stone floor with his great staff. When silence fell he struck the stone again. When the reverberation attenuated he once again raised his staff and struck the stone. On this third time, the doors opened before him. A man in similar but less spectacular garb bowed to him. Smiles of welcome played at the corner of his mouth. Behind him stood younger men with shaved heads. They wore only white linen kilts and sandals. Behind them stood older men similarly dressed. Arrayed in serried ranks, they bowed to Mustapha.

"We have awaited you with the highest expectancy, your Holiness," said Abdul, the Assistant High Priest. He had coal eyes, heavy brows, and a beaked nose. Abdul's hair was short but not shorn. His manner was fawning with hints of steel. Abdul and the others stood aside to let Mustapha enter. When inside, he was standing in a temple precinct. It was a simulacrum of the inner temple of Karnak.

Karnak. Karnak the great, Karnak the mighty. Karnak home of Amun-Ra, the Creator of All; Mut, his consort, the Mother of Everything; and Khonsu their Son, Keeper of the Sky. Karnak the largest religious site built in all of human history, larger by far than St. Peter's in Rome. Karnak begun in the 12th Dynasty, and elaborated and extended for over 2,000 years. Karnak was the heart of Thebes and soul of Egypt, source of all knowledge, repository of the sacred magic of pharaoh and his priests. Theirs was an effective magic. It let Egypt live for millennia, far longer than any other civilization. Karnak, gateway to the Valley of the Kings, and the sacred knowledge of eternal life. Karnak, where wisdom flowed like milk and honey. Karnak, whose greatness appeared to vanish with the pharaohs.

Thousands of priests lived in the temple precincts of the original Karnak, men whose only task was to care for the gods and to guard the knowledge the gods gave their people. These priests were privileged to live with the gods, for Karnak was not easy to enter. Egyptian temples were the private palaces of the gods. Worshipers did not have access, any more than commoners entered the palace of the pharaoh. The gods' servants—the priests—and their human member—pharaoh—entered to do them service. But no one else. Each day the priests bathed the living statues of Amun-Ra, Mut, and Khonsu. They clothed them in linen robes, adorned them with jeweled ornaments, offered them flowers and incense, and fed them wine, fruit, wheat, barley, beer, milk and meat.

Then in the 18th Dynasty, the pharaoh Akhenaten fell into heresy. He magnified one of Amun-Ra's attributes into a divinity he called the Aten, decreed it supreme, and compelled Egypt to worship this Aten to the exclusion of Amun-Ra and all the other gods. He tried to break the power of Karnak. Threatened by the great temple's wealth and wisdom in the capital Thebes, Akhenaten moved his capital to Amarna, a site in the empty desert halfway down the Nile towards contemporary Cairo. The power of Karnak declined. It was restored after Akhenaten passed over into the next world. This first decline of Karnak was a signal to the wise of what must eventually come. One of them decided to lay a foundation stronger than time.

Rameb, the High Priest of Amun-Ra after the reign of Akhenaten, wanted to ensure that no matter what any pharaoh did to Karnak, or what indignities history might inflict upon Egypt, the trinity of Amun-Ra, Mut, and Khonsu would always be served. One of the standout geniuses in the long history of Egypt, Rameb was equal to the task. Drawing on the infinite wealth of Karnak, he built a working model of the temple complex to serve the gods in times of siege. He built it as a bunker, a survivalist temple against the dangers of the world and the ravages of time.

He built Karnak in Exile. He sited it north of the ancient city of Memphis on the eastern side of the Nile eight miles east of the pyramids of Giza. In this way it was in the land of the living, as the Giza complex west of the Nile was in the land of the dead. The site mirrored its original: Karnak sits on the eastern side of the Nile while the Valley of the Kings, the burial place for generations of pharaohs, lies to the west.

Cairo was to grow over Karnak in Exile in later millennia. The Fatamid dynasty of Islamic rulers built their medieval city above it, and never knew it was there. For Rameb dug deep and concealed Karnak in Exile better than any pharaonic tomb was ever concealed. He reproduced Karnak in reduced but working scale. The motor of Karnak was the inner sanctum with the homes of the living gods. Once Karnak in Exile was in place, no matter what happened in the outer world, a dedicated cadre of priests would make sure that the gods were attended daily and never forgotten through millions of years.

Rameb's ambition succeeded because of its secrecy. The only ones who knew anything about it were the High Priest and those necessary for construction and the priestly duties performed there. The library of Karnak was copied in its essential parts—mathematics and magic—and installed. He built everything the priests would need: a small city underground with a bakery, infirmary, brewery, and sanitation facilities that let directly into the Nile. All were still functioning, and had been modified to keep pace with technology's leading edge. To make the temple sustainable, priests were allowed to spend time in the outside world, and most of them came and went as Mustapha did. The ancient code of secrecy survived, and anyone who broke it was erased from this world and the next.

In the Third Intermediate Period, about 1000 B.C., the stability of Egypt was eroding. In a vision, the High Priest of Karnak at the time saw the ancient ways interrupted. He wanted to ensure that the life of the gods continued without hiatus, and so he took a step that changed history: he had Amun-Ra, Mut, and Khonsu surreptitiously moved from their home in Karnak to their survival bunker—Karnak in Exile. Replicas were substituted in the original Karnak. In this way Karnak in Exile became the Center of the World, for the gods enter the world of men through the portal of their true images.

So it has been ever since. The pharaohs are gone. Their kingdom, together with the original Karnak, has lain in ruin for over 2,000 years. Yet in a sacred castle keep, beneath the old buildings of medieval Cairo, the heart of Egypt beats on uninterrupted. The gods have been served with never a single day missed. Priests are still called to service. The High Priest still rules Karnak for the pharaoh. Mathematics and magic are still studied. All of this happens every day in secrecy. For the initiates, it is the true world. It enshrines a reality more vital than the secular world outside. That world lost interest in the old ways generations before Cleopatra clasped an asp to her breast to end her affair with a Roman interloper. For the initiates, this parallel world beneath Cairo holds the seeds of truth that will once again bloom on the face of the Earth. Conditions must be right for this to happen. Like the seeds of desert flowers, those who serve Karnak in Exile are patient.

Mustapha stood with the priests in the underground temple's outer courtyard. It was a large stone room, and though of ancient construction, was now lit subtly by electric light. An opening pierced each of the courtyard's four walls. On the northern side, behind him, was the door through which he entered. On the western side, the precious library of Karnak. On the eastern side, the living quarters of the priests, together with the temple's vast support facilities. In the south, straight ahead of him, the pylon gate leading to the holy of holies, the inner sanctum wherein lie the living quarters of the gods from whom life, power, and magic flow.

Mustapha was now High Priest of Karnak. He was also Great Mage of Egypt. Ever since its founding, Karnak had been the seat of divine power and therefore also of magic. The gods entered the world of men to make magic, protecting Egypt, the pharaoh, and the people. When Egypt flourished, magic was upon the land and the gods were active. The Great Mage was charged with knowing all the laws and formulae required to bring the magic down from the plane of the gods to the human plane. To acquire and maintain such knowledge was a life's work. It was hard to gain and difficult to keep, precise and demanding. More than knowledge, however, was needed to make the magic work.

The burden Mustapha felt most heavily was the obligation of purity. The Great Mage of Egypt becomes the vessel for the will of the gods, the human form through which they act. He must be blameless. When one of us humans dies, even the pharaoh, the god Maat weighs our soul against a feather. If our transgressions weigh more than the feather, Maat casts our soul into perdition. For us this happens when we cross over into the next world. The Great Mage of Egypt is more frequently judged. Each time he seeks to be the vessel of the gods so as to let their magic flow through him, his soul is weighed. The vessel must be pure if the magic is to be effectual, and before manifesting magic, the gods will judge the Mage.

Each time he entered Karnak, Mustapha was reminded that the Great Mage of Egypt needs knowledge and purity. Only through knowledge can he become the vessel. Only through purity can the gods fill it.

The ancient burdens of the High Priest of Karnak included his obligations to maintain the temple, administer its finances, regulate the lives of the priests, and ensure that the gods were taken care of in their daily rounds. History had given Mustapha another burden: the need for secrecy. Karnak in its days of might was the heart of Egypt and the most impressive part of its capital Thebes. The High Priest of Karnak was second in importance only to pharaoh throughout the Two Lands, Upper and Lower Egypt, the Land of the Bee and the Sedge.

Now Mustapha must maintain Karnak while keeping its whole fabric secret from a world gone cold to the gods. Secrecy on a massive scale may be the most expensive commodity on Earth, and the wealth of Karnak helped the priests secure it. The wealth of Karnak, greater than the wealth of pharaoh, was based on the gold of the Eastern Desert and the gold of Nubia, it was based on vast domains of land and cattle and grain. This wealth was not lost when the Kingdom of Egypt left this plane like water runs through desert sands.

Keenly, shrewdly, always trying to manipulate the goods of this world into the service of the gods, the High Priests of Karnak infiltrated the new economies brought by Alexander the Great, then by the Caesars, then by the followers of Muhammad. No one knew Egypt like the High Priests of Karnak and their army of anointed and well-educated priests. To preserve the life of the gods, the priests deployed themselves into the new economies. Priests still, they became invisible.

Their investment and acumen built the Alexandria of the Ptolemies. Their shrewdness built the medieval Cairo of the Arabs. They had a hand in the Suez Canal and in the Aswan High Dam. They built pipelines in the Ukraine and ports in Kamchatka. After twenty centuries of building and extending the original Karnak there was little they could not do, and finance and construction were second nature to them. The priests' work in the world secured the safety of the gods in their underground temple, a safe haven for sanctity in the long years of strife.

Mustapha raised his right hand to bless the priests. He was their father, and gave them a father's blessing as he prepared to meet the gods. He took a measured step forward and felt the melancholy he always felt at this moment.

He should expect joy when approaching the gods. Instead he felt heaviness like a premonition of despair. In old Egypt, the gods lived and the people knew it. When a pharaoh needed guidance he would come to Karnak and visit the gods in their inmost chambers. They would speak and give him advice. Amun-Ra, Mut, and Khonsu were the pharaohs' familiars. In an earlier time, the Zep Tepi or First Time, the gods walked among men. Isis, Osiris, and Horus ruled as kings, before turning governance over to the divine pharaohs. The gods taught humans how to live, and how to compel the magic of the gods when they were in difficulty.

The gods had been silent for two millennia now. Although they lived, they had withdrawn from humans. Although they abided, they no longer spoke or communicated directly. In his blackest moments, Mustapha wondered whether the gods had ever appeared, or whether these were merely tales for children.

If the old stories were true, then Egyptian religious practice was based on knowledge. The ancestors actually knew the gods, who walked in the open and worked magic upon the land. If the stories were true, the knowledge the Great Mage acquired was not theoretical. When people were in need, the Great Mage could compel the gods to act through knowledge and purity. The magic would flow. But this too had not happened for millennia. The magic had lost its juice. Direct experience no longer tied us to the gods. We had only pale substitutes: faith and devotion.

Mustapha took a second step forward. He raised his staff to greet the gods, as ritual prescribed. The High Priest and Great Mage had come to see the gods, the all-powerful lords of the universe who were also in his care. At this point Mustapha took heart. He recalled the purpose of humans in the dark times of history: to care for the gods lest they be forgotten. A prophecy older than the pharaohs returned to him, and sent a warmth through his psyche that canceled the heaviness. The prophecy was attributed to Horus himself:

> *There will come a long night when the gods appear to sleep. Lose not your faith, oh men, nor neglect your duties. For if a few are steadfast in this time of testing, the Land of Gods and Land of Men will be made as one.*

Mustapha felt anxiety arise within him, edged with curiosity. Why had he received the urgent phone call? Were the gods stirring at last? He took a third step forward and quieted his mind so that he could invite the gods to enter into it. Abdul, the Assistant High Priest, who should have been following behind, broke protocol and came to his side.

"Your Holiness, I must speak to you before you enter the chambers of the gods. Something has happened, the reason I called you. Something disturbing and perhaps wonderful."

"Come with me. We will speak in the gods' antechamber, beyond the pylon."

They continued in ritual pace. They approached the pylon gate, that most characteristic Egyptian design: its cedar doors surrounded by fine stone rising high and angling inward toward the top, surmounted by a cornice and covered in images of the gods. They opened the pylon gate and entered the antechamber. Here, and beyond in the chambers of the gods, the light was by candle. Its soft illumination and beeswax perfume comforted Mustapha.

"Now, brother," said Mustapha, "tell me your news."

"Your Holiness. It is astonishing." The man was excited but wary. He was on ground that he did not know and had not mastered. "When I went to dress and offer food to the gods this morning, I went to Amun-Ra first as always. As ever, I bathed him, changed his linen robe and jewels, made offerings of wine and flowers, fruit, and so on. I recited the incantations..."

"We do this every day. Why are you so troubled?"

"Because of what happened next. I went to the chamber of Mut, the Great Mother. I bathed her, changed her robe and jewels, and made the offerings. Then something happened. I was standing back watching her while I made the incantations. Her right foot moved forward. She nodded as if to acknowledge us. The offerings disappeared. All at once, just gone, as if she wanted us to know she was accepting them. Your Holiness, nothing like this has happened for 2,000 years!"

"I am well aware of that. I must be sure it happened now. Are you certain it was not a trick of candlelight?"

"It was not."

"Let me smell your breath." The Assistant High Priest released a diffident breath while Mustapha gave a practiced sniff.

"No drugs?"

"I do not use any."

"Were your servers witnesses to this manifestation?"

"Yes, your Holiness. I had two men with me, both good witnesses. Jalal Sadr, the young attorney, and Hossein Nasr, the physicist."

"I know them. I can question them later. Let us enter the Chamber of the Mother now."

Straight ahead was the chamber of Amun-Ra, the Creator. To the left, the Chamber of Mut, Mother of all things, the god who in Mustapha's view gave her name to mothers in most languages, from Latin 'mater' to German 'Mutter' to Urdu 'ma,' English 'mother' and so on through the web of human tongues. To the right, the chamber of Khonsu, their son.

Mustapha turned to the door of the Mother. He bowed and beat his staff three times on the stone floor to announce his intention to visit her. He opened the door and entered. The candles illuminated a room whose floor was alabaster and whose walls and ceilings were entirely made of gold. In the purity of the chamber stood Mut upon her altar. She was life sized, human scale. Fashioned of black diorite, her statue invoked the essence of Mother, so that she could come through to her children.

Mustapha bowed and moved forward to examine the statue. The offering bowls before it lay empty. The statue's right foot extended to the edge of its plinth, a full twenty-five centimeters beyond where it had rested for millennia. Mustapha felt a growing excitement, but he had to pass through one more stage before be could believe. It was a stage prescribed in the ancient protocols.

Mustapha touched a scarab inlaid into the heavy cuff that covered his left arm from elbow to wrist. The scarab was fashioned of gold and lapis lazuli. From its head emerged a long narrow rod fashioned like the single horn of a Hercules beetle, a giant among the scarabs. The horn was folded back over the scarab's body. Mustapha detached the scarab from his cuff. He took it and bent the horn forward. It snapped up, and Abdul could see that the horn was actually a key of intricate design. Mustapha leaned over to the front of the plinth. He looked at a hole that a casual observer would not have noticed, or if he did would have put down to minor damage in such an ancient statue. This small hole became the center of Mustapha's attention.

He inserted the scarab's horn into the hole. It fit. When he turned it, it clicked into place. The scarab moved. It opened jeweled wings, as if it had just flown down from heaven to land on the plinth and so grace the day. In doing so it met the test the statue's ancient makers had crafted so that the High Priest could judge whether the statue was authentic or a counterfeit, should the need ever arise.

Mustapha watched the candlelight play on the scarab's open wings. He smiled. The scarab had proven that the statue was Mut herself.

"I believe in this manifestation," said Mustapha softly. "I am only concerned about what it means for the world."

15

"How are you doing with that equipment?" Wolfgang said. Petra was behind him, just about coping with the three titanium cases balanced and lashed on her dolly.

"Just fine. I'm used to this from airports. Girls always have a lot of luggage. Even in a pyramid."

Wolfgang laughed and they headed in. "This passage wasn't the original entrance," he said. "This one is level and crude. The original is above us—The Descending Gallery. It is elegant. We are in the one that Al Mamam, Mameluke and local potentate, opened in the 9th century. He had a team of goons break through here. They built fires to make the rock hot, poured vinegar on it to crack it, and then used battering rams."

"Ouch."

"They eventually broke through to The Descending Gallery where it meets the First Ascending Passage up ahead. We'll see."

They came to a flight of steps leading up out of the crude tunnel now used as the tourist entrance. The steps were steep, and Wolfgang hauled both of the dollies up. They stood in the First Ascending Passage, the authentic interior space of the Great Pyramid.

"Look at those big granite blocks," Wolfgang said, pointing back to where the Descending Gallery met the First Ascending Passage. "This way was blocked with huge granite blocks like those that fit and filled it. They were stored in the Grand Gallery ahead of us, and the workers slid the stones down from behind when they sealed the pyramid."

"From behind? Did the workers stay behind and die?"

"Apparently not. A narrow wiggly crawl space worms all the way down through the pyramid and bedrock to the strange subterranean chamber, a weird primitive cavern that no one has any good ideas about. Anyhow, the workers could have sealed this passage from behind and slithered down through the narrow shaft. They could have walked up out the Descending Gallery, which goes all the way down to the pyramid's sub-basement. Then they could plug the entrance with more granite blocks from outside. They finished the job by covering the whole pyramid in white limestone polished like a mirror, which hid the entrance."

"That's why they blasted their way in later?"

"The stone facing wasn't ripped off till a couple of hundred years after, to build the mosques of Cairo."

"Must have saved a lot of work."

"One way to look at it."

"Wolfie, what I'm wondering is: if this was never a tomb like you say, why seal it up so carefully at all?"

"Perhaps to store the magic. Maybe it was like a Leyden jar or battery and had to be sealed to generate a charge. Maybe we have other secrets to discover. Come on, let's do it!"

They pulled their equipment up the First Ascending Passage to where it connected with the Grand Gallery.

Petra looked up. "I had no idea the space is so huge in here. Amazing."

"Sure is. Straight ahead is the Queen's Chamber. If you go up the Grand Gallery you get to the King's Chamber."

They bent over to pull their equipment down the low corridor into the Queen's Chamber. They stood as they entered. It was now their laboratory. A granite room of five by five and a half meters, it had a four and a half meter pitched roof. Giant slabs made up the walls, roof, and floor. They bore no markings or decoration of any kind.

"This is called the 'Queen's Chamber' out of folk imagination," said Wolfgang. "Since there is a larger chamber above, it was named the 'King's Chamber'. So what else could this one be but the Queen's? The third chamber below ground would by similar logic be the Baby's Room, or maybe the Mother-in-Law's Apartment."

"How about the Alchemist's Basement?" Petra looked around at the Queen's Chamber. "You know, it's not claustrophobic in here. I was thinking it would be, with millions of tons of stone on top of us."

"Good. We'll be in here a while. Better not to freak out. Okay, let's set up here," said Wolfgang, moving toward the chamber's eastern wall. They took the six titanium cases off the dollies and lay them on the floor. Four of the cases stacked two-on-two would make an impromptu equipment table.

"I want to set up the monitor and laptops first," said Wolfgang, opening those cases and beginning to work.

Petra opened the case of cables. Then while Wolfgang was busy she opened the case that cradled the laser.

"What's this, Wolfie?"

"Oh," he said, "you're not supposed to see that. That's my secret weapon. I've come with a lot of questions. I intend to leave with answers."

Soon they had Wolfgang's video monitor and laptops set up. He ran some diagnostics. Satisfied, he opened the titanium case containing the jewel of the expedition, the minibot he had painstakingly fashioned and then tested by running it through the air conditioning ducts in his university labs in Germany. He took the cables that Petra had hauled in. They would be the lifeline between the brain and camera aboard the minibot and Wolfgang's computers in the Queen's Chamber while the minibot crawled up the narrow shaft into the pyramid.

Wolfgang laid the cable out in a tight and careful coil, much as the line would have been laid out for the harpoon in Ahab's whaler, and for the same reason—so that it would not snag during pursuit. He attached one end of the cable to the minibot, the other to his computers. He ran a diagnostic routine that checked the minibot internally: battery, electric motors in each of the six wheels, maneuverable arm, and crucially, the miniaturized video camera and lights. When the minibot's systems checked out, he ran diagnostics on the rest of the components: the minibot-cable interface, the cable itself, the cable-computer interface, and finally on the communications back and forth between the minibot, computers, and video monitor.

Everything checked out, but it had taken a long time.

"Time for lunch," said Wolfgang.

"Good!" said Petra.

He took sandwiches and coffee out of his backpack. They shared them sitting on the floor, the chamber's wall providing a cool backrest.

"When do we get going?" Petra said.

"We put her in the shaft this afternoon. The rest of today is more testing. If all goes well, we'll reach the door at the top of the shaft tomorrow. Then we shall see what we shall see." Wolfgang stretched, got up and walked over to the minibot. It sat on the floor of the chamber near the southern shaft, the one that interested him. He bent and stroked it like a favorite small dog.

Wolfgang had built his minibot with the skill, precision, and technological sophistication that NASA lavishes on space probes. Its six metal wheels were covered in rubber for traction. Wolfgang thought of it as a time probe designed to let him meet the pyramid builders. For him the minibot had a personality and charm. He had wanted at first to put it live online, so millions could watch its plucky ascent up the mysterious shaft. He decided against it in the end. He was a scientist. Better to see the results himself before showing them to the world.

His plan was a good one: send the minibot up to the door at the end of the shaft and use the mechanical arm to poke a video minicam and his laser through the hole the last expedition cut. With any luck, the hole would be wide enough to work through, and he could get right down to cutting through the second door, behind it. Wolfgang was counting on luck. Knowing that luck favors the prepared, he had taken pains to be as thoroughly prepared as Caesar putting his troops into battle.

Wolfgang hefted the minibot and inserted it into the opening of the shaft. "Okay, baby, let's have us a flawless shake-down cruise."

He crossed the room to the laptop and video monitor array perched on the stacked packing cases. The minibot was already alive from the diagnostics runs. It sat in the opening of the shaft. Ahead of it the shaft ran level, parallel to the floor of the chamber, for the first two meters. Then it angled up at thirty-nine degrees, the angle it maintained throughout its length.

At the keyboard, Wolfgang signaled the minibot to move. It crawled down the first two meters on the level and began its slow ascent. He had chosen a high-torque-slow-motion gait for the minibot. On the monitor he saw the rising shaft through its eyes and brain for the first time. The shaft was nicely crafted.

His mind clicked through possibilities of why the builders of the Great Pyramid made the effort required to fashion such a smooth shaft through the pyramid, using no more than copper saws. A shaft that lay concealed behind the wall of the Queen's Chamber until it was discovered in Victorian times.

Was the shaft a religious offering of some kind? Spiritual or magical technology? A third possibility pleased him most—an intelligence test. A puzzle for those who would come after. To fascinate them, capture their imagination, perhaps teach them something that would shake up their world.

This was a great game, the kind of puzzle Wolfgang lived for. Maybe it was the way to gain the recognition he felt he deserved too. Although he was on track to make his name in quantum cryptography, he was painfully aware that his field would never be as sexy to the public as relativity theory or string theory. So he hoped his pyramid hobby would make him famous.

He wanted his minibot to capture some fabulous prey for the whole world to see. That way he could get the celebrity his genius deserved. And then he snorted, shook his head, and quietly laughed at his adolescent ambition. He had after all nothing but a hunch. As the minibot inched slowly forward, Wolfgang worried.

"Look Petra, see how smooth the shaft walls are? More than I anticipated. So I hope I made the right choice of latex and tread for her wheels. The angle is steep and my little girl is pretty heavy. We have high torque but we're going to need all the traction we can get."

Petra watched the screen and saw the square empty shaft illuminated three meters ahead by the light on the minibot. She was going to be watching a lot of nothing for a long time, like sitting in a field and waiting for lightning to strike.

A couple of hours later Wolfgang relaxed. The minibot had moved ahead about forty meters flawlessly, all systems working well.

"Let's go get a drink," he said. "We'll toast the success of our system. Tomorrow we begin our assault on whatever's behind that little white door!"

16

Maria walked out onto the wide veranda of the Al Minah in time to witness the sinking of the Sun. She was relieved to be in the open air after the book dust in the Egyptian Museum's library. She had changed into linen slacks and a red silk blouse that seemed to concentrate the day's late light.

Mustapha sat facing west. Maria was pleased to find him. Her inner landscape seemed broader in his presence.

"This already feels like a daily ritual," she said, sitting next to him.

"The right rituals anchor us in the world. I am glad you are joining me in mine." He wore his linen suit. With it he donned a world-weary mien, the best disguise for his knowledge. He was drinking mineral water.

Wolfgang, full of the success of the minibot's shakedown cruise, strode out onto the veranda with Petra. Jack entered impatient to hear if Wolfgang had solved his problem of looking under the Sphinx.

Maria ordered white wine for herself and a Coke for Cliff, who arrived as she placed the order. After everyone had drinks, Jack told the waiter to put their drinks on his tab, not just for the night but for the whole research season. Their thanks led to a silence.

Maria was considering a conversational gambit when Mustapha broke the silence. With what she took as a hint of nostalgia, he said to no one in particular, "My ancestors believed that the sunset has a specific meaning. It is when Ra the Sun god sails the sky boat called 'Weakening', representing his nightly loss of strength. He sails it into the west to do his eternal nocturnal battle with the forces of darkness."

"Kind of stupid, huh?" said Cliff. "I mean that story just doesn't hold up at all!"

"In a way you're right," said Mustapha. "Yet imagine how little people knew about science 5,000 years ago. They told stories of the gods that made sense of what they observed."

"Science kills religion," said Cliff.

"Religion has three choices in the face of science," Mustapha said. "It can grow in sophistication, my own preference. It can wither away and leave our hearts bereft. Or worst of all by far: it can turn into the idiot animal we call fundamentalism."

"Mustapha," said Maria, "what happened to the gods themselves? Were they ever real, and if so what happened to them? Why aren't Amun-Ra and Horus, Isis, and Osiris present for people today?"

"Oh they were real enough," said Mustapha. "It is clear when you study the old texts. The ancient people here in Egypt really believed in the gods. Very sophisticated people like high priests, great mages and pharaohs give eyewitness accounts of actually meeting with the gods. The same is true for the Jews. In the Old Testament you find Moses actually meeting with his god, spending time with him, learning what he must do for the people." Mustapha paused. He sighed and stroked his mustache. After a while he continued. "But then something happened. Yahweh has not talked to his chosen people since the time of their Old Testament. The same thing happened in Egypt: the gods went silent. They were real in this land and active in the lives of its people. But then they went silent. We have not heard from them since. This silence of the gods has stretched over several thousand years now. I do not know if it happened because the people forgot the gods or if the gods turned their backs on us. Perhaps if the people forget, the gods can no longer speak. Perhaps when they are forgotten the gods cease to exist."

The tall date palms on the bank of the Nile caught the final effulgence from Ra's Boat of Weakening as Mustapha finished speaking. The palms' heavy fronds swayed pensively in the breeze.

Maria was willing to enter Mustapha's mood, but she saw that Wolfgang, leaning forward and ready to speak, was not.

"Come on, Mustapha" Wolfgang said. "I think those people were primitive, just at the birth of the human mind as we know it. They couldn't tell the difference between fantasy and reality. Those gods were like kids' imaginary friends. You should be less naive then they were."

"We've come a long way in technology and science, I'll grant you, though the pyramids aren't bad for 'primitives,'" said Mustapha. "When it comes to theology and philosophy—humans standing on the edge and gazing into eternity—I think they were at least our equals."

"I'm a scientist. Where is your evidence their gods were real?"

"Again, we've got eyewitness accounts of meeting the gods. You have to understand that these came from their best people: the pharaohs, high priests, chief scribes. To put it into the terms of your world, it would be as if your Chancellor, the head of the Deutsche Bank, and the editor of *Der Spiegel* all regularly reported seeing the gods."

Wolfgang looked out at the date palms fringing the Nile.

"Mustapha, maybe the gods don't cease to exist," said Maria. "Maybe they lie dormant. Maybe they sleep. I've worked with indigenous cultures, studying their plant medicines. With the Huichol, with Amazonian tribes who take psychedelic botanicals. They experience the gods and spirits. I started out as a Western scientist dismissing the notion that there was any reality in what these people were seeing. Then I did the medicines with them. There's truth in what they see."

"I've got the only mom I know who takes psychedelics," said Cliff.

Maria turned to see Cliff smiling. She thought his smile combined pride and nervousness. "Only in a professional context," she said, smiling reassurance. She returned to her thought. "I've now taken dozens of other skeptical Westerners into the experience. They've worked with the shamans, taken the medicines. They've seen gods and spirits. The very ones that the shamans believe in, gods the Westerners never heard of. These serotonergic plant medicines tweak the brain chemistry and then we perceive the gods. I believe the ancient Egyptian priesthoods knew this and made a serotonergic sacrament. With its help they saw their gods. They conversed with them and received teachings from them. We are in the land that these gods once walked. So maybe the ancient medicines would awaken the ancient gods for us too, I don't know. But I am sure that there are gods latent in the human psyche and that they can be awakened."

"Are you saying they are some fantasies or archetypes?" said Petra.

"No, I think they are as real as you and me," said Maria, "and I don't really know if they live in our psyche and wake up when we invite them to, or if they are on some other plane that we can reach when we get opened up."

Maria paused. She was moved by her speculations about meeting the Egyptian gods. She sensed something different in the air tonight. Something she had not experienced during her prior trips to Egypt.

"I would like to think the gods sleep and will awaken," said Mustapha. "Though I do not know why they are silent now, except that we failed to pay the attention that is due. I would like more than anything to meet Amun-Ra. And so I still have hope."

Maria had been watching Mustapha as he spoke. She sensed in him tonight a new depth, as if glints of light were catching something shiny in deep water. She would keep watching to see what was revealed.

"I think you're a romantic, Mustapha," said Jack. "If Maria's right, it sounds like we are hard-wired to believe in gods. Maybe it doesn't matter which ones. So when Rameses rules, we believe in

Amun-Ra. When Muhammad's armies sweep through the land, we believe in the god of Muhammad. If we believe anything it's by historical accident. Or if you prefer, by the evolution of culture."

Cliff had been listening but getting progressively fidgety. "I think we need a totally other way to look at it," he said. "I've been reading string theory. I'm pretty sure we can go beyond the gods and beyond culture into pure physics. Religion within the limits of pure physics alone."

Wolfgang had been studying the periodicity of the date palm fronds' slow swaying in the breeze. At Cliff's remark he turned and listened.

"It's fantastic stuff this string theory. I don't get all of it, but the basic idea is that everything is made of infinitesimal strings vibrating in ten-dimensional hyperspace. They are way smaller than atoms, smaller than quarks, smaller than any quantum unit. They flash in and out of being, vibrating in and out of existence in the hyperspace. They're what we're made of. So everything is a result of vibrating strings. You get it? Everything is a frequency: you, me, light, coconuts, and the pyramids. I'm sure you could make a new religion around this. I've sort of been trying so that I could have one that is totally scientific."

"What have you got?" asked Wolfgang.

"Here's what I've got." Cliff was excited and talking fast, afraid of being dismissed by the group, using his hands to mould their attention as he talked. "Everything takes place in this hyperspace and like I said the whole universe, or rather the Multiverse, because there's an infinite layer of universes, is made of vibration. So I started to think in terms of music: the music of these infinitely small strings vibrating. And this is where I am now."

He was a little breathless and stopped to see if they were still listening. They were so he went on. "The vibrating strings in hyperspace make a music we perceive as matter. Molecules are melodies. Solar systems are concerti. You can find this lovely correspondence all the way up the scale of complexity. Symphonies of this music are universes. Because there's an infinity of notes and note combinations in the music of the strings, the Multiverse holds an infinity of universes. To study the harmonics of the music of the strings is to do physics. If we could experience all the music directly, we would know ourselves as the mind of God. Because the mind of God has to be the totality of the music in hyperspace. I don't know how to get there. I'm guessing you start with math, and then add humility and wonder. That's what Einstein did I think."

As Cliff fell silent, Maria felt for her son. She had seen elation in him as he shared his private intuitions. Confidence had filled his chest and animated his hands. She watched it dissipate. He folded in upon himself.

The breeze filled the date palms. Distant traffic sounded. The Nile flowed before them from south to north with a soft profound insistence, like a bass baritone singing a lullaby in whispers.

Just as Cliff's vulnerability was becoming painful to Maria, Wolfgang spoke.

"Cliff, I'm not sure I buy it, but it is clever. You have a theory that captures my feeling of wonder in uncovering the structure of the universe. Or Multiverse."

There was a joy in being heard when you bared your soul like this. Maria watched Cliff warm to Wolfgang's words.

"You may make this skeptic into a believer yet," continued Wolfgang. "Make sure you are in the Queen's chamber with me tomorrow. I want your brain there."

"Listen Wolfgang, I'm sorry to take you away from this, but I need to talk to you about my problem of seeing under the Sphinx," said Jack. Jack stood and Wolfgang walked with him over to the balustrade leaving the others.

Maria had been waiting to ask Mustapha about something else entirely. Now that Jack and Wolfgang had left the group, she felt more comfortable bringing it up. Although Mustapha was a strong male presence, he seemed more sympathetic to the numinous than the other two men. "Mustapha," she said, "what about magic?"

Concern flickered across Mustapha's face. Maria was surprised by his response. The expression lasted only the smallest interval of time, and someone less astute than she would have missed it. Quickly, his courteous world-weary mien returned. When it was intact, he said, "Magic?"

Making a note of his reaction, Maria decided to press ahead. "When you talk about the gods of Egypt going silent, what about the magic of Egypt?"

"In ancient days, the way the gods moved through the world was magic. They could bend the quotidian to their will, and magic was an art of the sacred. White magic I mean, for a dark art has always shadowed it. The white magicians were priests of those gods who made the world and nourish life. The black magicians served the gods who seek to destroy the world and drain its life away."

"How do you know this?" said Cliff.

On guard but now apparently relaxed, Mustapha was skilled at walking unnoticed as the Great Mage of Egypt. He said, "It is part of my job. To understand the antiquities in my charge would not be possible without paying some attention to how the ancient ones saw magic. They were different from the later alchemists. Here in Egypt the white magicians sought not only to refine base matter. They achieved this, which I am not convinced the alchemists ever did. But the ancient ones went even further. They actually helped the gods to create and protect life. Their spells were effectual, not fairy tales. If you like, they knew how to play the strings of hyperspace to create the universe they were looking for. For thousands of years Egypt seemed eternal. Then the magic went dry when the gods went silent."

"Have you tried? Have you made magic?" said Cliff.

Mustapha parried. "Many have tried but none has succeeded. You can learn the hieroglyphs yourself and try it. I will teach you to read them if you want. But the magic no longer works, for it depends upon the gods. The white magician's purity of heart compels the gods into an act of co-creation. But the gods must be awake and listening."

"What about the black magicians?" said Cliff.

"A mirror image to white magic. The filth in the heart of the black magician calls forth the gods of ordure. Chief among them is Seth, Prince of Darkness and Scourge of the Desert. But when the gods are awake, the forces of creation are always stronger than those of decay."

"If dark gods are still awake then the black magicians could still do their damage."

"I fear, Cliff, that may be the case," said Mustapha quietly. "Perhaps that is why the world is as we find it."

Jack and Wolfgang rejoined the group. Maria could see that Jack's impatience had melted.

"Wolfgang's come up with a clever idea for using sound waves to look for chambers under the Sphinx," said Jack.

"Yah I like it," said Wolfgang. "We play some music we can characterize very accurately, feed it right into the rock. Something classical, like Kraftwerk."

"Run *Autobahn* right under the Sphinx and see what comes out the other side," said Cliff. "Cool."

Jack was a beat behind, and Maria decided to rescue him. "I'm sure Mozart would do it too."

Her ploy worked. Jack came back from the periphery into the center of the conversation. "Either way," Jack said, "Wolfgang will help me set up the experiment right after his robot reveals what's behind that second door in the pyramid."

"It won't take long," said Wolfgang.

"I hope not," said Jack. "I'm sure the Sphinx has a lot to reveal to us."

Wolfgang looked around at the group. "Everyone want to see what happens tomorrow in the Queen's Chamber?"

"I have other duties," said Mustapha, "but I expect to hear of marvels at sunset."

17

Before leaving Karnak in Exile, Abdul changed out of his priestly vestments. Abdul's job in the eyes of the world was to be a member of the special police force guarding the pyramids and other monuments under Mustapha's jurisdiction. As he often did, Abdul wore his police uniform home.

No one must see a trace of Abdul's role as Assistant High Priest of Karnak in Exile. Not even his wife, whom he loved like a rose in the desert. Nor would he show his sons, his two young sons, wonderful boys that any father would be proud to call his own. The boys, he knew, were also proud him, proud of their father being a policeman.

Abdul walked through the medieval Arab Quarter on his way home. He felt the strain of the day. He had seen Mut's statue move. He had called Mustapha. How could the ancient statue move like a living thing? Yet Mustapha had accepted the manifestation as real. Abdul took Mustapha as tough-minded and knew he had access to arcane knowledge. If Mustapha believed, his judgment was likely to be right.

The experience with Mut's statue was confusing. How could Abdul make sense of it? He walked quickly, his manner brusque. His confusion filled him with restless energy, and he needed to burn it off. His steps were random through the medieval Arab Quarter's warren of narrow streets. Abdul was oblivious to the jostling crowds and choking diesel fumes. He bumped into other men and took no notice of their protests. Abdul's eyes were lowered. His worries were more real to him than the other people in the street.

As he paced through the narrow streets, Abdul realized that a few years back, such a manifestation of Mut's statue would have excited but not troubled him. He was a believer then. He had been recruited into the priesthood of Karnak in Exile in his early twenties, after joining the Egyptian Antiquities security force. When he was a young trainee, the ancient priesthood's secrets seemed wonderful to him. The old gods were benign, the priesthood welcoming. He felt certain that his involvement in Karnak would provide a life of relative comfort for the family he intended to have. As he moved up in the priesthood, he was comforted by the beliefs in the old gods and hoped with the rest of the priests that the old ways would return once again.

When Abdul was in his early thirties, though, his belief in Karnak had dimmed. The hidden gods of the underground temple started to seem irrelevant to the woes of the Arab world above ground. He was an Arab long before he was a priest of Karnak. He watched the situation of Arabs in the world deteriorate. Anger grew within him. He shared a sense of powerlessness with other Arab men his age. Abdul's anger was nurtured by what he believed was an American crusade against Islam.

Abdul had been to university. He struggled with the anger as it grew. He tried reaching for an urbane view. He considered the sweep of history all the way back to the original Karnak. Empires come and go, he had told himself. Oppressors rise and fall. Only the gods are eternal. We must serve them and wait.

It did not work. Abdul's anger had taken on a life of its own, rooted in his identification with the Arab people. As he paced the medieval Arab Quarter, he felt his anger. The anger was in his heart now, dense and heavy. He remembered the final time he had tried to dispel it.

Mustapha had recently raised him to Assistant High Priest. One night, Abdul had gone to Mustapha. It was late. Mustapha was in a white robe, sitting in the High Priest's chamber in Karnak in Exile. He was reading a papyrus by the light of an oil lamp.

"Forgive me for disturbing your study," Abdul said.

"What brings you so late?"

"To speak about what troubles me."

"Speak."

"I cannot ignore the world outside our walls. The people suffer. Yet we sit here quietly, protecting the old ways. We need to do more! We need to relieve suffering! Our resources are great. Our religion humane. Our gods care for the people, and for nature. Not like the Western capitalism that sucks the lifeblood of the world."

"I agree with much of your diagnosis. What is your remedy?"

"Let us show the people a different way. Let us become engaged in politics again. Emerge from our self-imposed obscurity. Become leaders in the struggle for social justice."

Mustapha looked down at his desk. He was silent. Abdul felt his own heartbeat racing. Would Mustapha rise to the needs of the world? If so, Abdul would work with him tirelessly.

Mustapha looked up. "Not yet, Abdul."

Abdul felt his shoulders drop.

Mustapha continued, "The needs you speak of are real. I feel them too. This is no game we play. It is a struggle for control of reality. What reality will the people live by? Much in the world is baleful. I meditate always on how to help. I feel your heart's trouble. It is compassion you are feeling. But we are not ready to act. Our time will come, but it is not yet. We must trust the gods to let us know."

Abdul left disheartened. He spoke to other priests. Perhaps he could develop a consensus and return to convince Mustapha. The priesthood, however, was against him. Karnak needed to wait concealed and patient, Abdul was told again and again, letting the waves of contemporary injustice break overhead. The time would come. It was not now.

Abdul felt rebuffed by Mustapha and the priests. Betrayed in his hopes. All the priests were men of talent, capable of making a change in the world. They should not just wait passively. Abdul's sense of betrayal grew, and merged with his anger over the treatment of the Arab peoples.

Abdul's anger drove him to Allah. He began to talk to Islamists. In them Abdul found a vision and a passion. He sometimes feared their certainty and often deplored their violence. Their God was in the open, though, and their world the contemporary world. Abdul came to the conclusion that he would throw his lot in with them. He found his way to the Islamic Foundation and began to work for it secretly.

If Mut's statue had moved, though, maybe there was truth in the ancient religion after all. Maybe he should do nothing to betray it. Yet the mullahs knew of his association with Karnak, because he had told them. The mullahs would surely ask him to betray the priests of Karnak. They would ask soon. Abdul paced through the Arab Quarter, troubled in his thoughts.

As if waking from a dream, Abdul found himself near home. His *haras,* the alley where so much of his family's life was concentrated, was close by.

Abdul turned into the *haras.* The familiarity of his alley made Abdul somewhat more relaxed. He sensed the cooking smells of dinner in the *haras.* Turmeric, cumin, and sweet basil, coaxed by hot oil, released their savors into the evening. He greeted his neighbors as he approached and opened his own front door. Abdul climbed the stairs to his apartment. He was eager to take refuge from his troubles in the security and comfort of home. About to see his family, Abdul's heart grew less heavy. He knew how uncomplicated it was to be with his wife and sons.

Running up the last few steps, he opened the door.

"Daddy!" His younger son Osman, five years old, ran at Abdul and grabbed his legs. Abdul laughed as he picked the boy up and hugged him.

Abdul's older son Ahmad was nine. He had become a little diffident recently. Ahmad walked up, smiled at Abdul and said, "Dad."

"Come here Ahmad my son," said Abdul, grabbing the older boy with his right arm while he held the younger one in his left. "My boys!"

Abdul's wife smiled broadly at him from the kitchen doorway. Her true name, Faten, was known only within her family. The outside world knew her as Umm Ahmad, The Mother of Ahmad. Like many women in Cairo, her public name was an honorific based on the name of her eldest son. It kept her family's life private.

Umm Ahmad. Abdul loved her chestnut hair, clear skin, wide dark eyes, and symmetrical features. No wonder his sons pleased him so. How could they not be handsome with a mother such as this?

"Have some tea, Abdul," she said. "Dinner will be ready soon."

Abdul sat at the table in the simple kitchen. Light filtered in the open window, the purple of late dusk. His wife gave him mint tea. While the boys played in the front room, Abdul drank his tea silently. He watched his wife's fluid movements as she prepared dinner. Abdul would put the boys to bed early tonight, telling them a briefer story than usual. He would not wait long to take Umm Ahmad to bed.

Umm Ahmad was in the bedroom getting undressed when Abdul entered.

"Mother of my sons," said Abdul.

"Come to bed, husband."

She finished undressing and lay down. He undressed. Then he lay down beside her. She half rose, and turned toward him, resting on her arm.

"You are troubled, Abdul. I could see it the moment you walked in tonight."

"I cannot say what it is."

"Do you remember when we were children in the *haras*?"

"It was a good life, simpler times."

"Such a rich community in our little alley's world. Every night Mahfouz, the old man, would close the *haras* gate. It seemed we were safe from anything that might harm us in the entire world. Do you remember old Mahfouz?"

"He was always patient with us kids. I well remember the *haras* of our youth. But its feeling of security is gone. We know the dangers of the world now."

"Let's not keep coming back to now. Remember our life then. We've known each other always. Do you remember how I watched you when you were a little boy? I was little too. I would look down from the balcony and watch you play for hours. I could always tell when something troubled you."

"And I could always tell when you were watching. It made me feel like I had an angel guarding me."

"You still do."

Abdul lay quiet, looking up at her. "My refuge," he said, looking into her eyes.

She leaned down and kissed him softly, light as a girl's glance from a balcony.

"There's one thing I couldn't do to console you back then," she said. Her kiss became fierce.

Abdul made love to his wife passionately. She received him as the desert does rain, hungrily as if no rain had fallen before in history.

Abdul felt fortunate in his wife. He was certain he would make more sons upon her.

Spent, he rolled off and lay beside her. She soon dozed.

Close to sleep himself, Abdul's mind was bitten by worry again. What did the manifestation of Mut mean? He now accepted Allah. He saw the Egyptian gods as idols, harmless ones, no more than historical memories. Only the Karnak priests let the old gods distract them from the true faith. But if Islam was right, how could there be any power in Mut? He wished he could speak with his wife about it. She was so sensible. Yet he must hide his work for Karnak and the Islamic Foundation from her. These were the affairs of men. He would shield her from their dangers.

Abdul must have dozed more than he thought.

He found himself on a mountain in the desert. He was kneeling. His eyes were almost closed. The radiance from the being standing before him was painful.

"Why can't I see you?" said Abdul.

"It would blind you. Do not look, only listen."

"Who are you?"

"You know me as Him Who Gave the Law to the Prophet."

"Gabriel, God's messenger?"

"I am."

Abdul prostrated himself completely. He was right to have accepted Islam. "I am unworthy. Why am I here?"

"The Prophet needs your help against the infidel."

"I will help."

"The gods of Karnak are awakening."

"I have seen this."

"Their magic is of the Sun. It will help the infidel. The magic of the Night will be brought by dark gods. They serve the Prophet's jihad. You must stay at Karnak and wait for the magic of the Night."

"I will tell the mullahs."

"Do not tell them, under pain of death. Learn your place."

Gabriel vanished. Abdul woke in his bed. His wife was next him. Abdul was covered in sweat. He felt exulted and troubled at the same time. The vision had not eased his mind but disturbed it further.

Abdul looked over at his wife sleeping next to him. He smelled her sweet ripe woman smells of passion sated, more pleasing to him than jasmine, more consoling than prayer. Peace be upon her.

Then, from the darkness, a thought erupted into his mind: *reach over and choke her to death.*

Shocked, he clenched his fists by his side. "Never," he whispered. Frightened, he searched his mind, "What is happening to me?"

Abdul slept little and fitfully. The thought of killing his wife did not return that night.

"Allah hu'Akhbar!"

"Allah hu' Akhbar!"

It was morning. Abdul sat himself at a table in a small cafe in Cairo's medieval Arab Quarter. At the table were two dark intense men, bearded, wearing turbans. They were members of the Islamic Foundation. It was almost six months ago that Abdul had started working with them. The Foundation was an Islamist group dedicated to violent overthrow of American and other Western interests. They were dressed as mullahs and revered as holy men. Abdul accepted a glass of the sweet mint tea the men were drinking.

"Does he suspect?"

"No. Mustapha does not suspect," said Abdul. "He runs a large rich organization that he believes is secret. Karnak has penetrated into businesses everywhere. But he has no idea that his own organization might be penetrated."

"He is a fool."

"Perhaps." Abdul had once admired Mustapha, revered him like a father. Since joining the Islamic Foundation, he had started to see everything wrong with Mustapha. Abdul felt that all the years he had paid Mustapha respect were being repaid poorly. He felt betrayed. The longer Abdul worked with the Foundation, the more distant Mustapha became to him. The distance grew and grew until it was hard to remember the respect he once felt. Often when Abdul looked at Mustapha he now felt contempt. He knew the mullahs might ask him to take Mustapha's life, and it had become possible.

"How many operatives are safely inside?"

"Two others with myself," said Abdul. "Good men loyal to Islam and to the Foundation."

"Do you have any access to the accounts? We have international operations that require large amounts of cash soon. You have been working your way in?"

"I have been Assistant High Priest for a full year now, but only the High Priest has access to the finances. I can't draw him out on this matter without arousing suspicion. Over the last 2,000 years there have been several men in my position who were terminated when their interests in Karnak's wealth became too personal."

"There must be a system. What if he were to die?"

"There is a system," said Abdul. "That much I know. There is always a second man who has the codes and passwords. It is generally a young priest who is well trusted. That way if the High Priest dies suddenly, the young priest can tell the new High Priest how to have access to the money."

"Do you know who this young man is?"

"No. His identity is a deep secret. If I were to ask, it would arouse suspicion, and again I would be terminated."

"If Mustapha were to die suddenly, you would become High Priest?"

"Yes," said Abdul. The moment he had anticipated was upon him. They were asking for Mustapha's life. He would have given it to them more easily a few days ago. Now that he had seen Mut's statute move, he was no longer sure. But he was also vulnerable, as was his family. If he refused, the mullahs knew where he lived. The *haras* could not protect his wife and boys from the discipline of the mullahs.

"We are patient up to a point. But we also have crucial operations."

"Perhaps by removing Mustapha and assuming the position of High Priest I will gain access."

"You're willing to do this for Islam?"

"I must do what is necessary," said Abdul.

"We know from other members of the Foundation that a CIA operative is at work in the pyramids. This has happened in our country on and off since the SRI devils violated our monuments thirty years ago. We will let it proceed for now to see what they find. Be watchful. Mustapha helps them. Continue the operation and be here at the next regular meeting."

"Allah hu'Akhbar."

"Aallah hu'Akhbar."

Abdul left, and the next operatives went in to take his place, have a glass of mint tea, and face the mullahs.

A few minutes later and several alleys away, in another café in medieval Cairo, Abdul met with the men he had mentioned to the mullahs: Jalal Sadr, a young attorney in Cairo, and Hossein Nasr, a physicist at the university. Like himself, they had joined the secret priesthood of Karnak seeking meaning, seeking their people. They found it through Abdul in the Islamic Foundation. Now trusted in Karnak, they were his men, willing to do whatever they could to help him penetrate the secrets of Karnak.

As the mullahs ran Abdul, he ran them. Their loyalty was unquestionable; their oath was to the death. They had been turned from the accommodating religion of ancient Egypt to the harsh realities and unquestioned certainties of the Islamic Foundation. Although trained as a lawyer and physicist into sophistication, they took refuge in the simplicity of the Islamic Foundation's belief. In a world grown complex and threatening, it felt good to be told what to do. It was reassuring to be told what to believe, no matter how impossible it was to reconcile their harsh new beliefs with their former humane beliefs. They had been lost and now were found, normal men willing to commit murder because someone told them it was God's will. Their human hearts had been captured through ancient fears.

Abdul needed these men. He needed their help in what was coming. They had also by chance witnessed the strange manifestations by the statue of the god Mut. She apparently took their offerings and moved. Since they saw this challenging manifestation together, he was willing to take a chance with them. One he would never take with the mullahs. If the mullahs misheard him by a fraction, he would be guilty of heresy and his life would be forfeit. He could therefore never tell the mullahs about Mut's statue. Nor could he tell the mullahs about his dream vision of the Archangel Gabriel. If the mullahs thought Abdul were vaunting himself and comparing himself to the Prophet, then his wife and the spawn of his seed would also be destroyed. But he trusted these two men. He also needed to talk to someone.

"You have both seen the manifestation by the statue. Though Mut is an infidel god you saw some magic or miracle come through her. I will now reveal the vision I have had. It must stay among the three of us. You understand what will happen if it does not."

Their eyes looked down, their shoulders hunched. They were used to admonitions of death as part of the ritual of the Foundation. They thought of their wives, their children, uncertain of Abdul's intention and reach. They nodded and Abdul continued.

"I have had a vision of the Archangel Gabriel, who gave the Koran to the Prophet. The very same Gabriel came to see me in my dream. The Angel said the Prophet needed our help against the infidel. The Angel said that Karnak and its magic will serve the infidel and that we must stop it. I was told that the gods are awakening to help Karnak. But that other gods too would come. The magic of the Sun is for Karnak but the more powerful magic of the Night will serve the Prophet's jihad. We must stay at Karnak and wait for those gods who come to share the power of the Night with us, for they will be in the Prophet's service."

"How did Gabriel appear?" said Jalal.

"Blazing like fire, too bright to be looked upon," said Abdul.

"Must we keep this to ourselves?" said Hossein. He was eager to repeat the story.

"That was the admonition of the Archangel Gabriel himself. I do not know why we are chosen. He said it was under pain of death. He said the time to reveal it would come. He said we must wait and we must help. If the magic of the Night is a thing of the Prophet, we must wield it for him."

"Allah hu'Akhbar."

"Allah hu'Akhbar."

18

Morning found Wolfgang, Petra, Jack, and Cliff already in the Queen's Chamber. For Wolfgang, the dank air was as invigorating as an alpine spring. The computers and monitor were booted and the minibot lay on the floor near the shaft, ready. Wolfgang walked over, picked it up and kissed it. "Today's your big day baby. Go get 'em."

He placed the minibot in the shaft, returned to his keyboard and typed commands. The minibot moved smoothly along the first two meters on the level and began its ascent. They saw the shaft on the screen. If the pyramid were a body, this shaft was a capillary within it, embedded within layer upon layer of stone, two-ton blocks precisely cut and honed by hand to fashion the shaft. To what end? That was Wolfgang's sole preoccupation now.

The minibot crawled slowly up the dark shaft in the great stone body. It came to the place they had reached yesterday and went on. The shaft held to the same angle. As the minibot crawled up, they saw the shaft through the minicam. They could see that the dressing of the stones varied along the shaft walls. After two hours, the minibot was within three meters of the shaft's end. Here they saw the walls change dramatically from merely dressed to beautifully finished. They were clean, smooth, and finely made, polished white limestone like the entrance to a shrine. This high quality limestone, from the Muqattam Hills outside Cairo, was reserved for central chambers in sacred sites.

Wolfgang was happy to find that the minibot's traction was good on the highly polished floor. The minibot moved ahead and they saw the small white slab blocking the shaft. It looked like a portcullis that had dropped down to bar the way. The slab had two small copper bars about a third of the way down from the top and equidistant from the sides. The bottom right corner was chipped like a tooth, as if the door had bitten down too hard. At the center was the hole drilled through the slab by the last expedition. Beyond that was the second door, and whatever lay behind it.

19

Seven time zones west. In the White House, the vice president looked up from his desk. He had asked the secretary of state to join him for a late-night whisky. The secretary of state said amiably, "How's the family?"

"Fine, fine." The vice president put the secretary of state's repeated inquiries about the wife and kids down to his being Hispanic. It was hard for the vice president to feign reciprocal interest so he seldom tried. Some five months after a prostate operation, the vice president was less paunchy than his norm. His thick brown hair was just going gray. His soft brown eyes and calm voice contrasted with his manner, warm as a polar cap. He early on acquired the techniques that served a ruthlessness much admired among the cognoscenti of global capitalism.

He had learned that loyalty flows to the winner. He had picked a series of winnable games, and found that nothing felt as good as the energy jolt of loyalty flowing to him from others who were also players. Nothing except the winning itself. The games got bigger and deeper, leading inevitably to the office he sat in now, sipping whisky. From here he ran the Executive Branch smoothly and firmly like a good company. He saw it as a services company that needed, in the president, a celebrity figurehead for board chairman. Someone who could golf with client dictators and effuse to veterans' groups and gun lobbyists. Someone who could tell right-wing religious groups that his heart was torn by the bioethical questions that were beginning to take too much of the vice president's time. Why were all these people worried about cloning, whether animal or even human? It was a fine new industry waiting to happen. A knowledge-based industry of the kind America needed more of, as unskilled jobs migrated offshore. One he was already heavily invested in. There were risks associated with any new method of capital formation. Cloning was no different. The greens weren't stupid. Why did they never understand that new industries gave us new knowledge to deal with unforeseeable consequences? And the Christian right needed to see the competitive advantage to America that would come from pioneering the industry. The choice as always was stark: progress driven by profit, or atrophy. He would drive them forward.

The vice president raised his glass to the secretary of state, whom he didn't entirely trust. Was he sound? The man's background was wholly political. His mettle had not been fully tested in the marketplace. How reliable does that make a man? What made it worth having a late-night drink with Jose was his posting in a prior administration. He had been CIA director, and showed great political skill at retaining his information-flow relationships. To the vice president's way of looking at things, a former spook as secretary of state was a lot more useful than a human rights campaigner.

"The man we have in there's not a current operative," said the secretary of state.

The vice president had not been listening. He was musing. So few had the vision to run this country right. So few had the skills to help, or the guts it took. The will of the people and his ambition were the same. He would shape their will, move it forward, and explain their destiny to them. He noticed that his attention had drifted. It must be late.

"He's only on vacation," Jose was saying. "But he never wastes a move. He's our best crypto consultant, a real natural. If he's onto something, it's worth knowing."

"Who're you talking about?"

"Disch, Wolfgang Disch." Jose had learned the patience required to please men more powerful than himself. It was something he was willing to do on his way up. Then things would be different. But it was too early to show any sign of his own presidential ambitions.

"Watch him. Where is he?"

"Egypt. The pyramids."

"Do you have a network in place?"

"Good satellite coverage, but as the tide of Islamists rises higher in Egyptian government, it gets harder to penetrate the country effectively. We haven't found the key for bringing over Islamists we can use as agents, so it's hard to get men on the ground. Worst-case scenario, the space command's new battle station sweeps over regularly. We've never used it, but it's a beauty."

"Keep your eyes open. We haven't done a lot at Giza since we used SRI. And keep me informed."

The vice president took a long pull at his whisky, a single-malt Ardbeg from the peaty island of Islay. He felt the comfort reach into his heart. It would pump the precious Scottish juice to irrigate his whole body. God, he loved the taste of peat.

Part II
Across the Branes

Thereupon the rhinoceros of doubt once more raised his head.
—Hakuin Zenji

20

Wolfgang stopped the minibot centimeters from the door. He activated its arm and forced back a sudden sense of dread. He feared that what was called the "second door" was no door at all. Perhaps it was solid stone. Even if it were a door, he might find just blank solid stone behind it. He had seen false doors in tombs, and maybe this was one. Maybe this whole ensemble served some inscrutable Egyptian purpose. Was a symbolic door enough for the pharaoh's subtle *ka* to enter and leave the pyramid? Was this whole effort pointless? He was grateful that he and Mustapha had agreed to do this quietly.

As the minibot extended its arm, Wolfgang switched the minicam on. The monitor screen now showed a split image. The left was the picture from the minibot's maincam showing the limestone door. The right half showed the minicam image and drew their attention.

Wolfgang worked his keyboard. The minicam and laser were on the same equipment pod, narrow enough to move through the hole in the limestone door. As the pod advanced, the minicam image onscreen made it look like it was crawling through a tunnel. The pod emerged into the space behind. He moved it forward and they got a clear picture of their quarry, the second door. It was not as fine as the limestone door. More workaday, it appeared to be made of the same sandstone as the walls of the lower shaft.

Wolfgang had no way to judge how thick the door might be with the equipment he had. He searched for the spot where he would focus his attack and found it directly ahead. They were all watching over his shoulder.

"Yah, that spot will do," he said. "It's begging for it."

Wolfgang entered a sequence of keyboard commands, and the equipment pod arced forward. It carried the laser in front like a narrow finger. The minicam wore a filter to protect its sensitive eye from the laser's pointillist solar glare. Wolfgang's intention was surgically precise. He would remove only as much of the stone as needed to insert the minicam pod: its diameter plus a fraction for freedom of movement.

A fuel cell of his own design was attached to the minibot at the back, the power feeding forward to the laser. Control was entirely at the discretion of Wolfgang's keyboard. His fingers flew; he was entranced. Jack, Petra, Cliff, and Maria were tense, expectant.

"Here we go, boys and girls!" said Wolfgang. He struck a key, and the laser firing sequence began. They saw a spot on the door turn red and begin to glow.

21

Abdul, the Assistant High Priest, turned down an alley in the medieval Arab Quarter. His destination was an apothecary shop he had never entered until today.

Abdul pushed aside the curtain. The room was tiny. He had expected it to be dark and dusty, but it was orderly and brightly lit by an exposed bulb. Shelves lined the walls from floor to ceiling. The shelves were filled with bottles labeled in clear Arabic script. The labels announced contents whose uses Abdul could only guess at.

In Islam, as in the West, poison was the first branch of medicine thoroughly explored and understood. The knowledge had not been forgotten.

"Brother, you are welcome."

Abdul faced a small man sitting on a stool in the corner of the room. He was old, his skin smooth and tough, as if it had been cured by his potions. His hands, too large for his hunched body, were folded awkwardly palm up in his lap. A cigarette burned between the middle and ring fingers of his left hand.

Abdul breathed in as he prepared to speak. The scent in the room was peppery, sweet, musty. Abdul became nervous of breathing too deeply.

"I've come for a remedy that is invisible in its effects and certain in its result."

"A remedy for a life in your way." Like a spider in its web, the old man had not yet moved.

"Yes, there is someone in the way."

"By what route will you propose the remedy?"

Abdul felt uncomfortable in the old spider's company. "In a drink."

"You make it too easy for me." The old man smiled but did not otherwise move. The ash on his cigarette lengthened. "I will give you something we have known a long time. It came to Cairo by camel before the Prophet's truth."

"What do I do?"

"It is a powder. A mushroom extract. A few enhancers for good measure. Use the full dose. Mix it well with the drink. It is tasteless. It will be the drinker's last drink. It works quickly. A few convulsions, then nothing. Very clean."

The ash fell as he pulled the cigarette to his lips and drew deeply on it, as if recharging his own poison sacs. He spun around with agility, reaching out to the edge of his web, pulling bottles off top shelves. He used a small silver spoon to measure out precise quantities. Mixing his formula in a glass dish, the old man poured the mixture into a glass phial. He handed the phial to Abdul.

"Be careful with this. It is a treasure."

Abdul took the phial cautiously, as if the potion could act through the glass. "What is its price?"

"Only your brotherhood. I too serve the Foundation."

Abdul nodded and ducked out through the curtain. His relief in leaving the apothecary was soon replaced by anxiety over what he was about to do.

Mustapha had mentioned 'other obligations', when he begged off being with Wolfgang and the rest in the Queen's Chamber. They were obligations as High Priest of Amun-Ra. Once a month, the High Priest entered into a ceremony called 'Returning to the House of Amun-Ra'.

Mustapha was already in Karnak in Exile under medieval Cairo. He had performed the ceremony of entering the temple, and the ceremonies of robing and washing in preparation for the monthly rite. He was in the most sacred part of the temple, the chamber of the chief god, the home of Amun-Ra. He sat facing the altar, with its statue of the god, on a chair whose seat was broad enough so that he could sit cross-legged. Abdul, his Assistant High Priest, approached.

Abdul held a golden chalice. Mustapha watched the chalice fondly as it came towards him. It held the communion Mustapha would take, as he had monthly for all the years he had been High Priest, and as his predecessors in office had done for millennia. The Assistant High Priest prepared the communion. Its formula had not varied for more than five thousand years. The drink contained two plants sacred to Amun-Ra: the acacia and Syrian rue. The lacey-leaved acacia, well adapted to Egypt, was worshiped throughout its history. Its seeds contained a high concentration of DMT, a close relative of the brain's neurotransmitter serotonin. Syrian rue, a shrubby flowering plant partial to ancient ruins, had seeds full of powerful beta-carbolines. Mixed judiciously, they produced a beverage that would give the drinker powerful visions for several hours, a time to commune with the gods.

Though Mustapha did not want to acknowledge it at once, Maria had made good guesses about ancient priestly practices. When Mustapha spoke of the gods going silent, it was no vague sentiment but a report of his experience. He knew from the unbroken record that in the ancient days of Egypt, when the High Priest performed the ceremony of 'Returning to the House of Amun-Ra' he would see and speak with the god. This had not happened for more than two millennia now.

Mustapha had visions, as all his predecessors had done. He was transported through layer after layer of pulsing delicate geometries. They extended like flat membranes one above another. Each reached horizontally to infinity, their hierarchy reaching up without end as he mounted higher and higher through them. He sensed truth in these visions: he was witnessing the weaving of reality, as universe upon universe was fashioned on a loom of light.

Mustapha felt grateful for these communions. Reality pulsed with divine energy, and was reconstituted from it many times each second. He felt right being a priest because he witnessed this continuous divine creation through his succession of monthly sessions.

Still, Mustapha's heart was heavy. His human heart and emotional mind wanted to see and know the divine in personified form. He wanted more than anything to see, meet, and hear Amun-Ra, the Creator, embodied and individuated.

Mustapha took the golden chalice, its familiar shape a comfort in his fingers. He offered the cup to Amun-Ra, who stood in front of him in the form of his statue. Mustapha raised the chalice and drank. The bitter brown liquid ran down his throat. He handed it back to Abdul, and watched as his Assistant High Priest bowed and placed the empty chalice on the altar. Abdul returned and sat in a chair beside Mustapha as the ceremony prescribed, in case the High Priest should need assistance during his inner journey.

Mustapha sat cross-legged. He felt his back supported by the chair. He prayed for the sake of all beings and for the return of the gods, as he always did during the half hour or so it took for the communion to unfold. When the rush began, Mustapha felt a susurrus of fear, the sense of crossing a dangerous threshold.

Mustapha let go and abandoned himself to the gods. Eyes closed, he felt himself move rapidly upward. He moved through lattices of light. When he looked left and right, the lattices extended infinitely outward. When he focused on any one of them it opened into delicately pulsing fractals, stretching into finer structures without end.

Mustapha realized that he was pure awareness witnessing the continuous creation of reality out of emptiness. He filled with gratitude. Then he blacked out.

Abdul watched as Mustapha convulsed, shudders passing through his body. Abdul stayed seated. The difficulties Mustapha posed were about to end. The way forward would soon be clear. His duty to the mullahs would be fulfilled. He would become High Priest, and have access to all the wealth of Karnak in Exile. Wealth that would now serve the Prophet's jihad.

Abdul watched as Mustapha's head sank to his chest. Then Mustapha's body slackened.

Abdul stood. He went to Mustapha, bent close and listened for breathing. Mustapha was silent. Abdul felt relief. It must be over. He decided to lay Mustapha's body on the floor, and observe him for a little while longer before calling in the other priests. Abdul struggled with Mustapha's body, now a clumsy dead weight. When the body was laid out on the ground, Abdul sat once again in his own chair. He would wait a while, praying to Allah for peace of mind.

Mustapha found himself in a strange temple. This was new territory. The temple was one he had never seen before. It was as vast as the original Karnak. Mustapha had never entered a place of visions such as this.

His heart filled with a longing, almost unbelievably sweet, to see Amun-Ra at last. It did not happen. His wishes did not control events here. Instead, he found himself lying on his back in water. It was like a canal, narrow and cut into luminous white stone. He looked down and saw that he was dressed in a white kilt. He felt a headdress of some kind. Sitting up in the still water, he saw that he was wearing the Blue War Crown of the pharaoh. He sensed that he was to lie back in the water. When he did so, he was pulled head first by a gentle current, until he was sucked in under an altar, also of luminous white stone.

Then the movement of the water reversed, and he floated out in front of the altar. A second time he was drawn under the altar and a second time returned. When the water drew him a third time under the altar, he emerged head first into a large chamber.

In the chamber stood Amun-Ra, glorious. Light poured out of his eyes and suffused his skin.

"Arise and take birth," said Amun-Ra.

Mustapha stood and stepped out of the water. Wordless, he bowed to the god.

"Take courage," said Amun-Ra. "The great work is about to begin. You wear the Blue War Crown for a reason. Your help will be needed."

With this, the effect of the communion dissipated like a fog in sunshine. Mustapha was returned to the chamber of Amun-Ra in Karnak in Exile. He opened his eyes. The room was familiar. Mustapha stretched his limbs as if re-entering his body from a great distance.

Abdul was shocked out of his prayers. How could the old man not be dead? He had given him the entire dose of poison. Who or what was protecting him? This was more disturbing than the incident with Mut's statue. But there was no time for questions now. He must respond quickly and naturally. "Your Holiness, you seemed to stop breathing. I feared for you."

"Abdul, I was given a vision. The manifestation of Mut's statue was only the beginning. We will joyously embrace the gods' new workings."

Joy is not what Abdul felt.

22

The power of the Sun was focused in the heart of the Great Pyramid. The red spot on the second door glowed, bubbled, melted away. Then they were through.

"Yes, that was nice," said Wolfgang. He was relieved that the system had worked and that the fuel cell had held out with power to spare, though the door slab was thicker than he had guessed.

"What now?" said Cliff.

"Now for a little live video," said Wolfgang. He played his laptop keys like a jazz pianist. The laser retracted. The minicam emerged from its protective filter. Wolfgang maneuvered it nearer the laser-drilled hole.

They got a clear picture. It looked like the hole would do the job.

"Okay let's keep going," said Wolfgang. He took an involuntary breath. Unconscious of doing so, the three others followed suit. Wolfgang maneuvered the arm delicately forward with the care one would take docking a space shuttle. Any damage to the minicam would cost him precious time.

Slowly, Wolfgang found the perfect poise. The minicam approached the hole the laser had cut for it. By now the stone had cooled. Wolfgang began the insertion. The minicam's lights were in a ring around the lens like a medical camera. He could see clearly into the hole as he was working the minicam through.

Then he was through. It was onscreen. The room behind the door was a jewel seen from the inside. It was too much for his eyes to take in easily.

"Jack, you're the Egyptologist," said Wolfgang. "What is this?"

"This is totally different from anything ever found in Egypt before. I have no idea what the hell it is."

"So what does this all mean?" said Petra.

"Means it's an intelligence test," said Wolfgang.

"Cool," said Cliff.

23

Later that day they were on the veranda of the Al Minah. The Nile flowed by singing its soft song to the Earth. The date palms, with their stately formal wigs of fronds, so like those worn by women in the pharaonic court, were backlit by the setting Sun. Jack, Maria, Cliff, Wolfgang, and Petra were gathered in a semicircle with their drinks in their nightly ritual. Mustapha had not arrived, and it felt like the play could not begin before he joined them.

"I've already told Mustapha about my theory," said Maria, "so I'll tell you about what I've discovered today in the library of the Cairo Museum. My hunch had been that the ancient Egyptian priests used powerful hallucinogens in their rituals. I got there by comparative ethnobotany. I mean, these kinds of drugs were used in every ancient culture we know of where the substances were available in plant materials, as they are here. I didn't have any direct textual evidence, but today I hit pay dirt—a medical papyrus from the remains of the old library at Karnak. It talks about the spiritual healing powers of the acacia, when it is mixed with a plant called the 'Helper of Ra'. I'm pretty sure they are talking about the ritual use of acacia seeds with a plant that supplies an MAO enzyme inhibitor of some kind. A psychedelic ritual, like in all the other ancient cultures."

"Do you think they saw the gods?" Mustapha, elegant in linen, panama, and walking stick, had appeared as if from nowhere.

"I'm sure they thought they did," said Maria. "And yes, personally, I believe they would have. I'll spare you my theory on why just now."

"A theory I would enjoy hearing another time," said Mustapha, sitting himself down in the chair they had left for him at the center of the semicircle.

"And Wolfgang," Mustapha continued, "what have you found at the heart of our most durable mystery?"

"An intelligence test," said Cliff.

"It's totally unprecedented in the entire history of Egyptology, Mustapha," said Jack, abandoning his usual cool.

"Wolfgang?"

"Well first of all I have to apologize to Jack, because I'm not going to be able to help him for a little while with his sonograms under the Sphinx."

"Forget it," said Jack. "I'm helping *you* now, until we have this figured out."

"Wolfgang?"

"Well, okay. Here's what we found behind the door. Imagine a polygon. A geometrical shape with twenty-three surfaces, perfect planes, so many that the whole figure begins to approach a sphere. It's a very complex structure with no obvious analog in nature, though some virus capsids may be similar. Imagine yourself now standing inside it. You look around. Each facet is made of a different color of stone. Each facet has marks, a pattern of straight lines, slash marks incised on the surface. Totally unlike hieroglyphics. Or according to Jack, anything used as a form of writing or numbers in Egypt or elsewhere. The marks are repetitive, and it's not obvious at all what they might signify. Look."

Wolfgang opened his laptop and clicked through stills from the vid images of the surfaces. "Another puzzle: some places, seemingly at random, are blank."

Maria watched for Mustapha's reaction. When he saw the images from the polygon he went very still. His eyelids top and bottom opened wide. His nostrils flared. His lips parted and he breathed in through them. Maria saw that he was astonished. She also anticipated his next move, and waited for him to conceal his emotion from the others. She enjoyed watching how rapidly he picked up his world weary manner.

"Gibberish?" said Mustapha slightly taunting.

"Don't be ridiculous," said Wolfgang, missing the irony. "Who'd go to the trouble of concealing a geometry like that behind two stone doors at the end of a double-blinded shaft inside the pyramid to cover it in meaningless drivel? There has to be meaning."

"I'm intrigued, obviously," said Mustapha. He studied the images. "Jack is right. Nothing remotely like this exists. Not in the monuments, not in the papyri, not in other ancient cultures. How do you suggest we proceed?"

"Try to decode it. I have some mathematical cryptographer friends back at the university. They may help. I'll ask. Otherwise, I sit here and try to pierce the pattern like Champollion."

"I can help," said Cliff. "I've been writing some, like, pattern and meta-pattern recognition software that works pretty well. It's based on cellular automata. I've been studying Wolfram."

"Sure, thanks, you can help, my scientific theologian," said Wolfgang with a smile.

"Where do you start?" said Maria.

"What do you think they are trying to tell us?" said Petra at the same time.

"I have no idea yet," said Wolfgang. "I am thinking maybe math or physics. A message about their level of knowledge. Sending it down the ages. Is it like us sending out the Voyager spacecraft into deep space? Maybe they were sending a message forward into deep time."

Later, in their room, Petra said, "Wolfie, archaeology is so much more exciting than I thought it would be. I want to make love now with the man who will find the key."

"Okay, good idea," he said. "I just need to upload this email to my crypto friends first."

Petra came up behind Wolfgang, leaned over the chair, put her arms around his chest and pressed her breasts against him.

He took a deep breath and felt himself stir. "Hold it for a second baby, I'll get rid of this thing as fast as I can."

He sent off his report on the day to Washington with a copy to Langley. Then Wolfgang luxuriated in Petra's attentions. "A fit reward," he thought, "my due."

Mid-afternoon at the White House. The secretary of state walked into the vice president's office.

"Back for another round?" said the vice president smiling.

"Not quite yet for me, you go ahead," said Jose, returning the compliment.

"Look, you remember our little chat about Wolfgang, our crypto operative."

"Sure."

"Just got an email at my private address quantum encoded, impressive from a field operation. Sent these amazing photos of some sort of ancient code, very bizarre looking, deep in the pyramid."

"Why do I need to know this?"

"First, I thought you'd be interested. Second, he wants NSA supercomputer time starting immediately to work on the decoding."

"Scarce resource. Interesting enough?"

"If Wolfgang thinks so, yeah. Worth a shot."

"This isn't some sorta joke, right? There really is some bizarre code up the ass of the pyramid?"

"No joke. Wolfgang has no sense of humor."

"Last thing I need is some message from aliens up the ass of the pyramid, for Chrissake. But okay. Tell the NSA boys to take a look. I'm uncomfortable if I don't have operational control. That means knowing more than the other side. Wolfgang won't go to anyone else?"

"He's secure."

"Keep him that way."

24

Cliff knocked on Wolfgang and Petra's door. Wolfgang opened it. Carrying his laptop under his arm, Cliff said, "Thought it was time to get to work."

"Come on in."

Cliff pulled an armchair up to the coffee table. Wolfgang sat in his own armchair in front of his laptop. Cliff opened his and booted it. While waiting, he watched Wolfgang sink back immediately into contemplating the images from the polygon. Between them on the coffee table was a lamp with a red silk shade and tassels. Cliff felt a dislocation in time. Here they were working on a 21st century problem, while the surroundings made him expect a fat man in a fez to walk in and start talking to him about a Maltese falcon.

"I need a copy of the images if I'm gonna work on them," Cliff said.

"These are my images. Can I trust you with them? You're not going to share them with anyone without my permission."

"Look, I just want to work on them myself!' Cliff couldn't believe Wolfgang was making this difficult. "I need them. I'm helping you, okay?"

Wolfgang had established his primacy. He downloaded the images onto a CD. He stood and stretched, then walked over to Cliff. The male ritual of comparing laptops began.

Wolfgang watched as Cliff's laptop read the images off the CD. Cliff selected them all and imported them into one of his pattern recognition applications. The raw files appeared on the screen, one by one. A second window opened. It began to fill with high contrast black and white copies of the images from the polygon. Cliff saw the look on Wolfgang's face and said, "Extracting the actual images. The front end works something like an OCR program but doesn't try to match an ASCII text."

"Looks like a pretty souped up machine for a kid. Do that yourself?"

"Yep, no other way to get it this fast," Cliff said, proud of his modified machine. It would take a while to extract all the data, so he got up and went to take a look at Wolfgang's laptop, expecting to see the same machine he'd seen in the Queen's Chamber earlier in the day. Instead it was something he had never seen before.

"What the hell do you have here?" Wolfgang's machine was black, smooth, and chunky. It bore no logos. Its side and back were bristling with peripheral ports. It had the tech appeal of military spec.

"Oh just a little number on loan from friends I consult with. Too small for anything really interesting like weapons sim or weather modeling, but it'll hold the grocery list. Quantum crypto eats space. I've got special RAM chips, parallel overclocked experimental quad CPUs, all the I/O is triple firewire speed. Stuff the *hoi polloi* will never get their hands on."

"So who are these friends of yours, and how can I consult with them?"

"Get your Ph.D. first, then we can talk about it."

Cliff thought it had been worth a try, even if Wolfgang persisted in being secretive. He went back to the hardware in front of him. "I bet your laptop's fast enough to make some of my pattern recognition software blaze." Cliff wanted very badly to use Wolfgang's computer, but couldn't bring himself to ask. It would just mean another put down.

"Yep, that's the kind of thing it's good at. I'm going to start by seeing if the polygon is some sort of physics textbook. I keep thinking that these straight line combinations are a lot like the way we represented numbers on the Voyager."

"But there seem to be only four numbers if that's what they are. Unless there's a meta-pattern. Or unless it's some sort of weird base four system."

"Well I'm going to poke around with that. Our problem is that we have zero context. Enigma was cracked because Turing knew the Nazis were transmitting info about the war. Submarine deployment and the like. But this stuff could be anything. Secretly coded passages from *The Book of the Dead.* Some made up language the pharaoh was to speak when he was challenged in the realm of the gods. A set of twenty-three spells for such challenges is very possible. It's the way they thought. My friends at the university are good at linguistic code breaking, since that's what most code is for. If it's a text, some set of spells or whatever, they'll get it. No better crackers. So I'll leave it to them and look for ancient science."

"What's your gut feeling?"

"That it's beyond anything the ancient Egyptians could do. If it's from Earth, why doesn't it match anything else? If it's not from Earth, and I'm just leaving the possibility open, then it could be really hard to crack."

"I've processed the images, so I'll start configuring my pattern recognition program." Cliff felt outgunned by Wolfgang. But his own software was good. It was Linux-based, and he had radically modified it from the source code of a fast but relatively unsophisticated commercial program. He had to believe in it now. "I start with simple rules. Cellular automata. Then the rules grow themselves, like dendrites reinforcing patterns of input in a growing brain. I can run cycles through fuzzy logic routines too, and fractal analysis and a couple of others. So I can look for patterns that might not be intuitive to the human mind. If there's a meaningful pattern, we should find it."

Wolfgang looked at Cliff. "Interesting. Show me more later. Right now, let's roll." They each bent over their laptop, humble servitors of portable gods.

Several hours later, in the still of the night. The only light came from their screens and the lamp with the silk shade. From the next room, Petra snored. Cliff was slouched down in his chair, wondering what it would be like to be in the room with her, watching her as she slept. He wondered if she slept in the nude. He looked up from his screen at Wolfgang. Wolfgang felt the look, and returned it. Cliff found Wolfgang staring at him, with the look of an animal protecting its territory.

"Need some sleep? Why don't you go get some. Leave this to me," said Wolfgang.

"No way, man," said Cliff.

"Good luck cowboy, but you haven't got a chance."

"Forget it. I'm gonna crack this thing."

They were in their element, playing against each other and against the crypto team Wolfgang had called in. They were playing their favorite game: Who is fastest and best? Cliff intended to triumph, despite Wolfgang's computer. In a Western, the cowboy who won the gunfight also got the girl. Cliff wondered if the same could happen here.

"Hey there's some Cokes in the minibar," said Wolfgang, "why don't you get us some?"

"I don't mind." Cliff was careful not to get up too quickly, so that it seemed like his idea, not Wolfgang's. He got the Cokes, went to Wolfgang and looked over his shoulder. "Got anything?"

"Nothing yet. Four hypotheses down, twenty-eight to go. I have an array set up with all the possibilities I have available. Things we might expect to see in normal crypto operations. Looking for recurrences that might match a data set in my reference table. Next is looking at long astronomical cycles, like precession of the Earth's poles in reference to the fixed stars. It's something they might have figured out and thought deeply esoteric. Maybe they thought it was magic, worth both expressing and concealing, storing it up so pharaoh could use it in his star journey, I don't know. How about you?"

"Nope, it's running through the data. I set the correlation cutoff level at an 'r squared' of 0.5. If we get close to anything, it'll beep and alert me."

"Back to it."

So back they went. Their faces lit by their screens were intent. From time to time Cliff heard Petra snoring placidly in the bedroom, reminding him that the world went on and that he was losing sleep. But there was just no time for sleep right now. An hour later Wolfgang got up to stretch. He fueled himself with a couple of fingers of whisky. He held the bottle out to Cliff, who waved it away with a "no thanks."

A couple of hours more and a cock crowed. It was a strangled sound, the cock never managing to get through the loud last note in his song. He nevertheless announced the triumph of Amun-Ra over the gods of darkness. Sunlight slid through the window and the day would soon be hot.

When Cliff looked up, Petra was standing at the door of the bedroom in her dressing gown, eyes still puffy with sleep. She stretched her arms and rotated her hips, as comfortable in her skin as a wild desert cat. For a moment, all thought of the polygon left Cliff's mind.

"Hey you guys still at it? Incredible. Time for breakfast, smart boys. Mama says."

Cliff felt a little bleary now. He wouldn't fight her call.

"Got anything there?" said Wolfgang.

"Pattern after pattern after pattern. No meta-pattern, though. No correlation coefficients much above point one. Rich with pattern but not with sense."

"Nonsense?" said Petra with a yawn.

"It would be a little early for that conclusion," said Wolfgang. "I don't have anything either. I'm dead sure it's here though. Let's have breakfast, but I'll just go online and see if the university crypto boys have anything for us."

Cliff took a shower. Petra put on a red bodysuit and a wraparound black skirt that left little to the imagination. Wolfgang went online. He found a message for him from the NSA codeworks:

"No clear path."

Wolfgang sighed as fatigue mixed with elation. The polygon held a coded message. He was certain of it. And he was going to crack it before the master code breakers at the National Security Agency, hunkered in their crypto fortress in Langley, Virginia.

The sky was turquoise enamel straight from the kiln. A pair of doves cooed in the date palms. Roses pink in boxes flanked the walls. The three of them sat at a table heavy with linen under a green and white striped awning.

"What would you like for breakfast, Cliff?" said Petra.

"Lots of coffee."

She was amused by how valiant a tired teenager could look. He blinked and started to push back his hair with his right hand. The gesture changed mid way though. Elbow on table, he scratched his head.

"Where do we go from here, Wolfgang?"

"I really don't know. The university boys have nothing, and I've been through my main hunches. We're missing something."

"Life goes on. Get some sleep pretty soon or you'll fall over," said Petra.

A fly buzzed around Cliff's head, annoying him. He shook his head, long hair flying. The fly returned and landed on his nose. He swatted and missed the fly, hitting his nose.

"Yes! Got it! Hooray!"

"What?" said Wolfgang.

"Okay you were right, we needed the context."

"So what is it?"

"Life goes on. Fly lands on nose of man." He was giddy.

"You're being a little too Zen for me."

"Life! What book has twenty-three chapters?"

"Damn!" said Wolfgang. "The book of life! Maybe you've got it, bro."

"Look, sure, twenty-three panels equals twenty-three chromosomes. Repetitive sequences of four are nucleic acid bases. And the frequency of three-element repeats. Codons! Bingo."

"I like it," said Wolfgang, "but it's full of holes. First, how the hell did they know anything about DNA? Takes X-ray crystallography at a minimum. But two, I know something about genetics. Way too little on each panel to even sketch the chromosomes.

"On the first objection, I have no idea. On the second, you're right."

"But that doesn't mean you're wrong."

"What is going on with all these brain storms?" said Petra.

"Well, Cliff has the best idea so far. This code has to be about something, and DNA is by far the best fit. The human genome has twenty-three chromosomes. All the assembly information to make a person is written in pairs of just four bases. Repetitive sequences of four elements on twenty-three facets. Best fit to data yet. Just hard to believe they could have done it. We need to look at the panels again and see if they fit."

"Not before you finish breakfast," said Petra.

"Okay mama, we need the caffeine anyhow," said Wolfgang. Exhaustion gone, they were a happy little tribe.

25

Back in Wolfgang and Petra's room littered with empty Coke cans and a whisky glass, Cliff and Wolfgang were bent over Wolfgang's laptop, re-examining the panels.

"There's just too little information on each panel," said Wolfgang.

Petra entered. "My Exxon card, have you seen it?"

"Huh?" said Wolfgang, coming out of his thoughts.

"My Exxon card. While you geniuses are thinking, I'm going to take my Mercedes and do some research on the art in the Citadel, but I need diesel. Know where my Exxon card is?"

"That's it, you're beautiful!" Wolfgang rushed across the room, ran his fingers through her hair and embraced her. "You've got it! Exons and introns. We can chop them out and maybe get a fit!"

Cliff lit up, and hugged Petra too. "Twice in one day. 'Life goes on', and 'my Exxon card'. You're our muse."

"So what is all this?"

"Well we just take out the 'introns', the junk DNA, and maybe we're there," said Wolfgang.

"What's junk DNA?"

"Well probably lots of viruses that fused with our genome early on. And maybe also a kind of genetic operating system or global communication system, interesting work by this guy Mattick. Anyhow. There's a big chunk of the genome that's called 'non-coding DNA', made up of introns and other stuff."

"How much?" said Cliff.

"About 98% of the transcriptional output of the whole human genome, 95% at least."

"And if we knocked it out, do you still read it as human?"

"Yep, the Human Genome Project only decoded 5%. But you can probably do without another 2-3%."

"So our panels may have a perfect minimum description of the human."

"Looks like."

Petra was a little embarrassed for them in their enthusiasm.

"Look, you boys clean up the details while I go out. This room is starting to smell like a gym. Forget the cards. I'll get the diesel with cash."

When Petra returned several hours later, Cliff was looking over Wolfgang's shoulder at the laptop screen. They were tired and exultant.

"How's it going, boys?"

"Great," said Cliff. "We're beginning to make sense here."

"Okay, time for a nap for you both before lunch. Off you go Cliff, and up you get Wolfgang."

Wolfgang said, "I'm not having any 'nap' unless you have one with me."

Cliff knew when to leave. He walked down the hall to his room, feeling lonely. "I guess every dog has its day," he told himself in consolation.

Petra and Wolfgang entered their bedroom, undressed each other and fell into bed. The light of Egypt used their sweat to sculpt their bodies' curves. It was a victory celebration.

Lying there after, Petra enjoyed the languor that follows love. Eyelids half-closed, her mind entered a pre-dream wander. It was a comfort to have Wolfgang next to her, spent, warm. She drifted toward doze, when suddenly he was getting up.

"Hey where are you going?"

"Nice nap, but now I need to start looking at the blanks."

"Blanks?"

"Places in the panels are blank space. They look random. Scattered all over. Must mean something, so I've got to figure it out."

Soon he sat naked in the armchair, poised over his screen. A knock came from the door. He said absently, "yah?"

"Hi, it's me," said Cliff.

"Come on in."

Cliff entered, took in Wolfgang's nakedness, said, "Nice nap."

Wolfgang looked down at himself and smiled. "Okay, don't want Maria to think it's me corrupting your youth." As Wolfgang stood, Cliff had a chance to see what a woman would find attractive in him.

Wolfgang returned wearing jockey shorts. "I need to find a pattern in these blanks."

"I've got an idea about that," said Cliff. "Let's just line up what we've got against the Human Genome map. If the matches are good enough, maybe we'll see what the missing bits of DNA code are."

"Sure. We're not quite there, but will be soon. I've been working on the first panel. I've figured out how the permutations of the slash marks on the panel may represent the nucleotide base pairs. I have the coherent versions here. If we're lucky there will be a good fit to one of the chromosomes. Then we know exactly how to read the slash mark code, and the remaining 22 panels will be readable quickly."

"Can you just call up the Human Genome Map data?"

"Sure, let's do it."

Wolfgang went online and quickly had the genome map.

"How did you do that? I thought you needed a paid subscription to the database," said Cliff.

"I have a few tricks to pull when I need them." Wolfgang quickly sorted through the twenty-three chromosomes, hoping he'd find what they needed in the 5% of the genome the Human Genome Project had mapped. Was their intuition right that the polygon held a model of the 2 or 3% of the genome that remained after you removed all the non-coding DNA?

Soon, Wolfgang yelled, "Score. Genius. Got it!"

What they labeled Panel 17 was a good fit with the Human Genome Project map for chromosome 3.

"Let's rename the panel '3'," said Cliff.

"Sure, and look for the other correspondences."

Absorbed, they clicked and sorted, clicked and sorted. Petra ordered room service and they were soon celebrating with pizza Al Minah and drinking beer and coke. By mid-afternoon, they had the correspondences plotted out. Each panel matched the core data of a human chromosome.

"What about those gaps now?" said Cliff.

"Now we line them up and check what's known about the functionality of the missing bits. Let's start here." Click. "Yep, I had a hunch. Look, these missing chunks of the XY chromosome decide if we're male or female. A significant thing for them to leave blank."

"Why do you think it's blank? Didn't they understand that part?"

"No way. I bet these other missing bits are also key. I bet they are all central chapters in the instruction book on how to build a human."

Seven blank spaces appeared among the twenty-three panels. When Wolfgang and Cliff matched them to gene functionality maps, they found that the blanks were indeed crucial. In addition to sex, what belonged in the blank spaces coded for skin color, eye color, brain size, longevity, and one of the homeobox genes that control body size.

"Okay, what should be in the blanks are key gene sequences," said Cliff. "But why leave them blank?"

"Finding the polygon and decoding the panels was intelligence test number one. The reason for the blanks must be number two. We'll have to solve it before we get any further."

"Wherever 'further' is."

Maria left her desk in the library of the Cairo Museum to meet Jack for coffee. He sat waiting in the small cafe across from the museum's entrance. He rose to greet her and gave her a kiss. She sat with a smile and ordered coffee.

"So what have you been doing all day Jack, since your Sphinx work is on hold? Working with Wolfgang?"

"No, that's Cliff. They don't need an Egyptologist, and I'm no computer geek. I'm supernumerary at the moment, so I went and spent half the day with the Sphinx. Communing, I don't know. When I'm out there with the Sphinx I have this crazy feeling that it wants to tell me something. Probably silly fantasies of a guy who'd rather dig and can't."

"Poor thing, it's hard for you to be still." Maria wondered if all men remained eighteen years old on the inside for their entire lives.

Wolfgang composed an email to the secretary of state, put it into quantum crypto, and sent it off:

You can tell the NSA boys to back off.

Cracked the code. Get this: it's the human genome. Don't ask me how. Still fiddling details. Hell of a vacation.

26

Mustapha sat behind his desk in his office at the Cairo Museum. The secretary who guarded his privacy knew him only as the Director of the Supreme Council of Antiquities.

Within the chambers of his mind, he was contemplating recent events through the eyes of the High Priest of Amun-Ra and Great Mage of Egypt. He sat with his left elbow on the desk. His left hand scratched the crown of his head absently: pose of the primate in thought.

First the living statue of the mother god. Mut the Great Mother had come alive for a moment in Karnak in Exile. That would have been more than enough for a lifetime as High Priest and Great Mage. So much more, so very much more, had now happened. His lifetime prayer had been answered in yesterday's ceremony of Returning to the House of Amun-Ra. He had seen the god in his vision and the god had spoken to him. This had been his prayer for Egypt and the world as well as for himself—that the gods awaken. "Let the Gods awaken and heal the Land," had been the doleful beseeching of every High Priest and Great Mage for two millennia. An unbroken tradition of faith annealed with melancholy.

"We used to keep The Two Lands alive," he thought. "The Land of the Bee and the Sedge, Upper and Lower Egypt prospered. We served the gods and they lived among us. Sad and lonely, humans in a landscape empty of gods."

Yet what would it mean if the gods awakened? What would it mean for Egypt and for the modern world? Would they return to heal? Or would they be a scourge? Or both? His vision of yesterday unsettled him. He was born of water into the presence of Amun-Ra. A prayer answered. Yet he was wearing the Blue War Crown of pharaoh. Would war and destruction accompany the gods' awakening? What did Amun-Ra mean by 'the great work is about to begin?' What would be his role in it? 'Your help will be needed', said the god. With all his heart he would do what he could, but how could he help the gods?

Mustapha sat back, left hand now massaging his knotted neck. He looked down at his desk, at an ancient papyrus he had brought with him from the library of Karnak in Exile. It was a precious thing from the Old Kingdom, the earliest known version of a core text unknown outside the Karnak priesthood. The contents of this papyrus had been his particular study since he gained access to it upon becoming High Priest of Amun-Ra and Great Mage of Egypt.

It had become his familiar, his comfort and puzzle. The text was a treatise on sacred magic, regarded as perhaps the most powerful of all such texts. Mustapha felt the power of the text coiled up and waiting to grow. Its ancient title: The Book of the Power of True Names.

His eyes fell on a favorite passage he had chewed on often:

> *He who rightly speaks a True Name can call on its full power. For him who calls with a clear heart no good will elude him. Let him raise the dead. Let him smite the enemies of Egypt. The power of life and death over peoples is his. The greatest of all True Names is that of Amun-Ra. He is called 'Khepera' in the morning when he brings back the dawn. He is call 'Ra' at noon and 'Atum' in the evening. But who knows His True Name? Who possesses this True Name but Amun-Ra himself?*
>
> *Osiris was said to have it. But only a child could so believe. If he had it, Seth could never have defeated him. When Amun-Ra chooses to reveal his True Name, then will its power to loose and to bind on Earth, and below and above, be given. For the power in the True Name is the power of the god himself. Therefore pray for and fear the Day on Which the True Name of Amun-Ra is Revealed.*

Mustapha looked up from the papyrus. He had read this passage for years, its hieroglyphs as familiar as his own face in the mirror and much more resistant to change. He felt the words were connected to his vision and somehow animated by it. He wondered how his vision and this sacred text were connected with the polygon in the heart of the pyramid. What was manifesting? He prayed for and feared the Day on Which the True Name of Amun-Ra is Revealed.

The secretary of state walked into the vice president's office.

The vice president was sitting behind his desk. It was heavily built of mahogany to convey the power of the man behind it. A pair of Chippendale chairs upholstered in yellow silk faced it. The vice president looked up from the briefing papers he was reading. "Hey, Jose, we've got to stop meeting like this." He squeezed out a smirk. It was his nearest pass at a smile. "What you got? Pyramids?"

Jose sat and looked at the vice president levelly. "Yeah. Our boy cracked the code. Inside the pyramid is a secret twenty-three sided room. On its walls are written the entire human genome."

"Human genome. We haven't had that for all that long."

"That's the kicker. Time to tell the president?"

"The old man doesn't like details: history, science, that sort of thing. I'll handle this. Get me operational control. I'm uncomfortable without operational control."

The pink roses floated their perfume across the veranda where it mixed with the scents of the Nile flowing north to the sea. It was the time of day when Amun-Ra is called Atum, and it was still very hot.

As the sunglobe fused with the horizon they gathered in their semicircle, drinks in hand. Jack and Maria drank gin and tonic together, Petra arak, Wolfgang beer, Cliff Coke. Mustapha drank mineral water. With the ceremony of 'Returning to the House of Amun-Ra' behind him, Mustapha would be able to enjoy an

Ouzo in a day or so. The ritual would not require him to teetotal for another three weeks. Then, to prepare the body for the effects of the communion, he would drink only water for a week. He sometimes resented but always followed the proscription.

The excitement of the six was palpable.

"Tell me again, Wolfgang," said Mustapha. "I am an antiquarian not a geneticist."

"Right. Our polygon has twenty-three faces. Each of them bears one of our twenty-three chromosomes. What you could call the book of life."

"Just for humans?"

"These twenty-three are human, but our genetic code is based on the same four letters as a worm, a rose, everything, just arranged into different words."

"We share an amazing amount of our actual genome with other life forms," said Cliff. "Something like 98% with chimps. We share most of our functional genes with rats. Even a lot with fruit flies and lettuce."

"Western science cracked the human genome in the last minutes of the twentieth century," said Jack. "How could the pyramid builders have it?"

"I have no idea," said Wolfgang. "That's more your line of work,"

Mustapha wasn't listening. He was staring off into space.

Maria said, "Mustapha, what are you thinking?"

"The Book of Life inscribed in this polygon. We know the Book of the Dead. I never thought we might find a Book of Life. I know of nowhere that speaks of such a treasure."

"There's another puzzle, too," said Cliff. "These people have the human genome. They even edit out the parts you don't need. To show us how good they are. But they leave blanks. There are seven blank spots in the set of twenty-three surfaces. "

"What do you mean 'blank'?" said Jack. "Has the surface of the stone flaked off over time? Very common for some types of Egyptian monuments."

"Not that. It's like the faces were prepared but nothing was inscribed there. Each of the seven blanks is pristine, fresh as yesterday."

"What are the blanks? I mean what parts of the genome do they represent?" said Maria.

"Things we'd be interested in as humans," said Cliff. "Like determining sex, brain size, longevity."

"So the next intelligence test," said Wolfgang, "is figuring out why they are there."

They sipped their drinks. The waiter brought another round.

Mustapha felt a sudden excitement, a waterfall of happiness pouring down into him from the Sky of Khonsu.

"Wolfgang, tell me whether you know how to fill in the blanks correctly. Can you look at the genetic code and translate it into the slash mark notation used in the polygon?"

"Piece of cake. Why?"

"And if you did this, then you'd have the true description of how to fashion a human being from nothing?"

"Well essentially, yah."

"Why is this so important?" said Maria.

Mustapha worked to conceal his elation under a mix of pedantry and courtliness.

"The *Book of Life*. The polygon is the *Book of Life* with pages left blank for us. We will write the true name of the human being within the *Book of Life*. In ancient Egyptian magic, to call something by its true name is to gain great power to do good."

"Or evil," said Jack.

"Or evil, yes. But we would not use it for evil. Perhaps the gods are still on the side of humans, if it is we who have discovered this."

Petra was listening, but unsure where Mustapha was going. A minute ago he was an urbane older man. Not quite her type but interesting. Now he was acting a little mad. She decided she liked mad better. "What do you want us to do? To help," she said.

"I am not yet sure," said Mustapha. "Wolfgang. Once you work out the code for the blank spaces, could you inscribe it in the polygon?"

"What are you talking about?" said Jack. "That would deface the most important Egyptian artifact ever discovered."

"Perhaps. Or if this really is an intelligence test as Wolfgang suggests, maybe we have to take the test. What will happen if we pass?"

Jack was thunderstruck that the arch keeper of the monuments could suggest such a thing. Unlike the others, he was not borne along by enthusiasm. "I know you're all excited by this discovery. But I don't think it's a good idea to start chewing this thing up with lasers. What will happen?"

"Are you afraid of a curse?" said Cliff.

"I don't know what I'm afraid of. What I'm urging is caution. We don't know what we may be unleashing."

Wolfgang was not interested in caution. He was pondering Mustapha's question. Could he inscribe the relevant code on the blanks in the polygon? Could he burn the slash marks into its stone panels? He was in the contented space of an engineer weighing possibilities.

"It may be possible," he said. "When you start to think this question through you see something I'd missed before. You see that the seven blanks are all opposite the door we went through. It's like they thought about this problem and pre-engineered things so I can do what you're asking me."

"Cool," said Cliff. "How do we do it?"

"Well *if* a person wanted to do it, here's what you'd do. You'd have to make the hole in the door bigger. But not huge. Got to get the minibot arm through, so it can aim the laser. Needs freedom of movement on the other side of the door. We're talking a seven to eight centimeter diameter hole. Then the minibot inserts the minicam and the laser. We program a firing sequence so that it can etch the needed lines."

"Can the minicam survive?" said Cliff.

"I can protect it with a filter, and program it to shut down while the laser is firing."

"Would the lines look just like the slash marks on the panels?" said Mustapha.

"The match should be close to perfect."

"Sure you can cut those stones with the laser?" said Maria.

"Again the builders are helping us. The hard stones, diorites, porphyries, greywackes, are used in the sixteen complete panels. We'll be cutting softer stuff, sandstone, limestone and so on. Easier to work."

"Got enough power?" said Cliff.

"A backup fuel cell the size of a suitcase in my room. It could supply all of Cairo with power for a few hours."

"Does Wolfie need a special permit?" said Petra.

"I would not recommend he apply," said Mustapha. "For I would have to record the request and deny it. My ability to monitor what goes on, however, is very limited. If I got a subsequent report that something had happened I might have to issue a small fine. But the deed would already be done. A bureaucrat's power reaches only as far as his desk." Mustapha stroked his moustache and waited.

"Cliff and I will translate the missing bits of the genome into the polygon slash code tonight. Let's meet in the Queen's Chamber at 8 a.m."

"I guess you're all going ahead with this," said Jack, "but forgive me if I remain skeptical. I wish you'd all reconsider, slow down and listen to me. I just don't see this ending in a good way."

They talked more, but Jack was unable to dent their enthusiasm.

Mustapha was the last to leave the veranda. He adjusted his panama and buttoned his white linen jacket. If the 'true name of the human being' was on offer, when would the true name of Amun-Ra appear? He allowed himself an unaccustomed spring in his step. Jack was not wrong. But Mustapha found that anticipation swamped the all too reasonable fear.

27

Wanre sat in his office. He looked out at the lake and wished he were an airdragon, as he often did when some political fight arose. He smiled internally, catching this familiar indulgence, and returned to the business at hand: gathering the information he needed to fend off Benben and Bulbul.

The Consilium's scholar attached to the Committee on Earth Assessment sat before him making his report. Like many scholars, he came from a race that always struck Wanre as a bit monkish, more avid for theory than for life in the body. He wondered if such a bent in a species could influence its evolution. He imagined courtships in which females were swept away by extempore abstractions, put in heat by the recitation of recondite information, and brought to climax by dense knots of whispered theory. "One might evolve the pallid, avid face in front of me that way," he judged. "Now focus, old friend," he told himself.

"So in sum, there are no statistically significant changes in the projections we've been making. Typical end of Level 2 turmoil: the powerful are stuck in their patterns, may wreck their biosphere, and so on."

"Nothing else?"

"Well one thing, but it's impressionistic."

Wanre had a reaction when faced with a statistical mind: that such a mind lacked finesse.

"Impressionistic?"

"Nothing definite at all. But several humans are conducting an experiment in the Great Pyramid."

"How do you know?"

"Just our normal monitoring. The standard remote viewing that any planetary assessment committee's techs do by reg. We can watch most things. The problem's never seeing but sorting. Signal from noise."

"The Great Pyramid? I know it of course. But..."

"So. This group of researchers has found a fascinating artifact. A twenty-three sided polygon—an icosikaitrigon—deep inside the Pyramid. Left there from its construction presumably. Oddly it has the human genome inscribed in it, save for certain blanks."

"Significance?"

"Unknown. Insufficient data. It's not correlating with any known artifact in any civilization on any brane."

"Reason for the blanks?"

"Unknown. A test of some kind perhaps, to assess the level of human technology and resourcefulness."

"By whom?"

"Unknown. That's what most interests us. The fact that the artifact doesn't correlate isn't definitive. But it is most intriguing."

"Why didn't you find this artifact before?"

"Resources, really. We know a great deal more than humans about their probable futures, based on our cross-universe data. The pyramids on Earth have always interested us. But we can really only gather and correlate, not do original research. When this group started their research, it highlighted it for us. We'll miss nothing."

"Make sure of it." Wanre rang a handbell and the scholar, now dismissed, shuffled away.

Later that day Benben and Bulbul arrived for a scheduled meeting. Wanre rose to greet them.

"Look, I am more convinced than ever," Benben said. "I've heard the report from the Committee's scholar too. There's something totally unexplained going on here. I hate not knowing why events on a planet under my jurisdiction are happening."

"Why does this pyramid business bother you so much? You know perfectly well that we see pyramids on half the inhabited worlds across the branes."

"And you know equally that the Giza pyramids stand out as peculiar. Unlike the pyramid structures everywhere else, the scholars have never fully succeeded in correlating these ones. This new polygon riddle just convinces me I'm right. Something there may trigger a great awakening or a great crash. This is not just normal end of Level Two business. I'm beginning to sense we need to be there in force when the humans complete the puzzle. A great awakening could disturb Consilium policies across several branes. A great crash could damage all the civilizations in the Multiverse slice parallel to Earth."

"Look. I acknowledge the strength of your feelings. But there's no basis for them. Not yet. Good to watch, not to act. For all we know, this is just as likely to have minor consequences, even on the Earth plane."

"I'm not buying it. As Speaker, you can bring this to the Consilium tomorrow. As committee chairs, we can too, by emergency petition."

"You doing it would make it easier for everyone," said Bulbul, giving Wanre a conspiratorial wink from where he was draped over Benben's shoulder.

"I just don't see any reason to take this beyond committee study," said Wanre.

"Even in the Consilium, fear is more effective than reason," said Bulbul.

He was quoting a maxim of General Babel, a distant relative and one of the most important military writers of the Consilium worlds. The General's maxim dated from just after the Beginning. It formed a leitmotif in Bulbul's conversation when he felt aggression hormones rising into his hind segment from Benben's brain.

"We're willing to push fear's reliable old buttons if we have to," he continued. "We will bring this to the Consilium, and *now*. Spot of excitement, humm?"

"The good general was a fear specialist too," thought Wanre. "Parasite genes I guess." He spoke to them. "You know my views. I suggest you temper yours." He rang his handbell, signaling the end of the interview. He enjoyed for once the power of the Consilium Speakership.

Wanre asked Toran, the Second Speaker, and Saiki, a personal friend, to join him. The two women were his closest advisors. He was sure Benben and Bulbul would act tonight, demanding that the full thousand Consilium representatives meet in the morning. Emergency petitions like theirs were vanishingly rare. They should be. Little that can affect the worlds has not been studied since the Beginning. Little has not been debated by scholars and then deliberated in the Consilium itself.

Even the Consilium's scholars cannot predict the future, Wanre thought ruefully. The principle of computational comparability limited knowledge of the future, and made any predictive science of history impossible. Nevertheless, the projections and probabilities were well understood. Surprise has become rare, and emergency almost unheard of. Therefore it is piquant. Wanre was wearily certain that none of the representatives would fail to turn up in the morning. They would not miss gossip on so vast a scale.

Wanre had invited his allies for a cocktail to apprise them of the emergency petition. He turned to them because of their talent, and also because they were from his home universe.

Each universe was splayed across a membrane, its billions of galaxies like bacteria colonies in a Petri dish. These membranes or 'branes' floated in multi-dimensional hyperspace. Like a millefeuille pastry, layer upon layer of branes were sandwiched close together. Every one of them a universe, and there were infinitely many of them. The sum of the branes was the Multiverse.

The reach of the Consilium arced across the Multiverse. Its broad sweep of knowledge and cooperation meant that once a race had gained entry, it was partnered to the rest, all of them working to further the cause of life against entropy. The nature of the Multiverse, though, posed logistical problems. There was a potentially infinite number of races who would at some time qualify as members. No cooperative governmental structure could cope with the logistics of decision making as the number of decision makers approached infinity. The solution was to have a thousand races hold rotating consulships.

A thousand representatives would gather in the Consilium, and stand in for the rest. The representatives were drawn from the known high sentient species. Consulships were held for a cycle, and distributed in a way that combined selection rules with randomness. The selection rules meant consulships were held across branes, so that no one universe or set of universes dominated. Randomness in the selection meant that a race in power knew that any other race might hold power over them next. It was the karmic cycle translated into government.

Although not representative in a strict sense, the system had worked. The thousand races holding power at any time tended to act in the interest of all, which is to say in the interest of life.

Consuls met by projection to make decisions. The results traveled by webs of information flow, the same way data normally moved across the Consilium worlds. Spanning the Multiverse with shared information, the Consilium was the most complex and successful form of organization the Multiverse had ever known.

Physical travel, though, was possible only in one's home universe, which is why Wanre had chosen his advisors from the universe he was born in. Physics did not allow travel across the branes, and therefore everyone was physically confined to their universe of origin. Being on the same brane made face-to-face meetings possible. One's home universe was a neighborhood one could move around with the ease of instantaneous travel.

Wanre felt he needed to sit, eat, and drink with his closest advisors. Speakers often felt this, and like Wanre recruited their intimates from their home universe. It caused no controversy within the Consilium. The value of meeting in the flesh was intuitively clear to everyone.

Wanre would meet with Toran and Saiki at Toran's eyrie. Toran, the Second Speaker, was descended from avian hunters. Wanre liked her *sang froid.* She had long been his confidante, from early in their careers. They had watched, supported and tested each other as they rose in government. They now entered the inner rooms of each other's confidence without hesitation.

Wanre walked to Saiki's villa. They would climb Toran's mountain together. Where the path curved around the lake Wanre paused to look at the airdragons. Today there was a pair of dapples, large sinewy creatures, young males playing at what would later become serious territorial fights. One of them left his rough and tumble to plunge headfirst through the surface of the lake. He emerged with a glistening fish and leapt into the sky. Lying insouciantly on his back in the air, the young airdragon used his belly as a table to hold the fish while he chewed its head off, the start of a leisurely meal.

Wanre had never *seen* into the life of the airdragons. He put it on his mental list of enjoyments postponed. He turned right along the shore of the lake, following the path to Saiki's villa.

Saiki lived in a structure of wood and living crystal fronting the lake. Like Wanre, Saiki was a native of Leucandra. She was a sartist, and a well known one. Her specialty was inviting life into new forms. She took combinatorial biologics to the edge where it becomes art, and her house had been her first major work. She brought elements of a local ecosystem to a cusp where trees and bacteria conspired into columns and sheets of living crystal. The result pleased her and was widely admired.

Wanre saw Saiki waiting for him. He appreciated her skill. He had brought her into his administration. Council meetings included a group of writers, historians and sartists, so that proceedings were recorded in a multidimensional way for posterity. Because of her acumen, he had made her the lead sartist in the group. Walking up her path, he found himself drawn to her. Unlike him, she let her mane go luxuriant. They touched palms and greeted.

"Let's not talk about Benben and Bulbul till we get to Toran's," said Saiki.

They walked up the path sculpted from the mountain by microorganisms recruited for the task when Toran built her eyrie. Waters ran down the mountain's flanks under dense foliage. Beams of light pierced the canopy. Glassine insectiles hovered gemlike in green dark shadows.

Wanre and Saiki walked up, enjoying the pull of their muscles and the deepening of their breath as they climbed. Trees gave way to rock as they reached the summit.

Toran was basking when they arrived. Her membranous wings, dark as the basalt, stretched wide on the rock to let her blood drink light. She loved every photon of it. The light was hot and it drew a sharp oil tang off her wings. The smell filled Wanre's nose. When he first knew her he found the smell repellent. Now he had grown accustomed to it. He found the smell comforting, as Toran's own race did.

"I'm delighted to see you," Toran said. She got up slowly, stretched and folded her wings.

Wanre looked into her dark round eyes. She was not being merely polite. She was delighted to see them. He sensed it clearly, though most found the feelings of her race hard to read in the unblinking eyes. Toran bent down. She extended the bony digits that sprouted from her wing's mid-joint. Wanre, then Saiki, received her touch on their palm.

"Come in, we'll have *bil* and talk."

Wanre and Saiki followed her through a cave mouth. They entered the salon, whose main feature was the view, a mountain panorama extending in all directions. From here, with her raptor vision, Toran could track what happened within a radius of several miles.

Although it was Toran's home, it was Wanre's meeting. He had sent a bottle of *bil* from his private reserve ahead of them, and

Toran brought it out. Wanre poured the drinks, to offer respect. They felt the gesture as intimacy: he has put aside his power to serve us. It was a gesture that they would have to return. Wanre was famous for hearing the beat beneath protocol, and for playing its rhythms most skillfully.

Wanre poured the *bil*, a wine made from a Leucandran fruit of the same name. Admired by connoisseurs from all the worlds, *bil* was Wanre's favorite drink. "When I retire I shall drink *bil* and write poetry," he thought as he poured.

It is traditional to have silence accompany the pouring. Silence allows concentration on the aroma, the first of the four pleasures *bil* offers. Some hear the aroma; some see it. Traditionally, none talks of it. They each raised their glass, bowed to the others and tasted.

The first flavor was flowers: the nectar, aroma, the soil and sexiness of vegetal riot. This had made *bil* a favorite among the green magi. Then came a pause in flavor like cloud moving across a summer meadow. The second taste, having gathered itself on the palate, was upon them unexpectedly. Deeper, acid and fruit balanced, it was as graded as a rainbow and as variously described through the sensorium of each of the sentient drinking species. Nor are any two sips the same. Their structures vary, always with a set of harmonies. As the notes of flavor quieten, the third taste experience comes: a refreshing cleanliness, running down the scale as pebbles on the beach make receding music when the wave leaves shore. Cleansed, the palate is primed for more.

When members of different species drink *bil* together in the traditional way, they find themselves easy. This was why Wanre had performed the ceremony. He would have preferred to keep drinking until they were merry, but duty called.

"You know how Benben, with Bulbul in tow, has been harping on the Earth. It is a jewel beyond price to her and she must have it. Some new discoveries at the pyramids have given them a lever. Not of reason but of fear."

"Even in the Consilium, fear is more compelling than reason," said Toran, a compassionate woman whose raptor eyes belied the fact.

"Yes, I know: Babel's *Book of Destroying the Enemy by Fear.* I just don't know why we are their enemy. Or why Earth is."

"Can you delay the petition?" said Saiki.

"I don't think so, politically. I thought of having them taken on my order for psychological examination. It would give us a little time but perhaps make them martyrs. No, we let them speak."

"Who will lead the opposition to their petition? It has to be someone else on the Earth Assessment Committee, as well versed in the facts as they," said Toran.

"It'll have to be me," said Wanre. "I will pass the Speakership during the hearings to you, Toran. Then I'll be able to speak simply as a committee member."

They finished the *bil* and stared out from the eyrie into the distance.

28

Next morning, the Consilium met on Leucandra to decide the fate of the Earth. Consuls from Wanre's universe would come by wormhole. Consuls from other universes would project their avatars across the branes. Toran would fly down from her eyrie.

Wanre decided to walk. Latching his gate behind him, he headed into the woods. He walked briskly this morning, letting the forest smells fill him. Soon he was at the edge of the woods.

The meeting hall of living crystal rose before him. Toran was in the air. She tipped her dark membranous wings in greeting and he smiled. He waited for her outside the hall. Since the other delegates would arrive directly inside the hall, they could greet each other privately if he waited outside.

"Ready to confront them?" said Toran as they touched palms.

"Let's see how good she is."

Morning light filtered through crystal panels in the meeting hall. The light spilled crimson on the consuls and Wanre thought of blood.

As Wanre had anticipated, all the Consuls were here. The Second Speaker called the Council to order, her raptor eyes commanding respect. She announced Benben and Bulbul's emergency petition. Benben would speak first. Wanre would oppose.

Benben stepped to the platform in the center of the circular tiers of benches. She carried Bulbul around her neck. His head rested on her chest. His hind segment was attached to the hole in her skull by suction and teeth. She would do the talking while her symbiont enjoyed the rising and falling waves of neurotransmitters that coursed through her brain. He loved the salty, fatty, orange taste of her anger. But he loved a much rarer delicacy even better: the plummy yellow swirl of her fear. He wondered if he would taste it today.

"I come before you today because of events on Earth," began Benben. "You know I chair its Assessment Committee with my symbiont. You know I have paid particular attention to my charge. It is dual: to care for the Earth and to safeguard the Consilium worlds. I have reason to fear for your lives."

Bulbul felt a thrill of anticipation. She said she had "reason to fear." Was he about to taste her fear? He waited for the plummy yellow swirl to enter his hind segment so he could savor it. He was disappointed. The taste was salty, fatty, orange. She was not feeling fear, just making a speech. He gave a connoisseur's inward sigh and prepared to make do with her anger.

Benben slowly turned around, taking consuls by the eye, the better to bend them to her will. She thrilled to power and needed a theatre of influence more malleable than the well-organized Consilium allowed her. Where to achieve it but on a Level 2 world? What better one than the violent and unpredictable Earth, home to so much suffering and opportunity?

Because the Council met by projection they needed no life support. That and their use of High Consilium speech made for immediacy. Because they had all evolved, they shared a common feature: fear was a program embedded in the substrate of their sentience, no matter how refined they had become.

Completing her circuit of eye contact, she allowed just enough time for the note of fear she had struck to resonate.

"The reason I fear for your lives is on Earth. These humans have just found an artifact inside their Great Pyramid. Those familiar with Earth or versed in comparative sentology will know it: the pyramids at Giza are the only ones in the Consilium that we do not have full provenance for. When something so significant does not correlate, we watch. What threat may it conceal? Something unknown in the entire Consilium? Just now, this artifact was uncovered. It spells out the human genome in code of unknown origin. No authorized interventions from the Consilium could account for it. Nor any unauthorized ones that could have escaped our scrutiny. So we have an anomaly, an important one, a phenomenon of utmost power and knowledge unleashed on a Level 2 world."

She looked slowly around at the consuls, giving fear time to ripen. "Let me get to my point: something momentous is afoot here. Who laid this trap at our feet? They are unknown to us. Do they have powers we lack? Could they open the branes to physical travel? Have they solved this profoundest of cosmological mysteries? Is it about to fall into human hands?

"Let me outline a deadly scenario. What would happen if humans could smash the chirality mirrors and travel across the branes? Mark my words, humans are aggressive meat eating apes at an early stage of cultural evolution. If they could pierce the branes they would appear throughout the Consilium wielding nuclear weapons, to whose power they are still in thrall. We would be wide open to their threat, utterly vulnerable. We must intervene now. We must control events as they unfold. Though it is dangerous, I will lead a mission. I ask you to authorize it. I am not asking much when the fate of the Consilium hangs in the balance."

Wanre leapt to his feet. Bulbul savored the plush red taste of power unleashed in Benben's brain.

"Pure demagoguery!" shouted Wanre. "I am embarrassed for my fellow committee member. And I am concerned for her mental balance. No process of reason can support her claims. As a member of her committee, I exercise my peremptory right to request an examination. Let her be examined for mental balance within the range of her species!"

As he finished, cries and mutterings arose from half the Council. It took a quarter of an hour for the Second Speaker to regain order. Bulbul enjoyed the sustaining taste of Benben watching her prey.

When silence returned, Wanre continued. "We will return to my request in a moment. Now to the merits. We have undertaken formal crisis intervention in a Level 2 world only rarely since the

Beginning. In each case the danger was clearly documented and generally agreed upon, not fear and phantasms. Even so, the interventions seldom worked. Nor would this one. We have no need for it. Events on Earth may be interesting, but that is what we have planetary assessment committees for. Let the Earth Assessment Committee continue its work. Watch. Report. Appoint a new committee chair. This call for intervention is bizarre. If the co-chair is not ill, she harbors political ambitions that are proscribed by the Consilium's charter. There are two possibilities here: she is sick or she has criminal intent.

"My motion to have her examined, which I make by right of my seat on the Earth Assessment Committee, precedes her request for intervention, as it calls into question her competence to lodge the request, or to follow through on it should it be granted."

Wanre sat down amidst a call by several hundred consuls to be recognized. He never really enjoyed speaking in this way, but sometimes one had to discipline barbarians, and he found a satisfaction in that. He knew he would lose the request to have her examined. The debate on the point would aid his case though, greatly aid it. He would succeed in blocking her request for intervention. "Then," he thought, "if she acts on her own, she will be a criminal throughout the Multiverse. Her further steps will be more difficult." He relaxed into a procedural enjoyment as if it were a truly fine meal.

29

It was night in medieval Cairo. Mustapha had left the veranda of the Al Minah and come to Karnak in Exile underneath the city. Dressed in his white linen kilt, gold pectoral and gold cuffs made vibrant with gems, he lay prone. Beside him on the floor lay the electrum staff of the Great Mage of Egypt, the baton with which the Mage conducted the workings of white magic. Surmounted by the ankh of life, the staff was as ancient as the office Mustapha held.

He was alone in the holiest shrine, the House of Amun-Ra. Lying humbly, face to the stone, both hands outstretched in supplication, he prayed to the god. So much had happened that he never expected to see in his lifetime. The statue of Mut the Great Mother had moved. He had met Amun-Ra in the ceremony of Returning to the House of Ra. The god had spoken and said that the work was about to begin. He did not know why the gods had begun to awaken and speak. He did not know why he wore the Blue War Crown. What would happen next he did not know but yearned to find out.

"Amun-Ra, great God, hear me. Dear one, you are The Hidden One, grant me your ears. As your High Priest and Great Mage, let me become worthy to carry out your work. Awaken fully and do your work in the world again. Help your people. We have been faithful. We have made offerings every day for millennia, everything necessary for your maintenance: bread, vegetables, beer, wine, milk, incense, meat, and flowers. Generations have lived through the quiet millennia and died in the hope of your return. Awaken and help your people. Let your magic return, the magic by which you make the world fit for life. Let me be a pure vessel for your magic. Let me be judged by Maat, let the great Maat judge my soul against a feather, and if I am inadequate, strike me down and raise another in my place so that your work can go on. Awaken, live, and give me a sign. I beg for a sign to know if I am the one who you choose to let your magic work. Awaken now and show me!"

Mustapha had spoken the strongest aspirations of his heart. He was moved. Tears flowed. He was certain his words had been heard, and sat back on his heels to wait for an answer.

Amun-Ra stood in his shrine in his classic pose as he had for millennia. His left foot was out before the right. His right hand was lowered to his side with fingers closed. His left hand was raised, holding a short staff. On his head was a crown: two high plumes in gold surmounting a solar disk, the crown almost as tall as the god.

As Mustapha watched rapt, a pale blue light danced down the twin plumes in the god's crown. Amun-Ra raised his right hand. He opened it and held the palm toward Mustapha in the gesture known as 'have no fear'.

"Mustapha," said the god, and the room trembled. Mustapha wondered if he were mad.

"Mustapha!" Blue light flashed around the god's mouth as he spoke.

"Yes, my Lord!"

"You have been judged worthy by the great god Maat. She says you will be our vessel. The magic is being reawakened. It will flow when it is needed. Stand now, and pick up your staff."

Mustapha did so.

"Hold your staff in your right hand. Hold your left hand forward, palm out facing me."

When he did a blue light leapt from the god's outstretched hand to Mustapha's. It danced around his body, filling him with an itchy tingle from toes to brain. The light passed down his right arm to his staff. The light pulsed up and down the staff until it concentrated near the tip. The ankh glowed, passing from blue to crystalline white, a diamond light.

"You will be ready when the time comes," said the god.

Mustapha collapsed unconscious on the floor.

Abdul the Assistant High Priest was hiding in a dark niche off the sanctuary's main chamber. He had heard everything. He considered picking up Mustapha's staff and using it to bludgeon him while he lay unconscious. He thought better of it. The time was not yet right for another attempt. "Your time will come, old man. We shall see what good your gods are to you then."

Abdul slipped away into the night.

30

The debate raged on. Interminably as far as Benben was concerned. She had defended her sanity in a hundred different ways, and finally defeated Wanre's pre-emptive motion to have her examined. Annoying she had not seen that coming.

She had pressed her case for intervention. She had woven her web of fear, enjoying the delicate game. She would relish playing it on Earth, where no beings could match her. Wanre had seemed ineffectual, despite his shaven head. Yet he deftly cut away her webs as she spun them. She had underestimated him. In the game of feint and parry she was as resourceful as Wanre, but he was as skillful as she. Benben appreciated, from inside the game, the shadows Wanre hid his power in. She admired him for it.

As various consuls argued their points, Benben took her own counsel. She did not care what the results of this debate were. She had the power to act anyway, whatever the outcome. She would convince them she was acting for the good of the Consilium. Sacrificing her own good to the greater good. If she was successful on Earth, they would believe her. She would make them believe her truth as their own.

Once she had them believing her truth, her truth would swell till it engulfed them. Who more capable of running the Consilium than her? Who more able to manage its power and wealth? Who better able to centralize that power and wealth until it reached a pinnacle never seen before in the history of the Multiverse? Who, throughout the Multiverse, was more deserving of command than she?

"I am right about the threat Earth poses," she thought. "Anything we can't forecast and control is a danger. But the danger Earth poses is not nearly so great as the opportunity it offers me. If I act convincingly, I can be Consilium Speaker next cycle. My climb to majesty can start." Then she gave an internal shrug. "Even if I don't win any more battles in this round of the game, I'll at least have a good romp on Earth."

Benben stroked Bulbul absentmindedly. He floated in a sea of her neurotransmitters. They were savory as they welled up from her brain into his hind segment, attached by suction and teeth to the hole in the crown of her head. He was having one of the most absorbing and powerful rides of his life. How could he ever do without her?

The long debate ended. Benben's motion was tabled, the Earth Assessment Committee directed to continue its work. She and Bulbul retained the chair. Seven new members joined, five of them sympathetic to her point of view. This would increase her control in the long term, but not solve the immediate crisis. As the Council broke up and the members withdrew their projections back across the branes, returning to their parallel universes, she said to Bulbul, "Come my little friend, we have work to do."

He looked up at her. His eyes, half covered by drooping lids, were full of rapture and suspicion.

Benben and Bulbul returned home to consider their next moves. They changed the decor in their apartment every couple of months, taking turns. It had been her turn to craft the projection this time, and he had not yet seen it. These were magical moments for him.

They entered through a low door. It was dark at first, the walls warm and slightly sticky. Benben had to push her way through sideways, with Bulbul wrapped tight around her neck. The space widened into a twisting tube, dull red, pulsing in a peristaltic wave. It opened into a warm moist chamber entirely red, the color of arterial blood. No right angles only rounded curves. All surfaces red and yielding, spongy.

"What do you think?" said Benben. In a Level 5 civilization, everyone was an aesthete; even politics could not supplant the aesthetic impulse. A fashionable epigrammatist on their world had recently written: "At Level 5, politics are an aesthetic consideration." Benben did not go so far, though she enjoyed the aesthetics of dangerous play.

"It's fabulous! So atavistic. So parasitic. It revives ancient hungers." He finished with a voice gone husky with desire.

"Maybe later. Now let me bring you up to speed. While we were separated yesterday, I was busy preparing for the Earth work. Since we'll be vulnerable after we insert, I wanted some local heavies for support. Bodies who can throw stones and pull triggers for us. As you know, I've been tracking Mustapha."

"Of course my darling. We are concerned the gods of ancient Egypt are waking from their sleep."

"I don't know if it's true, but I have to find out. No one from any Consilium world has been credentialed to appear. So if these gods are about to awaken, it is due to some power unknown to the Consilium. Since the Consilium knows all there is to know in the Multiverse, who could be doing this?"

"Might that have been a good argument to make to Wanre and the others? Might we make it now?"

"No use. They would love it. They have been sitting on their multi-species asses far too long as it is. Imagine what they'd say: 'Oh something we don't know about—how wonderful. Let's study it forever!' That's what it would come to: degenerate dreaming about Level 6."

"Ah, Level 6. Myth or reality? A civilization like gods, able to control entire universes *sans* instrumentalities. As the Consilium is to an ant so are they to us."

"My nuclear threat didn't move those bureaucrats. The excuse of a Level 6 civilization to sniff out would only make them sit down harder."

"Where did you find our henchmen, my dear one?"

"Under Mustapha's nose. Some Islamic militants close to him. Their simple beliefs are easily manipulated by one of my skill."

"No one on Earth can match you. But how did you secure our henchman's loyalty? A yummy dream?"

"I went as the Archangel Gabriel."

"How did you make his flaming sword?"

"That's a different one. Gabriel was Muhammad's buddy. It's why he makes our Abdul swoon. Now relax, it's time for me to re-enter Abdul's dreamscape. I need to focus, put on Gabriel's glamour, then project it across the branes."

31

It was late night in medieval Cairo. Abdul arrived on his doorstep, tired from his meetings with the mullahs and his own operatives, and his surveillance work in Karnak in Exile. He entered his flat silently so as not to disturb his family. They needed their rest. He looked in protectively on his two sons asleep in the room next to his. They were fine boys and, *inshallah*, future warriors. He entered his room and stopped to enjoy his wife's peaceful breathing. A faithful woman, one to be treasured. He undressed quietly and slipped into bed. His wife stirred but did not wake, used to his late hours. Soon he slept.

In his dream he was lost in medieval Cairo, looking for a familiar street. Then a blinding light appeared. It was the Archangel Gabriel again. Abdul became lucid and attentive within the dream. He knelt in the angel's presence.

"Abdul, I have returned to reassure and prepare you. One is coming who bears the Magic of the Night. You will assist him and his companion."

"Archangel, I am troubled. What is it, this 'Magic of the Night?' Would it be black magic, for if so how could it be something of the Prophet?"

"Abdul, it is for you to obey not understand. I tell you this: whatever smites the enemies of Islam is the Prophet's true sword. The next time you will see not me but him who carries the Magic of the Night. Obey him."

Abdul woke in his bed. He was covered in a film of sweat. To his right his wife still breathed softly. He knew sleep was now denied him, so he resigned himself to await the dawn.

Slowly Benben came out of her trance. She lay on a red plush sofa shaped like an obscure inner organ. Lighter and darker veins passed in skeins through the fabric, pulsing. Bulbul lay by her side. His hind segment was still attached to the crown of her skull. He came out of trance with her, drowsy from tasting her neurotransmitters as she projected Gabriel across the branes. This time he followed the action at a distance. When she made her run he would go too.

She stirred, turned her head and looked at him. Blinked, yawned, "A good performance."

"As ever, dearest. Did you entangle our little Abdul's mind?"

"A little more than strictly necessary, for the fun of it. Parts of his memory and perceptions are now entangled with mine across the branes. He'll helplessly attune to my needs. He'll also have some of my thoughts, poor thing. He'll be looking out on the world with blood colored glasses."

"And now a little something for her to whom I am bound in love."

Bulbul contracted his hind segment, attached to the hole in the crown of her head by suction and teeth. He sent a pulse of neurotransmitters down into her brain. Lying on the red couch she went still and then almost rigid. Her topaz eyes scintillated along their dark iris slits with an inner fire.

32

It was eight o'clock in the morning at Giza, the hour chosen by Wolfgang last night for them to gather to work on the polygon. Now that they were once again in the Queen's Chamber, the passage of external time was remote, and they lived within the stream of their expectations. Five had gathered: Wolfgang, Petra, Cliff, Maria, and Jack. Mustapha was absent, and his absence surprised them. He had been interested in the polygon when they talked about it on the veranda. While he withheld official permission, he had almost insisted that Wolfgang use the minibot's laser to inscribe the missing lines of genetic code on the seven of the twenty-three panels that held a blank space.

Mustapha had said that when those blanks were filled in and the genetic code in the polygon completed, it would amount to the true name of the human being. In Egyptian magic, he had said, a true name gave the power of life and death. Their exploration was more than archaeology. This was now about the power of the gods.

Wolfgang had worked half the night on his preparations, alert with excitement. His slash marks would have to express the right content and be executed flawlessly. He was sure that he and Cliff had worked out the right code. To be certain, he confirmed it on the NSA supercomputers. What worried him now was getting the lines correctly inscribed.

His laser should be able to do such work, and he had been trying to engineer precision. His computers were now programmed to guide the laser so it inscribed the slash marks with correct length and depth, and a sharpness of execution to match the original. His goal was to make sure that not even the craftsmen who made the original polygon—however they did it—could tell the difference between the original code incised in the stone and that done by the minibot.

He went beyond mere programming. He was at Giza at dawn collecting small slabs of stone. He used them to test the minibot's laser and the program that would guide its cuts. Both laser and software worked smoothly in his trial runs. He hoped for the same in the polygon. He was hyper-aware that he had only one chance to do it perfectly. If Mustapha was right, and a true name required perfect execution, then the smallest slip would mean losing this chance forever. Losing this chance might mean closing down the human future, as if an ape 10 million years ago had flung away the chance for her descendants to walk into a cafe and order in French.

Though Mustapha was absent, Wolfgang began. It would take time to get everything in place, and maybe the old man would arrive by then. Wolfgang picked up the minibot and kissed it.

"Today is your big day, baby, go and get'em!" He placed it in the twenty centimeter square shaft, and returned to the computer. He keyed the minibot awake. It crawled forward horizontally and climbed where the shaft tipped to thirty-nine degrees. As it crawled it trailed its umbilical cables. They ran now not only to the computers and monitors, but also to Wolfgang's high capacity fuel cell. The size of a suitcase, Wolfgang believed it held many times the power the job required.

Cliff was not convinced. "How can something as small as a suitcase give your laser enough juice for the job? It would have to be nuclear, but then it would need a ton of cladding."

Wolfgang was not in a mood for technical talk. "Let's just say I'm a quantum guy and leave it at that."

"Okay, you're a quantum physicist." Cliff was pensive. Then his face lit up. "So I get it. You've got a quantum flux zero point source! Unbelievable." Cliff was almost shouting in his excitement. "Tell me about it!"

"I could tell you. But then I'd have to kill you."

Cliff laughed. "Come on, you couldn't."

"You're right. I'd make a call. Someone else would."

Cliff was still in his enthusiasm, and assumed Wolfgang was joking. "So where did you get this? Someplace like DARPA? You must have helped design it."

Wolfgang looked away. When he looked back it was straight into Cliff's eyes. Wolfgang's lips were stretched into narrow bloodless lines. He put his right hand on Cliff's shoulder. He squeezed hard. "Look, Cliff. You're a smart kid. I want you to live long enough to get your Ph.D. So drop it right there."

Cliff looked into Wolfgang's ice blue eyes. Wolfgang's words stung like a slap in the face. "Okay, sure." He looked down at the floor and went quiet.

Maria, Petra and Jack watched the exchange in stunned silence.

"Come on, everyone, let's get to work. We've got a live robot." Wolfgang drew their attention back to the monitor. Onscreen, the minibot climbed higher, its laser and minicam in their protective pod. The five gathered around the high rez monitor to watch its progress up the shaft through the maincam image. It seemed to take an eternity to crawl all the way to the door at the end of the shaft.

"Don't you have a higher gear on that thing?" said Cliff. He wanted to get beyond the put-down he had just suffered.

"No, but impressive torque is more important," said Wolfgang. He looked up and smiled, happy to be in the middle of an experiment, their earlier exchange forgotten. "Hold your horses."

The white limestone door was clear on the monitor in the view of the maincam. The minibot inched forward until it was in position. It passed its arm through the hole in this first door, and they could see the rougher sandstone door they had cut through yesterday.

"Good morning ladies and gentlemen." It was Mustapha's entrance line. He doffed his panama and looked debonair in his white linen suit. He walked over to the high rez monitor, stood with both hands on his walking stick, and peered into it.

"What do we have here?"

"The minibot is in position," said Wolfgang. "First we enlarge the hole in the second door, the one we drilled through yesterday. That will let us insert the arm with the laser and minicam directly into the polygon. Then we can cut the code into the blanks."

"Let the fireworks begin," said Mustapha.

Wolfgang punched in code. The laser unsheathed itself and moved forward on the arm. Its light flashed out and hit a spot on the door. It moved slowly around, widening the hole they had cut. When the cut was done, Wolfgang judged it fine. He let the stone cool and keyed the next commands.

The laser arm and minicam arm moved through into the polygon. The audience of six gave a cheer. The minibot seemed as valiant and distant as if it were on a moon of Jupiter, picking through the artifacts of a departed civilization.

The picture on the monitor let them see the polygon from inside. Wolfgang was right: the seven panels with blank spaces were on the far side. On each panel the blank was a fairly small part of the code, in the way that a royal name in a cartouche is a fairly small part of an inscription on a stela. If Mustapha was right these small blanks were the key to great power.

"Okay, here we go," said Wolfgang. The laser was pointed at the first of the panels that it would slice into.

"A burst of the light of Amun-Ra comes to the heart of the Great Pyramid," said Mustapha reflectively. He bowed his head as if in prayer.

Wolfgang, with automatic respect, waited until Mustapha raised his head, then punched in the firing sequence.

The laser sprang to life, lancing across the polygon. It flicked over the first blank space, incising a precise straight line. It stopped.

"Now we look while we hold our breath," said Wolfgang. He manipulated the minicam so that he had the right shadow and perspective for the computer to judge length and depth of the cut.

"Impeccable." The six gave another cheer and Wolfgang engaged the rest of the firing sequence for the first blank. When the remaining lines of code were cut, Wolfgang checked the whole panel. All impeccable.

Wolfgang moved to the next panel, and let the program direct the cuts. When the blank was filled, Wolfgang checked. Impeccable. He repeated the procedure until all seven blank spaces had been filled with code. All impeccably.

When the last one was done, they all exhaled together, tensions for a moment broken.

"What do you think, Wolfgang?" said Jack

"Couldn't have gone better."

"What do you think, Mustapha?" said Maria.

"What can a simple scholar know? I can only think that the true name of the human being has been spoken in the secret language of the Great Pyramid, and that history is therefore about to change."

33

They sat in their semi-circle facing west. They were numb after the long day and unreasonably disappointed. They had hoped for some response to their work on the polygon. Though they would have agreed it was foolish, they had hoped for something big to happen, something in Technicolor and Sensurround. They wondered if they had passed an intelligence test set by creatures of genius or merely despoiled an ancient treasure.

"What will you have?" The waiter was asking Petra. He had taken the other orders.

"Arak. Make it a triple."

The usual evening calm prevailed on the veranda. The Nile flowed north while the date palms shifted their fronds in cadence to the breeze. Tonight it was less easy to be lulled by ancient rhythms.

"Where did we go wrong?" said Jack.

"I don't know," said Wolfgang. "We are certain of the polygon slash mark code. There's no doubt. The fit is perfect and there is no other logical possibility. No other message in the universe can be there. The lines we cut were just right too, their depth and length precise. You cannot tell ours from theirs. We completed the puzzle."

"Maybe we have to be content with that," said Maria.

"No way, mom," said Cliff. "This thing has got to lead somewhere. The polygon has to be a key."

"What do you think, Mustapha," said Jack. "You live with the monuments."

Mustapha sat looking west in his immaculate linen suit. His panama and walking stick rested on a nearby table.

"I know no more than any of you. But I will tell you my dream, if you would like to hear it."

"Sure," said Jack. They were all a little relieved for a momentary distraction.

Mustapha looked around the semi-circle, and felt they were all attentive. He took a pull on the Ouzo he was enjoying, since his next communion ceremony was weeks away. He set the Ouzo down and began.

"My dream is that what we did today has a specific point. That it connects somehow with the re-awakening of Egypt's gods."

"What would that mean?" said Cliff, not noticing that he was interrupting.

Raising his left eyebrow, Mustapha continued. "The gods of Egypt are tolerant. It was a humane period, the three and a half millennia they lived among us and spoke to us." He was moved almost to tears to be talking about the old gods in the open air, not hiding his understanding of them below ground. "In a culture of rich polytheism, you see no religious wars, no ethnic hatred based on religion. Great Egypt fought wars, but they were for land, territory, resources, and often to protect its borders. In Greece and Rome at their heights, when they were working polytheisms, you also see no religious wars. When you study the monotheisms, you see something else. Judaism, Christianity, Islam, each is more intolerant than the last. Progressively, each is more willing to slaughter you if you do not accept their dogmas. This happened in Egypt only once, 3,500 years ago, before the first of the modern monotheisms knew its name. We experimented with monotheism, but only for a generation. The Pharaoh Amenophis IV, called Akhenaten, chose to make his favorite aspect of the Solar Personality supreme over all. Aten became his only reality. With all the intemperance that characterizes monotheism, Akhenaten defaced the great Temple of Amun-Ra at Karnak. The pharaoh destroyed the shrines of the Ennead, the Nine, in Heliopolis, not far from where we sit. It lasted only for a generation. His successors wiped his name and his intolerance from Egypt. His name was chiseled off monuments, his funerary temples knocked down, his statues trampled into dust.

It became possible again to worship all the gods. A generation of civil strife in the name of monotheism ended, and Egypt returned to her prosperity."

"But what can the gods of Egypt actually do?" said Cliff.

"And aren't you putting yourself in danger to even speak this way in Egypt?" said Maria. "Aren't there Islamists around alert to heresy?"

"Second question first," said Mustapha. "I would be in danger if I broadcast such views, certainly. But I do not. Certain wise men reside in the bosom of Islam, Sufis mostly. They understand, and I consort with them. Those who see deeply see the same. What concerns me are not these few but the many. It is the propensity for widespread aggression coiled within monotheism that worries me. And Cliff, now your question. The gods of Egypt are, I believe, very special expressions of the Immensity. Beings suited to humanity, who helped and taught. Were they to return, I cannot know what they would do. I can only trust that they would attempt a great healing in this world of ours."

They fell silent, moved by Mustapha's hope. Their minds settled into a more Nilotic rhythm. Mustapha's dream of the return of the gods to Egypt was so much more spacious than worries about whether they had cut the slash marks correctly. His hope stirred them. The mystery in his story held them.

Maria wanted to enter Mustapha's world. She struggled to suspend her disbelief. Was his vision no more than an elaborate fairytale? Wasn't the real world the one we struggle through every day on our own, mothers bearing children, many in the world hungry, all of us finding love where we can and hoping it lasts? What place did Mustapha's gods have in all of this? She looked over at him. Perhaps Mustapha had depths of knowledge hidden from her. Maria sensed Mustapha's conviction that he had a basis for his belief. She knew he was no fool. She hoped he was right, despite the evidence of everyday life.

While Mustapha took another sip of Ouzo, a waiter arrived. He appeared to be in some distress.

"I am sorry to disturb you, Excellency," he said to Mustapha. "But I have a message for you. It says you are needed at once at the Sphinx."

"Thank you," said Mustapha, in his role as Director of the Supreme Council of Antiquities. He finished his Ouzo deliberately, stood and walked to the nearby table. He put on his panama and picked up his walking stick. Addressing the semicircle he said, "Ladies and gentlemen, shall we see what the Sphinx is up to?"

34

Wanre decided to meet with his advisors again. He had just left the Consilium discussion on Benben's emergency petition to intervene on Earth.

No *bil* today, this was all business. Instead they drank tea made from the bark of a flowering tree on the Second Speaker's world. The tree grew only on Mount Noberu, and its tea was one of the delicacies of her world. It was described as such long ago in the classical text called *Twenty Chief Delights of Those Who Fall From the Sky Upon Prey.*

The latter part of the title was what her avian ancestors called themselves in a less urbane millennium. Other delights described in the text included "small rocks from Mount Noberu which when seen from a height resemble succulent songbirds."

A smile came to Toran's eyes as she recalled the ancient book. She poured the tea. Mount Noberu was near where she was born, and it was the only place to be mentioned twice in *Twenty Chief Delights*, a cultural honor still much valued. On the table in an appropriate lacquer stand rested one of the fabled rocks from Mount Noberu. While she poured, they all admired it, conscious of the associations. They tacitly agreed through their attention that civility is stabilizing when crisis impends.

Wanre sipped the fragrant tea. Having gathered his thoughts he said, "I think her intentions are clear. Lacking patience and diplomacy, she has called upon fear to stir up support for her idea of intervention, though we succeeded in tabling her emergency petition."

"That will hardly be the end of it," said Saiki. "The Consilium has studied Earth for centuries. More study won't satisfy her."

"She may intervene on her own," said Toran.

"I'm sure she will try," said Wanre. "She will hardly be able to help herself."

"I'm sure too," said Saiki. "She's a skilled branerunner, Bulbul too. How will she appear, and where?"

"I would guess Giza," said Wanre. "It is what has captured her interest. As for how, I would imagine as a god."

"What is her aim?" said Saiki.

"Chaos. To interfere with a higher order unfolding that we are all ignorant of," said Wanre.

"What's our best response?" said Toran.

"She'll act quietly," said Saiki. "So a first step is to place her under observation."

"What if she projects in?" said Toran.

"Follow carefully by remote viewing," said Saiki.

"If she goes in, I'm going in after her," said Wanre.

The two women were speechless for a moment.

"Wait and get authorization," said Saiki. "You'll be able to. Otherwise you'll be subject to impeachment and the same criminal penalties as her. Go in accredited if at all."

"You know how lugubrious the Consilium can be," said Wanre. "How long will accreditation take? A week of debate? If she goes in there'll be no time for that. Someone has to be there to counter her. Humans won't be able to resist her."

"I've never heard of someone being able to ride in pursuit of someone else across the branes," said Toran. The thrill of the chase had moved her off the wisdom of the idea. "Can you do it?"

"I'm good," Wanre said.

"Let me come in and help," Toran said. "I'm a skillful branerunner. You'll be safer with me there, and won't face the opprobrium alone."

"I'll be all right."

"I want to come," said Toran.

"I need to do this alone," said Wanre. His tone made it clear he would not bend.

"If you insist. But are you really prepared to take her on?"

"My mind is a match for hers."

"What about your will?"

"I can't be sure. Hers is honed by bloodlust. I can only contest her."

"How will you project in?"

"I'll follow her, planning to put on the glamour of a god." He smiled to reassure them.

"Why go in?" said Saiki. "You know you'll be throwing your life away."

"History has no meaning, but we can give it meaning. Earth may be just one small planet, but I'm determined it will not be Benben alone who shapes the history of its peoples."

35

Benben and Bulbul were relaxing in their blood vessel of a boudoir. She had slept soundly after her neurotransmitter binge. She was lazing contentedly, hatching plans.

"What news, my little worm?" He had been awake and engaged.

"Wanre is having us observed, and if I didn't know better, I might be tempted to say it is tantamount to house arrest." He appeared somewhat shaken by these developments.

Benben laughed, and Bulbul was soon giggling. He could not play the victim for long. It was one of his favorite personae, but it was so contrary to his usual disposition that he could not maintain it.

"They can restrain our bodies but not our minds, worm."

"Oh yes they can, dear." He was suddenly serious.

"I know old Wanre. He'd never impose mindlock at this point. That would make it seem he had something to hide."

"So we intervene on Earth?"

"Naturally, but at the right moment. We need a clearer sense of what is brewing, so we can go in at the right time and place. We'll be physically apart, so we'll have forty-eight hours safety. We've got to make this trip count. Once we've played our hand, Wanre would be a fool to let us have another jaunt on Earth."

"I do so hope we won't push the time limit. Not only do I hate being separated from you, I hate the idea of death by separation even more. A high price to pay for this kind of fun."

"What a courageous and sentimental darling you are," she said with a hint of contempt. "No gain without risk. We'll withdraw our minds in plenty of time to reanimate these bodies we leave in the boudoir, and reunite them with a celebratory brain flush."

"What do we look like when we project in? I love costume parties."

"I've given it a fair amount of thought. This is about the pyramids. And it looks like some program older than Egypt is waking up. So we go for an Old Kingdom look. Say a pair of Egyptian gods."

"Bold. Fresh. And they had the *best* headgear."

"It gives me room for unexpected action. It meets the cherished fantasies of the key players."

"Mustapha? That pretentious old dear?"

"He lives for the return of the gods."

"Which ones? I can never keep track. All those crocodiles and heifers and hippos."

"That's where the fun lies. Get cozy and I'll tell you a story."

Bulbul loved it when she played mummy. He snuggled around her neck, and tweaked the hole in the crown of her head with the teeth in his hind segment to signal he was all ears.

"Mustapha's gods went silent millennia ago. When they were active, they were presumably projections from somewhere, maybe the Consilium, though I haven't been able to find out. Anyway, his secret band of hideaway priests has woven together two great strands of religion in pharaonic Egypt—the gods of Karnak in the south and the gods of Heliopolis in the north. Toiling away underground the priests of Karnak in Exile have re-arranged the gods to suit themselves."

"Rearranged?"

"Sanitized. In the old days you had the Karnak Trinity: Amun-Ra the sun god, Mut his wife, and their goody goody son Khonsu. Boring, but a clever front for the biggest landholdings in Egypt. The Great Ennead of Heliopolis is much more fun."

"Do tell."

"It all starts with Atum. It was the beginning and he was alone in his universe. Nothing else in all of existence, just Atum and empty space. So what does a fella do when he's lonely? He whips it out and whacks off. Atum comes explosively and everything in the universe is made from his jizz."

"You're making it up. It's just too good."

"Nope. That's Heliopolis theology for you. The Egyptians must have been a fun-loving crowd to have a theology like that. So Atum spawns the other gods in the Ennead. First generation are Shu and Tefnut. Shu is a boy and Tefnut a girl, the Dry and the Wet. They put an end to Chaos, and produce a male Earth god—Geb, and a female sky god—Nut. This incestuous pair have four children: Isis and Osiris, another incestuous couple, and their evil siblings Seth and Nephthys."

"I love the incest but I'm losing the thread. If that is the Ennead, then what did Musty's priests do to rearrange it, while hiding in their basement?"

"They never liked Seth or Nephthys. All because Seth hacked his brother god Osiris to pieces and then he and Nephthys hid the pieces. So poor Isis had to search all over Egypt for her brother-lover's body parts. The hardest bit to find was his willy."

"Surely this is Egyptian theology according to Benben. It's just so *you*. It can't be what they believed."

"Oh yes it is. Just my kind of folks. But what humorless old Mustapha and his boys did was unforgivable. They booted Seth and Nephthys out of the Ennead."

"No, they couldn't! Just when we found some gods we can believe in!"

"Just for butchering Osiris and playing hide and seek with the body parts. They substituted the Karnak crowd. Khonsu and Mut. And to keep the Ennead to nine, they merged Amun and Atum.

"Where do humans get off treating their gods like that?"

"The Egyptians merged gods as happily as capitalists merge corporations. No one ever seemed to mind, and whoever was running the divine projections was patient with their humans. But we needn't be."

"The picture begins to clarify."

"Seth and Nephthys are the fun ones. We go in as them."

"So Musty's big dream comes true. The gods come alive. But it's his biggest nightmare too—it's the wrong gods who show up."

"One more thing, my macho. We cross dress. I'm the murdering Seth and you're his evil sister Nephthys. For I, my dear, am far the better butcher."

"Have you been preparing Musty? Perhaps entangling him?"

"I've tried to enter his dreams, but he has some protection around him. No idea where it comes from, it's no Consilium technique. Part of the Earth weirdness, like someone else is watching. Doesn't trouble me though. Mustapha's never going to pose a threat, so there's no need to neutralize him."

"I'm not sure I heard you right, Jose," said the vice president. He sat behind his desk. He picked up a china coffee cup too delicate for his thick fingers and took a sip.

The secretary of state stood before the desk, ready with his answer. He enjoyed the tension in the room. From whatever angle the vice president attacked, he could answer. He smelled a tang in the air. He wondered if this was the smell of history in the making.

"It's bound to be a surprise," Jose said. "As per our conversations, we're keeping close tabs on Giza. Recon shows us developments at the Sphinx. Right in front of the Sphinx is a massive ruined temple. Its floor, a huge flat panel, has slid open. It's big—about twenty by thirty meters, Egyptian scale. All we can see from above is a staircase leading down."

"Connection with the polygon?"

"Perhaps. Not enough data."

"Our operatives?"

"Will be among the first in."

"I need operational control. Let's get a KH-15 up there to sit in a fixed-sky position. I want constant telemetry. I want our battle-sat ready too. I don't know what the game is yet, but I expect to win."

36

Wolfgang was at the wheel of his old white Mercedes. Mustapha sat in the front passenger seat. Jack, Maria, Cliff and Petra were jammed in the back, so they could all ride together. Petra sat on Cliff's lap. As Wolfgang pulled out of the Al Minah, Cliff decided to stay calm by studying the snake tattooed across Petra's shoulders whose head and tail were peeking out of her blouse. It was not his best idea.

"What's going on, Mustapha?" said Jack.

"No idea. But I'd guess that Wolfgang and Cliff have helped us pass our first intelligence test. I would anticipate another."

They arrived. The monument police had reacted quickly to events, cordoning off the area. Mustapha's role as Director of the Supreme Council of Antiquities took them through. The area was floodlit, and only the police and Mustapha's group were present.

They approached the Old Kingdom Sphinx Temple in silence. Built on the typically grand Egyptian scale, it lay before the Sphinx's paws, and the Sphinx towered above it. The temple, never completed, now lay in ruins. They entered, and moved toward its inner courtyard open to the sky.

Where the courtyard had been they found an opening in the ground. The opening gaped twenty by thirty meters, most of the temple's great court. Stairs led down. They never stopped to wonder whether they should descend. The steps themselves looked like ancient Egyptian work. They were beautifully shaped granite, fitted together with a jeweler's precision. From below, a pale blue radiance emerged.

Mustapha led the way. A few steps down he stopped. Something did not feel right. He looked at the great slab that had slid back to reveal the steps. The slab carried the rubble it had made in opening. They were now level with its leading edge, and with the tracks it had slid in when retracting.

"What is this?" said Mustapha.

"Not stone," said Maria.

"Some kind of metal, I think," said Wolfgang, "but nothing I have ever seen."

The substance was black, so dark it appeared to absorb rather than reflect light.

"None of the sensing runs picked it up," said Jack. "How could so much metal so close to the surface not register?"

"The SRI work in the 70's should definitely have seen this," said Wolfgang. "And this cavity too. Whatever this stuff is, it has properties unlike any this engineer has ever seen, or this physicist thought possible."

"God stuff," said Cliff matter of factly.

"Maybe," said Mustapha. "Maybe, Cliff, you are exactly right. Let's go down."

The staircase took them out of view of the KH-15 recon satellite perched above in fixed-sky. They stood in a chamber fashioned of cyclopean blocks. Enormous stones, perhaps twenty tons each. They matched in size and style the stones of the great Valley Temple of Khafra, adjacent to the Sphinx Temple above. Khafra's Valley Temple is connected to his pyramid by a causeway, and until this moment, it was the only known place in Egypt where stones had been worked like this. The great blocks were cut like soft clay. They bent around corners, to knit together in a way that was aesthetically satisfying and almost impossibly difficult to build at this scale. The power and virtuosity of the Valley Temple's execution looked designed to lead later generations into wonder, and so Jack had included it in his list of Holy Anomalies.

As they stood in the chamber Jack and Mustapha took in the similarity in construction. It was arresting that this subterranean chamber was built like the Valley Temple. What did it signify, finding this kind of construction in conjunction with the black transhuman metal? But these were the concerns of the specialists.

The other four were staring at the stela in front of them, a monolith ten meters high. It was of alabaster, the hieroglyphs turquoise inlay. It was glowing, illuminated from within. The turquoise characters were burning with a blue flame.

The blue light from the hieroglyphs radiated throughout the otherwise dark chamber, penetrating into its farthest corner. No way led out but the stairs. The chamber looked like the forecourt of a temple, but the temple pylons and gateway were missing. Why would this astonishing stela be sited in a cyclopean chamber leading nowhere?

Mustapha and Jack studied the hieroglyphs.

"Beautiful classical diction," said Mustapha. "Old Kingdom, perhaps, but it feels somehow beyond it."

"Elevated and direct," said Jack, "but different from any known text."

"Enough literary deconstruction," said Maria. "What does this monster say?"

"The style is important, Maria, because it can help us date it," said Mustapha. "This is clearly as old as anything ever found. It seems older, different, and purer. As if this were the source of the ancient tongue and the ancient writing. As if we are being spoken to by something older than Egypt."

"A message from the gods?" said Cliff.

"In so many words, yes," said Mustapha. "That makes this unique. The message is as unique as the stela itself, as this chamber. As the polygon. We spoke the 'true name of the human being' when we inscribed the polygon. This chamber opening must be a response. We worked through the outer complex layers of a puzzle to its perfect heart. We completed the polygon and now we have a direct communication. Who knows how many millennia it has waited here? Who knows why it is awakening now?"

"The polygon was a test to see if we were technologically advanced enough to find and solve it," said Maria. "If we hadn't unraveled the human genome we couldn't have done it. Is this another challenge to our level of civilization?"

"Yes," said Mustapha. "You could say it is a challenge to our level of civilization. But not to our technology. Or rather to our inner technology."

"Come on, guys, what does it say?" said Petra.

"Jack?" said Mustapha.

"You are the master, Mustapha."

"All right, my friends, here is the message of the stela." As he prepared to read, his face suffused with blue light, he became happy and grave. "Our destiny emerges," he thought. "Not just mine, but that of the Land of Egypt, and by extension, all of humankind. Oh gods, I long to meet you. Help me to do my part for your return." His lips parted and he spoke the words of the glowing stela:

From the time before time we speak to you.
From the time before humans we command you.
From the time we made humans we speak to you.
To this turning point in your destiny we welcome you.

We are the Nine, the Ennead.
We made this universe from nothing.
We separated light from dark, dry from wet.
We ended the reign of Chaos.

You have learned much.
You have forgotten much.
Now you face hidden dangers.
Now your own hearts may destroy you.
O humans, a time of testing is coming to you.
O humans, without our help you will not survive.

Call upon us now.
Speak the heart syllables of our True Names
Be sure that the one who speaks is true.
Let him be our High Priest and Great Mage.

O humans, your time of testing is coming to you.
O humans, without our help you will not survive.
Call upon us now.

Mustapha fell silent. While reading, he'd felt an energy pouring through him, an energy at once familiar and strange. The silence lasted for some time.

"The message isn't signed," said Cliff.

"Oh yes it is," said Jack. "They said they were the Ennead. That is a specific group of gods worshiped at Heliopolis here in northern Egypt: Atum the Creator, who begat Shu the Dry and Tefnut the Wet who together ended Chaos. They begat Geb the Earth and Nut the Sky. They begat four: Osiris god of the Dead, Isis his consort. Also Seth and Nephthys. These are the Ennead. Seth and Nephthys are enemies of Isis and Osiris, and are ultimately vanquished by Horus the hawk god, who is their nephew and the son of Isis and Osiris."

"Can it be real?" said Maria.

"Circumstances suggest so," said Mustapha.

"What is the danger they are talking about?" said Petra.

"We can't know yet. The gift they are giving is that they are willing to intervene now before the danger is upon us."

"But it's no good, Mustapha," said Jack. "Even if you're right, and this is a genuine message from the gods of the Ennead, we fail. They say that we must call on their true names. We can't do that."

"Why not?" said Petra.

"There's a lot of ancient Egyptian magic at play here Petra," said Jack. "The true name is the source of all power. One source says, 'He who can speak the true name wields the power of what he has named.' This invocation of the true name is the source of all ancient magic, even of the debased Western forms. But the profane can never know a true name. There would have been an esoteric tradition where the magicians would have claimed to know it. Speaking the true name of the gods, if you knew them, would mean you were participating in the gods' power, creating the world with them. I think this was always a primitive religious fantasy. I doubt even if at Egypt's height, its sacred magicians knew the gods' true names. How could they? It would be as powerful as wielding atomic power. If they'd had this knowledge, how could Egypt ever have fallen?"

"There's a worse problem," said Wolfgang. "Suppose you're wrong about Egyptian magic, Jack. Suppose the true names worked. Maybe they opened you to the gods' power, rather than gave you control over the gods. I'm willing to entertain the hypothesis that true names are effective. Look at what happened when we inscribed the genetic code in the polygon. It can't be an accident that this place opened up. But here's our problem. The text on the stela is quite clear. It says only the High Priest and Great Mage can do it. Where do we find one?"

"Forget it, Wolfgang," said Jack. "The High Priest and Great Mage is an extinct species. Dead as the dodo. Deader in fact, since there hasn't been a High Priest and Great Mage for about two thousand years."

Mustapha took a deep breath. He sighed deeply. Maria took it as a sign of weary resignation. She felt disappointment blunt her hope. She was angry with Mustapha. She had expected more of him. She had half thought he could pull some magic out of his hat, and make the gods appear at last.

Mustapha's sigh echoed in the chamber. They fell silent again before the stela, bathed in its ethereal light. How could they have cracked the polygon and now be told by the Ennead on a burning stela that human history hung in the balance, only to come to an abrupt dead end?

"Can't we try?" said Cliff. He was certain he could do it. "Why can't we read all the old texts, learn what the priests knew, and see if we can do it?"

"Wouldn't work," said Jack. "The High Priest and Great Mage went through all sorts of secret initiations into power and magic that we can only guess at. It took years, and was a person-to-person transmission. They say it was the sun god Amun-Ra who made the first High Priest and Great Mage, and who anointed all his successors. We might as well try to make the Holy Grail in a lab."

Cliff went silent, the spring of hope dried up. They again stood in silence, washed in the blue light.

"That's not what worries me," said Mustapha.

"What are you talking about?" said Jack, his frustration flashing into anger.

"What worries me is knowing which true names," said Mustapha. "My sense is that, as with the polygon, we will have only a single chance. There, if we drew the wrong glyphs, it was done forever. Here, if we recite the wrong true names, or even the right ones imperfectly, the opportunity to open the ears of the gods may perish."

They had all been facing the stela. But as Mustapha spoke, they had turned to him. He continued.

"Reciting true names is never easy. Timbre and pitch are crucial to get the incantation right. Pronunciation of the ancient Egyptian must be unfailing. The purity of heart of the magician is even more important and much the harder accomplishment. The worst problem, though, is that the Ennead has evolved. It is not static, it is no longer the same as it was. The Ennead Jack listed a moment ago has long been out of date."

Maria stood next to Mustapha. Her anger with him was gone. She saw him with new eyes. While the others were agitated and off balance he was calm, confident, in his element. He looked like a man come home after a long voyage. Her hope returned. He spoke to her.

"I am who you think I am, my dear, and other things too."

"Where does all this come from that you're saying?" said Wolfgang.

"Personal experience."

"What the hell are you talking about?" said Jack.

"I have a little confession to make," said Mustapha with his usual charm. "The traditions are not as dead as most people think, especially most Egyptologists. A continuous tradition runs down to this day unbroken from ancient Egypt. What was known in Karnak is known today. What was known in Heliopolis is known today. And what was known is considerable."

Maria had long felt something hidden in Mustapha. Now she was seeing through the surface reflection to the animal in the depths. "So when you long for the gods," she said, "you're longing from inside what was revealed."

"From deep inside."

"Are you talking about the sacred magic of Egypt?" said Jack.

"Among other things."

"Let's go find these people and talk to them," said Cliff.

"How do we find them?" said Maria.

"No need," said Mustapha.

"What do you mean, 'no need'?" said Jack. Things were changing faster than he liked. The polygon. The stela. The claim that the traditions of ancient Egypt were alive. He'd earned his Ph.D. based on the fact that the traditions were lost, embalmed. "Of course there's a need."

"Jack, there is a need, of this I have no doubt. I only mean we don't need to go find them. They are aware of what is happening. They will help."

Jack, Maria, and Cliff started to ask more questions. Mustapha held up his hand for silence. "Friends, give me a moment." He reached into the breast pocket of his white linen suit, glowing blue in the light from the stela. They expected some magical emblem to emerge. Incongruously it was a cell phone. He punched a speed dial number.

"Please come down now," he said into the phone. Putting the phone away, he studied the stela. "You know, in all of Egyptian history, we see nothing like this text. All the stelae we know, all the inscriptions we know, purport to be by men. By pharaohs to posterity, or passages from *The Book of Going Forth By Day,* what you call *The Book of the Dead*, on the walls of tombs. Nothing like this. Nothing that communicates a message from the gods directly to humankind. It feels somehow as if history were starting all over again."

He fell silent once more, and they all gazed again at the stela, waiting for a response to Mustapha's call. They did not know what to expect, and half assumed a brightly clad Egyptian magician would materialize before their eyes.

When he arrived he was more prosaic. A policeman, one of those guarding the perimeter of the Sphinx. He was the one in charge, who had waved Mustapha through when they arrived in the white Mercedes. A trip that was a lifetime ago now. The first policeman was followed by three others, walking a few steps behind as they descended the staircase into the stela chamber. The one in charge led the procession with a leather bag the size of a small suitcase. Made of tooled Moroccan leather, it was a case a Saudi prince might use for an overnight stay. The policeman carried the case in a formal way, as if it were precious, more than just a suitcase. Mustapha turned from the stela to face him. He approached Mustapha and put the case down. He bowed, then knelt and touched his head to the floor. They all watched.

"Your Holiness," the man said, still kneeling.

"You have done well," Mustapha said. "A time is coming that we have anticipated with formless longing through the generations. Return to the temple. Tell the others, and keep vigil there. Leave these three priests with me," he said pointing to the three others dressed as policemen. "Make sure you post an adequate number to stand guard above."

The man inclined his head. Mustapha raised his hand in blessing. The man rose and ascended the staircase, leaving the three others who stood silently. Mustapha blessed them as well then turned back to the stela and his five friends.

"No need to find those who can help because I am their leader," he said. "Our tradition stretches back to the dawn of Egypt. It is unbroken, and I am the unworthy vessel in which it now reposes. Know that I am the High Priest of Karnak and Great Mage of Egypt."

"Unbelievable," said Jack.

"Believe it, Jack."

"Why didn't you tell us?" said Maria.

"Although you are my friends, we have required secrecy for two thousand years. By the time of the first Ptolemies, the ancient culture was becoming degenerate all around us. The world as we knew it was ending. People listened no longer to the message of the gods, and would have corrupted or destroyed the knowledge, had we not kept it secret.

"While we protected the knowledge, two other things happened. One pleasing to us, the other dire.

"The pleasing thing was an evolution in the Ennead. I told you Jack's version was out of date. The reason is that the Great Ennead itself evolved, but outside the view of ordinary men, so scholars know nothing of it. When we built our hidden temple to safeguard the knowledge, we put it, as I said, under what became medieval Cairo. We were not far from Heliopolis, the Ennead's home. We merged the priesthoods of Karnak, the religious center of Upper Egypt, with Heliopolis, that of Lower Egypt. Karnak was the greatest of all temples built by man. It was the gateway to the Valley of the Kings, the eternal resting place of pharaohs.

"When we merged Karnak and Heliopolis, the gods were still with us. They joined in. They directed things. And they reformed the Ennead. The gods Seth and Nephthys, who murdered Osiris, were expelled by the others.

"Ancient Egypt went into exile in its own land, in a secret Karnak that was also a sarcophagus for its former glory. As it did so, the gods expelled the dark gods among them. Then Amun, the face of the Sun and Creator at Karnak, merged himself with Atum, the face he wore at Heliopolis. So Amun-Ra is Creator, and the Great Ennead's chief god. Then there are:

Shu and Tefnut

Geb and Nut

Isis and Osiris

And in place of Seth and Nephthys, the Creator put Mut his consort and Khonsu his son, from the Trinity of Karnak.

"What followed then was dire. The gods had sustained Egypt for thousands of years. We knew them intimately because they spoke to us. Faith, conjecture, and speculation, which have played so large a role in religions in recent millennia, played little part in ours. Then suddenly, silence. The gods stopped communicating. We have sought to know why. The silence of the gods gave birth to theology.

"In the end, no answer satisfies. We rejected the idea that the dark gods had defeated and destroyed the Ennead. Human life would have ended if the gods had died. So we waited. We kept the traditions, the lineage, the knowledge, yet it all was in a vacuum. Without the gods, the sacred magic lacked power. Our spells had once changed the course of battles and shaped the tides of history. Now they felt like empty fantasies. We waited, nurturing hope that one day the gods would return to Egypt. Now, my friends, I believe they have."

"I read once," said Wolfgang, "that if technology were light years ahead of ours, it would look like magic."

"We must get the juice back into this divine technology and have the magic work again," said Mustapha.

Their eyes were drawn to the great stela before them. Its turquoise hieroglyphs burning with a blue light, like flames without heat, it gave every appearance of being the kind of technology Wolfgang was talking about. Mesmerized by the light, it was as if they stood on the shore, waves rolling in, gazing out at a new and unknown horizon.

"You said we had just one chance," said Maria after a little while. "Why just one?"

"Because of the structure of magic, and the nature of the Great Ennead," said Mustapha. "I have the power to utter the 'heart syllables of the true names'. Not the whole true name of any god mind you, no man has ever known them. To have the true names themselves would be to have the gods' full powers. So we have just the kernel, to call upon the gods. These heart syllables have been taught and handed down in the lineage of the Great Mage.

"But it is not easy, it never was, even for the early masters who knew the gods. It must be done just so. One wrong note, one misinflection, and it all goes awry. We take it as a rule written into the fabric of the universe: in all truly important matters, you get only one chance. So if through failure of intention or ability I perform the incantation incorrectly, we may never know what the gods intended to come about.

"The next thing is harder yet. I must call on the 'heart syllables of the true names of the Ennead'. All right, but which Ennead? The original or the evolved one? I am tempted to think that my predecessors at Karnak would have known if this amazing stela were built during their time, which suggests that it was earlier, leading us to the original Ennead of Heliopolis. Yet I must believe it is the new Ennead I am called upon to invoke. The gods seem able to suit these manifestations to our contemporary knowledge, witness the polygon's genome puzzle. So I believe it will be the new

Ennead, substituting Khonsu and Mut for Seth and Nephthys, and merging the Creator's Amun and Atum aspects. If I am wrong, however, we may be at a dead end forever."

"Mustapha," said Petra. "What if the ones you take as gods built this and walked away? Maybe they were spacemen. Maybe they meant to come back but couldn't?"

"My dear girl," said Mustapha. "We can never know by playing around with ideas. It is time for action. Wolfgang and Cliff opened the first door. I must open the next."

Mustapha picked up the tooled leather case lying at his feet. "And now, ladies and gentlemen," he said with a conjurer's flourish. "I must change into my work clothes. So as not to offend the ladies, I will do so behind the stela." He walked up to the stela, and touched the cartouches that bore the names of the Ennead. Then he disappeared with his case behind it.

They heard the clasps pop open. Mustapha began to chant an eerily beautiful ancient tune, in a language they had never heard and which Jack had thought lost forever: the Egyptian of the pharaohs. The chant was his ritual robing spell, sung to awaken the garments of power of the High Priest of Karnak and Great Mage of Egypt.

He emerged before them as strange as if he had been one of Petra's spacemen. He wore the vestments of Karnak in Exile, at once simple and splendid. A kilt of pure white linen, luminescent in the blue light. White linen sandals with gold straps. Broad wrist collars in gold, with intricate inlays. Though he wore no shirt his body was covered from neck to waist. A wide pectoral collar in gold spanned his chest. From this hung the Sun and the magic symbols of the nine gods of the Ennead. Jeweled sculptures in gold and precious stones, they hung separately but combined into a single breastplate. Each of them was tuned to the energy of one of the gods. Together they allowed the High Priest to communicate with the gods. When he acted in his other role as Great Mage of Egypt, the breastplate allowed the gods to possess him and work their magic through him.

On his head was a simple diadem representing the solar disc supported by scarabs. He carried his staff of electrum over cedar wood. His staff was the same one borne by the ancient mages. When Karnak went into exile, the staff was refashioned. Originally one piece, it was now in three, so that it could be carried concealed and reassembled at need.

"We say that the breastplate allows communion with the gods. The wrist collars provide strength. The kilt, sandals, and diadem symbolize purity of heart. And the staff of electrum catches the divine spark and allows the magic to flow."

Again they fell silent, as if in a dream. Mustapha's transformation was complete in their eyes. It now seemed possible for anything to happen.

"I will stand close to the stela to perform the working. Please move back to the steps with my acolytes," he gestured to the three men dressed as police, "for your own safety. If the gods judge me an unworthy vessel, they will certainly destroy me. Whatever happens now, only observe. Under no circumstances may you intervene."

Jack, Maria, Cliff, Wolfgang, and Petra took Mustapha's direction. When she stood on the steps, Maria looked up and saw a slice of the night sky above. She felt they had been plunged into a space opera of immense reach. Other stars, other sentient species, even the gods were plausible. Perhaps they were more than projections of the collective unconscious. She shivered despite the warm night air.

Mustapha faced the stela. His policeman-acolytes bowed their heads reverently. Slowly, Mustapha raised the great staff in his right hand. He raised his left hand to chest height and extended it before him, palm facing outward. He breathed in. When he let the breath out, it was in chant. As with his robing spell, it was eerily beautiful, modeled on the natural music of the ancient Egyptian language. The chant was an incantatory spell of power. It preceded speaking the heart syllables of the gods' true names, that most powerful spell of all, unused during the millennia of the gods' silence.

As the spell grew and swelled, Cliff felt it fill the room. He felt an energy, subtle but real. It came down and tickled the crown of his head. Then it moved down through his body, gently down, until it reached his groin. He looked over at Maria. She looked back. He saw surprise in her eyes. She was feeling the same thing.

The chant continued, paced and melodious. The energy in the room grew more palpable. Mustapha had broached the great spell, the recitation of the heart syllables of the true names of the gods. Then a blue flame leapt from the stela to the tip of Mustapha's staff. The light played about the ankh at the top, and maintained itself, a band of blue connecting the staff with the stela.

Mustapha was in the great spell when a tentacle of light reached out from the stela to his breastplate. Cliff half expected it to incinerate him because the gods found him unworthy.

Mustapha chanted on, resonant and powerful, cadence perfect, no interruptions. The blue light now surrounded him. He was on fire but not burned. He and the stela were one. The chanting reached a crescendo and then sank, gliding into a low bass note. The blue fire trembled and began to dissipate. He turned to face them. Blue flame still danced along his staff and breastplate, and in his moustache and eyebrows. He spoke.

"It is done. We had communion. Now we must wait to see what they do."

They did not have long to wait. The huge cyclopean blocks of the stone walls began to transmute. In a sweeping flicker of color, they were transformed, now covered with hieroglyphs, bas-reliefs, and colored portraits of the gods. They found themselves standing not in the empty chamber with the stela, but in the forecourt of a temple of ancient Egypt, flashing into focus.

Another wave of color, and a great pylon gate appeared in the wall behind the stela. At first it was only a two dimensional image, like a fresco. Then the stone dissolved away and the gate swung open. They walked towards it and stood before a corridor high, wide, and lit bright as daylight in the desert, though no source of illumination was visible. Fashioned of polished stone, the corridor angled down into the Earth.

A panel of hieroglyphs appeared above the corridor, supported on each side by a winged scarab and surmounted by a cobra. They all pulsed with life. The hieroglyphs glowed red and threatening.

"This is not some reproduction of a known temple," said Jack. "This is fabulous. Wholly new territory."

"It looks like we passed this intelligence test too," said Wolfgang. "What now?"

Petra was standing next to him holding his hand. She felt him keyed up, his hand sweaty and trembling.

"You okay, Wolfie?"

"Sure."

"Let me tell you what is written in fire," said Mustapha. "It says:

I am the Gate of Life and Death.
I am End and Beginning.
Let no one enter this mystery
Whose heart is heavier
Than the Feather of Maat.

"What does that mean?" said Petra. She continued to hold Wolfgang's hand, feeling his twitchy excitement.

"Maat judges each human at death, even a pharaoh," said Mustapha. "Maat holds a scale. She weighs the person's heart against a feather. If the person's faults weigh less than the feather, she judges them to be pure of heart, and allows them to continue their journey into eternity. If their heart outweighs the feather, the person is cast into the underworld."

Wolfgang slipped his hand out of Petra's. He moved toward the corridor.

"I have to be the one to go through first," he said. "I have to see what's down there. I solved the first puzzle. This is some advanced technology, not magic. I have to be the one."

Wolfgang rushed past Mustapha, who reached out to stop him. Taken off guard, Mustapha only got a hand on Wolfgang's shoulder, which the younger man easily brushed off with the advantage of his momentum.

"Come back!" yelled Mustapha.

"Don't do it!" wailed Petra, her voice breaking.

"I've just got to. It's going to be amazing."

Wolfgang was in the corridor and moving fast, following it down. When he had gotten only ten meters though, he ran into something. It was invisible, like transparent cotton. He could not push on.

"What's happening?" said Petra. She had stayed with the others in the stela chamber.

"Some sort of barrier, maybe an energy field of some kind. Interesting."

"Turn back now, Wolfgang," said Mustapha.

Hearing Mustapha's instruction, Wolfgang tried to unstick himself. It did not work. He struggled with all his strength. He was as thoroughly stuck as if in a hug web.

"Wait, I can see something," said Wolfgang.

"What?" said Petra.

"I can't quite make it out. Very strange. It's red. A red landscape, black rocks. A creature appearing. Body of a crocodile, head of a jackal. Oh god, it's seen me. It's coming this way!"

37

"This is Hillary Holloway reporting to you live on CNN from the pyramids in Egypt."

Her full lips smiled slightly, showing perfect teeth. The eyes were almost too large for the face and looked lit from within. Wit lay behind the smile, and detachment from what she reported. She had been a pop star, but always too bright to be comfortable as a girl act. As a CNN reporter she had her best role. The numbers of young males watching the news soared. Few of them learned much about current events, but all picked up fantasies. When she gazed into them with her detached smile reporting bombs in Somalia, global warming, and the crash of the NASDAQ, her seduction was complete.

"We're here at the pyramids because something unprecedented has happened. A huge vault has opened, apparently spontaneously, near the Sphinx. Security guards are keeping us away, but you can see the mysterious vault in this footage taken from our helicopter just minutes ago."

The picture showed the Sphinx, the Sphinx Temple in front of its paws, the great rectangular opening, and the steps leading down. It was still night in Egypt. The blue glow from the stela was visible.

"We know that an international team of scientists is down there right now. Will they emerge with some Egyptian treasures to rival King Tut or will some mummy's curse make sure they don't? Stay tuned to CNN and find out."

The camera went dark. She said to the cameraman, "Hokey but fun. Everyone loves this pyramid stuff."

"How the hell is she on it so fast? This thing just happened," the secretary of state said to an aide.

"She's in Cairo for a UN conference on women's' rights. Typical CNN lucky break."

"Our people there?"

"Should be down that hole. No reports in a while."

"Let me know. Still, I don't mind. I like that girl. Always makes you think she's going to show you more. We should get her in here to do an interview one of these days."

"What's happening to him?" said Petra.

"I fear that the caution inscribed above this gate is very real," said Mustapha. "Somehow, Wolfgang is seeing directly into the Duat."

"The Duat?"

"The Duat is where we will all go. The Land of Osiris, who rules there. The Land of the Dead."

"Oh my god, we've got to help him!"

"This is his test alone."

They looked down the corridor at Wolfgang. His arms were raised and he was struggling as if caught in an invisible web that kept getting tighter. He cried out.

"This jackal/crocodile is coming closer. It's here now, oh my god, it's going to bite!"

They watched in horror as Wolfgang's right foot simply disappeared. They could not see the attacker who was tormenting him. It was as if Wolfgang were a figure in a painting that the artist was painting out.

"It hurts, agony. It is real, weird. It is eating my leg and I feel fire and ice."

His right leg had disappeared completely.

"Now he's about to take my left leg. The pain is outrageous. I don't know why I'm not passing out. I should be dead from shock by now but I feel the whole evil thing. His teeth biting through. This intense fire and ice. He'll be eating my guts in a second."

They watched in disbelief as Wolfgang's body disappeared before their eyes. His waist going, his belly going, his chest going. He stopped speaking.

Petra yelled at Mustapha. "Can't you do something old man?"

"Not about this. Daughter, it is Anubis himself who is devouring Wolfgang. It is, it must be, his fate. We can only pray that when Anubis brings Wolfgang in his belly to the forty-three judges of the Duat, and spits him out for judgment, they are merciful to him. We will ask that they commend him to Osiris, who rules all powerful in the Duat."

Too much in shock to move or even cry, Petra and the others watched as Anubis, invisible to them, continued devouring Wolfgang before their eyes. When only his head remained he managed to speak one last time.

"My god I'm dying, I'm going." Wolfgang wept loud gasping sobs that tore the hearts of those listening. Just as he was about to disappear wholly from view, a red light filled the corridor. A jackal's howl, blood curdling in its intensity, raised the hair on the back of their necks.

Then it was over. The corridor was empty.

38

"I know you had fun, I can taste it in your brainmix," said Bulbul. "What did you see in your trance?"

"There's good reason the Consilium forbids anyone unlicensed to do remote viewing. Might learn too much. Control the information and control the Multiverse. Don't you think the Consilium has been drifting towards fascism under Wanre?"

It was Benben who was drifting, a problem whenever she came out of a remote viewing trip. The Consilium's remote viewing staff had support—assistants, handlers, exquisitely tuned brain cocktails. Because hers was a bootleg operation, Benben was on her own, with the help Bulbul could provide through intuitive modification of her neurotransmitters. It worked, but she drifted a bit afterward, affected by the touch of paranoia always present in her internal landscape, like shadows around the edge of the brightest day.

"I don't know anyone else who can remote view like you can without all the training and backup, my clever darling."

He was coiled around her neck to offer reassurance. His hind segment was attached to the hole in the crown of her head by suction and by teeth. When you were coming down you wanted everything comforting and familiar.

"What did you see?" he said.

"Strange things. At Giza, the lands of the living and dead are interpenetrating. Something big happening. Can't look into future. Not sure what."

"Do you sense it's time for us to make our grand entrance?"

"Not quite yet, darling. Timing. Is everything."

"Do you have ancestor dreams?"

"All my race does," said Toran.

"What?"

"Falling from the sky upon prey. It must have felt wonderful. I sometimes envy the airdragons."

Wanre and his raptor-eyed Second Speaker looked out. The airdragons flew lazily in the sunny afternoon, occasionally plunging into the sea to rise with a huge fish. They would eat at leisure, lying on their backs in the air as on a couch, using their stomachs as tables.

"I'd like to become one when I retire," said Wanre, "and this afternoon would be fine." He sighed. "What do our remote viewers see?"

"Things are picking up their pace. A strange stela appeared in a vault by the Sphinx and a member of the research team dematerialized."

"Dematerialized? That's not within their current technological capability."

"No, but it fits a story line in an ancient text. Looks like anomalous technology. We can't place it."

"Benben?"

"No movement, but she's been remote viewing again."

"I can't fail to like her irrepressibility." He smiled. In the moments when he could feel it was all a game, he enjoyed playing. And winning. "Let me know when she makes her next move."

Wolfgang had vanished from the canvas before their eyes. The weird howl that marked his disappearance was dying in their ears. Petra was incredulous and angry. "The idiot! What did he think he was doing?"

"I'm going in after him!" said Cliff. He moved too quickly for anyone to stop. His graceful figure dressed in black was moving down the corridor already. Maria gasped, the instinctive fear of mother for child. She followed in after him.

"Beware the cautions!"

They heard Mustapha but did not listen. In another moment, Cliff would be in the place where Wolfgang had been trapped. He was not sure what he would do to help Wolfgang; he only knew that he had to try. Maria was right behind him. Cliff reached the deadly place. He passed on through unscathed. Maria too.

"They are pure of heart in the eyes of Maat," said Mustapha. He moved into the corridor. "Impetuosity is not what is needed now," he said to them. "Wait. I know these gateways. I know their names. I know the words of power to make us safe."

Cliff and Maria kept on, and Mustapha moved after them at a measured pace, intoning a spell. The pace of his footfalls was as critical for this spell as the right pitch, pronunciation, and volume. Now that the ancient spells were coming alive, he was grateful for his tenacity in learning the old knowledge. His fear that he would never be a maker, only a scholar, was proving unfounded. As he moved down the corridor, its blank walls transformed in time with his progress. The spell he cast in passing was what these walls had yearned for. It was like spring moving through the countryside. The walls filled with bright paintings and bas-reliefs. They depicted the Two Lands festive and fertile along the Nile: papyrus and ducks, peasants and pharaohs, swallows and geese.

Then Mustapha approached the place where Wolfgang had been trapped. He knew that he must not falter in his footfall or his spell. He nevertheless felt fear. Was he worthy? Yet what did he fear? Did not Amun-Ra himself say he had been judged worthy by the great god Maat? But life was moment to moment. Was he worthy now, right now, this very second? He pushed on. He had to protect Maria and Cliff.

Mustapha moved through the place of danger. The spell continued to unfurl color and form along the wall. The Sphinx and the pyramids emerged fresh as new, made yesterday or the day before. There were gods interacting with people, teaching them, and receiving offerings. The gods assured the return of the Sun, the rise of the Nile, and the bounty of harvest. Mustapha longed to stop and study the images. But he kept moving.

After fifty meters of mural, the corridor opened into a space. While the corridor was brightly lit, it was dark. The light from the corridor was swallowed, the darkness impenetrable.

Cliff and Maria stood at the end of the corridor, hesitant to move into the darkness. Mustapha soon was with them.

"You have been fortunate. Your good hearts protected you. But now, please follow me. Until the words of power are said and the making done, this place is no place. It exists in no time. It is no more and no less than empty, pregnant eternity."

They saw no reason to argue.

"How could Wolfie be so stupid?"

Jack was standing with Petra in the stela chamber. He was not sure how to console her. It seemed like consoling a wildcat: he was not sure she wanted it, and he was afraid of getting scratched.

He was a gentleman. He would try. "Wolfgang had just done such brilliant work. He was overexcited. There was no way he could have foreseen that trap."

"Brilliant, sure, look where it got him. What a smart guy. You men are all the same. Now you're telling me he did the right thing. If you expect me to believe that you're crazy."

Jack felt the scratches were coming. "I'm just saying it was an accident, a terrible tragedy."

"Not for you! For me! What do I have to hold on to?" Petra started to cry. She brought her hands up over her eyes.

Jack reached out to her. He could feel her back tremble under his hands. She did not scratch. She was so fragile. He felt her sobs move her breasts against his chest. He smelled the freshness of her hair. He also smelled the fear mixed with her anger.

"Maybe Mustapha can think of something that will bring him back." Jack sensed he was offering false comfort, but did not know what else to offer.

"You heard Mustapha. Wolfie is in the underworld, whatever that means. I just know he is gone. I don't see why I should forgive him. And I don't see how I can ever be happy again. Maybe I'll just forget about men."

"I've been wondering, darling. What would make you truly happy?" He was still coiled consolingly around her neck, though he had detached his hind segment from her skull. Her mood had returned to near normal, recovering from her remote viewing trip. She felt that she had almost full command of her mind and her will, the only real comfort in the end.

"Well let's see, darling. That would be the elimination of all my enemies. Followed by the elimination of everyone who annoys me."

"Ooh, I love the vision. But that's getting pretty extreme in terms of numbers, isn't it sweetmeat?"

"Well yes. It means the total elimination of any life form that can talk back. Except you of course, my dear and faithful worm. But even I could never achieve such a luminous and perfect result. It is only a dream. A beautiful precious dream."

"What a romantic you are!"

"I am correctly accused. The sad fact is that a genius of my kind will never achieve true happiness in her lifetime."

"Your vision is too ideal for this Multiverse."

"What is there to console me?"

"I have just the ticket, treasure." He winked and reached his hind segment up to her head, attaching it to the hole in her skull with suction and teeth. Flexing his body, he squeezed a flood of custom blended neurotransmitters directly into her brain.

"If we can't empty the Multiverse," he said, "at least we can empty ourselves for a while before the action starts and we have to be on duty."

The chemicals poured into her brain, and docked at a cunningly chosen array of receptor sites.

"What a great mixmaster you are, worm," she sighed, as she began her liftoff. She zoomed into a dimension of pure geometry satisfyingly devoid of life. He tasted the reflux from her brain through his hind segment and lost himself in a wash of color.

39

Mustapha stepped forward chanting a spell into the darkness. They saw a stone floor materialize under him, keeping pace as he moved. A blue spark danced around the ankh at the tip of his staff. The spark grew in intensity until its light created a bubble of visibility around Mustapha.

Maria and Cliff instinctively hung back. They faced an abyss. As Mustapha stepped forward, stones appeared hanging in empty space, a bridge into vast emptiness, more fragile than an idea.

Mustapha raised his staff and spoke words of power. They were melodious, loud, precise. They made Maria wish with her whole heart that she understood ancient Egyptian.

The words were efficacious. The blue light from the tip of the staff grew stronger and the stone path widened, still suspended in emptiness.

"Come," Mustapha said to them gently.

They walked tentatively onto the stones until they stood with him. Then blue light began to radiate from his jeweled breastplate, from the precious figures of each of the nine gods of the Great Ennead. As the light emanated from the jewels, they came alive.

Suddenly an intense beam leapt out from the figure of Amun-Ra, chief of the gods, the Creator. An image formed in midair. It took on life. The figure of the god hovered in the emptiness. It was not flimsy like a hologram, but as real as the humans who stood before it.

Then a second beam of light leapt off the breastplate. It too brought a god to life in the empty space before them. It was the god Shu, the male of the pair who put an end to the primordial chaos. Another beam exploded into Tefnut his partner. Then a series of beams of light exploded off the breastplate, revealing in the emptiness the other gods of the Great Ennead: Geb and Nut, Isis and Osiris, Mut and Khonsu. The Great Ennead of Karnak in Exile, the gods who made the world.

The three humans stood silent before the gods.

The Creator Amun-Ra raised his right hand. In a blaze of light, a vast temple complex sprang into being out of the emptiness. It was greater by far than the original Karnak. Here the pylon gate stood a hundred meters high. Behind the gate, now closed, stood a forest of stone pillars in the hypostyle hall.

Mustapha fell to his knees. Then he lay down his staff and began to prostrate himself before the gods.

Unlike Mustapha, Maria and Cliff had not been trained in the protocol of ritual. The gods of ancient Egypt were before them in human form. They had seen them depicted with the faces of raptors, jackals, rams, but here they wore human faces. Or almost human, because they were more vivid than we are. Their faces had an idealized ancient Egyptian beauty with large eyes, high cheekbones, elegant noses, and copper-gold skin.

The gods of the Ennead radiated a vitality greater than human in the same proportion by which the Sun's brightness outshines a lamp. They also radiated power, partly conveyed by their scale. The gods were huge by human standards, standing some three meters high. Among men, only Rameses the Great projected himself at the same scale, and then only in stone.

Maria saw Mustapha going down in his bow, and felt it would be rude to stand there. She tapped Cliff on the shoulder to get his attention. When he took his eyes off the gods to look at her, she nodded and pointed down. She started bowing quickly, to catch up with Mustapha, watching him, trying to do the same. Cliff quickly joined in. By following Mustapha, they soon found themselves prone on the floor, arms wide.

Mustapha completed his prostration. While he rose, he picked up his great staff. Maria and Cliff followed suit, rising quickly.

Mustapha stood and looked at the gods. His eyes feasted upon them. This divine manifestation had already moved beyond anything in the conscious memory of humankind. Even in the First Time when the gods walked the Earth, humans were never invited into a making such as this.

He was sleeping when the call came. The mobile by his pillow woke him.

"I thought you should know, Abdul." It was the chief security officer at Giza.

Abdul was groggy, almost as if he had drunk some of the alcohol with which the infidel offends the will of the Prophet. "What is it?"

"Mustapha has asked me to let the brotherhood know. You are Assistant High Priest, so it is you I am first calling. Here at the Sphinx, wonderful things are happening. Mustapha is below ground, and we are securing the area. I suggest you come for yourself first of all." He rang off.

Abdul was still waking. "Below ground?" He had just passed through a series of bad dreams, but could not pull their images back into awareness. He had answered the phone lying down and now raised himself on his elbow. His wife was still asleep beside him, faintly visible in the light leaking through the shutters. His immediate thought was to hit her, beat her until she bled.

This woke him completely. He felt a momentary panic. His devotion to his wife was real. She had borne him two fine sons and he treated her tenderly in return. He loved the comfort of lying near her in bed. He loved her softness and her scent in the night. Here, it came again: the impulse to beat her while she slept. The thought had no power to move him to action but disturbed him nonetheless. He got up, dressed, and slipped out.

When he arrived at the Sphinx, he found reporters, lights, the beginnings of a crowd of spectators. They were held back by barricades and Mustapha's armed security police. The head security officer greeted Abdul with a warmth that acknowledged they were both priests of Karnak in Exile. He was glad to have Abdul there, whose forcefulness would be welcome, since events had already spilled beyond known boundaries.

Abdul greeted him and saw his automatic weapon. Into Abdul's mind flashed the idea of taking the weapon and spraying its shells into the people assembled behind the barricades. He blinked to get rid of the thought. While it was there he was not in his own mind. When it passed he was left uneasy.

Out of nowhere lights and a camera were in his face.

"Hi, I'm Hillary Holloway reporting from CNN. You're clearly an official of some kind, perhaps a high ranking police officer. You're about to go underground, into the cavity that has opened beside the Sphinx as if by magic. Can you tell us anything about this? Is it magic? What's happening?"

The thought arose in Abdul to shove the camera so hard it would put the cameraman's eye out, and then to strangle this woman reporter.

"Look, I cannot comment or help you." He turned away.

The chief of security led him down the stairs to the stela. Was this something from Allah or from Satan? His next thought was that if only he had enough plastique with him, he could destroy the stela. Somehow the mind he had awoken with was more complex than the one he had taken to bed.

40

Mustapha, Maria, and Cliff stood before the gods. The divine faces bore enigmatic smiles, conveying no sense of threat. Maria wished she had paid more attention to the typology of Egyptian deities, so she could correctly distinguish each of them.

The Ennead stood before the closed pylon gate. The high pylon took the characteristically Egyptian shape, wider at the bottom and narrowing near the top, surmounted by a lintel. The pink granite of its walls was finely polished and incised with reliefs of the Ennead creating and sustaining the world. Before the gateway stood wooden flagpoles bearing pennants that snapped in the breeze. On either side a giant obelisk rose, symbol of the light of Amun-Ra.

Aside from the vast scale of the temple, the only jarring note was the pair of doors in the pylon gate. Maria would have expected heavy doors of some precious wood, perhaps cedar. These doors were made of no wood, but rather of the same material as the slab that slid open in the Sphinx Temple floor. Dense black, it absorbed light rather than reflected it.

Amun-Ra stood at the center of the company of gods, and slightly in front of the others. Maria recognized him. She felt drawn to the notion of a sun god as a beneficent deity. She had always been a little jealous of his headdress too: a pair golden plumes rising from his crown so high they were almost as tall again as the god. She smiled at herself for having such thoughts as they faced the Ennead.

Mustapha spoke. "How can we serve you?"

Maria expected Amun-Ra to say something in return. Instead she felt a sudden pain in her chest. It was terrifying. "I'm having a heart attack!" she thought.

Then the pain vanished and she felt a flood of love. It was like nothing she had ever known. The gods stood before them with smiles. She looked over to Cliff and Mustapha. Cliff was leaning over, shoulders hunched. Mustapha held his hand over his heart. She judged that they had been given a similar gift, and that it had been equally surprising to them.

Then Amun-Ra spoke. They felt it as a vibration in their chests. "For the making to succeed you must propose the offerings."

They looked at the eight gods flanking Amun-Ra, four on each side. These eight gods of the Ennead each held an empty golden bowl.

Mustapha was not certain how to proceed. These empty golden bowls, like begging bowls of the gods, corresponded to no known story. Nor did the Creator's request for offerings have any precedent.

"What may we offer?"

"What is needed must be given."

"Help us understand," said Cliff.

"We will bring anything if we know what is needed," said Maria.

"Bring only what is needed," said Amun-Ra, whose voice, while not actually threatening, now made their chests vibrate in a way not entirely comfortable.

"How shall we know?" said Maria, bravely persisting in the face of what was starting to look like divine indifference.

Mut, the Mother of All, answered Maria. The consort of the Creator, Mut stood at his right hand. She wore the double crown of Upper and Lower Egypt. "Look deeply inside yourselves," she said, "and you will find the way."

Although Maria could not name Mut, she felt the intensely nurturing energy that poured through her. The mother in Maria knew the mother goddess in Mut. She trusted that her advice, gnomic as it seemed, would prove enough to guide them.

"We must now do what the Lords of Creation require," said Mustapha. He bowed and this time Maria and Cliff bowed with him. They turned and left, eager to fulfill a mission they did not yet wholly understand.

They walked back up the corridor, past the newly minted murals and bas-reliefs. Maria quietly marveled. Cliff had other things on his mind.

"Why does this have to be another intelligence test? Now that Wolfgang is gone, how are we going to solve it? Why can't they just tell us what to do? And if they are gods, why do they need our help anyway?"

"Don't be so hard to please," said Mustapha gently. "We humans have to play by the rules the gods set. Who wouldn't give their eyeteeth to be involved in a game as deep as this?"

As they neared the end of the corridor, they saw Jack and Petra still standing in the stela chamber. When they entered, Petra spoke, shaking with anger.

"At least you're back! About time! I thought you might be as stupid as Wolfgang and disappear."

"Everything is going to be all right, Petra." Mustapha said.

Maria considered going to Petra to support her. She held back when Mustapha went to Petra and held her by the shoulders. Maria saw that Petra's anger arose against men and needed them to complete its cycle, like a wave rising against and breaking on a beach.

Petra looked into Mustapha's eyes. "Don't be stupid, old man. You're full of fairy tales."

Mustapha was undeterred. He saw tears behind Petra's anger. Holding her shoulders he spoke softly. "It will really be all right. It's hard to believe, but it will be all right." There was something in his voice that penetrated the anger. She listened, still sure that things would never be all right again. Yet the way Mustapha cared brought some comfort, and the way he absorbed her anger let it subside.

Abdul and the guards waited at the foot of the stairs.

"What is happening, Your Holiness?"

"Something wonderful, Abdul. I don't have time to explain now. "

He turned to the security chief. "Get more of our men here." He looked up through the open slab and saw the sky paling into dawn. He had lost track of time. "The day is upon us. Maintain security. Under no circumstances is anyone to enter this site without my express permission as Director of the Supreme Council of Antiquities. And Abdul, organize a meeting of the brotherhood in the temple, and I will make everything clear."

He turned to Cliff, Jack, and Maria, who was holding Petra. "It is time for us to go. But not before I change into mufti. Wouldn't do to be seen like this."

He went behind the stela to change, and they waited for him by the steps. He took off his vestments of office and objects of power, and carefully secreted them in the Moroccan leather case. He disassembled his electrum staff into its constituent pieces and added them to the case. He donned his white linen suit, left neatly folded on the floor, and his panama. The case felt small in his hand after the staff. He strolled over to the stairs in a relaxed, worldly gait and said, "Follow me. Ignore whoever has gathered up there. We will go to the Al Minah to have breakfast and consider next steps. A member of my security team will drive us." He motioned for the guards to come along.

They followed him up the stairs. The crowd had swelled with the morning. Hillary Holloway was poised to speak with Mustapha as he headed for the car. Camera running, she said, "I understand you are the Director of the Supreme Council of Antiquities. You've been down under the Sphinx all night with these experts. What's going on down there, and when will we get to see it?"

"We've made a find of some pristine archeological material. We were inspecting it. Because of its fragility, we'll have to conduct tests before letting the public have access."

"What about pictures?"

"Soon, after our preliminary examination."

"What's in your suitcase? Are you carrying away some ancient treasures?"

"This?" he said, raising his case. "Just some tools of my trade. Be patient. The Supreme Council of Antiquities will be happy to work with you."

Mustapha turned and walked away.

"So there you have it. Stay tuned for further updates on these startling developments. This is Hillary Holloway, for CNN, reporting live from the Sphinx."

As Mustapha stepped into the car, he heard a thunk. Looking back, he saw that the metal slab in the floor of the Sphinx Temple had closed again. He hoped his door opening spells would work.

The hopefulness of dawn became the oppressive heat of morning as Abdul re-entered medieval Cairo. He would organize the meeting of Karnak in Exile. First though, he wanted to return to his family. Things that made no sense were piling up. He would reenter the zone where he was master. He was a loving master. He had gained the respect and not just the fear of the circle of people with whom he lived, and who depended on him.

He entered the kitchen. His wife smiled sleepily at him. Morning light filled the small room. The motes at drift were as bright as the stars over Giza a few hours ago. His wife was feeding their younger son. Abdul looked at the two of them and his anxieties lifted. He approached to touch her hair and offer a greeting. He noticed a sharp kitchen knife on the table. An image smashed into his mind: he would pick up the knife and slit his son's throat. The image went, but he stumbled as he approached them.

"Are you all right, Abdul?"

"Perhaps not enough sleep."

He sat down and she brought him coffee, bread, oil, and dates. The food was reassuring.

"You had to work last night?"

"Something unexpected."

She knew very little about his activities, either with Karnak in Exile or with the Islamist mullahs. She accepted that his work required discretion. She was grateful that he supported his family well.

Abdul finished his food. He put down his cup and walked from the kitchen. His older son Ahmad, his favorite, was in the hall kneeling to tie his shoes. Abdul stood before him, watching with pride.

An image punched through the surface of his consciousness: he would slam his knee hard under the boy's chin, throwing him backwards, shattering his skull on the stone floor. The image floated away. The boy looked up, then stood, ready for the day and his father's approval. Abdul gave it: his son, his hope.

Abdul walked into the bathroom. He washed his face with cold water. He felt his hands on his face. The most familiar feeling. He looked in the mirror.

"Who am I? Am I crazy? How could I dream of killing my wife, my sons?"

Looking deep into his reflected eyes he wondered if he should go away, or kill himself, to protect his family from these new feelings. "But then," he thought, "what man would take care of them?"

Abdul shook his head. He lowered his face and pulled more cold water onto it. His impulse was to go to the mullahs. As he thought it through, though, he realized they would not help him, and dared not show them weakness. Under his fingers the skin of his face felt slick, alien.

He reached a decision. If these episodes persisted, he would go to Mustapha. He would do what he had never done before as Assistant High Priest. He would speak truth and seek guidance.

41

The morning was fair and hot, the linen thick, the silverware heavy. Coffee, juice, croissants, butter and jam were spread before them. For most of them, attention was elsewhere. They were still in shock at losing Wolfgang. They wondered what Amun-Ra could have meant by 'Bring only what is needed,' and what Mut could have meant by 'Look deeply inside yourself' to find the answer. They felt emotionally numb, and were short on answers.

Cairo was waking up around them. Cars murmured and buzzed like swarms of insects, and would soon foul the air with the day's stinging smog. The Nile flowed on eternal and indifferent. A pair of crows landed in the crown of a date palm near the veranda. The birds cawed rasping and raucous, tearing holes in the sky to mock their ignorance.

Mustapha ate his breakfast methodically. The way he worked through his rolls, butter, and jam suggested the world was in its first springtime. He stroked his moustache with the knuckle of his right index finger to dislodge a croissant crumb. He sipped coffee and replaced the cup in the saucer with a click.

"I've just gotten it," said Maria.

"So what's 'needed'?" said Cliff.

"I don't know *that*."

"What's the deal then?"

"I have a way we may find out. Mut said to look deep within ourselves. One thing that might mean is that we go on an inward journey."

"How?"

"You all remember the research I was doing before all this happened?"

"Sure. You think the ancient Egyptians tripped."

"In a sacred way, yes. I think maybe if we do the same, the gods will help us find the answer."

"Far out, Mom."

"It's crazy," said Petra, thick-lipped and withdrawn. "Wolfie is dead and you're talking about tripping. I can't believe it."

"It won't bring him back, Petra," said Maria. "But it may help us understand what the gods want from us. Wouldn't Wolfgang have wanted that?"

"I really have no idea. It's all too stupid. You can keep your gods and their deadly little games." Petra pushed her chair back, scraping the floor like chalk on a blackboard. She narrowed her eyes and walked to the balustrade. Maria looked after her, and gave a sigh of sympathy.

"What exactly are you proposing Maria?" said Jack, concerned.

Maria turned to Jack. She decided she would get the others to agree to her idea, then go and take care of Petra. "Well you know the dual components of the chemistry. My guess is sacred acacia and Syrian rue. But I don't know anything about the formulation."

"Mustapha," said Jack. "If she's right about the ancient rites, you must know all about it."

"Well," said Mustapha, flicking a crumb off the left sleeve of his linen jacket. "Yes, I believe I do."

"Can you tell us?"

"Only initiates can know. There are few of them. It takes years of devotion to the way of the gods, but I think it's fair to say that the gods themselves have initiated you all in varying degrees. The higher initiation went to Maria and Cliff who joined me to witness the gods and bear their message. So I can share this information with them. I'm afraid you and Petra will have to sit this round out, Jack. I hope that's all right with you. Petra is too fragile right now in any case, and she needs someone she trusts to be with her."

"That's fine, Mustapha. So Maria and Cliff will go with you."

"That's right. Maria and Cliff, you need to know that what I will share with you are perhaps the most closely guarded secrets on Earth. They are almost certainly the oldest. Though the gods have shown you favor, their favor is also a burden. If you reveal what you have seen the personal consequences for you will necessarily be of the most drastic kind."

Their minds turned to Wolfgang. They agreed to discretion.

Maria stood and went to Petra. She found Petra leaning on the balustrade, left arm propping up her chin. Maria stood quietly next to her. The crows started up their rasping clatter.

"These black birds at least remember Wolfgang. They are singing for him. Croaking his requiem."

Maria listened to the harsh sound for a moment. "You loved him. He was taken from you suddenly. Your pain must be terrible. I know how you feel."

Petra rounded on her. "How can *you* know what *I* feel?"

"I can't get inside your heart. But I lost my husband Akira. He was also a brilliant young physicist, he also died suddenly, it was also through his bravado. And I loved him too." Maria saw that she had reached Petra.

"I didn't know," Petra said. She looked Maria in the eye. "How did it happen?"

Maria felt the pain again. "He had just discovered something important about black holes. Wouldn't say what it was, just that it would change physics forever. He wouldn't talk to anyone about it. One night he said that he was going to drink a lot of bourbon and drive his car fast, like John von Neumann, a mathematician he admired. I couldn't stop him. A couple of hours later he was dead, wrapped around a tree."

"You had Cliff."

"Taking care of him got me through the grief." She was quiet for a moment. "You have a whole life before you. I know you'll find a way through."

Petra pursed her lips. They both looked out at the Nile, and Maria wondered what Petra's next move would be.

Maria arranged for Jack to stay with Petra at the hotel. He tried to make sure she got some sleep. He saw her to bed and then sat in the living room of the suite she had shared with Wolfgang. None of them had slept. Jack dozed off in the armchair.

Maria was squeezed into the back of Mustapha's Cinquecento. She wanted Cliff to be able to talk with him as they drove across Cairo.

For Mustapha, this was his familiar run to medieval Cairo and Karnak in Exile. For Cliff, it was a dive down through slices of history. It reminded him of the float trip he had taken with Maria down Utah's Green River. Floating at first past rock of recent origin, he was drawn by the river through canyons it had sculpted in some of the oldest rock on Earth. Here he was leaving modern Cairo for the medieval city, to be led down into the oldest working human edifice, toward a psychedelic ceremony.

The ride was a kilometer and the traffic moderate. Maria let Cliff chat away with Mustapha. Her mind floated. She looked out as the city passed by and thought again of Akira. Cliff was now eight yours younger than Akira when she had met him. She still thought of Cliff as a boy, but more and more saw his father's genius flashing out. As Mustapha turned off Sharia Muski to park in a narrow side street, she wondered if Cliff's genius, like his father's, would uncover something that so frightened him he would reach out for the comfort of death's embrace.

The men were already out of the car and waiting for her. She roused herself and climbed out. Odors exploded into her tired mind: livestock funk and acrid diesel then sweet basil, turmeric, and cumin.

She followed as Mustapha led them down an alley where the buildings leaned in and nearly touched above. They turned into a narrower one to squeeze around a donkey and then a boy who pushed a wheelbarrow piled high with purple carrots.

"Isn't this great, mom?"

Maria enjoyed Cliff's excitement at being in a vivid medieval world. "It really doesn't seem like it's changed at all for centuries."

"Don't be too easily impressed," said Mustapha. "This is a modern town, two millennia newer than where we're going. Now follow me down into the real world."

He took out his high tech key, inserted it in an apparently old lock, and took them down.

Mustapha brought them within the temple to the room where they would conduct the ceremony. It was not the inner chamber where he conducted the monthly rite of Returning to the House of Amun-Ra. They could never be allowed in there.

The room he took them to was like a jewel box. Its stone walls were joined with micrometer precision, and covered with paintings whose color was more emphatic than nature. Mustapha was again in ceremonial dress. He explained that the formula Maria had guessed was correct, and had been used for millennia. He satisfied her curiosity about how the decoction was prepared, and her concerns about its safety. He mentioned that a ritual diet would ordinarily be followed, but the exigencies of the circumstances warranted swift action.

"Have you ever used hallucinogens, Maria?"

"A long time ago, in college."

"Cliff?"

"Well, not so long ago. Just a tiny blotter."

"Cliff, I didn't know," said Maria.

Cliff shrugged.

"That's good," said Mustapha. "Much better that we don't have naive subjects for this ritual. It's too important. I don't want to worry about whether you are going to get lost on another plane and need help. We want to focus on hearing the message of the gods clearly, whatever it is."

"Do you think they will speak through the plants?" said Maria.

"I cannot doubt they will speak. I only hope we will understand."

"Okay," said Cliff. "Let's trip."

"Understand that this is sacred, Cliff. We go in with the intention of listening to what the gods have to say. It all depends on the clarity of our intention. We want to help the gods move humankind wherever they mean it to go."

"Okay. Just show us what to do, I'm ready."

Three sleeping couches in the ascetic ancient style were arranged to form a circle with heads pointing inwards. In the center of the circle was an altar bearing small images of the Ennead together with lighted lamps and offerings. The altar was covered in sheet gold. The offerings of grain and fruit, beer, wine, milk and meat were in alabaster vessels. Rich incense perfumed the air.

Cliff and Maria were drawn to the strangeness of the couches. They were made of woven reed over a rectangular frame of wooden poles. The legs were carved into the form of bull's legs complete with hooves. The head of each couch was slightly higher than the foot, and held a curious object in place of a pillow. It looked like a stand of some kind, a pillar rising about fifteen centimeters off a base and supporting a narrow piece of wood whose ends curved up to make a crescent.

"What is this thing where a pillow should be?" said Cliff.

"A head rest," said Mustapha. "What ancient Egyptians used instead of a pillow. Try it, but it may not be comfortable unless you've grown up with it. If not, you can remove it. Now to work. We will each sit on our couch. The attendants will bring us the communion. We will drink, lie back, and wait for the gods to speak. We will share our visions when we have all returned to this room. It should be three or four hours."

"Ready," said Cliff.

Mustapha smiled at his eagerness "I hope my manner isn't too severe for you to understand this is a joyful experience. We are privileged."

Each of them sat on the edge of their couch. Three men came in, each carrying a chair. They wore linen kilts like Mustapha but without his array of gold and jewels.

"These are our attendants. One will sit by each of us. They are experienced, and will ensure we fare well."

The men placed their chairs next to the beds. They left and returned with three alabaster chalices.

"This is the communion. Drink it mindfully, lie down, experience what comes, and we will confer later. May your journey go well."

Maria held the alabaster chalice and looked in. It was dark like tea. She drank it all at once, a large mouthful. An oily bitterness crossed her tongue. She felt it clearly as it moved down into her stomach, as if it had an energy and intelligence of its own. It felt like the soul of the vegetable world had entered her body to teach her.

When they lay down, Cliff and Maria found the headrests fiendishly uncomfortable. The attendants removed them and replaced them with white linen pads. The room was quiet. The lamps cast a flickering light that gave life to the rising incense. From a distant part of the temple a rhythmic chanting drifted in.

Nothing happened for a while. Cliff wondered if he had drunk enough. Just as he was thinking this, the thought was replaced by a wave of experience. He lay with his eyes closed and felt words rising in his heart like flower petals bubbling to the surface of a spring.

Neurosis is endlessly repetitive
Why stay in the grip of it?

Consciousness is boundless
Why not explore it deeply?

Human life is brief
Why not use it wisely:

To swim in the true Ocean
And know the taste of bliss?

Then a soft energy penetrated him from the crown of his head down through his throat. It moved into his chest. Out his arms to his hands, which moved and stretched of their own volition. Down to his belly, his groin, the tips of his toes. He breathed easily and more deeply.

Then came a sudden fear. "What have I done, what will happen now?" This passed, and a wave of happiness replaced it, like some familiar and long lost happiness was returning. It became a summer afternoon in his inner landscape. Hope and possibility blossomed. Suffering was banished to a distant shore.

"Maybe this is how the gods feel," he thought. The next thing he knew, the gods of the Ennead were standing before him. He was with the gods in the courtyard before the temple that Amun-Ra brought into being below the Sphinx. The gods were alive and breathing, just as when he met them. They looked directly at him but said nothing. They held the golden offering bowls he saw them hold. The Creator, Amun-Ra, held no bowl, and so there were eight.

Then as if at a signal he had not seen, the eight gods with bowls began moving. They performed a stately and dignified dance, weaving around each other in complex pairing combinations all along a line. Weaving in and out around each other up and down the line the gods danced.

When they stopped he thought it was over, and felt regret. It was only a pause, though. The gods began again, dancing a complementary but different pattern. Trying to catch the figure, he saw that they were dancing a mirror image of the dance they had done before. It was not like running a movie or a game of chess backwards, but the same dance in mirror variation. Cliff, always eagerly seeking patterns, was pleased by the symmetry.

Then as suddenly as before the dance stopped. This time the eight dancers gathered in a circle around Amun-Ra. Each of the eight in turn bent down and emptied their golden bowl. Cliff had seen nothing in the bowls, so he was surprised when what looked like colored sand pour out. From each bowl a different color. Eight small piles of color around Amun-Ra.

The Creator stood still. What came next delighted Cliff. Each of the eight gods reached down, picked up some of the color, and floated into the air. They moved as freely in the air as he had always dreamed of doing. As they flew they fashioned something out of the colors. Two gods at a time came together and a bicolor platform hung in space. They did this again and again in varying combinations. A spiral staircase took shape. It grew higher and higher until Cliff lost sight of the gods.

Then Amun-Ra moved. He mounted the staircase, spiraling higher and higher until he too disappeared. Cliff with all his heart wanted to follow. When he tried, he remembered that his body was lying in a room underneath Cairo.

The images shifted from the staircase and temple into more abstract geometries, grids of color and patterns of paisley. He slowly returned to the room. Opening his eyes, he saw his attendant sitting by his side. The attendant, a man some years older than himself, was reassuring. He said quietly, "Everything OK?"

"Sure," said Cliff, stretching and sitting up slowly. "Very much so. Yeah."

Mustapha and Maria were already sitting up. Maria had been watching Cliff for the last few minutes. She felt her perceptions cleansed by her experience. She saw for the first time that Cliff was crossing over into manhood. She appreciated his beauty as she had so often during his boyhood. With his long black hair, jet eyes, and golden skin, he could have been fashioned of sheet gold and ebony. She thought he looked at home among the Egyptian gods. She spoke to Mustapha.

"Did you see them?"

"Oh yes." He stretched and rubbed the back of his neck.

"You, Cliff?"

"You bet."

"And you, Maria?" said Mustapha.

"Happily, yes."

They compared experiences, and found that all three had shared the same vision through to the details. Mustapha was moved by this.

"This almost never happens—people having the same vision—unless it is induced. And I did nothing to induce it. I take it as a mark of authenticity, of the gods inducing it."

"But what does the vision mean?" said Maria. "What do we do now?"

"Logistics first. We will confer here for a while. Then the attendants will take you back to the hotel so you can get some rest. I must meet with the brotherhood here. So, back to our vision. Any thoughts?"

"In the dance and in the staircase, they were making something," said Maria. "Any clue in the ancient texts? Are they acting out a known story?"

"Other than obvious metaphors, like the gods make the world by their dance, their play, and that the realm of the gods is above us, no. These are not known scenes from any texts, or even folktales."

"It's got to be related to the two pieces of the puzzle," said Cliff. 'Bring only what is needed' and 'look deep within yourself.' When we met the gods, their offering bowls were empty. We're meant to bring that colored powder they used to build the staircase. Whatever it is."

"Maybe the geometries in the vision provide a clue," said Mustapha. "In a hieroglyph, we reduce something to its simplest geometry. In the dance and in the stairs, we have a spiral. If we used a spiral as a hieroglyph..."

"You'd be creating an ancient Egyptian word for DNA!" said Cliff.

"I don't know, Cliff," said Maria. "It solved one puzzle. Why use the same test again?"

"I learned something about DNA," said Mustapha. "It is built up out of four chemical building blocks. The gods had double that—eight different colors were used to build the staircase. If each color is one DNA building block, we have double the number we need."

"Maybe, just maybe, I've got it," said Cliff. "If I do, I tell ya, I'm the man!"

"Okay, what is it?"

"Suppose that 'what is needed' are the bases that build DNA. There are four: A, C, G, and T."

"That leaves four empty bowls."

"That's the point. Maybe this is not about humans any more. Maybe there are eight building blocks, eight bases. The eight colors in the vision were a clue."

"Maybe," said Maria. "There's good science that says the four building blocks used in Earth DNA are not the end of the story. Others could be used to make different kinds of DNA."

"So not Earth life?" said Mustapha.

"That's the cool part," said Cliff. "Aliens. It would be alien DNA. Maybe the gods are aliens. Maybe we're about to help them make a whole bunch more!"

"Tell us," said Mustapha. "Are there just four other amino acids that could be used?"

"No," said Maria. "Once you open it up there are many choices."

"How do we narrow it?"

"Got it," said Cliff. "Meta-patterns. We go on a hunt for permutations that stand out by making sense. Then we guess."

"And hope," said Mustapha. "It looks like with each of these tests we get only one chance."

"It's worked so far," said Maria. "One: we find the polygon. Two: we crack its code. Three: we've got a Great Mage who could speak the heart syllables of the true names. So far so good. The next stage in the game may be whether we grasp the possibility of alien DNA."

"I most rambunctiously and funkily do!" said Cliff.

"And figure its components."

"We'll get it. I just need my laptop, an internet connection and a little time. Too bad Wolfgang isn't here, he would have loved this." He went very quiet.

"You shall have what you need," said Mustapha.

"I'll help you," said Maria. "I may not be Wolfgang, but I'm pretty good on plant genetics. It'll help."

"Great."

"Why do I get the feeling," said Maria, "that these tests have all been programmed a million years ago for us? That we are passing tests left by an ancient race who wanted to be sure we had a specific set of attainments before unleashing something we can't possibly imagine?"

"We shall soon know. Meanwhile, I must bring the brotherhood up to date. We'll meet later."

All the members of the brotherhood who could come on short notice were sitting cross-legged in the temple precinct of Karnak in Exile. Mustapha was conferring with several of the senior priests before he addressed the group. Abdul approached him.

"Your Holiness?"

"Yes."

"Before you address the brotherhood, I must confide in you a disturbing matter." Abdul told Mustapha about the eruptions of violent images, and asked if he were going mad.

"Our tradition describes such experiences. Dark powers can attack us in this way. We can work to protect you. I will help. Come to me soon. We will explore this more thoroughly."

Abdul felt relief at being comforted by this man he ordinarily disdained. It was like reaching back to an earlier and simpler time in their relationship.

Mustapha told Abdul to attend to some administrative details. When Abdul left to do so, Mustapha called over another priest. He told him to have Abdul watched. Mustapha wondered if he had lost Abdul, and what the cost would be.

42

"Were we able to break through and view their visions?" Wanre looked up from his desk at Saiki. He had increased the scope of her duties. She was now a security advisor to the First Speaker in addition to being the Council's lead sartist. The combination of posts gave her access to most day-to-day work of the Council. Wanre could thus consult her on whatever matters were occupying his mind.

He was happy he had found her on his home planet. Having her here with him in the body was good. The relief he originally felt in her company was from her clear perceptions of events. Now there was much more, a relief from solitude and deepening trust that gave onto need. "I need as much sense data as possible. To see if I can get a feel for the Earth anomaly."

"We didn't break through. Almost with Cliff. The signals were somehow shielded. We could almost read him, but not quite. He is highly attuned. For a human, he has a very powerful mind."

"We must watch him. He is young. He has not yet had to choose between good and evil. I wish I could ensure his choice, whenever it comes, is the right one. Humans—and we—may need him."

They watched an airdragon perform a relaxed barrel roll. Then Saiki rose and left. He considered calling her back, just to have her near. Then, thinking that sartists must fly free, he smiled and let her go.

After the meeting of the brotherhood of Karnak in Exile, Abdul drove to the souk for his next scheduled meeting with the mullahs. He saw a car filled with a family coming in the opposite direction. His mind filled with the thought: turn the wheel, veer into them, hit them head on.

He kept driving. He parked and walked. He was now calm and when his turn came he sat with the mullahs. It was familiar. Then, as he was listening to the mullah sitting closest, a thought arose: *reach out, grab him by the throat and choke him to death.*

The thought went and he found himself telling them about what had happened under the Sphinx. He told them much of what Mustapha had told the brotherhood. He wanted to stop his recitation and ask for their help with the storms in his mind. But he did not, knowing it would mean being sidelined or eliminated. He finished his report, wondering what the mullahs would make of the appearance of the ancient gods of Egypt.

The mullahs muttered among themselves. Then the eldest of them spoke to him and said, "These foreign scholars who were down there with Mustapha are from the United States?"

"Yes."

"They have high positions there?"

"They are educated. University professors."

"Then they must be agents of their government. These monuments and all they contain are our birthright. We believe Mustapha must be coming close to betraying us, to selling our birthright to the West."

"Are these ancient things not pagan?" said Abdul. "How can they be our heritage?"

"Were they not built by our Arab fathers before they had the benefit of the Prophet's truth? If our ancestors made these things, are they not ours?"

Abdul had no further questions.

The mullah continued, "If you see the least sign of Mustapha betraying our Arab heritage to the Western devils, eliminate him. Do not ask questions."

Jack sat in his hotel room in the Al Minah. He was trying to come to terms with what he had witnessed. Seeing Wolfgang disappear fit no pattern that Jack could make sense of in his rational mind. It was more suited to the mythical world the ancient Egyptians must have lived in. Jack wrote up a description of the events. He would send them to his contact in Washington.

Jack had been approached when he was a student. The approach came when he was doing his doctorate at the Oriental Institute in Chicago. He was a natural linguist, adept not only in hieroglyphs but also in Arabic. It was a time when the intelligence agencies were recruiting top young Arabists. Jack felt that he would be doing his country a service. The connections should also help smooth the way for his work.

The demands from his contact were never onerous. When he was in Egypt, he filed regular reports about what he saw and heard. Occasionally he would arrange meetings with agents or others he was asked to meet. None of it felt wrong. He was just an observant researcher.

As Jack's contact worked his way up through the system, Jack began to feel that he had privileged access. It was lonely being an Egyptologist. Research budgets were paltry, and universities could barely make room for Egyptology any more, given the vogue in biosciences. When Jack's contact eventually climbed to secretary of state, Jack felt like he participated in the success. The habit of access to power made up for a lack of actual power.

For this field season, Jack's instructions were to report what he saw as always, and to pay special attention to any sign of Islamist activity.

Jack typed his last paragraph:

> *It's difficult to turn these events into any sensible rational account. And it's particularly hard for me to grasp the disappearance of Wolfgang, a German researcher in our party. I should perhaps say "death," as he apparently died before our eyes. He is certainly gone, vanished in a below ground corridor of unknown origin under the Sphinx. Spaces and passages have opened under the Sphinx that conform to no known historical account, and seem inexplicable by the laws of physics. I suppose as an Egyptologist I should be happy with these wonders appearing, but they honestly make me nervous. I can only continue to participate, observe and report.*

Jack reread his last paragraph. He was feeling a discomfort in sending the report he had never felt before. It was not the events themselves that made filing the report hard. It was the fact that he was reporting on situations that involved people he cared about. Was there any way that Maria could be hurt by his report? He had left out the part about the psychedelics. Was there anything else? He decided there was not. He encrypted the email, and got ready to send it to Washington.

Maria knocked on Jack's door and entered. She found him with his laptop.

"Oh hi," Jack said, "I'm catching up on Oriental Institute correspondence. About done, let me just send it to Chicago." He was uncomfortable at having to lie to Maria, but it was part of the role he had agreed to play, and the lie was small. Jack sent the email.

"How's Petra?" said Maria.

"She was resting when I left her. What happened in your ceremony?"

"I have an extraordinary son. We did the journey and he cracked the problem. 'Look deep inside yourself' is about DNA code again. But eight base code, not four base terrestrial code. When we understand what the eight bases are, we bring them to the gods, thereby bringing 'only what is needed.'"

"Non-terrestrial DNA?"

"Don't know where this is taking us."

"Next step?"

"We help Cliff figure out the bases."

Jack was sitting in an armchair with his laptop. He put the laptop on a side table, stood and went to her. "By the way, do you know how beautiful you are in the grip of a scientific puzzle?"

Maria smiled and held his hand. She led him back to his armchair and sat in one next to it. They were all tired. She chatted with Jack until he dropped off into a light doze.

Maria looked over at Jack. She wondered where she wanted to go with him. He was reliable, even doggedly so. He was bright, handsome and wealthy. Yet he had none of Akira's fire. Nor the appealing tang of cad that Wolfgang had about him, nor the mystery and power of Mustapha.

Maria remembered Nietzsche's line that marriage is ninety percent conversation, and smiled to herself. Maybe daily life was better with dads than cads.

She looked over at Jack in his improbably perfect khakis and tried to imagine him fitting into her life in Berkeley. The picture did not come easily. She tried to imagine herself in Chicago, in a Frank Lloyd Wright house with Jack, but soon left that stream of thought. Maria had let no man close since Akira's death. She had devoted herself to work and to Cliff.

Maria looked out the open hotel window into the dusty light of Cairo. A muezzin's voice drifted in as he called the faithful to prayer. The sadness in his voice again raised the loss of Akira. What had so upset him about black holes that his drinking became an invitation to death? Her great worry slid out into daylight: when Cliff inherited his father's brilliance, had he also inherited his shadow?

Jack woke from his doze. "Everything okay?"

It called her back. "Yes, Prince Charming," she laughed. The image that came to her mind, however, was not Jack as Prince Charming. It was Mustapha cloaked in his mystery and power, the High Priest of Karnak and Great Mage of Egypt.

Maria and Jack went to Cliff's room. They knocked and went in. Cliff was bent over his laptop. Maria watched Cliff's intensity. It was almost as if she were looking at Akira.

Petra entered without knocking. Maria saw Petra was startled to find her and Jack there.

"Oh, hi," said Petra. "I was looking for some company. Guess I found it." Petra walked over to Cliff. "Hi there."

"Hi." Cliff didn't look up.

"Like Wolfie, lost in a problem for hours," said Petra.

Petra smiled wanly, and Maria felt herself clenching. She knew from Petra's manner what she was planning. She would make her move on Cliff.

"Okay, genius, what do you have for us?" said Jack.

Cliff still did not look up from his screen. Maria thought ruefully that the one thing she shared with Petra was men who lost themselves in complex problems. She noticed that the laptop he was using was not his own.

"Where did that laptop come from?" Maria said.

"I decided to borrow Wolfgang's. It's superfast. I thought it would run my pattern software better, and it does."

"I thought it was a good idea too," said Petra.

Maria did not like the way that Petra's tone had become proprietary over both Wolfgang and Cliff.

"All this is actually beginning to make sense," Cliff said. "I started by downloading papers on novel amino acid building blocks for DNA. I read them. Some help. There's a lot of chemistry trying to build alternative nucleic acids, and people have been modifying the bases, the sugars, the backbone. But none of them works very well. Also there are too many possibilities, no good way to prioritize—and we only get one chance. The four terrestrial bases work so sweetly I decided to keep them. So I went back to the vision. Remember the dance? We haven't used it yet. Remember how the gods stopped halfway through and then danced a mirror image of what came before?"

"I guess I didn't see it was a mirror image," said Maria.

"Well it was, guaranteed. Anyhow it gave me a clue."

"So where are you headed?" said Jack.

"Here's the deal. We've got four terrestrial bases. The DNA they make all spirals in a right handed way. You could make it spiral left. It's called chirality, molecules being right or left handed.

All terrestrial DNA is right handed, though no one knows why. Change direction of rotation to left and it should work just as sweetly. Complementary but different. With right handed DNA you can make anything alive on Earth. With DNA spinning in both directions, who knows what else? We've got our solution."

"Makes sense to me," Maria said.

"Then time for dinner," said Jack.

"Let's see if this dump can pump out a decent pizza!" said Cliff.

"And some Jack and Coke," said Petra.

"You trying to corrupt me again?"

Maria felt herself sigh.

"The price of brilliance," said Petra.

They agreed to convene for dinner after freshening. Because this meant engaging with their laptops for Cliff and Jack, the two women were ready first.

Maria walked out onto the veranda of the Al Minah. She found Petra reading *The Egyptian Gazette*, the Cairo English language daily. It was laid out for guests along with *The Herald Tribune, Le Monde,* and *The Financial Times.*

"What's in the news?" Maria said.

"The Egyptian government is cracking down on Islamist groups. Reports of The Islamic Foundation infiltrating government agencies."

"These crackdowns happen here periodically."

"I was just reading about the shooting of all the tourists at the Temple of Hatshepsut. Never heard of that. Pretty scary," said Petra still looking at the paper.

"That was a long time ago. Nothing like it has happened since."

"Makes you feel less safe."

Maria wanted to probe Petra's relationship with Cliff. It would be hard to do it skillfully. This was as good a time as any. "About Cliff," said Maria.

Petra folded the paper and put it down. She lowered her head and looked at Maria as if ready to charge. "What about him?"

"He's still very young." How else could she say it?

"Look," said Petra, angry. "Why don't you take your cross-generational hots somewhere else? Why don't you go get yourself serviced by Mustapha?"

Maria was taken aback. "Just who are you?"

"A woman like you. In a world where we're put down for it. We women need to take what we need."

Maria was at a loss about how to respond to this manifesto. Her concern for Cliff was hardly alleviated. Anger at Petra's crudeness was mixed with admiration for her pluck. Maria was relieved when Cliff and Jack, arriving together, came onto the veranda.

After dinner, Cliff and Petra were on their second Jack and Coke. Maria drank Chartreuse. She let her feelings about Petra steep in its vapors.

Mustapha arrived in his white linen suit. He sat his panama and cane on a side table.

"Good evening friends. Let me introduce my associates Ibrahim and Abdul. When Ibrahim is not a priest, he is a chemistry professor at the university, working with DNA. I thought he might help in our preparations. Abdul is my Assistant High Priest, with a role in our security service. You may need to know him as events unfold."

Maria appraised Ibrahim, and found the calm that comes from confidence in one's talents. Ibrahim and Mustapha sat.

Abdul remained standing. Maria studied him. The Assistant High Priest displayed none of the gravity and composure of Mustapha. Abdul seemed nervous, almost shifty. His glances at Petra were not appreciative but disapproving.

Petra noticed the glances too, and decided to investigate. There was an empty chair near her. "Abdul, why don't you sit down?" she said with a smile. She was used to men taking every opportunity to be near her. Abdul shook his head, and waved his hand dismissively.

He moved further away from Petra. She decided he represented the worst streak of Islamic macho. Maybe the kind of twisted Islamist she had just been reading about in the paper. What other kind of man would treat her this way?

Cliff was bringing Mustapha up to date on his new theory. Maria turned her attention to him.

"So you believe this set of chemical compounds is 'what is needed'?" said Mustapha.

"Yes," said Cliff. Maria nodded agreement.

"I had no doubt our charmed semi-circle would find the key. Write out what you need. Ibrahim will obtain it tonight."

Cliff scribbled out the list and handed it to Ibrahim. "When you've got this stuff, we can cook ourselves up an alien."

Ibrahim stood to leave, and Abdul accompanied him. Mustapha ordered a mineral water. He sipped. The Nile flowed north to the sea. "I welcome tomorrow," he said.

"How do we get in?" said Cliff. "The slab slammed shut."

"I know a way. Let us meet there tomorrow at five."

"Mustapha," said Jack, "Before this goes any further, I have to be the skunk at the party. My gut says you'd be a fool to go ahead with this. You don't know what you're getting into here. What you may be unleashing. The results could be devastating to the world. You've been sucked into the excitement of the game, solving all the puzzles. But Wolfgang is already dead. If you march in there tomorrow, you may wind up dead too, not to mention the rest of us."

"Jack, for me there is no question. I must to go ahead tomorrow. I deeply trust the Egyptian gods. They are coming back to heal not destroy. I am sure of it, though their cure may be painful. The world is suffering. The gods are asking that we invite them back. How can I do anything else? If I must die, I do so willingly. For the rest of you, you must make your own decision."

"I'm in," said Cliff.

"Me too," said Maria. "Jack, I know your concerns are real. What is happening here, though, is too important. We can't walk away from it."

Jack shook his head, knowing he was not going to change anyone's mind.

Mustapha took his leave.

Maria and Jack left, still talking.

"I think they're getting together," Cliff said.

"Maria and Mustapha?"

"No! Mom and Jack."

"Maybe. How would that make you feel?"

"Okay. She needs someone and I like him."

"How about us?"

"How about us what?"

"Getting together?"

"You don't lose any time."

Petra's flinch was brief and ended in a smile.

Petra felt how vulnerable Cliff was. She could use her anger to dominate him. Or she could let her tenderness forward. Petra put her anger aside for now. She needed intimacy to fill her loss.

She lay in the bed in his room. She had undressed quickly. As he took his clothes off, she saw that every one of his familiar gestures had become something new to him because she was watching. He lay on his side looking at her. She followed his eyes as they moved to the snake tattooed across her shoulders. She felt his eagerness and nervousness.

"Okay smart boy, we need to get you out of your head." She reached over and gently stroked his right nipple. He sighed. She stroked both his nipples and kissed him lightly.

He gasped at the unexpected pleasure, then offered mirroring caresses. She lay back and enjoyed him over her. As she felt him relax into arousal she reached down to bring him in.

Petra lay quiet after. The intimacy she needed was beginning, and she held onto it like a mezzo holding a velvet note until it finds a natural silence. When Petra returned to herself, she found she was crying. She opened her eyes to find him crying too.

She brushed his tears away. "What do you have to cry about, hmm?"

"I guess I thought this might never happen to me."

Petra smiled through her own tears.

"What about you?" he said.

"Sorrow and happiness mixed up together. Losing Wolfie hurts. A lot. But maybe the reason I came here was to meet you. That's the happy part."

They lay quietly together.

"So Jose, what's the deal?" It was noon in the vice president's office.

"Night over there. They're putting up some sort of a tent over the Sphinx Temple site, the kind they use at archaeological digs. Big one."

"Clever."

"Our main operative is a casualty."

"Got backup?"

"I've just gotten a full report from our second man." Jose had doubts about how reliable his second man was, but kept them to himself.

"Orbital battle platform ready?"

"Yes, it is."

"Operational control?"

Jose reassured the vice president. Then he paused at the Rose Garden on his way back to the State Department. Pacing, he set the events at Giza within his framework of meaning. Chaotic situations were dangerous opportunities. He would take any actions necessary to protect the interests of his country. He would also keep his eye on the opportunity. It was not for his good alone but for the good of all Americans that Jose nursed presidential ambitions.

Benben came around.

"What news, worm?"

"I've been busily plugged into our network. Things are hotting up. I'd say we might want to insert in another four or five hours. And Musty, I am tired of him. Ever pretentious, getting worse."

"Don't worry darling. He can't help it. Just the way he is."

"You're awfully forgiving today."

"You know how preparing for battle always puts me in a good mood. Did you say four or five hours?"

"It's what my little head says."

"Then how about one more squirt into my head from your little tail?"

Part III

Bridge of Dreams

Suddenly the mystery...became perfectly clear. It was just like looking at the palm of my hand. The rhinoceros of doubt instantly fell down dead and I could scarcely bear the joy of it.

—Hakuin Zenji

43

The Sphinx Temple at 4.30 a.m. The press and the gathering crowd were behind security lines and away from the black metal slab, which now sealed off the stela chamber. The capacious khaki-colored tent that Mustapha had set up covered the site. Mustapha was inside with Ibrahim and a handful of security guards, all acolytes of Karnak in Exile. He had changed into his priestly vestments. The gold pectoral collar and great breastplate were in place. Ibrahim assembled the staff of electrum and handed it to him.

The others arrived and Mustapha greeted them. Ibrahim held a gold offering tray. Sitting on it somewhat incongruously were not flowers or meat or wine, but eight neatly labeled plastic vials. They held two sets of the chemicals that they thought constituted what the gods needed for whatever they had in mind. Mustapha hoped that they had got it right. This stage of the puzzle was even more outside his realm than sending the robot up the shaft in the pyramid. He simply had to trust his team and hoped they had all accessed the right inspiration.

Mustapha advanced to the slab of transhuman metal that sealed the stela chamber. The others were behind him.

He lifted his staff, and the ankh at its tip glowed with blue light. He thumped the black metal with the base of the staff. The sound propagated strangely through the slab, first amplified then dying quickly away. Then he beat a second and third time. He waited for the sounds to die away, and intoned a melodious spell in the ancient tongue.

The slab responded by sliding open about two meters, plenty of space to enter. Holding his staff high, Mustapha descended into the stela's blue light, and the others followed.

They stood before the stela and Mustapha read out the final stanza of its admonition:

O Humans, your time of testing is coming to you,
O Humans, without our help you will not survive.
Call upon us now.

Mustapha made a quiet prayer, then led them around to the corridor that would bring them to the gods. Surmounting the corridor were the red hieroglyphs burning bright. Mustapha read:

I am the Gate of life and death
I am End and Beginning
Let no one enter this mystery

"But here the text has changed. It used to say '*whose heart is heavier than the feather of Maat*'. Now it says"

Unless they are ready to give
This world back to the gods.

Mustapha turned and faced them to make his dispositions. "Jack, I appreciate you coming, despite your reservations. Please stay here with Petra. Ibrahim, give the offering tray to Cliff. He has seen into 'that which is needed', so he will assist me in making the offerings. You stay here as rear guard. Cliff, let me show you how to hold the tray. Raise it to just above the level of your eyes. Good. Now follow me, and Maria, you come third."

The procession moved down the corridor. Cliff held the tray above his eyes as instructed. It let him see where he was going. That was not his worry, however, as he headed down the corridor.

Last time he had made it through the place where Wolfgang died. He survived because of his purity of heart, according to Mustapha.

Since then Cliff had made love to Petra. It was his first experience. It was thrilling. It also brought guilt: Wolfgang's death was fresh. Had he dishonored him? Cliff had also coveted Wolfgang's laptop supercomputer. He now used it. Had he ever wished Wolfgang dead and out of the way? How did his purity of heart rate now? He wondered if he would make it through.

As he approached the place where Wolfgang got stuck, Cliff braced himself. What did Wolfgang feel when he got stuck? Was it sticky? He expected to run into something like a giant spider web. It was hard to balance the tray. Then he was through. He breathed deep and hoped that Maria, following him, had noticed nothing.

Mustapha walked silently this time, admiring the bright paintings and bas-reliefs of the gods and scenes from ancient Egypt fresh as day. They came to the end of the corridor, and the courtyard of the temple Amun-Ra had called into being. Mustapha had a feeling of dislocation, as if they were not underneath the Sphinx, but under the blazing turquoise sky of Egypt, and the gods had brought them to a reality tangent to our own.

The gods awaited them, tall and radiant before the closed metal gates in the high pylon.

Flanked by Cliff and Maria, Mustapha addressed the gods. "We have looked deeply within ourselves and brought only what is needed. We will offer it to you now."

The gods said nothing. They waited, wearing hieratic smiles and holding their empty golden bowls.

Cliff said softly, "Is there some order we need to do this in?"

"Does your knowledge suggest any?"

"Only that the chemical bases work in pairs. The pairs can follow any order."

"Let us follow your rule of pairs then. There is a parallel in the Ennead. While Amun-Ra stands apart, the eight who await our offerings are also paired."

Mustapha motioned for Cliff to come with him. They approached the gods together. Mustapha felt each movement of his body with the utmost precision. There was a heightened clarity in this experience, and Mustapha let himself wish that life might always be like this.

Mustapha approached Shu and Tefnut, the Creator's children. The Dry and the Wet, they brought an end to Chaos. Shu wore an ostrich plume upon his head, and Tefnut a solar disk. Cliff handed Mustapha the first pair of chemicals. The gods reached down their golden bowls to accept Mustapha's offering.

He went next to their children. To their son Geb the Earth and their daughter Nut the Sky. Geb wore a simulacrum of his sacred goose upon his head, and Nut a water-carrying pot. They reached down gracefully to receive the offerings.

Mustapha went next to their daughter Isis, mistress of life, and their son Osiris, lord of the dead. Isis wore a solar disk over cow horns upon her head, and Osiris the *atef*, the white crown of Upper Egypt flanked by striated plumes. They lowered their golden bowls to receive the offering.

The fourth pair of gods were Mut, the Great Mother, and Khonsu, her son with the Creator. She bore the double crown, and he wore his lunar disk and crescent. They received their offerings graciously.

When Mustapha and Cliff came before Amun-Ra they realized they had nothing to offer him.

Before Mustapha could apologize, the Creator spoke. "You have done well." The god's voice was more delightful to their ears than the first taste of chocolate to a child's tongue. "You have brought only that which is needed. Now we will use the gifts to invite forth Him Who Is To Come."

Amun-Ra turned to the great gates of black metal and raised his hand. The doors responded by swinging open silently. Through the open gate Mustapha saw the temple's inner courtyard, open to the sky. Its plan looked like Karnak but the scale was wrong. Karnak itself was built to a monumental scale meant to induce awe, with pillars ten times the height of a man. The scale here was altogether different. It had no reference to the human frame at all. Long after Karnak was built, the Greeks would say that 'man is the measure of all things'. In this temple where the pillars were ten times as high as Karnak's, man was the measure of nothing. Maria imagined herself a fly in a house. Cliff imagined himself a lizard on the Great Pyramid.

"Who is this made for?" said Cliff.

"I don't know," said Maria, "but we'll need to look up when we talk to him."

Amun-Ra walked through the high pylon gate. In pairs, the gods followed, moving at a stately pace. Mustapha, with only a momentary hesitation, joined the procession. Maria and Cliff looked at each other and followed Mustapha.

Inside the courtyard double rows of pillars stretched before them, the pillars soaring as tall as a sixty storey building.

Maria said, "I don't see how stone pillars could ever be so high. It doesn't make sense. And I sure don't see how all of this can be under the rump of the Sphinx."

"Only one way out," said Cliff. "The gods must be able to make a parallel universe. Maybe the stela is a black hole generator, I don't know. But we're not in Kansas anymore."

"Parallel universe?" said Mustapha.

"If you could open one, you could change the rules, build stone pillars tall as skyscrapers. The normal rules don't apply here."

"Let us see which ones do," said Mustapha.

They followed the procession of the gods across the courtyard and up a ramp into the hypostyle hall, a forest of colossal pillars roofed over. It was darker, the darkness of a forest whose high canopy absorbs most of the light. Entering the hypostyle hall brought a foreboding. The world they were entering was yet more alien with less possibility of escape.

The procession made its way through the hall and finally approached the holy of holies, the shrine at the temple's heart.

Mustapha spoke to ease the strangeness. "Egyptian temples are unlike modern places of worship. They are homes of the gods.

Normal people never entered. Lay priests would enter on certain feast days, but the rest of the time only those who were fully consecrated. In the most important shrine rooms, only the pharaoh and the high priest were allowed."

They watched as the procession of the gods crossed the threshold and disappeared within. When they tried to follow, they felt a buzzing tingle as they approached the threshold. Mustapha used his staff as a probe. He angled it forward. When its base touched the threshold, sparks flew and he could push it no further. They were disbarred.

"Not even the High Priest gets in this time," said Maria.

"They have no need for one in there," said Mustapha.

Looking in, they could see it was a shrine room like no other. No statues were present, nor any images. A great stone basin dominated the room. Its size suggested that the gods had decreed a sarcophagus for something the size of a mountain. Next to it, like a bee next to an elephant, lay a small open sarcophagus, human sized.

"What happens now, Mustapha?" said Cliff.

"We can only stand and wait."

Amun-Ra stood at the head of the great stone basin, the gods flanking him. And then the gods began to dance. Holding their golden bowls high, they danced in pairs, weaving a helical pattern. The dithyrambic dance of the gods twisted away from the Creator, around the edge of the great basin.

"The dance in our vision," said Cliff.

"Yes," said Mustapha quietly, engaged in watching the gods.

The first born of the Creator, born of his seed directly, born to help shape the world, creating existence out of emptiness, Shu and Tefnut danced. They were the eternal Light and Dark, Dry and Wet. It was they who brought an end to primordial Chaos and fashioned the coherence and security in which the rest of life might come to be. Now they danced the dance of creation once more. Their children Geb the Earth and Nut the Sky danced. They were the gods who brought forth the fullness of life in this world from their own loins and hearts in the peace that came when Chaos was vanquished. Now they danced the dance of creation once more. Their children Isis and Osiris danced, who cared for human life on this Earth and in the land of the dead, the pair who guided each human life through the intimate experience of life and death. Now they danced the dance of creation once more. Mut and Khonsu danced. She was the eternal Mother of All Things, the generating principle and the repository of universal trust, and he was her son by the Creator, symbol of the Creator's presence in the human world. Now they danced the dance of creation once more. Each pair circled each other and weaved among the other pairs, a helix snaking around the great stone basin. The Great Ennead danced. The powers that called this world out of emptiness, caused life to flourish, and nurtured humankind. Now they danced the dance of creation once more.

They danced around the basin until they returned to Amun-Ra. He raised both hands in power and blessing. Pair by pair the gods poured the contents of their golden bowls into the basin, commingling the letters of life's alphabet.

"Since this was like the dance from our vision," said Cliff, "what about the staircase up to the world of the gods?"

"Whatever the gods are making," said Mustapha, "will become that staircase."

Standing on the threshold, Mustapha, Cliff, and Maria strained to see what was happening in the stone basin. At first they could see nothing, only feel a stirring within themselves. It was like hope rising in their hearts, like fish pressing against the sea in which they swam. It was their dream of a world without suffering mounting layer by layer closer to reality.

Fear was also present, the fear that pervades liminal moments, when one approaches a threshold of change that threatens to sweep away the known. It was fear born of a cellular suspicion that what comes would be less comfortable than the familiar suffering.

The gods now also waited and watched. Their smiles showed their anticipation was unmitigated by fear. They were overseeing creation again.

Suddenly the light dimmed as if birth demanded a share of darkness. Whatever grew in the basin knew how to suck the light and energy of the world to create itself.

A mist appeared in the basin and rose above it. Colors cycled rapidly through the spectrum. Slowly, forms emerged: geometric solids, animals, human faces, all rising into perception then sinking into the mist, replaced by others. More and more quickly the images shifted as if the mist were a huge brain thinking thoughts at once made visible.

The images moved like visual music through every form of life that had emerged on Earth and many that had not. Bacteria and apes and dinosaurs passed by, morphing into impossible monsters in twelve dimensions, things from the nightmares of mathematicians gone mad.

The cascade of improbables faded. The mist became purplish. It grew dense from within, as if the gods had charged it with universal possibility and it was now settling down to choosing a discrete physical expression. Waves moved through, disturbing its density to the extremity of the basin. Whatever it would become, it would be gigantic, the thing that this mountain sized temple was scaled to.

Cliff stood on the threshold, his eyes shiny with eagerness. He caught Mustapha's hand, the first time he had ever touched him. He said, "Will you teach me magic? I want to devote the rest of my life to it!"

Mustapha turned to him. "Cliff, the only true magic flows from a pure heart. You have one. Guard it. Let yourself ripen. We can work together. We must also see what magic means after this great unfolding." He squeezed Cliff's hand.

44

Coiled around her neck, he nibbled her right ear. "I've been keeping track and it's still getting hotter down there."

"Time for my big entrance?" Benben stretched, languid as a big cat before the hunt, avid as a diva about to break hearts. She looked around at the walls and floors slick with red, and the warm soft furniture peristatically pulsing. What other decorating scheme could ever seem so cozy? "Hard to bestir oneself from happy atavisms, but there is work to do."

"Worlds to dominate."

"Chaos to sow."

"Fun to be had at the expense of others."

"The code of the parasite. Now on to battle plans. I go in first, projecting myself as Seth. Maximum disruption of the game being played under the Sphinx's butt."

"I adore your *mise en scene.* But how will you find the right spot to project into? And what of your faithful worm?"

"Let's talk about me. Our henchman Abdul will serve as my beacon. It's why I've been cultivating him. I've entangled his mind with mine, so I can find it."

"Isn't he more of a guttering candle than a beacon?"

"No worse than most humans. His mind is crude, unable to appreciate the fluid subtleties of my malice. So the little thing's brain knots up whenever he feels my touch, and he wants to murder the nearest thing to hand."

"Vibrant."

"It opens possibilities for later on."

"Parties come to mind. We take a group of friends on safari—why not a little business! We entangle human minds and use them to hunt other humans with a range of horrifying weapons. We enjoy the experience of the hunters from inside. I suppose a race descended from a prey species might want the thrill of entering the minds of the hunted."

"More parasitically still, we go into deep entanglement and peel down a human mind aptitude by aptitude, defense by defense, memory by memory until nothing remains but carrion."

"It's the sporting life for me."

"Play later, brainworm, now back to work. I'll use Abdul as my beacon. He expects to see me as a figure from the life of his Prophet, my way of keeping his attention focused."

"I thought you were going in as Seth."

"I am. I toyed with the idea of making the projection polyvalent so those who believed in the Prophet would see him. But it would require greater concentration to hold the polyvalency across the branes, and I need to have all my powers at my disposal. Better to play the main game. Besides, I don't mind disappointing Abdul. I have no use for him except as beacon."

"And I try to follow you."

"My wake will sparkle. I go in as Seth, whose bad manners got him bounced out of the Ennead. Seth the scourge of the desert, bringer of death and destruction. The elemental force they've tried to exclude. Seth the overturner of civilizations, the personification of entropy, the one who always wins in the end."

Wanre scratched the back of his head. Toran had just brought him up to date on Benben and Bulbul's plans.

"Will you still go in?"

"I have to. We don't really understand what is happening at Giza, the only such anomaly in the Multiverse. It's too important to let her disrupt it."

"Can you stop her?"

"I have a chance. Before battle, isn't that the best one can hope?"

He had learned to read the expression in her unblinking hawk eyes. They offered few clues. He often reflected that species that had not co-evolved, or at least evolved in homologous ecosystems, could never easily share non-verbal cues to inner states. Bringing himself back, he sensed her unease.

"I'll be all right. My body will be safe here. I am a match for her."

"How will you find your way in?"

"I'll follow her. She'll be too preoccupied to notice my light."

"What avatar will you use?"

"You say she will be Seth. Who does that make me?"

"I'm not sure about going in as Nephthys," said Bulbul. "I've been reading up on her, and the old girl wasn't all bad."

"Look, I have a game to play. If you want to tag along, fine. But this is more than a costume party."

"Oh all right." It was never possible to win an argument with her, and it made him peevish. "Nephthys it is."

"Let's begin." They lay down on a warm red couch. "Before I start scouting gravity waves, I have to turn on our beacon's hot little brain."

"How did you entangle our henchman? I didn't see you do it. As far as I know entanglement takes proximity. 'Nearer my love to thee' sort of thing."

"Clever wriggler. I slipped away one day while you were passed out, did a quick surf, and groped Abdul's brain."

"But you could have killed yourself without a beacon, not to mention leaving your poor worm bereft."

"It was a thrill darling, and you love me for more than my brain chemicals."

He was happy to go back to his hunger. "Yummy as those are."

"It's safer now I've laid the way. And good to know this girl's up to the most dangerous rides."

"Benben the Outlaw Branerunner. Tasty. Mind if I have a little old hook-up?"

"No time, playmate. But here's another game. We should each visualize a fantasy before we go in. Its imprint on the aether will help us find our way back. So where does your fancy take you?"

"Same as ever."

"You're in a crowd."

"A crowd of mixed sentient species. I have magic wings so I can fly just above their heads like a little white dragon. I move from head to head at leisure. In each one that appeals to me I drill a hole in the top, attach my hungry hind segment and sample the wares. I drink them according to whim until each brain is dry."

"Silly really that the Consilium doesn't allow such pleasures. Most people would be better off if you had your way with them."

"Bureaucracy is the enemy of refinement." He sighed heavily. "And you my dear? You're carrying a knife."

"In a foreign city. I meet strangers of all ages. Virile men, old women, children. I slice each of them up slowly. I observe within myself the passion of our race for nurturing ourselves on the suffering of others. I am not helpless to stop myself, but I am a traditionalist." She came out of her fantasy. "Maybe our kind gave up too much to melt into the Consilium."

"I have a nostalgia for the old ways too. What a nice couple we make."

"You just relax while I turn on the beacon. It'll take a few minutes."

She focused on Abdul in another universe. She saw his apartment, and got a feel once more for being inside his mind. Bulbul had argued that once she was inside it, it was no longer 'Abdul's' mind. More pragmatic, Benben enjoyed the feel of being human, hardwired as an aggressive carnivorous ape. She sensed the human impulse to love locally and hate globally and to resolve all disputes by murder. Humans were so much like the children of her species. They would be putty in her hands. She looked out of Abdul's eyes and saw his wife lying next to him. It was dawn and Abdul was still dreaming behind half closed lids. She entered his dream.

Abdul was walking through the souk in medieval Cairo. Its sights and sounds were lurid. All the women smiled at him, a foretaste of the houris that would reward him in paradise. All the mullahs showed him the reverence he deserved. She decided he was having too much fun. She needed to heat her beacon up. Abdul was an open book that she would edit.

Benben made Abdul feel under his cloak until he found a scimitar. He took it out and tested the edge with his thumb. It was like a razor. He felt the heft and balance of the weapon. He concealed it under his cloak again. The next time they passed a mullah, he acted. When the mullah bowed, he kneed him in the chin. When he fell, he grabbed his beard and slit his throat.

Abdul woke in a panic. His heart raced, sweat poured from his armpits. He looked at his wife and understood he had just awoken. He did not remember the dream, but felt hot shame before his mullahs. He would have to do something for them to expiate the shame, something important. What? The mullahs worried that Mustapha would hand their heritage to the West. He would make sure it did not happen.

Benben stirred.

"Beacon switched on?"

"Woken up."

"Will there be collateral damage?"

"A little mayhem is seldom a bad thing. Now relax, empty your mind and I'll look for a good wave."

A good gravity wave is hard to find. Before she could scout one, she had to climb a psychic hill: Mount Fear. She knew that the fear of losing control would have to be surmounted. From the moment she caught a gravity wave until the moment she re-entered her body she would be surrendering much of the control she usually had. She would be vulnerable. Her gravity wave could fail and strand her. She could fall into the flesh and forget to return to her real body. There were many ways to wander off into the funhouse of the Multiverse. She would be attacked on Earth, one of the greatest temptations to overidentifying with the robe of flesh she would wear.

Looking at her vulnerability, she summoned her will. Like a splendid fierce warhorse coming to its master's call, her will arose. It entered her consciousness adamantine. Like prehensile armor for her actions, it would ground her purpose. Like lead shielding for a sensitive instrument, it would protect her mind from outside influence. She explored the contours of her will as a veteran checks his shield and sword. Well satisfied, she passed over Mount Fear. She knew Bulbul would have a harder time with it, but that he would surmount it too.

Time to start the countdown. She focused her awareness fully on her body. She felt her body fall into the couch immobile with heaviness, appreciating the gravity she usually ignored. She would need to feel the local gravity clearly before detecting the ripple of a gravity wave. Such a ripple is a difference most subtle, almost intangible. This subtlety was the greatest challenge to the old solo ops and remained so for branerunners. Some early branerunners let their bodies bloat. Their corpulence amplified gravity's fine structure, and the body, after all, was left behind on the ride.

Aware, relaxed, open, Benben waited for a wave. "It's not coming easily, worm."

He had just emerged from his fear. "Try lying on your right side. It seems to work better for you."

"Then you come around so I don't crush you if I roll over."

She turned and he wriggled around to face her. She held him like a fireman holds a pole. They could not ride brain to hind section as they would prefer because it might cause too much crosstalk between their nervous systems. They could nevertheless be reassuringly close. Bulbul kissed Benben's nose. It was a gesture the young of their species use to cause a parent to regurgitate food. In an adult it potently signified nervousness. He was not as skilled a branerunner as she.

He would follow her on the same wave. She would be his beacon, making his ride much safer and easier than if he were on his own. She opened her eyes and looked into his, centimeters away.

"Ready for another gay adventure?"

"Want to get tweaked first? Just a little tweak to boost your serotonin, get more confidence and clarity?"

"No, best stay at baseline. Got your avatar clear?"

He checked. He had been practicing the necessary visualizations. When his mind arrived at Giza, he would need to project his avatar by reflex to call forth his robe of flesh. Though not as deft as Benben, he was good: they were among the only branerunners left in the Multiverse who could summon the flesh.

She taunted him. "You wouldn't want to wander off and inhabit a hippo." He was vain about his figure.

"Cobra more likely." The banter loosened his jitters. "Got it. Nephthys, my very own Queen of the Night."

"Away we go!"

Her eyes closed and he sensed her mind and will focus. He closed his eyes and searched for her light. He found it in his field, a luminous red. Comforted by her color, he breathed and relaxed. He was on the starting line waiting for her gun.

Aware of the local gravity, Benben focused her mind, pulling its tendrils out of all parts of her body until it was concentrated in the head alone. She placed her awareness at the crown, at the hole where Bulbul attached. Using her will, she pushed her mind up out of her body. She was poised: if she pushed her mind out further she would die, if she caught a gravity wave she would ride.

She felt a gravity wave and it was fine. She caught it and pushed into it. She became one with it. Until her will disengaged her, the wave now *was* her mind. The wave carried everything in her mind as minor perturbations in its flow. Perturbations that could pass instantly through branes, crossing universe to universe as light could never do. She was now pure mind and will, transcending the constraints of matter.

It was delicious. Every species that braneruns loves this moment, and describes its sensations in images centering on fulfillment and liberation as they are encoded in the oldest brain strata of the species. For Benben it was as if an entire universe became a juicy host body for her larval stage to burrow into, its vital fluids made poignant by fear flooding in to fill her body gone universal in size. The ultimate triumph of the parasite and satisfaction beyond the wildest dreams of lust or avarice.

This intoxicating moment must be kept short for it is a dangerous one. Dwell in it too long and the will relaxed. The branerunner would forget it was a game and would ride the wave until their body in their home universe wasted away and died. It is believed that at this moment of death, the mind loses touch with the pleasure. When the body dies, most scholars believe the mind dissolves to reorganize at a higher level. Others believe the mind lives through eternity in empty longing like a hungry ghost. The smallest contingent believes that the pleasure itself becomes universal and you can feel it for the duration of the Multiverse. Some from this faction have chosen to ride this way. But they cannot, even in principle, report back on whether they win the argument.

These thoughts flashed through Bulbul's mind as cautions while he waited to shove off. He put them aside and sent his mind up through the crown of his head leaving his body, like Benben's, vegetative and vulnerable until they returned to reclaim them.

He saw Benben's light move forward and catch the wave. He must now move fast, and catch the wave at the speed of thought.

Bulbul moved, connected, felt the merger bliss and taste of satisfaction. After a brief delight he recalled it was a trap, and focused his will on her red light.

Wanre lay on a simple couch. The floor was covered with mats of woven grass. The window looked onto a pool backed by trees. In his own quarters he could live as he wished.

Saiki sat on a chair next to him. She touched his forehead, then rested her hands on her knees. She was helping Wanre visualize the avatar he would call as his robe of flesh. If she could not prevent his branerun, she could at least help.

"I've got it," he said.

A chime sounded. "Just in time. That means they're set to go."

Wanre wanted to chase Benben and Bulbul across the branes rather than ride his own wave. It was dangerous. He might get lost with no hope of return, as Benben would be the one to bend the wave. They might find and destroy him. But waves were unpredictable. If he waited for the next one, she might spawn chaos on Earth before he could stop her.

Wanre hoped to view Benben's mental landscape secretly while it was spread out along the wave, something he could only do if he was with her. If he went undetected, seeing into her could give him the advantage he needed.

The chase would also let him enjoy his virtuosity. To ride the same wave, even with team effort, was extremely difficult. No records existed of anyone riding in hostile pursuit, as he planned, and surviving.

"Come back safe."

"Under your orders, ma'am." He returned her smile and closed his eyes.

He quickly negotiated the fear. It was something he met in his practice every day, so it held no challenge. He pushed up through the crown of his head and prepared to leave his body behind.

She was riding again! Benben felt wild joy, dangerous fun beyond the constraints of matter. She moved at light speed but without light's constraints. For the few who could do it, outriding was the best feeling in the Multiverse.

Alone and naked, mind and will could move with complete clarity at light speed and jump from brane to brane, universe to universe. Because of the brain you left at home you felt physically present. At the same time you were ephemeral, pure information encoded in the perturbations of the wave you merged with. You felt no fear of anything in the Multiverse.

No fear in passing through galactic centers with stars so densely packed no life could thrive. Benben shot the rapids of the gravity wells around the largest stars, tasting the heat of nuclear fusion and its metallic tang.

Nothing was impossible for her; there was nowhere she could not go. She was a god. Easy seduction for those whose will ebbed in a cosmic joyride they would never leave. Joyriding Benben too felt the pull, the temptation to let the will slide, put aside all thought of embodied Benben, and merge with the gravity wave forever.

She let herself enjoy the temptation. She enjoyed all temptations, and enjoyed best beating them.

"Not yet," said her will. "You must remain differentiated to accomplish your fell purpose." It was time to bend the gravity wave to that purpose.

Her joyride had been in her home universe, the pond the gravity wave was rippling through. She must now cross several branes to reach the universe Earth resided in. Once merged with it, she could refocus the gravity wave by sheer force of will.

Though the branes were only centimeters apart, an entire universe bestrode each one. Between the branes lay hyperspace, a plenum of higher dimensions. The Consilium's scholars had deduced fourteen dimensions beyond the four that embodied beings felt in their home universes.

When a branerunner surfed between branes they experienced these extra fourteen dimensions. Benben knew the experience would be shattering. She scanned for her Earth beacon, fixed on him, and prepared to refocus the wave.

When she left the brane her mind went wide with ice. The entire universe heaved up as her mind's horizon and froze as if dipped in liquid nitrogen. She felt raw pain, scalding fear, and full body orgasm combined. She shattered.

She became more complex than the four dimensional Benben of everyday. There were fourteen extra dimensions like a Cubist hologram in pure consciousness beyond the realm of thought.

This was a new danger point. Some branerunners entered a multiple schizoid madness here. These ones should never have stepped beyond a joyride on their home brane. Like a mirror smashed, they fractured with no hope of mending, mind and will not strong enough to hold onto a unitary consciousness under the relentless pressure of hyperspace.

Benben held together. In another moment she tumbled down from eighteen dimensions into the familiar four. She still felt brane chill in her mind but here it was a comfort, a sign she had perdured.

She looked around at the universe she was in, noted that there were no spiral galaxies in this one, and prepared for another jump. She would have to cross four more branes to reach Earth. She would freeze-shatter-reform, freeze-shatter-reform until she got there. Her Earth sojourn, whatever dangers it brought, would provide a respite from having her consciousness dealt out like a tarot pack, until she made her way home.

She checked to see if Bulbul had followed her through the first jump. His glowworm light was present to her, so he must have reassembled. She could count on his addiction to her brain juices to carry him through.

She ran the branes to Earth's universe and was soon in Earth space. She scanned again for her beacon. He would stand out like a star on the surface of Earth, as he had from across the branes. Because she had quantum entangled him, a portion of his mind was in synch with hers, had become hers. Her fantasies were his nightmares. Abdul's mind offered a reflection of herself. When she looked across the branes and found her beacon, it was she who welcomed herself across.

Bulbul had followed well by focusing on the bright red light of Benben. When she headed across the branes to Earth he felt some trouble. He was afraid he was losing her, but that was not it. So after his first brane crossing, he waited to reassemble, then looked behind. He thought he saw something in the distance, a white light. When he checked it from across another brane it looked like it was following them. Then he lost it. Was there something there? It should be impossible. He would have to tell Benben when they were safely at Giza.

Wanre caught sight of Benben and Bulbul's lights. They looked like a large and small star locked into a binary system and feeding off each other. As they pushed into the wave he followed.

The bliss of merger filled him. He knew its danger but let himself enjoy it, trusting his ability. For him merger bliss was a release into nothingness, pregnant with possibility, empty and open. He let his personality and its attachments fall away while he expanded into universal spaciousness. This wide-open comfort would come at death and he would welcome it.

Not yet though, he must not go there yet. He must follow through.

Putting temptation aside, he summoned his will and it came clear as a sharpened blade. He followed Benben's joyride, trying to stay clear of the suspicious Bulbul. They were not expecting to be followed and that was his best defense. He sheltered in their overconfidence.

The shattering at each brane crossing was for him like a long run, an icy dive, a strong drink. In each he found an aspect of himself.

Within every universe they crossed, he looked into her mental landscape. He caught the glimpses he needed and she did not see him, intent on her goal. Bulbul saw him once and Wanre got ready to destroy him. Otherwise the two of them would have him. Perhaps he could make Benben believe she had lost Bulbul on the run.

First though he would try a feint. Wanre hid his light. Bulbul lost him. The worm's concentration was not enough to follow Benben, track Wanre, and keep his own mind together all at once, so he let Wanre go.

As the three poised to enter Earth together, Wanre summoned his avatar. Then he allowed himself a moment to savor his mastery.

45

Abdul looked over at his wife with familiar tenderness. Her softness as she slept was an erotic perfume. He sensed her appeal like it was the first time, and it comforted him. He was about to awaken and take her, when an image—him breaking her neck—entered his mind. He felt gripped by the mandibles of the night.

He got out of bed. Though it was early, he would go to Giza and see what was happening. He would look for an opportunity to act. Getting dressed, he belted on the holster and pistol that he had a right to wear as one of the monument guards under Mustapha's orders as Director of the Supreme Council of Antiquities. The ten kilometers from his bed in medieval Cairo to Giza would be a wild mess of traffic in a few hours. Now the streets were relatively empty. He made good time in his old Citroen.

Abdul parked in an area reserved for staff and walked to the lighted tent stretched over the Sphinx Temple. He passed a white van parked nearby, the CNN action news truck where Hillary Holloway and her techs were taking catnaps in turn, waiting for a newsbreak.

Abdul entered the tent and greeted the guards on duty. They were all brothers in Karnak in Exile, all familiar. He inquired about the two men in his militant cell. They were off duty, would be back later in the morning.

Abdul approached the duty officer, who happened to be the man charged by Mustapha with keeping an eye on Abdul.

"What brings you here at this hour, Abdul?"

"I had trouble sleeping. I was worried about Mustapha and all the events taking place. So I thought I'd come back for some extra voluntary duty to safeguard our High Priest."

It was a good line but left doubts in the duty officer's mind. He sensed Abdul's agitation and suspected it might have less elevated origins. He decided not turn Abdul away, thinking it better to keep him in view.

"Mustapha and the others are below," he said, "and I plan to take a turn guarding the stela. Why don't you join me on the next watch?"

Abdul agreed and they walked down the monumental staircase. Abdul's agitation grew in the presence of the stela, whose admonition from the gods still suffused the chamber with its turquoise light.

Petra found herself once again waiting for a man. It had been Wolfgang in the pyramid, now it was Mustapha, with Cliff and Maria in tow. Petra sat on the floor of the stela chamber feeling chilly. She was wearing a short-sleeved shirt that let the tips of her snake tattoo poke out. To pass the time she studied the blue light from the stela, which gave everything a painterly quality. "Like de la Tour on neon," she mused.

Two sets of male legs appeared, headed down the staircase. The stela's light gave their blue gray uniforms a surreal luminescence. Petra wondered who the men would turn out to be, and whether they would help relieve the tedium.

The men's faces came into view. Petra was irritated to find that one of them was Abdul. She still felt snubbed by his behavior at the Al Minah, when she had offered him a seat.

When Abdul saw Petra, he gave a reflexive frown and looked away. It was as if she was offensive to him through the mere fact of being a woman. Home in Germany Petra had met lots of men who should learn to treat women better. She had never met one who appeared to have contempt for her on the basis of her sex alone.

The duty officer relieved the two guards in the chamber. Weary, they headed up and home, away from the action that would dominate global news later that same day. The officer greeted Jack and Petra, then took his position and stood at ease. Abdul paced, an animal penned by his feelings.

Petra's own feelings stormed around her mind and heart. Wolfgang was dead. How could he be so stupid? How could he throw his life away? She was enjoying him. She understood his ambition and could live with it. She was a painter. His sharp analytic mind was a good contrast to hers. Their sex was getting more interesting, unusual in this stage of a relationship for her. Why had Wolfie been such an idiot and thrown it all away?

Petra needed to uncoil. She stood and walked to the stone staircase. She put her right foot on the third step, stretched, and leaned into it. It felt good. She decided to do a light workout to pass the time. She changed legs and continued stretching, working through her routine.

The repetitive quality was familiar. She would like to be in her dojo now, the movements of aikido would have felt right. Aikido had guided her through tight places and rewarded her achievement with a black belt. The toughness of the training had empowered her to set up her women's art collective back home in Germany. She thought of her community of women artists with satisfaction. Who needed Wolfgang?

The thought of Wolfgang brought an eruption of grief that surprised Petra. The grief came as a wave that froze all other thought. The grief filled her body. The power drained out of her. She felt tears come close. Tears she did not want to show anyone today.

She stood still, arms wrapped around her chest to hold the feelings in. As the feeling of tears stayed, she softened and thought of Cliff. Her time with him was less exciting than with Wolfgang, but easier.

How long would Cliff be down that rat hole with Mustapha? It seemed that hours had already passed while she waited in this room. Was she about to lose Cliff too now? And Mustapha had come to seem almost like a father, a distant father, but one who wouldn't abuse you. Was she about to lose him as well?

Anger returned. Mustapha and Cliff were no more responsible than Wolfgang. Why did they leave her here waiting?

Petra launched into her routine again, and threw more energy into it. She looked over at Abdul pacing and saw that her exercise made him uncomfortable. She found this encouraging.

Jack found that the time passed slowly. Petra was lost in her own thoughts and he was not about to interfere. As minutes stretched to more than an hour, Jack watched Abdul.

Abdul kept pacing, like a wild animal newly caged. The duty officer moved and stretched from time to time. Abdul's pacing was a stark contrast. His agitation was unnatural. There was something wrong here. What led a man to this much inner conflict?

Jack's curiosity was combined with the habit of gathering intelligence. He would touch the sore spot and see what happened. Maybe there was intelligence to gather, maybe not. Either way, he had the time. There was no sign of Mustapha, Maria, or Cliff. It could be hours yet.

Jack spoke to Abdul in Arabic. "My brother, are you all right? You seem to be nervous."

Abdul was startled. He had not taken Jack seriously. Jack was another vapid rich American, not a man with fluent Arabic. Abdul felt exposed. What else could Jack see? The duty officer had heard Jack's question and was now watching too. Abdul must think quickly. "I am only concerned for Mustapha. He is in danger."

"Don't you trust the gods to treat Mustapha well? You are his Assistant High Priest."

"Yes, yes, we must trust," Abdul muttered, and began pacing again.

The scene between the men pulled Petra out of her own thoughts. She stood, hands on her hips. "Jack," she said, "what's the matter with him?"

"I asked him, but he didn't really answer."

"Maybe it's something wrong with his family."

"My brother," said Jack in Arabic, "you heard the lady. She is concerned if all is well with your wife, your children."

"That is no lady." Abdul looked at Petra's tattoo snaking out onto her arms. His look was a sneer. "No lady looks like that. She is a lower thing." Abdul glared at Petra and kept pacing.

"What did he say, Jack?"

"It wasn't polite."

Petra's anger flared within her. Were she a man, she would hit Abdul. Instead, she would wait for the time to strike.

Jack was not satisfied with Abdul's answers. Something was not right. He would probe deeper.

"It is written that the man is nervous who serves two masters," Jack said. He was quoting a currently notorious Islamist cleric. He would see if Abdul went for the bait.

Without thinking, Abdul replied, "But we must have only one master."

Abdul had completed the Islamist cleric's line, saying it with conviction. He realized what he had done as soon as he had finished. There was no way to pull the words back into his mouth. Abdul looked at Jack, and then at the duty officer, a fellow priest of Karnak in Exile. He felt trapped.

"And who is that 'one' who is your master?" said the duty officer, whose own hand moved towards his holster.

"Jim, any action yet?" Hillary Holloway stretched, rubbed her eyes and forehead, and checked the time. She'd been out for an hour. That was about right. Longer and she'd be dopey, hungry for more shuteye. Less and she wouldn't be sharp when the action started. If the action started. She was beginning to doubt it ever would.

"Not yet princess."

She winced. Jim liked to put her on a pedestal. It was definitely not pc to enjoy it. Hence the ritual wince. Since she was hoping to get a break that made half the world put her on a pedestal, though, she didn't wince too hard.

"I'll take this watch. My news nose tells me that something big will be happening before long."

46

Mustapha, Cliff, and Maria watched from the threshold while the gods of the Ennead enacted their mysterious rite. The gods stood before the great stone basin big as a lake. Something huge was moving in it, something whose contours were not yet clear. Strange waves, shifting patterns, a squall on a colloidal sea.

"Nanomachines?" said Cliff. "It's purplish-gray and formless like there are billions of nanomachines making something there. What do you think?"

"It may be something way beyond that," said Maria. "If these are the gods, who knows what they can do. Mustapha?"

"They can do whatever is needful."

"Are you sure it will be good?"

"Experience and faith say so, but it is fair to ask."

"Do you have any idea what they are making?" said Cliff.

"I have a dream. We will know for sure very soon."

As the other eight gods faced what was coming to be, Amun-Ra, the Creator, turned aside. He raised his hands and before him appeared a helical staircase. As its leading edge grew higher, it disappeared from view.

"It's the same staircase as the vision," said Cliff.

Now Amun-Ra turned again to face that which was coming to be. He raised his hands and spoke.

"Arise now mind of our mind, stuff of our life from before time began. Arise Him Who Crosses Over, come to life One Who Walks the Stars to Rostau. Fulfill your present destiny, and awaken that of humankind. Arise."

As Amun-Ra spoke, that which was coming to be took form more definitely. Like a picture developing, it resolved into reality. A great head formed. It rose from the stone basin as if surfacing from a lake.

"What is it?" said Maria, "A huge god?"

As it rose up, they saw a face, the head wearing the *nemes* headdress of a pharaoh. "It reminds me of one of the pharaohs," said Mustapha. "Perhaps Menkaure."

"Wait," said Cliff. The figure rose further. "It's some kind of human-beast combination."

"A chimera," said Maria.

"Most of the gods have a chimerical form as one of their aspects," said Mustapha.

As the thing rose further, they saw it had a cat's body. The legs were lithe and powerful, the paws vast and leonate.

Mustapha said in a loud whisper, "There can be no doubt what is before us."

"The real Sphinx." said Cliff. He adjusted his black baseball cap.

"I am so fortunate to be here," said Maria.

"As are we all," said Mustapha.

"Now it's clear why everything is so big," said Cliff. "It's Sphinx-sized."

The Sphinx blinked. It was alive and real and as big as the stone Sphinx, its simulacrum on the Giza plateau above. He was the largest animal on the planet, if animal is what he was.

The Sphinx blinked again. A sound like a bomb exploding came from above. Amun-Ra spoke.

"Mustapha, you must go up and protect the Sphinx while he finishes his coming to be. You will find an old friend of ours up there in a typical distemper. Do not fear, for you go with our powers. Remember to carry your staff. You will need it."

The Creator turned back to the Sphinx but added, "Cliff and Maria, you may remain. Now hurry, Mustapha."

Mustapha made a quick bow to the Ennead and the Sphinx. He felt no fireworks this time. No flows of energy or feelings of bliss. It was time now for action. He said, "You are fortunate to remain. We will be together again soon."

Mustapha raised his staff, turned, and hurried away. He raced back through this Sphinx-scaled Karnak. His mind was nothing but questions: Why the Sphinx? Why now? What would it do? He forced the questions aside and felt the blood pulsing in his temples. He was not used to hurrying, and this temple seemed as big as Cairo. He kept at it, out through the hypostyle hall, down the ramp, through the courtyard. He stopped short just inside the high pylon gate, viscerally remembering that this was empty space until his conjuring. Seeing stone still where empty space was, he crossed over into the passageway whose paintings and bright bas-reliefs had emerged at his command.

The vivid designs were still there but the passageway had changed. It had become a monumental corridor twenty meters wide, nearly as wide as the stela chamber it led to. Mustapha raced up the corridor toward the blue light in the stela chamber. As he neared its threshold, however, he saw that the stela itself had gone, and the black metal slab above had slid back to reveal the entire chamber. He realized what the widened corridor, absent stela, and fully open roof meant: the Sphinx would come this way.

Mustapha's footsteps rang out from the corridor. Jack and Maria had a clear sightline to Mustapha. The duty officer and Abdul did not.

The duty officer's hand was on his pistol.

Abdul heard Mustapha's footsteps. He realized that the moment to act was upon him. His holster, like the duty officer's, held a Glock 17. It fired 9mm rounds. Arms aesthetes preferred the 9mm Beretta, since the Austrian Glock was mostly molded plastic and therefore not as sweet looking. The Glock, however, was miraculously light. Mustapha, with the traditional Karnak attention to technology, considered it the sidearm of the future and had chosen it for his men.

At this close range, it would rip him to pieces.

Abdul knew he would take the Glock from the holster and please the mullahs. He would clean up the consequences later. His hand reached down and felt the cool plastic.

Jack saw the duty officer and Abdul drawing their weapons. Abdul was nearer the corridor opening than Jack and Petra, but only they had the direct line of sight to Mustapha. Abdul's view was blocked by the stela chamber's stone wall. Abdul would not have a shot at Mustapha until the High Priest and Great Mage entered the stela chamber.

Jack started running towards Mustapha, with Petra close behind him.

What happened next happened very fast.

The duty officer raised his gun a second before Abdul drew his.

Mustapha crossed the threshold as Jack neared the spot. Jack held up his hands and yelled, "Mustapha, no!"

Mustapha stopped just inside the room. Abdul could now see him, and get a clear shot.

The duty officer shouted, "Abdul, put down your weapon!"

Abdul turned to the duty officer. Without hesitating, Abdul shot him. The shot took the man in the leg. He went down in an explosion of blood.

Jack's awareness was heightened by the danger, and the adrenaline it pumped into his bloodstream. The effects were immediate and profoundly altering. Time distended. All the action went into slow motion. He watched Abdul fire on the duty officer. The man fell in a bubble of bright blood. Jack found he had time to think, time to act. He would seize the moment. With timing and luck he could protect Mustapha. It would take a couple of seconds for Abdul to refocus his attention, turn to Mustapha, take aim and fire. Without thinking of his own safety, Jack launched himself at Abdul.

Abdul saw Jack coming, and swung his arm around to take a shot at him.

Petra was right behind Jack.

Just as Abdul was about the pull the trigger, Jack slammed into his arm. The shot went wide. But the explosion of the Glock so close to his face shocked Jack, stunning him for a crucial second. Abdul was about to get in another shot. This one would spray the wall with hieroglyphs of Jack's brain.

Abdul was so focused on Jack that he did not see Petra coming. She stepped out from behind Jack, to the side of Abdul. As Abdul targeted Jack for his second shot, Petra aimed an expert kick at Abdul's right knee. It connected. The knee tore apart with a loud wet crunch. Screaming with the pain, Abdul reeled back. The Glock went off, but toward the ceiling.

Abdul crumpled.

Jack recovered quickly enough to pounce on Abdul while he was down, and pin him to the floor.

Petra removed the Glock from Abdul's hand with a kick that shattered several bones in Abdul's right hand. Petra heard the bones go, one after the other. The sound reminded her of running her fingers over the high tense strings in a baby grand. Petra picked up the Glock.

"Maybe you won't take women for granted so quickly next time," she said as she pointed the Glock at Abdul's head.

"Friends, I owe you my life," said Mustapha. "And Petra, you embody the fierce lioness aspect of the great goddess Hathor. Glad to have you on my side, young lady."

Petra nodded to acknowledge Mustapha's remark, while she kept the gun on Abdul.

Mustapha continued, "I'll alert the security guards above. They'll take care of them both. Hakim," said Mustapha to the duty officer, "you will be all right. As for you, Abdul, you and I are not finished yet."

Jack looked up from where he held Abdul. He started to speak.

"Later, Jack. I must go now."

Mustapha climbed the stairs feeling energy he had not felt for thirty years.

47

At the sound of the explosion, Hillary had the doors of the van open. She was out on the ground yelling.

"Jim, get me on camera. Wake Tom instantly and tell him to put in our bid for going live."

She quickly checked her hair. She smoothed her tan Armani safari-style jacket, and straightened the white silk blouse underneath. Giza may not be the veldt, but she would make it *Out of Africa* for the folks in Iowa.

Jim and Tom were pros. While they waited for a live feed, Jim had the tape running. Tom signaled they had a live feed. She was ready.

"This is Hillary Holloway coming to you live from the pyramids of Egypt. Amazing things have been happening here. Hours ago the head of the Supreme Council of Antiquities disappeared with armed guards into a huge hole in the ground under the Sphinx. Seconds ago we heard gunfire from down there. What is happening? You want to know and we'll be finding out. This is..."

She was about to sign off when Jim saw Mustapha appear, coming out of the tent, holding his staff, moving fast.

"Keep rolling Hillary, we've got a live one."

She turned and saw Mustapha and ran to intercept, Jim and camera with her. On camera still, she telegraphed her excitement. "Can this be, yes, folks it is, the head of the Supreme Council of Antiquities, a high official. Sir, what is going on here? Why the gunfire, and why the fancy dress? Is this some kind of ritual?"

Mustapha, ever suave, stopped for a moment. He looked as composed standing there in his linen kilt, gold pectoral and breastplate, while holding his staff of electrum, as if he were at the head of a slowly moving procession.

"No time to chat now, my dear, I have work to do."

"Can't you tell our viewers what is going on here?"

Another explosion rocked them. Mustapha pointed to the stone causeway leading to Khafra's pyramid.

"That, I'm afraid."

A stone causeway passed close by the Sphinx's right flank. The causeway was raised up from the ground. A person standing on it, a hundred meters back from the Sphinx, would be roughly on the same level with the Sphinx's rump. They would also be on a direct line of sight from the pyramid of Khafra to the Sphinx.

"I don't believe it," said Hillary, as she stared in the direction Mustapha had pointed.

"Now forgive me, I must go." Mustapha moved off.

Standing on the causeway was a black pig some five meters high at the shoulders. The pig had flaming red eyes and gave off a reddish glow. It radiated aggression as a nuclear reactor radiates heat.

Next to the great black pig stood a beautiful woman. With the bearing of a queen, unperturbed by the hellish vision next to her, she wore a pleated shift in gauzy green linen, a long black braided wig, and a tall headdress composed of a collection of papyrus scrolls surmounted by a house.

Jim was zooming in. Hillary was reporting. "People, I don't know what's going on here. But we're not fooling around. You see what we see. We need to find out what it all means."

Jack and Petra emerged from the tent. Hillary recognized Jack from the last time. She liked the look of him. Liked his khakis, which would complement hers onscreen.

"Jim," she said. He had her on camera with Jack in seconds.

"You've been down under the Sphinx. Are you an expert?"

"Well, I'm an Egyptologist."

Petra was off-camera enjoying Jack's performance. Jack was being both pompous and nervous and therefore, thought Petra, entirely male.

"Great," said Hillary. "Can you tell us what is happening?" She pointed to the great black pig and the stately woman in the strange headdress.

"Mustapha's nightmare."

"What?"

"Well I'd say it looks like the gods have returned to Egypt. But these are not the gods you'd want to meet. What looks like a pig standing over there is Seth. He is the opposite of the creator god Amun-Ra. Seth is traditionally known as the Lord of Chaos, the Prince of Darkness, the God of Sin. We might think of him as the Chairman of Entropy. He takes the form of animals when he is in the mood for battle. Next to him is Nephthys, a goddess and his wife. Her headdress is the hieroglyph for her name. She is Seth's helpmate in all his works."

"Sounds like bad news."

"Imagine Genghis Khan in a really bad mood. Imagine him moving in next door. This is worse. Much worse."

48

"So mom, er, Maria, what now?"

She looked at Cliff and smiled. She had never been 'Maria' before. She looked at him standing there with his thumbs hooked into the pockets of his black jeans. "We see what happens next, I guess."

The Sphinx sat before them in the stone basin of its birth, in much the same posture as the statue above ground. Amun-Ra took a step toward it and said, "Now we will Open the Mouth. What is your name?"

The Sphinx spoke for the first time and answered the Creator. "I am the Light of Amun-Ra."

The god Shu stepped forward and spoke. "What is your name?"

The Sphinx answered Shu, "I am Him Who Opens the Way."

The goddess Tefnut stepped forward and spoke, "What is your name?"

The Sphinx answered Tefnut, "I am Him Who is the Bridge."

The god Geb stepped forward and spoke, "What is your name?"

The Sphinx answered Geb, "I am the Bringer of Truth."

The goddess Nut stepped forward and spoke, "What is your name?"

The Sphinx answered Nut, "I am the Scourge of Innocence."

The god Osiris stepped forward and spoke, "What is your name?"

The Sphinx answered Osiris, "I am the Life of the Gods."

The goddess Isis stepped forward and spoke, "What is your name?"

The Sphinx answered Isis, "I am the Will of the Unbegun."

The goddess Mut stepped forward and spoke, "What is your name?"

The Sphinx answered Mut, "I am Fate."

The god Khonsu stepped forward and spoke, "What is your name?"

The Sphinx answered Khonsu, "I am Destiny."

All the gods of the Great Ennead spoke together and said, "Arise mind of our mind, life of our life."

The Sphinx stirred, tawny like a lion, commanding like a pharaoh, beautiful and terrible beyond imagining. He spoke to the gods.

"I have returned to render judgment."

Then Amun-Ra spoke and said, "You are the True Name of Amun-Ra." At this all the other gods trembled.

Mustapha headed for the left flank of the Sphinx. He came to the great statue's paws, patched with brick from restorations ancient and modern. He moved fluidly, keeping the statue's great stone body between Seth and himself. He was heading for the back of the statue, to get closer to Seth. Had not Amun-Ra told him to protect the living Sphinx who was coming to be? How was he to protect the Sphinx from Seth and Nephthys? He would have to trust that the experiences the gods had vouchsafed him worked at a cellular level to implant aptitudes he was unaware of. Trust, like fear, had a threshold he had to cross anew every time. He would trust the gods had given him what he needed to face this test.

Bulbul stood on the causeway dressed as Nephthys. From where he stood next to Benben, he was about a hundred meters behind the Sphinx. He was musing and not altogether sanguine. He was proud of his Nephthys drag. He looked every inch the part. But how typical for Benben not to tell him that her version of Seth was a pig the size of a house.

When would he ever upstage her? He wanted too to tell her about the light he had seen tailing them, but had no time. Not even a friendly 'hello how was your ride, horrifying?' She was all eagerness and business. As soon as they were enfleshed she set about attacking the Sphinx. He would have to remember to ask her how she managed to project those red lightning bolts from her eyes.

There were just so many extra things you could do with a robe of flesh. She had not really left him anything to do, though, so he might as well relax and enjoy the show. There she went again, another lightning bolt. Sounded like a bomb going off when it hit the mark. This was fun after all. So much fun, no wonder it was illegal.

Mustapha ran along the Sphinx's flank, where the sandstone was soft. This part of the statue once rippled with the ribs of the beast. Horizontal bands of stone stood out clearly now. Erosion was severe. Still, the statue's vast bulk was providing the cover Mustapha sought as he made his approach.

Mustapha neared the Sphinx's left back paw, when one of Seth's red lightning bolts lashed out. Aimed at the Sphinx, it exploded some distance from it scattering into thousands of sparks. These fell away, outlining with fidelity a dome-shaped field over the great statue.

The living Sphinx, Mustapha realized, was being protected by the gods while it was coming to be below. Yet what if the repeated attack of Seth's fiery bolts broke through the protection? He realized that he was inside the field and felt joyful: harmony on his side opposed the chaos of Seth.

Mustapha raced on. He had the inspiration that if he could stand on the statue's back, he would be a little higher than Seth and have a clear vantage from which to return his attack. Running at speed, Mustapha held this image clear in his mind and raised his staff. Blue light sprouted from the ankh at its tip. He was lifted off the ground and flew up to the back of the Sphinx, standing on its rump facing Seth. "Better not get used to traveling that way, old boy," he chuckled to himself. He raised his staff and prepared to do battle with the Lord of Chaos.

If anger were clover, Benben was a pig in clover. She had focused her anger and chosen an avatar who expressed it clearly: Chaos, Darkness, Bringer of Storms, Death by Desert. A distillation of all the fears of the ancient Egyptians, projected into their god of all things anti-good. From the inside she was experiencing the value of Seth: anger wielded as a weapon of cleansing. Elimination of everything substandard, boring, annoying, and sentimental. Anything beyond my reckoning must be destroyed. She was proud of her discipline too. She could have enjoyed trotting through the souks of Cairo as Seth sowing destruction. But this was more than a tourist outing. She was concentrated on the source of the anomaly. Control or destroy that and she had every chance to control the Consilium.

49

Mustapha was beyond where the tradition could take him. There were stories of the gods battling each other to be sure. The great continuing battle was between Seth and Horus. Horus, Lord of Light, depicted as a falcon. Horus, grandson of the Creator. Seth the god of darkness forever battles Amun-Ra, source of the Sun. So Horus battles Seth on his behalf. A separate conflict fueled their fighting too: Seth and Nephthys murdered Horus's father Osiris. They chopped his body in pieces and hid them throughout the Land of Egypt. Isis the mother of Horus journeyed from Upper to Lower Egypt, gathering the Body of Osiris. She found all the pieces save the phallus. She reassembled the body and gave it a sacred burial. Osiris was resurrected as Lord of the Duat, god of the dead. For the murder of his father Osiris, Horus sought revenge.

As night follows day, the battle of Horus and Seth continued, each sometimes gaining the advantage. It is said in a famous ancient prophecy that the battle will end one day:

Horus shall defeat Seth
When the Gods return to Egypt.

His scholar's eye had framed the situation before him in an eyeblink, but understanding offered Mustapha no joy. He faced an implacable foe.

"Trust, only trust," he told himself.

When Seth saw Mustapha atop the Sphinx, he snorted obscenely to the sky. The darkness came. Where it had been morning turning bright, dark clouds boiled in bringing darkness like an eclipse. Nevertheless, Mustapha saw Seth and Nephthys clearly in the darkness from the hellish red glow Seth emitted. He saw Seth readying another bolt. He feared for the Sphinx taking birth below, sensing that the protective field was exhausted. If it did not hold, the Lord of Destruction would win his game.

Anger rose now in Mustapha. He could feel it clearly. It started in his groin and rose through his whole body. He saw his staff energize in parallel. Mustapha concentrated on stopping the next red bolt. The anger rose into his head. At the same moment blue light rose to the ankh. Seth let loose his bolt. At the same instant the light from Mustapha's staff leapt away. It formed a patch of daybright blue sky, a disk of light to swallow the fruits of darkness. It shot toward the bolt of chaos like a shark to prey and they met. The red exploded in a fireburst that lit the Giza plateau. The blue disk had disappeared, but taken Seth's bolt.

Mustapha's lungs felt tight. He had been holding his breath. He breathed fast and deep. The air smelled of ozone from the fiery exchange.

Mustapha realized he had just won the first round of combat with Seth. Then he felt a new fear: Seth's bolt had come close. The first bolt had shattered on the dome shaped field around the Sphinx. The second bolt had come so close that it must have pierced the protecting field. Now only Mustapha stood against the Prince of Darkness. If he failed, it meant the destruction of the Sphinx who was coming to be, the certain death of Maria and Cliff, and a reign of chaos.

Seth realized too that he had breached the protective field. He gloated over his impending triumph, stamping his heavy hooves until they shook the ancient causeway. He bellowed the coming victory of Nothingness. It was a sound terrible to hear, painful to the hope that lives in a man's heart and chilling the very marrow in one's bones. Seth raised his great head and bellowed again, wanton in his bloodlust.

Mustapha's hope drained away, reversing the course of the anger that so recently rose in him. In place of the youthful energy he had felt when he hurried into battle, he felt age and weakness beyond his years. He could not hold Seth for long, maybe not for another bolt.

Just then a gentle breeze refreshed the air, which had grown dank in darkness. A golden light came over Mustapha from behind. He feared to turn with Seth on the attack before him, but could not help himself.

What he saw behind him was no less fearsome than what he faced in Seth, but opposite in character. A falcon flew down from the skies bearing the solar disk as headdress. Like Seth the falcon was of monumental scale and when he came to stand was no less high. Horus had come to face Seth. Horus spoke to Mustapha in the language of ancient Egypt.

"Turn and give battle to Seth. My arrival surprises him. We must now unnerve him."

Mustapha turned and Horus stood behind him, one wing touching each shoulder to give him strength.

Seth looked across at Horus. The evil rejoicing in his heart wavered. Wanre-Horus knew that it was Benben who was Seth. He knew that she could not yet grasp that it was he who came as Horus, and would have to assume that it was another Earth anomaly, this one set against her. He was gambling in his opening gambit that Benben, the master manipulator of fear, would now know fear herself, and he was ready.

Wanre had already inferred a great deal of the inner Benben from their long course of dealings. She had become one of his hobbies. As they surfed across the branes to Earth, he found the keys to her. When you mind melded with a gravity wave to surf it, your mind was stored as perturbations in the wave. If another had access to the wave and knew how to read those perturbations they could read the structure of your mind as you might appreciate an ink brush painting. Wanre had had access. What Benben could not know is that he had the skill to read; a skill that was, insofar as he could tell, a mastery unique to him.

His bow had another string. He had kept his connection with her mind when they descended from the gravity wave into their avatars, and she had not noticed. This method did not give total access; it was not like mind combat. Nevertheless, he had his first precious look inside her.

So Horus could see into the mind of Seth. Seth stood on the causeway glowing in his red effulgence and faced Horus, Bringer of Light. He appeared to be readying another bolt.

Wanre looked calmly into Benben. Fear was not her normal feeling tone. He saw rapacity, anger, aggression, protectiveness toward Bulbul all glowing in her mind like fire. Something else, though, had emerged in response to his arrival. Something small and wet and slimy, like a misshapen bubble of poison. Just what he was looking for: fear. He concentrated on her fear, seeing it with his mind. He projected energy into her bubble of fear with all his force, and watched it grow and grow until it spilled over onto the fire in her mind and extinguished it.

Then Seth the Lord of Chaos and Father of Storms faltered. He trembled on the causeway as if stricken with a palsy. He fell heavily onto all four knees, and then onto his belly. The sound of the crash came back as a loud report echoing from the faces of the pyramids.

Mustapha watched, empty of thought. Horus's wings squeezed his shoulders for encouragement.

Seth shook his bristled head. He rose slowly to his feet, gathering his forces. Wanre looked again into Benben's mind and saw the fires refulgent. She was enraged and that energy would sustain her projection. Yet he had changed the tone of her mind and thereby accomplished a long-term objective. A pool of fear had collected there now, and it would remain long after he lost direct contact with her mind. He noted it with satisfaction as the battle turned to externals.

Seth bellowed again in challenge and squeezed a lightning bolt from his eyes.

"Raise your staff," said Horus. When Mustapha did, a golden disk shot out and met the bolt, consuming it. But Wanre worried. The disk consumed the bolt too close in. Benben had rebounded and was strong.

Another bolt quickly followed, answered by another golden disk. This time the disk gained greater purchase on the space and consumed the bolt closer to its source.

Another bolt and another, their fiery red energy lighting the still dark sky, an ozone smell of arc-welding in the air of Giza. Each of these bolts was consumed by a solar disk and as the fight continued the bolts were pressed back and destroyed closer to home. Registering the pressure physically, Seth stepped back a pace, his great hooves cracking ancient stones.

"Now!" said Horus. A solar disk flew from Mustapha's staff towards Seth not to counter a bolt but as an offensive weapon this time. Now they were on the attack. While Wanre had the advantage, he reached again into Benben's mind. He grew the pool of fear till it again lapped at her mind's fires.

Furious this time, Seth released three bolts in quick succession. The first neutralized the solar disk coming towards him. The second and third flew forward.

Horus and Mustapha destroyed the second at a middle distance but the third came close. They fired back four solar disks. Seth destroyed them but the fourth came very close to Seth. It would have annihilated the Lord of Chaos had it connected. With her avatar destroyed Benben would have been in grave danger. One needs time to withdraw from a robe of flesh and return to one's body. When the enfleshment is destroyed the real body can go into shock and die, and the mind wander ghostlike.

50

A beam of white light flashed out of Rostau, the place in the heavens where the pharaohs went to join the gods. The beam flashed down from the southern sky and far behind Seth's back, who did not see it. Just before the beam hit the pyramids it split into three. Each of these three beams smashed into a pyramid.

Mustapha and Horus could see all of this from where they stood but could not stop to wonder. Benben was now consumed by hatred for whatever or whoever Horus was, whoever had the gall to deflect her plans. Her only thought now was to eliminate this new enemy.

The pyramids drank in the light, and the beam from Rostau ceased. Just then all at once the rainbows came. Rainbows arced out from the pyramids as if they had been stored there forever. They momentarily lit the Giza plateau with soft warm color. They were glorious to behold, like a vision in a dream. Then as suddenly as they had come the rainbows were gone. They sprang off the face of the Earth like live things, launching themselves into space.

Jim was capturing all of this on live TV unaccompanied for now by commentary since Hillary and Jack had both become silent with wonder.

The wrath of Seth knew no distraction, and he pressed his attack. His bolts were now reaching closer to Horus and Mustapha. They worked hard to stay focused as the unearthly fireworks played out before them. They dared not let their attention stray: a single one of Seth's bolts would incinerate them.

In the heat of the battle, Nephthys was getting bored. The attack was Seth's and there was no room for moral support. If only he had access to Seth's brain. But was this going to go on all day? She walked a little way back from the heat of battle and sat down on the causeway trying to look like a lady.

The fortunes of battle were about to shift. The three pyramids became miracles of petrified sunlight. They glowed and the light gathered itself up to their apexes. Then the pyramids of Khufu and Menkaure beamed light into the central pyramid of Khafra and went dark. The tip of Khafra's pyramid glowed gold. It was then it shot its bolt of light.

It was a golden light, as if the white beam from Rostau had been honeyed by the pyramids' stone matrix. The golden light flashed forth as a coherent beam and headed toward the Sphinx.

Mustapha and Horus flinched. Seth gratulated with himself at this sudden advantage and squinted off the bolt he knew would kill them. But the bolt veered off course. The shaft of light on its way from the pyramid to the Sphinx found an obstacle never meant to be there. Seth's left flank was grazed by the light. The skin exploded. The stink of burnt hair, fat, and flesh would reach the TV crew moments later.

Undeterred, the beam slammed into the Sphinx with a shock wave so strong it made the statue shake. Mustapha lost his footing. He was too close to the edge. Horus tried to hold him, but Wanre was confounded by having flight feathers not fingers. Mustapha fell, and hit the stone floor of the Sphinx enclosure with a sickening sound.

51

Amun-Ra spoke to the Sphinx and said, "You will go forth by morning banishing the darkness. Today we return to you our powers over life and death. Receive them."

The gods of the Great Ennead raised their hands so that the palms faced the Sphinx. They said, "Be full of light."

At that moment the stone wall behind the Sphinx dissolved. Though it was eternal daylight in this monumental temple, the day was eclipsed. Not by darkness but by light. A golden energy poured in so powerfully that Maria instinctively covered her eyes while Cliff fished his sunspecs out of his pocket. Dark as they were, he still squinted.

The Sphinx turned and faced the light. His body absorbed it as a sponge absorbs water. As the light poured in, the Sphinx began to glow. His body drank in the light as a baby suckles his mother's teat and desert sands guzzle the rain of a summer storm.

When the Sphinx turned to face the gods again, he smiled at them. A smile of happiness, completion, beatitude. Cliff had never imagined so much happiness could be concentrated in anyone. As if the smile were a cue, the inpouring of light ceased.

The gods were well pleased. Amun-Ra said, "You hold the keys to life and death. You know what you must do."

The Sphinx inclined his head and Amun-Ra turned. He approached the helical staircase he had called into being. He began to climb. The other gods of the Great Ennead followed. One by one they climbed the spiraling stairs until they were well beyond the vision of Cliff and Maria.

Mother and son looked at each other. It had just hit them both: they were underground, maybe in a parallel universe, with a gargantuan living Sphinx whose loyalties were well beyond their reckoning. Then the Sphinx turned to look at them directly.

Hillary was not speechless for long. If she would ever get the chance to move from network twilight to limelight, this was it.

"Folks, we are watching what will be remembered around the world as one of the most extraordinary events in human history. We will all remember where we were when this happened. Like with Kennedy's assassination, and 9/11. Though hopefully this will have a much happier outcome."

"Now that was some well-sliced ham," she thought to herself. She continued.

"Throughout history people have wondered what the pyramids are for. I guess we just found out they are giant devices of the gods, but we don't yet know what the pyramids just *did.* There must be something incredible happening under the Sphinx."

Hillary turned to Jack, ready to ask a question.

At the same moment, Jack saw Mustapha fall from the Sphinx. "Look," he said to Hillary over his shoulder, "I have to go take care of my friend. "

Jack was running. Petra ran after him. Since they were in front near the Sphinx Temple, they had about a hundred meters to cover until they reached Mustapha, lying on the ground at the back of the Sphinx.

"Folks," continued Hillary, "You can see how eager these people are to help their friend, fallen in heroic combat. We'll have all the coverage on how he is, whether he is wounded, whether he survived that fall. You all want to know what lies under the Sphinx too, and what the beam of light from the pyramids has to do with it. And you will know, because we'll find out for you. You need to know what we're about to discover."

"Jose, another Ardbeg?"

"Sure," said the secretary of state. "It's past quitting time."

The vice president poured. They sat on sofas in his office. It was midnight, and they both had been through full days. The TV news was playing with the sound off. They sat near it as their forebears sat drinking their whisky by a roaring fire.

They were chatting and sipping when their attention was caught by the TV images. Dark screen, flashes of intense light, the signature of modern high-tech warfare.

"Volume, Jose, damn it!" The vice president was upset he couldn't place this conflict. Jose felt the same. What world situation had so spun out of control in the last few hours that particle weapons and guided munitions were in play? "Hell, we're the only ones *with* workable particle beam weapons, Jose, what gives here? Who's doin' the shootin'?"

Jose pumped the volume and they heard Hillary and Jack discussing the Egyptian gods.

"Gods, what kind of horseshit is this? We're talking modern munitions!"

"I don't know anything about the gods," said Jose placatingly, "but we've been expecting things to get weird in the pyramid zone."

"You know what I need, Jose."

"Operational control."

"The space battle station ready?"

"Maneuvered into a temporary fixed position right over the Sphinx."

"Good. I'm going to finish this drink and go to bed, safe in the knowledge of our firepower. Don't hesitate to use it."

"I'd prefer it if the president were in the loop."

"I've got the authorization. If things get too hot, fire. We'll talk in the morning."

52

Petra was running with Jack towards Mustapha. The sky was now bright. The light had won its battle with darkness. What comfort to her if Mustapha should die? Too recently she had watched Wolfgang die. Mustapha had been strong then. If he were to die too, who would comfort her? She'd barely had time to feel Wolfgang's loss with all that was happening, there had been too much to get through moment by moment. The time alone with Cliff had been some relief. Then for a little while the grief itself had erupted, while she waited in the blue chamber with Jack and the guards. She had felt like she could weep, but that was too public.

Now Petra's grief started to erupt again, Mustapha's accident calling it forth. Tears flowed as she ran. She used the backs of her hands to clear her vision. She felt like she would never get there in time. Her only thought: Mustapha.

They were the first to reach him. They knelt. It looked like Mustapha had fallen on his left side and then rolled onto his back.

Mustapha's left temple was smashed. Blood pooled under his head, ruby coagulating into garnet. Mustapha's left shoulder was broken, rolled over on itself like a coat thrown over a chair. Mustapha's eyes were closed.

Jack leaned close and heard shallow breathing from the damaged body.

"I think the best thing for him now is prayer."

Jack put his arm around Petra. While she wept, he was angry. It was no consolation that he tried to warn Mustapha off this whole business from the beginning, from the time Wolfgang first talked about using his laser to cut into the polygon. If only Mustapha had listened to him then. Look what had happened. Mustapha was gone now, following Wolfgang. Nothing was worth this price. Jack felt his tears begin.

Bulbul had been saved by boredom. The smell sickened him. He knew only too well what it meant: Benben could die and him along with her. Had Benben entered too far into this big singed tub of lard? She had intended a game, a witty one, in which she used her avatar to muck around in the mysterious business here. Instead she had let Horus draw her into a rage and forget the fun. Seth the puppet and Benben the puppet master. Had she forgotten the joke and fallen into the flesh? If she'd forgotten when Seth was hit, her body back home in their cozy red love nest could go into shock. It would read the vital signs here as its own.

Bulbul feared the worst as he rushed toward Seth. If Benben were lost he would be too. There was no way he could be sure of finding the way home across the branes. Even if he got there, he would still die, since he couldn't survive separate from his symbiont more than fourty-eight hours.

As he raced to Seth in the full regalia of Nephthys, he was close to panic. Thoughts chased themselves through his mind: he would at least make good use of this Nephthys number. He'd run screaming through medieval Cairo, climb a minaret, leap off keeping his awareness dual, and surf away just before she hit the pavement headdress first!

"Come now, worm."

A commanding whisper. Did he hear it? As he neared he felt a sudden rush of optimism: Seth's flanks were quivering. She must be alive!

"I'm down but not out, worm." She looked up and winked one large eye. "I'm a tough old pig in anybody's universe."

Nephthys bent down, almost losing her headdress in her happiness. She wept all over Seth's snout for the joy of life returned and the possibility of revenge.

Mustapha knew he was falling. In dreams he had fallen. Near the edge of high places he had imagined what falling would be like.

Now he was falling, and it was nothing like he had imagined. Time had changed. He remembered the shock that had knocked him off the Sphinx. He remembered the primary feathers of Horus' wings trying and failing to hold him. Time was stretching. He had all the time in the world. Nothing was wrong. Amun-Ra had asked him to go into battle. Had he not done so? Horus had come to help him. What now could be wrong?

He looked about him. The pyramids were there. Seth was there. The Sphinx was there. Only the perspective was askew. Try as he might there was nothing he could do to right it. He had all the time in the world. He would make it work.

He was approaching a wall. No. It was the stone floor of the Sphinx enclosure. No matter. Mustapha welcomed the stone. This was the body of Geb, the Earth Father, the loving provider, the living breathing body of the planet. He trusted Geb, whom he had seen live not an hour ago, dancing. Geb must be calling him. Yes, he was coming closer. Geb was calling him! Geb was raising his arms to welcome Mustapha into his body!

Geb took Mustapha and all went black.

The blackness became luminous, not hard, welcoming. What was stone became time, and Mustapha fell through it. He fell through time, deep time. He rested in time. He was in time for whatever would happen. In time he opened his eyes. This was all the time in the world. He moved freely through time as he had once moved through space.

He asked himself if this was a dream and discovered it was not. There was a clarity, coherence and volition he never had in dreams. He chose to look around. The place was both thoroughly familiar and strange at once.

There was the Nile, but huge wide and angry. In this mood the Nile would lay down no life-giving alluvial mud. It would scour away the banks and shelves, meadows and fields it had built up during more placid eons.

Then Mustapha understood. Who knew the history of great Egypt in more detail than he did? This was the Wild Nile, which had chased all human beings from the valley. Melting glaciers joined Ethiopian monsoons to turn the gentle river angry. People withdrew to the savannahs that would dry to desert.

Mustapha now knew. The river would not tame itself for another three thousand years. Then it would accrete the Black Land grain by grain. Only then would people venture back, tentatively at first. They would set up villages and gorge on fish that the river, now relaxed, would offer them. While they gorged, people in the west would go hungry. Sophisticated astronomers and farmers, the western people's land would turn against them. It would get steadily drier until green savannah became sand punctuated by oases. When the oases dried, the people would leave what was now the Red Land and move east. They would meet the simpler river people in combat and camaraderie until they fused into the world's first nation state: a ribbon of life a thousand kilometers long ruled by King Scorpion, the first pharaoh.

All that lay in the future. Egypt with its gods and glory was hidden in the future more thoroughly than mummies would ever be hidden by rock and sand. Mustapha knew now that he had fallen tens of thousands of years into the past. He laughed, only to find he had no body.

Part IV
The Judgment of the Sphinx

In every age the divine intelligence has scattered forerunners in the world. They are those who are ahead of their time and whose personal action is based on an inward knowledge of that which is yet to come. If you and I should happen to be forerunners, let us be thankful, even though, living a century or two too soon, we may feel ourselves to be strangers in a foreign land.

—Abbé de Tourville, *Letters of Direction*

53

The Sphinx looked straight at them. Instinctively, Maria and Cliff reached for each other's hand. The Sphinx looked down at them, and they felt that time had stopped. Each felt the other's hand tremble. They looked up into his face, fearsome and beautiful. The face was more intensely beautiful than anything they had seen, as if more life had been poured into this one being than they had ever met. The sheer intensity of him pushed them back a step within their own minds. Power radiated from him like light from a star. They did not know whether he was hostile or friendly, only that he was beyond. He was beyond their scale, beyond their comprehension. They could only gape at such a wonder.

Before they could speak to each other, he spoke to them.

Or rather, they heard him. The Sphinx did not move his lips. They saw the sound as color. They felt it with their bones. Their minds filled with it.

"Follow." The Sphinx gave them just that one word.

There could be no question whether they would comply. They would have done so anyway, even at their peril. To be told to follow, whether it was invitation or command, was more than they could hope for. Squeezing each other's hand, they stepped to the side of the doorway to make room for him.

The Sphinx passed through the door of his birth chamber and changed. His tawny, lion-colored body became diaphanous, a shining emptiness covered with stars. It was like he was a slice of the galaxy. His new body was pulsatingly alive and retained the contours of his familiar shape. He passed by, ignoring them.

Cliff was tempted to plunge in his hand and try to catch a star. Then he thought better of it. They had to jog to keep up.

"What if he gets annoyed with us?" said Maria.

"I hope we don't find out. Wasn't he a good god?"

"The Arabs call him The Father of Terror. Let's keep a little way behind him."

They jogged behind the Sphinx through the outscale narthex and courtyard. As his muscular misty shape moved, stars coruscated along its surface. They saw through his great body to the high pylon gate. Then they were outside the gate and moving up the corridor to the stele chamber.

When the Sphinx reached the stairs he leapt up them, as a wide wave crossing the ocean leaps powerful and high when it meets a rocky cliff-bound coast. As he leapt, the Sphinx raised his right paw. The khaki tent that covered the site became confetti on the desert sands. The few people on site skirled away.

Cliff and Maria were just behind. What they first saw were the birds.

The air was thick with them. Hoopoes looped like tropical butterflies. Purple swamp hens fat and iridescent shared the sky with shy coucals and tiny avadavats. Curve-billed glossy ibis, so beloved by the ancients they mummified them in thousands, loped along in skylines. Egyptian vultures and eagle owls, scavenger and predator, flew with hooded crows with piebald faces, stolid, strong, and smart. Nightjars set their jagged calls against the honk of Egyptian geese. Barbary falcons, sakers and lanners left off hunting and flew barrel rolls for the Sphinx. Desert larks, rollers and glamorous bee-eaters searched out interstices, while swifts and swallows in endless numbers stitched their way across the sky and chittered in greeting.

So many birds had never been seen above this desert. As they would have done at a total eclipse, they circled around and around, the living Sphinx their centerpoint. When he looked up and acknowledged them, the birds streamed away to all corners of the sky as suddenly as they had come.

The Sphinx turned and looked at his statue. All of the people onsite, and Hillary's TV cameras, were focused on him. He stood silent, ignoring them all. Even in the broad daylight of the desert, he looked like a three-dimensional slice of the galaxy: empty space illuminated and defined by stars. Yet he was the Sphinx.

Everyone was waiting for him to do something. When he did, it was not what they had expected.

He walked up to the stone Sphinx and sat down in front of it. His paws touched the statue's. He smiled an enigmatic smile at it, mirroring the one in stone. Then he melted into it.

"Melted." That was the word Hillary would use on her newscast. He flowed like mercury into the statue. As he did, the statue came alive. First the paws, patched and restored with brick over the centuries. The paws became lion's paws, huge and living. The transformation worked up the legs, and came to the chest and head.

The statue was alive. The Sphinx blinked and opened his eyes from a living face. The crowd drew breath together. Some wept. His beauty filled their eyes to overflowing. When a large photograph is reduced, the image gains in clarity. Despite his size, the Sphinx was clearer, sharper and more distinct than anything they had seen, as if he were more densely pixilated than ordinary reality.

The Sphinx sat there huge, alive, and dazzlingly beautiful. No one knew his powers or intentions. They expected some sort of announcement from him: a short speech, some indication of motive. His human features and obvious intelligence raised expectations.

The Sphinx remained silent. He sat and stared in the direction of the rising Sun, as his statue always had.

54

Cliff watched with everyone else as the Sphinx poured himself into his statue. Then the Sphinx spoke.

"Mustapha needs your help."

The voice was so loud Cliff feared it would shatter his skull. He looked around, expecting that everyone else had heard it. They were still watching the Sphinx's face, waiting for a word.

"Maria, did you hear anything?"

"No, honey."

It came again, not as loud this time, as if the Sphinx were tuning to his capacities.

"He is lying behind me in grave danger. Take him to my birth chamber and lay him in the small stone basin. You will know what to do."

"We've got to help Mustapha," he said to Maria. "The Sphinx just told me."

"Told you?" She looked blank.

"I'm not crazy. Mustapha needs our help. He must be hurt. He's behind the Sphinx."

They started jogging again and soon reached the spot where Mustapha lay on the ground.

"Listen, everyone," said Cliff. When he arrived with Maria, he found Jack and Petra already there. "The Sphinx told me we have to get Mustapha down to the chamber where the Sphinx was born, and pronto. Put him in the stone basin. Maybe we can revive him, I don't know."

"The *Sphinx* told you this?" said Jack.

"It may sound crazy but it's real. What other chance does Mustapha have at this point anyway?"

Nephthys bent close to Seth.

"Time to go home old girl. Can you?"

"Easy. We'll be home in no time. Spoiling for a fight."

"With?"

"Wanre."

"You think it was him?"

"Who else would have the nerve to spoil my fun?"

"I didn't know he could surf."

"Just like the bastard."

"Time to chuck that bulky hulk you're wearing and get home."

"You're fetching in that drag, worm."

"That one earns you a good brain boost when we're safe in our little red hideaway."

For anyone who might have been watching, the two gods disappeared into thin air.

Mustapha filled with profound peace. He could feel his breathing. He was alive and in a body. It was his own body. He opened his eyes. He saw through a tight frame what was above him. He was lying on his back. He tried to move. He could not. He had no command over his body. His mind was clear but his body was thoroughly still. He knew then that he had fallen from the Sphinx, and that his body lay broken around him.

He looked up. People were looking down at him. It was like looking up from the bottom of a well. His visual field faded to darkness around the edges, but was clear in the center.

Hearing was also acute. One was crying, a woman. The others were discussing what to do with him. He recognized them. He was back in the time of his life. The embodied life he had known among them.

Their voices were clear but distant. They were anxious in their concerns about him. They were missing what was important.

They had no need to worry about him. They should not get lost in their fears and feelings.

"I'm dying," he realized. "This is what it's like. My soul is still in my body. Not for long. Body so still, unmoving. Peaceful. How heavy the grace that stills my limbs." He lay soft, appreciating.

Then he needed to speak to them. He tried and found he could move his lips. They leaned closer.

"They are in the summer of their mortal love," he thought. He was struck by their beauty and felt an access of emotion for them. "I must tell them what is important."

He spoke. "Remember: love each other." They heard. His breath went silent. The four of them lay their heads on his chest and cried.

55

Jack and Cliff each picked up one of Mustapha's arms, Maria and Petra one of his legs. With the four carrying him, Mustapha was a manageable burden. Nevertheless, it was a long haul to the Sphinx Temple, down the stairs to the stela chamber, and then through the temples underground.

By the time they had negotiated the stairs with the body they were all tiring. Only Cliff and Maria understood the reality of how much further they had to go before they got Mustapha to the chamber where the Sphinx came to life. Both of them doubted that the four of them could bear Mustapha that far.

When they crossed from the stela chamber into the corridor, their worries evaporated. In crossing the threshold, they stepped immediately into the chamber they needed to reach. Somehow all the intervening space had been broached.

"What just happened?" said Petra, alert to the fact that she had safely crossed over the place where Wolfgang died.

Jack said, "An old text says of the Sphinx, 'He will make the way short for you.'"

"I'm not complaining," said Cliff.

Mustapha was alone. He was not moving through time. He was moving through death.

He was free. Free of his body with its pains and limitations. Free of his burdens as High Priest of Karnak and Great Mage of Egypt.

A radiance emerged in the darkness. A mound rose from the waters. He stood on the mound.

There was the emptiness and the radiance.

He knew what came next.

He would birth a world.

He understood it for the first time. This was the story of Atum the Creator. The One radiated love. He gave birth to all the elements. He gave birth to the world. He gave birth to life.

Mustapha was now Atum. He could create a universe out of himself. He would be coextensive with his creation.

There would be less suffering than in the world he had known. Mustapha entered the rapture of the Creator.

"The Sphinx said I would know what to do," Cliff said.

They entered the sanctuary and lay Mustapha in the stone basin scaled to the size of a man. Cliff found a golden bowl and spatula at the foot of the smaller basin. He picked them up, went over to the Sphinx basin, and climbed into it. There was a little moisture like dew. He collected it. In returning to Mustapha, he looked around for the helical staircase the Great Ennead had climbed. It was gone.

Maria and Petra removed Mustapha's elaborate breastplate and loosened his kilt. The wounds thus revealed ran all along his left side from head to hip. His temple had been smashed in the fall. There were more bruises, broken skin, broken bones now visible. Without stopping to discuss it, Cliff used the golden spatula to touch the wounds with the fluid he had collected.

A blue light danced along the wounds. The four friends kept vigil but not silence.

"I keep wondering," said Cliff, "if we're watching science we don't understand."

"How do you explain what Mustapha did?" said Jack. "His spells really did things."

"Maybe they were triggering things long programmed. Maybe they themselves are programs that boot aspects of reality we can't see."

The blue luminescence faded.

Mustapha's lips fluttered.

Maria was the first to notice. "I think he's coming back," she said.

Cliff leaned in, heard breathing. "He's coming around." There was an excitement in Cliff's voice that brought it close to tears.

There was a whisper. Cliff had his ear close to Mustapha's lips.

"No."

"What did he say?" said Maria.

"No," said Cliff, "that's what he said. No." Cliff kept listening. "He's stopped breathing again. I think we've lost him."

As quickly as their hope had revived, it was taken away. What was a miracle now seemed a false promise, a shabby dawn rising on disappointment. Maria covered her face with her hands. Her cheeks were wet with tears. Jack touched her shoulder in comfort.

Mustapha saw the Earth, full of suffering. He was being drawn back.

He knew Cliff needed him. One human being needed him. A human being's need called him back, and his heart responded.

Mustapha would help. He would go back.

But no, he could not. His new creation called him. There would be less suffering there. He needed to create this world more than he had ever needed anything.

"No," he said. "No, I won't go back. My time on Earth is over. The new world is about to begin. I gave them everything I had. I can make the new world better. I won't go back. No."

Mustapha moved into the space of his 'no'. It was comforting, but held the radiance distant. He stood on the mound in darkness. He could not move forward into creation. The love he needed to pour into it was banked like a fire overnight, invisible to him, unavailable. He stayed in the space of his 'no' for an indefinite, empty time. It became numbing. It did not flow like time. It did not move like feeling. It did not ramify like thought. It became the abyss.

Then Mustapha *saw*. He could hold back his love. He could guard it, keeping it to give to his creation, his world. If he chose this path, he would stay in the abyss. Perhaps the abyss would endure for eternity.

Or he could give love to one who needed it, one to whom he was tied by shared experience through more than one life. One with whom there was work to do. His creation would be delayed. Perhaps it would never happen. But he would move again, he would flow, his power and brilliance would manifest. His love would enter others. He saw Maria too, and felt a movement toward her.

Mustapha chose to return. He would reenter his broken body. He would accept the pain. He would become again the High Priest of Karnak and Great Mage of Egypt. It was a free choice and he made it. He would pour out his life, with consequences he would never be able to foresee.

"Where am I?"

Cliff was kneeling near Mustapha's head. "It's him, he's back."

Maria dropped her hands from her face. Cheeks still wet with tears, she said, "You're back in the land of the living with me, with us," she said.

"Under the Sphinx," added Cliff.

Mustapha sighed heavily. His empty lungs filled. He eyes opened. He looked up at the ceiling not at them. "I didn't want to come back. You won't, not once you get there."

"What made you return?" said Cliff.

"In a way you did, Cliff. I saw there was work to do together. I saw things. We were together before, when Amun-Ra was only a local god. We served Amun-Ra. I was your teacher. We did a ceremony in the King's Chamber. We lived once as Unas and Qaa, priests who played a pivotal role in Amun-Ra's life. We must do the ceremony again. It needs to be completed. Will you do that with me, Cliff?"

"Yes. You mean we're reincarnated?"

"Reincarnation was only theory for me before. Now I know it." Mustapha sat up and looked at them all. "My friends, I wish I could say it is wonderful to be back. Perhaps it will seem so in time."

"We're grateful you came back," said Maria. It felt odd to have to encourage someone who had just received a new life. She wondered if Lazarus had been grateful to Jesus. Perhaps he was angry instead.

"Come on, let's get you out of there," said Jack.

Mustapha let Jack and Cliff help him out of the stone basin. Maria thought he seemed softer, as if death had removed the knots in him.

56

"Your distress pains me, love apple." What a relief to be back in their intestinal décor. It was so good to be back in his own body too, now coiled like a cobra on a cushion beside her.

She had been having intestinal cramps and diarrhea since she re-entered hers. "Small price to pay for such an outing."

"Shall I give you something nice?"

"Just to take away the nausea and sharpen the mind. We can't take any real trips now. Work to do."

"Revenge?" He wriggled over to where she lay stately on the red bed gently pulsing. He attached the teeth on his hind segment to her skull around the opening into her brain. He exuded judicious drops of a mild neuro-transmitter mix. He restrained himself from pumping in the uplifting flood he felt he owed her.

"Revenge most sweet, worm."

"Sure it's Wanre?"

"Every cell in my body screams it. If he had children I would lie in wait to eat them. Since he doesn't, I think it's time the Consilium had a new ruler."

"Don't you mean 'Speaker'?"

"The job could mean so much more."

"Why leave the power distributed throughout the Consilium worlds?'

"When it should be concentrated in my hands."

"How will you get it?"

"Craft, subtlety, my genius for power."

"Do you think you can beat him? He sure beat you in Egypt."

"Be fair, vermin," she said, sitting up and wincing with the discomfort.

"Oh 'vermin,' are we? You *are* mad."

"He didn't beat me at all. I was wearing him down. I was close to incinerating him in his silly bird rig. No, it was something else entirely, whatever created that big spooky dog."

"Well it's not a dog really, but I'll grant you the Sphinx is spooky."

"So are you with me in my campaign? Revenge as a lever to ultimate power. Revenge under pretext of protecting the Consilium. It needs a stronger leader to protect it from the evils Wanre let loose. Had he not delayed me, I would have destroyed the Sphinx before it was birthed. Well, worm?" She looked up. His small head dangled down over her forehead.

"Why else do I live, gorgeous monster?" He gave a little squeeze to his hind section. A gout of bliss entered her brain as a sacrament of their enduring union.

Hillary was wearing her Gaultier bush jacket today. It was a relief that Cairo had the fashions and convenient you could shop all night. Breaking events and desert heat put demands on her wardrobe.

She was standing in front of the Sphinx Temple. Behind her loomed the living Sphinx, before her the multitude that had gathered. They had started to come as soon as the Sphinx appeared. First they filled the *son et lumière* theatre. Then they spilled over onto the desert. Hordes took buses or walked in the heat from Cairo. Well-heeled foreigners arrived by private jet at Cairo airport and hired cars and drivers.

"Okay Jim. Ready to roll?"

"In one."

"Folks, behind me you see the Sphinx, apparently living and breathing, though he has made no statements and won't react to questions. The view around the world right now is that something has shifted in human history. Everyone feels it, though the Sphinx came among us only hours ago. The shift shows itself in a lot of different ways. Several thousand websites are already dedicated to the Sphinx. We can expect that new religions will be springing up based on him. The strangest reports are that people playing video games are, well, seeing things. They see the Sphinx or the Egyptian gods showing up right in the middle of games–even first person shooters. These figures stare out at the players, who feel like they receive some sort of direct communication. Whatever it all means, it's clear that people are excited. Take a look at that crowd."

The camera panned over the crowd.

"Just look at the numbers of people already here, and they're still pouring in. They're peaceful, quiet. They just want to see the Sphinx, to be here in his presence. The crowd is already at least a million, and I bet it'll be a lot more by the end of the day. This is Hillary Holloway, live from the pyramids."

Bulbul wriggled up to her nose as she came around.

"Have a nice ride?"

She blinked, stretched. Benben was still a little dreamy, but there was a luxurious sense of physical power playing through her body. "A good mix, worm."

"Any dreams?"

"Other than revenge?"

"Start there, biscuit."

"Time for a shake-up in the Consilium."

"Can you turn our Egyptian escapade against Wanre?"

"He was wrong, I was right."

"But the Sphinx hasn't really *done* anything yet."

"He's more useful to me if I act before he does. A perfect screen to project Consilium fears onto."

"What they don't know *will* hurt them?"

"Clever wriggler. They're so used to knowing everything and controlling everything, the mere inability to find our Sphinx in their codex of species should be enough to put them in my grip."

"They'll need a strong leader."

"One not afraid to oust the bureaucrats."

"Wanre had some pretty fancy footwork."

"I've learned his tricks. Besides, we may have a new friend to help."

"Who could it be? We don't do friends very much. A blackguard?"

"Of the very worst kind. When I was running the branes home, I got a glimpse of the lord of the Milky Way."

"What good is a black hole to us? They just eat stars and piss radiation."

"He is corrupt to the core."

"Our kind of guy. But what does he do? Does he have a taste for stars with inhabited planets?"

"Worse."

"No."

"Yes, he's a rare one. He eats mind."

"So we cozy up and enjoy the spectacle."

"I thought we'd strike up an acquaintance."

"I don't think so. No. I am shocked at the thought. Shocked!"

She thought he was playing as usual. To her surprise she realized he was serious. She listened.

"Even your blackest darkness is white and shiny compared to one of these dark stars. What makes you think he won't suck down your—our!—minds too if you go calling? His suction has a galaxy behind it."

"He's big but slow. I'm fast."

"How could you hold him to a bargain?"

"I can't, just stay nimble."

"What do we gain?"

"Untold power in Earth's universe."

"But he might ride you straight back to our comfy little home universe."

"He could power my control of the Consilium. Imagine the fear I could project. Ponder what I could do to those who stand in the way."

"Does he have any sense of humor?"

"No, but he's so *big*." It was exactly the wrong thing to say. Benben found it hard to understand how touchy Bulbul was about his size.

"Size isn't everything," he pouted.

She needed him. "You'll always be my big boy."

"You mean?" He wriggled in anticipation.

"Not yet. I have to crush my opponents." He was always after her. But it was never easy to fit sex in. Let alone a reproductive cycle that could tear your guts out. On the other hand, she knew what a cute daddy he would make.

She had not given him much hope, but it was enough to mollify him. She need make no further concessions. He felt like he had made some progress and so he played along.

"You have to admire someone whose daily grind is soul sucking, I guess. When do we make contact?"

"After I destroy Wanre."

57

It was after nightfall on the day the Sphinx came to life and Mustapha re-entered his living body. He told Cliff that there was a ceremony they must perform in the Great Pyramid, and Cliff agreed. Mustapha felt a sense of urgency, and so they would perform the ceremony that very night.

Mustapha's men had set up a small tent near the entrance to the Great Pyramid, so they would have both access and privacy. Cliff was fasting for the ceremony. He was unused to doing without food. He was hungry and edgy. He entered the tent with Mustapha while the others waited outside. The light was from oil lamps.

"How do we know this will work?"

"We can only try it."

"But isn't this dangerous? Aren't there dark forces who might take advantage of us? I watched the battle between Seth and Horus."

"Cliff, the world is full of forces both good and bad. They compete for our mind and soul."

"You mean like angels and demons?"

"That is one way they fall into language."

"Can we do anything about them?"

"You might think of it this way: each of us is possessed, always. What distinguishes the wise is knowing how to choose who it is that possesses you."

Cliff was silent for a while. "Are there guides?"

"One I know well: The *Book of Possession by Light and Darkness.*"

"Shouldn't you teach me before we do this?"

"These are not concerns for now. Here, let's get ourselves ready with the right ritual. Each of us has a basin of clean water and a towel. You see that linen kilt and sandals. When you have washed thoroughly, put them on."

"That's all?"

"Yes. Back in the time of Unas and Qaa, they wouldn't even have worn sandals. You are actually getting off quite easily."

"How's that?"

"In the old days, you would have to remove every bodily hair except your eyelashes and eyebrows. We no longer do that."

Cliff was both intrigued and relieved. It was good to worry about hair, clothes, and washing his body instead of worrying about unknown dangers. He washed, donned the kilt, and Mustapha showed him how to tie the waistband. When they were ready, they left the tent.

"You sure look the part," said Jack.

"It's a real statement!" said Petra.

They entered the Great Pyramid. Cliff was familiar by now with the pyramid, though going in at night dressed like this was disorienting. Maria, Petra, and Jack came with them as attendants. They carried oil lamps to light the way.

The group reached the King's Chamber in silence. Mustapha helped Cliff into the sarcophagus. He lay in the open granite box, his head facing the door through which he had just entered. Mustapha explained that the cold would challenge both of them in the night. Then he asked the other three to withdraw and return at dawn. They said goodbye and made their way out.

The light reaching Cliff in the sarcophagus quickly dimmed as the three crossed the chamber. He felt a wave of panic: he was in a coffin, and it would be utterly dark in seconds.

"Mustapha," he said to allay the fear. "Is there anything special to do?"

"Ask for a vision. Beyond that, don't give in to fear. I am here. We have plenty of fresh air coming through the star shafts. Tomorrow we will greet the dawn together. Remember, if no vision comes, you are not a failure. This is just an experiment."

Cliff felt chilly. He lay on his left side and must have dozed off.

He was filled with a golden light, bright as the Sun. It filled him and was him. The light connected him up with everything in the universe—filamentous light reached out from him into reality, and from all of reality back into him. He was a local field in a universal energy. He opened his eyes and found himself standing in his light body before the Sphinx. He stood between the two paws. In front of him was the Dream Stela of Thutmose IV, up against the Sphinx's chest. He walked toward the stela and realized it was a doorway. It beckoned to him. He was near it. Then his right foot went through.

Next he was shivering in the dark. No light body any more. He touched himself. Bare chest, linen kilt. He realized where he was.

"Wow."

"I felt you go. What was your vision?"

Cliff told Mustapha.

"You know what you must do," said Mustapha.

"Go back to your place and trip?"

Mustapha laughed. He had found a good one in Cliff. Sincerity and aptitude were a rare combination. "I think you should walk through that door."

"The real stela?"

"Why not? It's sitting there between the Sphinx's paws."

"Thousands of people are there; millions are watching on TV."

"If you get through, I doubt anyone can follow. If not, they won't have a clue what you were doing."

"When do we try?"

"We will follow the ritual. Dawn is not far off. You deserve a good breakfast. Then you try."

Cliff lay in the sarcophagus, replaying the vision in his mind. He also remembered how the Sphinx spoke directly to him, and wondered what was next.

58

"NORAD, this is Mother Goose," said the vice president. He would have preferred a more martial handle, like 'Sidewinder,' or 'Thunderhead.' Still, it was not going to puncture his mood. He had taken direct command and he was going to enjoy it.

NORAD, the American space command, was lodged under Cheyenne Mountain, Colorado. He could have given instructions and let them do the job. But this was too important. History needed a major figure to bestride its turning points. He was willing to step up.

"Mother Goose, this is Space Command. The battle station is in place."

"Begin charging sequence."

"Begin charging sequence."

The critics of the space defense initiative were about to be proved wrong.

"Charging sequence complete, sir, particle beam weapon at full capacity."

"Acquire target."

"Target acquired, sir."

"Fire at will," said Mother Goose.

The Sphinx moved for the first time since he had assumed the posture of the statue. The crowd, transfixed, saw him raise his right paw and turn it palm up, angling it in what looked like a precise gesture.

From the battle station poised in the upper atmosphere, an endo-atmospheric charged particle beam strong enough to destroy underground missile silos streaked down towards the Sphinx. The beam of charged particles, invisible in itself, ionized the air it passed through. The beam shot down distinctly visible, a focused cascade of diamond. To an ancient Egyptian, it might have looked like one of the Aten's rays of light in the bas-reliefs of Akhenaten.

The deadly beam hit the Sphinx's upturned paw. The Sphinx batted it, like a cat playing with a fly.

A few seconds later, there was an explosion far above. It was bright enough to be seen in the daylight, like a white rose opening against the sky.

59

Mustapha suggested that Cliff and the others join him at the nearby Mena House for breakfast. Mustapha wanted Cliff to make his attempt that morning, so he did not want to drive into Cairo against all the traffic swarming toward the Sphinx.

The Mena House was an elegant old hotel, a former hunting lodge of King Farouk, the last degenerate vestige of royalty in The Two Lands. Near the pyramids, it was where Roosevelt and Churchill drank while they ordered D-Day.

As they sat down, Jack said, "It's on me. We could all use a top-flight breakfast today."

While the others acknowledged Jack's hospitality, Cliff's mind was elsewhere. In the refined old dining room, his vision felt a world away. "Is there anything special I have to do to cross through the stela?"

"We have to trust to your vision," said Mustapha.

Cliff relaxed a little into the others' buoyancy. They were used to working as a team. As long as there was a next puzzle, they shared a feeling of purpose.

After breakfast, they returned to the Sphinx. Mustapha was guiding them when Hillary intercepted.

"Folks, I have with me the head of the Supreme Council of Antiquities, and the scientists who were with him below the Sphinx. Sir, what do you make of the American attack on the Sphinx? The Sphinx apparently destroyed the American space battle station with his bare paws."

"You have to expect the Sphinx to defend himself."

"Is the Sphinx good or bad?"

"He was worshipped as a beneficent deity."

"We have just had reports that earthquakes in two dozen world capitals followed the attack on the Sphinx by some five minutes. Retaliation?"

"Was anyone hurt?"

"Apparently not."

"Then it was nicely judged. Perhaps a message."

"Its meaning?"

"Maybe we should show the gods some respect. Now excuse us." They moved off.

"Folks, stay tuned as we continue our coverage from the pyramids. Is the Sphinx a threat to the United States military? Is something apocalyptic about to happen, or is this all some sort of dream?"

Mustapha stood with Cliff at the Sphinx's paws. He was struck by the detailed beauty of the tawny fur. The Sphinx's enigmatic smile towered above them. The Dream Stela of Thutmose IV was straight ahead. Cliff approached it as he had in his vision.

He stopped right in front of it. He hesitated to try, afraid that if he touched the stone it would be unyielding and the dream would break. But he had to do it. He took a breath and stepped forward with his right foot.

It went in. He looked down to watch his whole body move smoothly through, turning into a golden light body on the other side.

Jack watched Cliff step through the Dream Stela. He was a radical Egyptologist, but still an Egyptologist. He had a scientific, skeptical view of unexplained phenomena. Even though his Holy Anomalies pointed to a non-standard view of Egyptian history, he had never imagined the possibility of what was happening in front of his eyes.

He had opposed the interventions the others were so eager for. He had feared the consequences, and felt more than justified when Wolfgang and Mustapha died. The experience of the last few days, however, laid siege to his skepticism. When Cliff walked through the Dream Stela, his resistance collapsed.

He would join the others and trust that what was happening was good. What followed swift and hard was the bite of conscience. He had sent reports to Washington detailing events.

Washington had just tried to destroy the Sphinx. Was he responsible? Was it because he had relayed his fears that they had acted with hostility? He did not know. He was ashamed that his government sought to destroy what it did not understand.

He decided to give them no more ammunition. He would send no more reports. Or if he did, they would help his friends not hurt them.

After his decision, the sunlight felt warmer. He had a greater claim to it somehow. Jack looked into Maria's eyes and saw the anxiety she held for Cliff. He knew then he was not abandoning what was best about his country, but choosing with requisite care where to place his loyalties.

Cliff was inside the Sphinx. He looked around. He expected to be in some Sphinx-shaped space, but there was no sense of being inside. He had left the morning behind. Here it was night. Brilliant stars filled the sky. He looked around. Modern development was absent. No electric light, no modern roads. The pyramids were pristine. They were immaculate crystals reflecting starlight. No buildings clustered around them. The funerary temples for Khufu, Khafra and Menkaure were long in the future. Instead, lush savannah studded with groves of acacia, sycamore, and date palms grew all around.

Cliff looked down again at his light body. Despite its radiance, he knew he was himself. He could see and think. He heard an owl calling. He smelled jasmine on the night air.

"Why can't I see you?"

The response came inside his head, resonating as before.

"There is no need."

"Why have you brought me here?"

"I invited you, but you came freely."

"Did you cause those earthquakes?"

"Yes."

"Because the U.S. fired on you?"

"That was of no concern. I looked into the health of the Earth. It angered me."

"You mean this is all some over the top green thing? Some enviro stunt? Is that all you care about? What about people? You could have hurt people with those earthquakes."

"If I feel you deserve it, I will destroy every human without thinking twice."

This stopped Cliff. He found himself pleading the case for humanity. In this court, he could not see the judge and did not know the rules. If he lost, humanity would get the death penalty.

Cliff was debating his next move when the voice said, "Let me show you."

Cliff was underwater. The water was warm. Before he looked around, he felt the others. Their fields were clear, strongest in the center and overlapping at the edges. His field touched the others, softly interpenetrating. There was an intimacy here he had never felt. The pack moved and he moved with it: ten in all.

When he looked, he was surprised to find he was a shark. He had an exaggerated tail fin as long as his body: a thresher. He loved the supple slip of his body through the water.

Ahead he could feel the tiny pinpoint fields of a thousand herring. The pack moved faster, to encircle the smaller fish whose flanks flashed the sunlight from above like a blaze of silver chaff. The pack encircled them. Then began the threshing. Cliff felt his long tailfin flail the silver shoal in a broad line of bright blood. The blood's sweet smell and iron tang were irresistible. A fervent greed swept through him, electric.

> *The sharks all turned into the shoal to feed and Cliff knew the abandoned joy of blood. His delight was sharpened by the satisfaction of all his pack mates. He could feel it in their fields.*

Then he was back under the night sky.

"Wow." It was a pleasure more raw than any he had felt. Returning to himself, even his light body, left him feeling several steps behind the sharp edge of life.

"Now," the voice said.

> *Cliff was again in the ocean and knew by feel that he was a thresher. He tried to find the others, but there was only one, whose field was weak. They swam together looking for herring and found only a few squid.*

Cliff was back under the stars.

"How do you feel?"

"I don't know. Sad. Lonely."

"When I last slipped through the veins of life on your planet, it was a paradise, and your species showed great promise. Now the web of life is fraying."

"Can't you help?"

"I could change everything for you. But then you would no longer interest me."

"Is this all about whether we amuse you? What about the value of human beings? Are we your lab rats? What about our inherent dignity and right to live as much as any animal?"

"Too much help would kill that dignity. You are free. You can realize your genius as a species. You may also choose the path of death."

"Is this all our fault?"

"You are fully responsible, but not entirely at fault."

Cliff was stretching to understand this. The voice said, "Let me show you the lord of your galaxy."

The sky emptied of stars. Two glowing cocoon-like bodies approached each other in slow motion. They crashed into each other, tearing their cocoon shapes. Stars spilled out and Cliff realized he was watching primitive galaxies. He saw three more cocoon shapes approach. Each was torn open, its stars confiscated by the growing shape.

"This is your galaxy 10 billion years ago."

Cliff saw a band of dark stars circling the growing patch of bright ones. The ring of dark stars was like a giant flywheel. As the flywheel turned, the bright stars moved into the graceful pinwheel of the Milky Way.

"Look at the center." Cliff saw a black open spot.

"A black hole?"

"It grew as each galaxy joined. Yours is a galaxy made up of many smaller ones. Each had a black hole at the core. They merged. Every black hole is a being, but some are composite. Normally the personae merge, harmonize and stabilize. The black hole fulfils its task of herding the galaxy. Like any lord, it feeds off those it controls. Normally it eats stars and stellar gas. But sometimes they become unstable, like a human schizophrenic. The personalities don't mesh. Then they may do what is forbidden."

"Forbidden? By who?"

"That is not for you now. As to what is forbidden: the lord of the galaxy is allowed to cull the matter and energy of its core. It is forbidden to eat mind."

"Mind?"

"Mind, matter and energy constitute your universe. Your greatest potential for achievement lies in the mind field. The lord of your galaxy is draining some of this. He is nourishing himself on mind."

Cliff saw a group of people on a city street hurrying to work. An immaterial mist was rising from them, fugitive in the morning light and hard to see. It looked like the steamy fog one sometimes sees above the surface of a lake.

The view pulled back and Cliff saw this mist streaming into the black hole as cosmic dust and gas should have done.

"Can't you just stop this?"
"I could."
"And we'd be your lab rats."
"Yes."
"Meantime the lord of the galaxy is sucking our souls."
"Yes."
"Is there anything we can do about it?"
"Yes."

60

The Council met on Wanre's home world. The chamber was a traditional design. Benches set in oval tiers were worked in gray metamorphic stone, its surface textured. The design was harmonious and sober. It was meant to extend this effect through the discourse.

The harmony and sobriety did not touch Benben. She had decided not to call another emergency session. It would only alert Wanre. Instead, she would make her move at the Council's monthly consistory. She would not have a full audience. Not for round one.

"Relax," said Bulbul in her ear. He was draped comfortably around her neck, his hind segment fastened to the hole in the crown of her head by suction and teeth. "Like a little squirt?"

"Not now, worm."

He could taste the tension in her brain and it excited him. "When will you spring our little trap?"

"Soon."

The meeting was moving through an agenda of no great interest to Benben. Trade disputes between galaxies and the inclusion of new species within the Consilium. She was waiting for new business.

The chair of the consistory rotated each month. Today the chair was from a planet in a system near Benben and Bulbul's home world. It was a pinniped, streamlined by adaptation to a world of heavy water, whose race was brilliant and phlegmatic in equal measure. A large female, she was stretched out comfortably on the stone bench as if she had hauled herself out into the sunshine. She gave every appearance of nodding off as the meeting ground through the agenda.

When new business was called, Benben was on her feet.

"I notice the chair has not put the Earth situation on the agenda." There was a long history between the pinnipeds and Benben and Bulbul's species. None of it was friendly. Despite the Consilium's comity, asperity edged their diplomacy.

"I saw no need," said the chair fully alert. "Little has happened to concern us. The situation is being monitored. You and Wanre will be examined for possible breaches of Consilium statutes in connection with your dual intervention there. Are you here to plead your case? If so you are early."

"I demand to discuss the fate of the Earth as new business."

"The chair reminds the consul of her time limit for the introduction of new business."

"I will need only a little while."

The tension between Benben and the chair added a pleasant stimulus to the meeting. The consuls gave their attention. Benben's sense of purpose was vivid, and there was magnetism in that.

"I went to Earth to protect the interests of the Consilium. An anomaly is unfolding that we need to confront. The Council would not give me leave, so I had to act. I went. I found the source of the problem—the Sphinx. Wanre prevented me from taking care of it. My intervention may have been in technical breach. But he criminally endangered my life and the entire Consilium. I could have stopped this Sphinx. Wanre has let it loose to wreak havoc."

The chair rested her head on her flipper. "I am indulging you by letting you speak like this. Those matters will be investigated."

"Here is my new business. From the founding of the Consilium there has been a way to redress injustice and prove right. I do not want a mere investigation. I demand justice. I challenge Wanre to mind combat in this house. Let the one who survives be judged innocent and the one who dies have their property confiscated."

There was a stir among the consuls.

"Mind combat has not happened in at least a thousand years," said the chair. "It is barbaric. And no one is meant to know how to do it any more."

"Wanre and I are the last who know."

Wanre knew she was lying. Bulbul was an adept. Wanre expected him to intervene in the fight.

The chair addressed Wanre: "You do not need to accept this. If you refuse, it will be no stain on your honor. What do you say?"

Wanre stood slowly. He stretched, nonchalantly rolling his shoulders. Then he looked across the chamber at Benben.

"I accept."

It was arranged that the mind combat would take place in the same chamber at first light the next day. There was certain to be a full house.

They sat quietly in his office. Saiki looked out at the airdragons. Wanre saw the sadness in her eyes.

"You could die tomorrow."

"I defeated her last time."

"I see no guarantee in that. You took her by surprise. Still it wasn't easy, and the finishing shot wasn't yours."

"There's something I can share with you alone. My practice has reached a new level, as if on its own volition. I have entered a place that none of the old masters described."

"Does that make you invincible?"

"It would make death easier to accept."

"For you perhaps." She looked out at the airdragons. "Have you tired of life?"

"No. She's a threat."

"She's manageable. The Sphinx is more of a threat, more unknown."

"I worry less about him."

"There's some other reason for your doing this."

"Benben is a perfect enemy. In the Consilium, a man is seldom privileged to meet one."

Saiki smiled despite herself. She rose, walked behind the chair he sat in, and held his shoulders. Two solitaires drawn together by mutual respect and shared purpose. Now there was something more. He realized that it had been developing for a long time. It was her touch that brought it into focus. He would take care of her. He would protect her. But he could not withdraw from tomorrow's combat. They gazed out together at the airdragons.

"I will do my best tomorrow."

"Yes."

"Will you spend the night with me?"

"Yes."

He woke before she did, relaxed from a satisfaction he had not known in years. She was turned on her side. He moved closer and pushed his face into her luxuriant mane of hair, its colors becoming visible in the early light. The feeling of her hair against his face touched something earlier than memory. He lay quiet, absorbing the perfume of her.

When she woke he made her tea. They drank it quietly, bodies just touching.

"I'll do my best today."

"You'll come back."

61

Cliff realized that he stood where the Sphinx's heart would be, were the Sphinx made of flesh. He imagined the great heart beating. It brought the power of the thing down to a more intelligible scale.

"The Sphinx is holding me in his heart," he thought.

"I am," resounded the voice in his head.

It took Cliff off guard. He had not realized the Sphinx was reading his mind. Still, he preferred to speak. It gave more sense of control.

"What can you do to help us?"

The sky was full of stars again, a close view of the center of the Milky Way and its black hole.

"The lord of your galaxy."

> *Cliff saw an emptiness ringed with stars—the black hole. Then one of the stars spun away from the others. It followed a spiral orbit closer and closer to the black hole. A red giant, it fell in and disappeared. A jet of radiation shot from the black hole's center.*
>
> *It was captivating. It was hard to believe that something you couldn't see—the black hole—was so powerful it sucked in stars and captured their light.*
>
> *Then another large star, blue and hot, moved down the spiral path until it too disappeared beyond the black hole's event horizon.*
>
> *The black hole shot out a jet of radiation like a tobacco chewer spitting.*
>
> *One after another stars left their orbits and spiraled into the black hole.*

"Is this really happening?"

"Not yet. It will take time. It would be dangerous to shift the dynamics of the core too quickly. The first star will enter the black hole in ten of your years. Then another star every year for another hundred. It will fully occupy the lord of your galaxy, force-feeding him."

"Like a French goose!" thought Cliff. The thought amused him. The Sphinx ignored it.

"That leaves a window of ten years. It is your most critical time."

"How do I stop him in the meantime?"

"Each must act on his or her own. You must deny access to your lord."

"How?"

"Become aware. When he takes you, turn away. Then he can do nothing."

"What does it feel like when he isn't getting me?"

"What do you feel like now?"

"But you're protecting me."

"No."

62

The chamber was predictably full. No consul in the Multiverse would miss the duel between Benben and Wanre. It was certain to end in death for one of them or brain death for both.

The chair could have decided to link both combatants to brain monitors. The monitors would let viewers see what the combatants were experiencing. It could be simulcast throughout the Multiverse, or at least replayed and studied as an example of a lost mortal art.

The chair, however, was a traditionalist. She refused to conscion any intrusion into the duel. The ancient way would serve. Each combatant would enter into the mental landscape of the other. They could use any stratagem they could devise to break the mind and will of the other.

Each combatant could also alter their own mental landscape as they wished. Throughout history, though, most had let the enemy enter their actual inner landscape. It required concentration to project alterations. The further from your actual inner landscape your projection became, the more concentration it cost to hold it, reducing the speed, strength, and guile you could muster for the fight. Most trusted that the elaboration of their consciousness throughout their life and practice would confront the enemy with diversions and traps enough.

Benben stood on one side of the chamber, stone benches full of consuls behind and around her, like a gladiator in the ring. Bulbul was draped around her neck, but not attached to her crown by suction and teeth as usual. To Wanre, this confirmed that Bulbul too would enter the fight, and wanted his attack cleanly separated from hers.

Wanre sat on a stone bench opposite. He would remain seated. It would suggest that he was relaxed, and the rough old stone would supply a grounding comfort.

Wanre looked straight at Benben across the chamber and

grinned, as if to say that he was going to enjoy destroying her from the inside out. As if he were a parasite within her very sense of self, eating away at her mind until it was a small dry husk.

Benben regarded Wanre with contempt. Her primary intention was to cause a crippling fear. Then, his mind rendered passive for a moment, she would destroy him. She was eager to remove him. Who else could block her from gaining control of the Consilium? She would also enjoy her triumph over his worldview. He smugly believed in the civilizing power of the Consilium. He knew nothing. All sentient beings remained beasts in their hearts, ravenous and wild. She would let their true natures emerge, when the Consilium was hers.

Wanre's dominant feeling tone was anger. Benben embodied everything he had worked against all his life. Since she had asked for the combat, she deserved the results. He would lance her like a boil.

"I will act as the referee," said the chair. She wished she could prevent this, but Wanre's rash consent had deprived her of any hold over the situation. She could now only officiate at the deadly ceremony.

"Are you ready, Wanre?"

"I am."

"Are you ready, Benben?"

"I am."

Both Benben and Wanre ordinarily held their minds well shielded. No one entered without their invitation, not even psychics and far-seers. Only the security forces could have entered against their will. Wanre had let no one anywhere near his mind since long before he had achieved mastery. He was certain Benben had let Bulbul into hers, so the worm would know her whole mental landscape. Wanre expected an ambush. He believed this advantage on their side was balanced by one on his own. The brane run had partially opened her mind to him. In their last fight he had found her fear and improved it.

In the days when mind combat was created, experiments were done. The parties jointly imagined a world they could share as a killing ground. This, however, proved too artificial a solution to be really satisfying. It was riskier and stranger to allow the enemy into your mind as you went into theirs. You must try to defend your own mind while seeking and exploiting the weaknesses in theirs. It was possible that Benben would not open her mind on cue. Then she or both of them could try to enter his mind with such overwhelming force that they disabled him before he could shield his mind again. But he was too confident of his strength to worry. He could lock them out if that was their game.

The chair spoke again. "Then let the combat begin."

Wanre pushed across her shadowy frontier and was in. He saw the whole of Benben's inner landscape ranged before him. As he expected, it did not gladden the heart. In the foreground lay a fetid swamp. Behind it in rough ground stood a twisted forest, dark and dripping. Where mountains should be were pulsing inner organs of a multitude of species, piled to a leaden sky. They puffed bilious vapors as their slimy surfaces pumped intestinal rhythms.

In the swamp were snakes and crocodiles lying in wait. At the edge of the forest lurked tusked pigs. Ravening beasts of nightmare aspect filled the shadows. Webs covered the forest canopy where huge spiders moved, grinding birds the size of vultures in their fangs.

He knew what he was looking for, but he would have to take on an avatar suited to this world before he could act. He became a dragon. Not an airdragon; those were more suitable for landscaped parks. Instead he became a black-scaled, winged beast of malevolent mien and disposition, which breathed out unquenchable fire with pleasure. This kind of dragon was long extinct throughout the Multiverse. They were destroyed in the dragon wars fought by most social species before time.

Wanre felt the landscape tremor as his dragon materialized. All the beasts here bore its image in their unconscious as the model of danger and untimely death.

Wanre pushed himself into the dragon. He would deploy it to ravage the landscape of her mind. His dragon flew fast over her forest. It breathed down fire, burning wide swaths through the pestilential morass.

In the chamber, the assembled consuls from a thousand worlds watched Benben twitch and jerk. Some muttered that she would spasm soon, and Wanre would finish her off. With small gestures they placed and amended bets outside the view of the chair.

Benben was furious. She had been let directly into Wanre's inner landscape. It stunned her. She was expecting to find all kinds of life. She anticipated neatly arranged gardens, flowering orchards, and pristine wild landscape. She expected a soft mind to destroy, or at least a mind with soft and vulnerable places.

She found none of it. There was only bare sand under a big blue sky. Nothing else. It was an inner landscape totally empty, totally devoid of anything but the blue sky above and the clean sand below. Not even snakes or scorpions, scrub or cactus. Nothing.

What did she have to work on, who make fearful, what destroy? How could she attack sky and sand? She looked to see if he was lolling in the sky, a sentimental airdragon. Nothing.

The damned thing was that there was no way to enter *into* this landscape. She tried being a rattler and a vulture. Nothing worked because there was nothing to get a grip on.

Meanwhile she started to suffer. It came first as a headache, when some old and indistinct fear arose. She could not see it or fight it. Then a burning in her mind. She would have to find some way to hurt him in return, and fast.

Wanre's black leathery wings were spread. Burning the forest, he flew until he saw what he was looking for: the lake of her fear. He had touched it in their fight at Giza. He rushed to it now through the smoke and fetid air.

The dragon flew down to the edge of the lake. He tasted its bitterness. Throwing his head back he snorted fire and bellowed, "The drama closes."

Wanre let the dragon disassemble into mist. He refashioned the mist as a stream running into the lake. He concentrated on the stream, pouring his energy into it. The stream grew into a mighty river, swelling the lake until it broke its bounds and flooded the landscape.

In the chamber, Benben gasped. She was close to full-body panic and she knew it. Livid that she could find nothing in Wanre's inner landscape to harm him, she knew that he would destroy her quickly now. She had to act before the panic set in and Wanre reduced her to a bundle of twitching reflexes waiting for the kill.

"Worm," she rasped.

"Hunkered down and ready, sugar."

She managed to conjure a thunderstorm over the desert. In thunder she spoke and Wanre heard.

"The worm has Saiki by the brainstem. She was totally unprotected. He is in position to decerebrate her. He will do so happily. Surrender or he will kill her, torturing her first. Kill me and he will do it in revenge, and in the vilest possible way."

Wanre was shaken. He had not anticipated the attack on Saiki. Nor would he have cared enough to be shaken, until she had touched him. Before he would have assumed that Saiki would willingly give her life for the Consilium. He would have finished Benben, and then tried for a such a quick kill with Bulbul that he would have no time to act. But things were different now. When Saiki touched him she brought into reality the feelings that had been growing within each of them for the other. They had been solitaires. Now they were one. Wanre would do anything to protect her.

"What do you want?"

"I want you to stand naked and helpless before me so that I can destroy you."

"Will you promise to spare Saiki?"

"Why not? She is no threat to me with you gone."

While he listened, he continued to study her mind. At the ultimatum, he saw something he had never seen before. There was a shadow, dark and powerfully attractive, that appeared beyond the pulsating mountains of organs. He sensed it was infinitely larger than her mind, had access to it, and was hungry. He noted it for further study. Then he realized he was about to die.

"All right," he said. "I will concede."

63

"Okay," said Cliff. "Keeping out the galaxy lord is key. But the real job is taking care of the planet. How can I get everyone to act? I'm just one person."

"I will help."

Cliff looked up. He was under the sea again. This time he was an observer. They descended to the ocean floor. Cliff saw shelves of dark ice honeycombed with holes.

"What's this?"

"Methane ice. When it melts it will bubble up through the oceans. The heating will accelerate."

"That's crazy. Why do you want to speed up the greenhouse? You were talking about helping!" Cliff was confused and angry.

"Only a crisis will move your species. This is an appeal to your brain's hard wiring."

"It may be enough to wipe us out! Maybe we'll get motivated and it'll be too late."

"The future is irreducible. What is certain is that you will not survive without a motivating crisis."

Cliff saw a light-like energy enter the methane ice.

"When will it melt?"

"That will depend. It will not be long."

"It's going to be a real big deal for our hard wiring."

In the White House, the secretary of state was briefing the vice president.

"You mean we didn't touch the damn thing?"

"It destroyed our asset. We inflicted no damage."

"How did that happen?"

"We don't have any idea."

"It's gone, just gone? The tapes give no clue?"

"None."

"We need to go on a heightened military alert."

"I'm not sure it's a military threat."

"You saw what it did, of course it's a military threat."

"I think it may pose an even greater threat to our society. A sinister and fundamental challenge to authority. And hence to our way of life. People all over the world love the thing. Websites, TV shows. Apparently Islamists are claiming it is some kind of message. Saying it confirms the West is corrupt."

"And there's no way to control it."

"That's right." Jose went into disconsolate silence.

The vice president took Jose's idea as his own. "The Sphinx poses the idea—no, the illusion—of ultimate freedom. No respect for properly constituted authority. It upsets the very basis of civil society."

"I'm reaching here. You mean it's Prometheus and we're the gods."

"You know what the gods had to do to Prometheus."

"Figure out how to get him in chains."

"And rip his liver out. "

The secretary of state was uncomfortable. "The only thing left is nuclear."

"Small nukes," said the vice president. He was an advocate of the new generation of small and acceptable battlefield nuclear weapons. "I want you and the head of the Joint Chiefs back here in an hour."

64

In the chamber, Benben's histrionics had stopped. Bulbul was rigid around her neck, concentrating on Saiki and ready to strike. Wanre was seated in apparent composure. Saiki knew nothing of the threat to her, since Bulbul was concealed in the foundations of her mind.

Inside Wanre's mind, Benben waited for him to disclose himself and make himself vulnerable.

She saw a single cactus appear in the desert. It was a saguaro, old and noble, its many arms reaching high.

She stoked the thunderstorm and sent down a bolt of lightening. It struck the saguaro, cleaving it and then pulping it.

In the chamber, Wanre's head fell onto his chest. His body slumped to the floor.

Saiki ran over to him, held him and listened to his heart.

"He's dead."

"As required by the statutes of this Council and the Constitution," said the chair, "the Speakership of the Consilium now passes to you, Toran."

The consuls gasped, talked, stood, most in disbelief. Wanre was so strong. How could it be?

Saiki cradled Wanre's head.

Toran let out a raptor's hunting keen as mourning.

Benben called Bulbul off. "Relent, worm. We have destroyed him."

As Bulbul withdrew from the foundations of Saiki's mind, he sensed romance in Wanre's death. But first he had a message for Saiki.

As Benben left the chamber with Bulbul around her neck, she passed close to Saiki. Saiki looked up in shock from Wanre' body at his killer.

Bulbul leaned down close. "I was in your brain. I was going to kill you. Wanre gave in to save you. Killed by his chivalry, very old fashioned."

As Benben moved on, Bulbul considered the celebration mix he would pump from his hind segment into his victorious sweetheart's brain, and dreamt of what might follow.

65

"You've judged us."

"I find you still full of possibility." The voice boomed in Cliff's head. "I will open a door but you must walk through it."

"Will you stay and guide us?"

"I go to my companions. I leave you the burden of freedom."

Cliff looked around, instinctively searching for the Sphinx. He saw only the night sky and Giza as it was before civilization. He looked out on the pyramids in their perfection. More than anything else, he did not want to break the spell.

"I want to come with you!" His shout rang out. There was no response. "Will you come again?" His question died away on the soft night air.

Then the night, like a solid thing, lifted up. Daylight came in under it. Cliff stood soon in daylight, in his normal body, in contemporary Giza.

Mustapha stood with Maria, Jack, and Petra near where the paws of the Sphinx had been. Petra began moving. She left the three others behind to run to Cliff.

Petra saw how alone Cliff was. He looked both drained and radiant. He was not the same. She needed to be with him.

As she ran to Cliff, Petra raised her arms to embrace him.

Cliff blinked, and looked at her coming. He smiled, and raised his arms. He stood still. There was no place for him to run, for he had just stood at the center of everything. He looked at Petra and saw her as if for the first time. She was the Earth and its future generations. She was all of life and energy pulsing towards him to embrace him.

Cliff held his arms open and Petra ran until they held each other. Without speaking, they looked into each other's eyes and kissed.

Together they looked up. The Sphinx had spread wide wings like jewels of gold, cornelian, and lapis lazuli. He was just above them when his shadow fell. It came down like a normal shadow at first, a spot of darkness proportional to his size and distance. Then the shadow expanded outward like a tsunami in all directions. As the shadow grew, blotting out the day, the Sphinx appeared to grow.

He was moving away, flying toward Rostau, the place where pharaohs went to join the imperishable stars. As he flew, the Sphinx confounded the eye. We expect to see something become smaller as it grows distant. He became larger. As he flew, he became ever larger, blocking out ever more sunlight.

At Giza they looked up into darkness. It was not the darkness of the night sky, shot through with stars. No stars shone; a velvet darkness filled the sky. Soon all the Earth was in the Sphinx's shadow as it folded out from him to embrace the entire planet.

Then he pulled his shadow back into himself and moved toward the center of the galaxy.

Astronomers trained space and Earth based telescopes on him. What they recorded ruptured expectations of what is possible. As his distance grew his size continued to swell. He became an ever expanding expression of pure geometries, blotting out an ever wider swath of the sky as he gained distance.

He neared the center of the Milky Way. His speed made no sense. He crossed light years like meters. When he neared its center, he blocked all view of the entire galaxy.

Telescopes could see his outline by the absence of stars, giving the astronomers who watched in realtime, and everyone after, the feeling that he could extinguish the galaxy should he choose.

When he reached the core he veered up and held himself above it. The galaxy reappeared. In their telescopes he looked like nothing so much as a bat formed of three elongated black diamonds. He reached down and pushed a succession of giant red and blue stars like a child playing at marbles.

Then he was gone. His dark form folded in upon itself and vanished. In one moment he spanned the galaxy and toyed with stars. In the next he was gone like the memory of a dream.

66

"He's gone."

"Good riddance."

"But the way he went is something you need to understand." The secretary of state sat down in a Chippendale chair facing the vice president's desk. "The boys at NASA say his shadow didn't get smaller as he went. He eventually blotted out the galaxy."

"So?"

"That means he was as *wide as the galaxy*. You see what I'm saying? He bounced around stars like basketballs. He's not bound by physical constraints like light speed."

The vice president was thoughtful. The secretary of state continued. "This thing has limitless power. It's a limitless threat."

"A limitless threat doesn't serve us, Jose. A limited threat like terrorism serves us. A limitless threat does not. If this thing wanted to harm us, it would already have done so. Therefore the Sphinx is no problem. The situation is now nominal."

The secretary of state knew when not to say more.

The vice president sat back and put his feet up on his desk. He put his hands behind his head, interweaving their thick tips. The crisis was over. "We're back to a business as usual scenario."

"Folks, you saw it too. Or at least his shadow. And now he's gone." Hillary looked lost. "What will the crowds gathered at Giza do now?"

Mustapha leaned close to the others. "I know what *we're* going to do: head back to the Al Minah before the Giza Road becomes impassable."

They packed into Jack's Range Rover. He was pleased he had rented it.

67

The shock was complete. Wanre was dead. Saiki sat by the lake. She moved between numbness and emotional pain so strong it scorched. Numbness was the only respite.

"How could Wanre have done it? He was stronger than Benben. He could have destroyed her, the bitch. I wish he had. She'll try to spread her poison now. How could he let her win? Was the worm telling the truth? Did Wanre do it for me? Was the worm actually going to kill me? Did Wanre really sacrifice himself?"

Her mind went numb for a while. "He would have, yes."

Love and loss flooded her. She cried herself back into numbness.

She was roused by an airdragon, the first she had seen all day. It was an old red male, its flanks striped gray and magenta like a sunset before a storm.

Looking at the airdragon brought an idea. The idea brought the first solace she had felt since Wanre's death.

Reds were the only species of airdragons that would eat people. Even so they were ordinarily no danger. The average swimmer displays four limbs clearly. Although the reds had the dullest senses of any airdragons, they saw the display of limbs from a distance. Disdaining the taste of meat, they avoided people taking exercise in the water. But they could be tempted. Ancient Leucandran aristocrats committed suicide by seducing reds. It had not been done in ages, but it should still work.

Saiki would have to make herself look like a fish.

She would seduce the paunchy old male. She would seduce death and make it come to her. She would make the airdragon take her to Wanre. She got up and walked quickly into her house. She stripped, then began to cut her rainbow mane. It felt natural to cut it away in her grief.

When she looked in the mirror, she realized she had made herself look like Wanre, with his shaved head. It was a comfort. She would go join him now.

She walked out naked to the lake. The air dragon flew over indifferently. She jumped into the warm water. Holding her breath, she dove under and swam out. When she surfaced, she held her arms and legs close by her sides.

She floated. She saw the airdragon fly over and then leave. She had to call him back. She tried to propel herself through the water without moving her arms or legs away from her body. She had to look like a large fish come to the surface. She had to swim without betraying the fact she had four limbs. If she only floated, he would not bite. She would look dead and he would ignore her. She could be a wounded fish, that would be fine, but she had to move. He liked his fish fresh.

She struggled at it. Finally she got an undulation going, then a pattern of undulations. The red circled over, lower.

"Come get me you fat bastard. Bring me to Wanre."

The red came still closer to appraise her now.

She knew how they hunted. Once he decided to make the kill, he would hold out his talons and stoop, using gravity to fall upon her. She was counting on the impact being strong enough to kill her before he chewed her head off.

"Do it now, monster."

The airdragon positioned himself. Looking down at her, he extended his talons. He plunged. She would not have long to wait.

Just then, a thought entered her mind with great force. "He's not dead! Wanre told me he got to a level beyond the old masters. I'll bet he got rid of his brain shadow. He's not dead! I know it!"

The airdragon was seconds away, falling from the sky upon her.

Saiki spread her arms and legs wide in a desperate semaphore to the airdragon: I am warm-blooded flesh. Go away!

Was there time? Had the inspiration arrived too late? Would the airdragon see her signal? Even if he did, could he change course now that he was committed? He was an old one, his reflexes might be slow. What had she done? Had she thrown her life away?

Life had never seemed so precious.

Saiki closed her eyes, certain she would never open them again on her world.

At the last second, the air dragon threw out his wings and pulled up. She felt the hot breath of his snorted disgust.

She opened her eyes. She was alive. She breathed and the air never tasted so good, despite the rank musky stink of the airdragon still so close.

She was overcome with giddiness. "Sorry, fat boy," she yelled to the airdragon as it pulled away and gained altitude, "I've got other things to do than play with you!" She was elated. She swam to the shore.

She did not know how to search for Wanre. His body was dead. If he had really gotten rid of his brain shadow, he could be anywhere in the Multiverse. As she stood shaking the water off, the texture of the sand beneath her feet was delightful. The sky reflected in the living crystal of her house was unusually beautiful. She saw her naked reflection and wondered if she would ever get to share her body with Wanre again. She saw her shaved head. It gave her a clue.

"I'll have to learn something about the techniques he mastered if I want to find him."

Turning around to the lake, she waved at the big old red in the sky. She laughed when he ignored her.

68

Toran sat behind closed doors in the private chamber of her eyrie. She was disheveled and keening softly. She had not been looking out as she usually did, and had missed Saiki's drama with the old red.

There was a knock. No one could see her this way, now that she had taken up the mantle of Speaker. She preened and made herself presentable.

"Enter."

A Consilium scholar walked in. Toran knew it was one who had advised Wanre. Seeing the scholar's face brought back Wanre's death. It was so recent and hurt so much that Toran maintained her decorum only with difficulty.

"What do you have for me?"

"I must report a major anomaly."

"Go on."

"We were monitoring the Earth as you know. Suddenly the Sphinx left Earth. It moved with near instantaneity to the galaxy's core. It disturbed the orbits of large stars with no seeming effort. Strangest of all, it assumed the apparent size of the galaxy. Then it disappeared entirely."

"Surely you are mistaken."

"We've been meticulous. But it gets stranger: the Sphinx flew across the branes. Physically. The good news is that it didn't rupture the branes. But it leapt right through the chirality mirrors from universe to universe as easily as it rampaged through the Earth's galaxy. This is beyond the rules of the physical Multiverse as we know them.

"Explanation?"

The scholar was clearly shaken and spoke hesitantly. "We have none. No race in the Consilium can offer even a theoretical explanation, let alone do such thing."

"Where is this Sphinx now?"

"We lost it. It disappeared, apparently at whim."

"Did it communicate, acknowledge us in any way?"

"No."

Saiki and the scholar fell silent.

"It can only mean one thing," the scholar said. "It's only been a theory till now. Nothing else can explain these events, though. There must be a civilization at Level 6. They must be so far beyond us that we are like children to them."

"And that," Toran said, staring out from her eyrie at the crystal meeting hall where Wanre died, "gives me reason to go on."

69

They sat in their semicircle facing the Nile drinking tea, coffee, and Coke.

Maria looked around at Jack, Petra, Cliff and Mustapha. She smiled. "Since we were here last time, Mustapha was raised from the dead, the Sphinx came to life and disappeared..."

"But not before Cliff walked into his belly and lived to tell the tale," said Jack.

"Like Jonah and the whale," said Petra. "What did you find out?"

Maria reappraised Petra. While her reservations remained, the way Petra had seen Cliff's need at Giza and responded to it was real.

"I'm trying to make sense of it all," said Cliff. "Basically it's like this. We don't have long to save the planet. We haven't blown it yet, but we're close, very close. The Sphinx is giving us one last chance."

They sat looking out. The Nile flowed calmly, the date palms rustled in the breeze. They heard Cliff, but it was hard to believe in a crisis when your senses reported that everything was fine.

"There's something bothering me," said Petra. "I may be a painter and not as smart as you guys. But it was creepy the way the Sphinx threw a shadow over the whole world like a blanket. Is he really giving us a chance? If I was painting the shape of evil, it would be that big shadow smothering us all."

"I think he's beyond our good and evil," said Cliff. "He is helping though. How can I explain this?" He paused. "There's a black hole at the center of our galaxy, but not an ordinary one. It's the lord of the galaxy and it's sucking our souls."

Maria experienced a sharp intake of breath.

Cliff continued. "The Sphinx is going to distract the galaxy lord. That's why he was playing with the stars. He's going to force feed him. But there's a window of ten years before the stars start falling into the black hole. So our most vulnerable time is this next ten years."

"What can we do?" said Jack.

"There's a trigger point soon, he wouldn't say exactly when. That apparently depends on us. The seas will look like they're boiling. A lot of methane will seep out and speed up the greenhouse. There's an awful lot to figure out."

"May I suggest that we go to Karnak?" said Mustapha. "We can live and work there as long as we need. Cliff and Maria saw only a fraction of it. It will be comfortable, private, and I can welcome you all there now."

"How about some pizza first?" said Cliff. "I'm starved."

"Our pizza à la Karnak-in-Exile is rather tasty," said Mustapha.

"Is Karnak still in exile?" said Jack.

"I was forced to appear in public," said Mustapha. "We'll have to see about Karnak, and much else." He looked down, thoughtful.

"I say it's pizza à la Karnak now and I want some!" said Maria, laughing. Her laugh pulled a smile from Mustapha.

"What are we waiting for?" said Petra. "I'm hungry too."

They piled into Jack's Range Rover and headed toward medieval Cairo. As they drove through the city, the world was full of danger and of hope.